THE MASADA PROTOCOL

BY
LEE BROAD

This book is dedicated to all men and women who stand the wall in defense of freedom, enduring much, often in obscurity, for the benefit of many, and, very especially, to America's combat veterans.

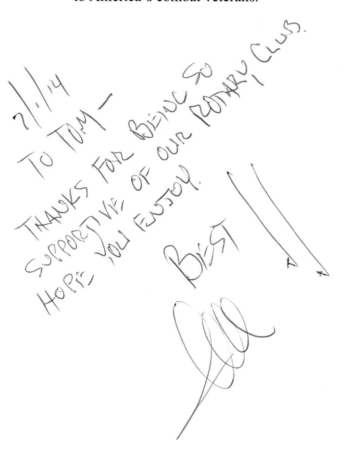

Historical Note:

About thirty miles from Jerusalem lies Masada, which means "fortress" in Hebrew. Masada is a steep rocky hill rising over 1400 feet from the Judea Desert on the southwest shore of the Dead Sea. In 40 BC, during one of the turbulent times noted by his reign, King Herod along with his family fled from Jerusalem to Masada and later, between 37 and 31 BC, fortified and furnished it as a personal citadel.

After the fall of Jerusalem and the destruction of the Jewish Temple in 70 AD by the Romans, Zealot resistors and their families numbering less than 1000 fled Jerusalem to Masada, which had been occupied by another Zealot, Menachem Ben Judah, in 66 AD at the outbreak of the Great Jewish Revolt. After the fall of Jerusalem in 70 AD, Masada became the last site of organized Jewish resistance.

In 72 AD, the Roman governor Lucius Flavius Silva marched against Masada commanding the Tenth Legion, which had in tow thousands of Jewish war prisoners. The Romans established camps at the base of Masada and laid siege to it. To approach the top of the mesa on which the actual fortress was constructed, they built a rampart of stone and earth on the western side of the fortress. Two years later, in the spring of the year 74 AD, the Romans moved a battering ram up this ramp and, at the end of the day, breached the wall of the fortress. Tired from the effort of breaching the walls and assured of victory, the Romans decided to enter the fortress the next day.

As recounted by Flavius Josephus, that night Elazar ben Yair gathered all the defenders and persuaded them to kill themselves rather than fall into the hands of Romans. Because Judaism strongly discourages suicide, as Josephus' story notes, ten people chosen by a lot killed all the other defenders, then each other, down to the last man, so that only one would take his own life. Josephus also reported that Elazar ordered his men to destroy everything except the foodstuffs as evidence that, not lacking an abundance of supplies, the Masada defenders deliberately chose death over slavery.

Masada today is the most recognized symbol of Israeli freedom and independence. The site is so important to Israelis that elite units of the Israeli Defense Forces hold induction ceremonies there pledging, "Masada will never fall again!"

Chapter One
Wednesday, December 11, 2013; Somewhere in Egypt

Steve Barber unlatched the trunk of the ancient Citroën and opened it an inch to hear the sounds of the night. Fresh air rushed in and he filled his lungs. He held his body frozen, legs cramped and neck stiff from eight hours in the confined space, and absorbed the village through his eyes, ears and nose. Voices were distant, the tone easy. It was pitch black, with just a wisp of lantern light coming from a mud-brick building fifty meters away. Dinner fires still offered a touch of garlic and onion mingled with the wood smoke.

Raising the lid higher, he climbed out with just the whisper of his clothing rubbing against his pack. He held a Glock equipped with a 17-round magazine—he'd attached the silencer while waiting for nightfall. He planted his left foot on the stony ground, cringing at the crunch his boot made on marble-sized pebbles scattered along the road. Slow and steady, he retrieved his pack, lowered the trunk lid, and crouched behind the right rear side of the twenty-seven-year old French car. After a 360-degree scan, he darted to the north wall of the building against which the Citroën was parked.

He had been in the trunk since being driven to the village and, even though the temperature had not exceeded 20 degrees Celsius that afternoon, sweat soaked his clothes down to his Phenix Fast Assault soft boots. But now it was a cool 9 degrees. A relief. A few quiet stretches and isometrics. Ready to move.

He had memorized the layout of the village, every detail from the bends in the streets to the depths of the wells, from the collapsed wall on the outskirts near the graveyard to the grove of broad-podded Acacia trees where the ground sloped toward a dry creek bed. Even in the dark, Steve knew this was the southwest corner.

He checked his watch—2334 hours. He drank some water from the pouch in his pack while he assessed his environment. Although there would be a full moon later, it was not yet visible. Steve didn't use night vision goggles. He relied on his training and eyesight, and dispensed with the ten ounces of equipment. As usual in December, it had not rained in this part of Egypt for days. A layer of dust covered anything that had not been recently touched or didn't move—like the ancient headstones in the graveyard, the names and dates obscured. Steve didn't think about death. No point. *What will be will be.*

He pondered the operational plan, the one he'd gone over twenty times before. The intel briefing just before he climbed into the Citroën for the long ride indicated his targets would be found in or near the village town hall. He'd find that building on a street thirty meters from its intersecting with the west side of the village square. He'd recognize it from the other battered buildings around—it had two stories and glass windows, the only such building in this tiny village. He had ninety-six minutes to make the kills.

Steve removed his short-barreled Micro Tavor assault rifle from his pack and slipped the strap over his shoulder, fixing the weapon to his lightweight combat vest. The Tavor was fitted with a 30-cartridge magazine and, like the 9mm, a silencer. He moved furtively through the village, avoiding a local police station that would be easy to take, but which would certainly alert the village—and the targets. Two or three times he pressed his back against the wall of a building, frozen in shadow as someone passed nearby, the rippled camouflage paint on his face and hands blending with the mottled brick. He carried two knives to silence potential alarm-givers, the new KABAR Marine combat knife and a Gerber TAC 2, but he would only take that action when absolutely necessary. He was not a killer. He was a warrior.

Moonlight broke over the horizon as Steve reached the street where the village town hall stood fifty meters away in crumbling disorder, its roof tiles chipped, panes of glass in the arched windows cracked and gray with grime. It was as though the building reflected the cruel minds of those inside. *That building might be a deathtrap. Avoid the debris by the front door so you don't alert those inside.* Steve's habit of talking to himself was annoying, even to him. Sometimes he said the words aloud. But he wouldn't make that mistake here.

An emaciated dog of mixed breed rushed out of a narrow side alley, snarling. Steve drew a light pistol from a holster strapped to his right thigh; the gun loaded with a veterinarian's dart filled with a strong sedative. He knew dogs could give you away, but didn't like killing them. He made sure the op-order provided this equipment. *Good thing you aren't ten pounds heavier, Fido*, he thought, as he fired the dart into the middle of the dog's rump, instantly silencing it. *I'd have shot you.* He bent to one knee, gently removed the dart, and placed the dog against a building.

Close now, he slipped into a small alcove and spoke into his communications microphone. A technician read satellite infra-red image information into his earpiece: two targets inside the building in the northwest corner; a third outside the building in the middle of the north wall; a fourth across the street from the town hall entrance on the south side. Remainder of exterior was clear for fifty meters. All four targets had been almost motionless for at least the last forty-seven minutes. Steve whispered acknowledgement.

He scanned the area. *There.* The man across the street from the entrance was leaning against the wall of a small doorway, asleep, his weapon lying across his lap. He would take out that man first, then the two inside and kill the fourth as he left the village to the west. He focused for a few moments, visually measuring everything, and then, pulling his Glock, counted off in his mind the precise cadence of his paces and actions. *One, two, three, four, five, six, shoot number one. Turn, one, two, three, four, five. At front door. Open. One, two, shoot number two. Turn, one, shoot number three. Turn back, one, shoot number two again. One, two, back at door. Look. Get out, close door, turn left, one, two, turn left, one, two, three, four, shoot number four. Leave town.*

He moved effortlessly, focused, trained to do, not feel. As he reached the first man and verified the target, their faces memorized—burned into his brain—he fired two silenced rounds into the head and one into his heart. *That's three.*

Steve reached the entrance to the town hall and pried the door open with his KABAR knife. His eyes had adjusted completely to the deep darkness long ago. He found and confirmed his targets. Two shots in the head of the first target; two shots for the second. One shot into the heart of the second, back to the first for the same shot. *Nine.*

As he returned to the front door, and as the news crackled through his earpiece, he saw that two women had discovered the man across the street. They did not yet know he was dead; he could tell because they were not yelling. He instinctively raised his weapon and aimed at the woman on the left. Even at this distance, he could kill each instantly with one shot. *Why the hell are they out this time of night?* Steve asked himself. *Shit!* He kept the target for a split second, assessing scenarios and outcomes. He pulled his weapon down. *I don't need to kill them. I can finish this and get out. Okay, move it!*

Steve slipped to the north side of the building and as he approached and verified the fourth target, the women shrieked like wounded animals, long and loud, as he knew they would. Undistracted by them, he put the standard three shots into the target and continued westward out of the village at a measured run. *Twelve. An even dozen. Keep that thirteenth shot in the chamber for luck.* He holstered his 9mm and unstrapped his assault rifle.

After fifty meters, he barked into his microphone. Someone barked back into his earpiece. The village behind him exploded with shouts and curses. A dark figure stepped into his path raising an AK-47. Steve veered slightly left and raised his Tavor. Without breaking stride, he sprayed the man with fire, sharply shifted two meters to his right, and kept running as the dead man soared backward, his shattered weapon firing wildly into the night sky.

Time for evasive action. He darted left down an alley, just a space between two buildings large enough for him to run through, then turned right as he emerged, heading toward the edge of town. He knew this would lead to a small group of Acacia trees and then to a dry creek where he could run first north and then west in the small depression next to the bank. *Look! Listen! Pay attention!* He pushed smoothly but quickly through the branches of the Acacia trees, twisting and turning to let the branches snap back into position, letting himself be hidden from view of the town as he reached the other side of the dense thicket. Fifty more meters and the village lay behind him.

Steve maintained an eight-minute mile pace, continuing first west for two kilometers, then south to the extraction point—the time had been moved up thirty minutes during the exchange back in the village. He heard the roar of engines and knew that pursuit would soon follow that sound. His advantage was the darkness and his stamina. Soon the sounds faded as he covered the distance to the designated point.

Forty minutes later, Steve reached the agreed-upon coordinates. He spoke into his microphone, heard a response, and unpacked his retrieval harness and balloon. As he waited motionless, crouched against a rock, he saw lights moving in the distance and heard gunfire. He sensed a snake nearby and held himself stock-still until he saw that it was a sand viper—judging by the horns and girth. Steve watched it slither north, its wide back illuminated by a sliver of moonlight. He blew it a kiss goodbye as it disappeared into a cluster of rocks.

Soon he heard the low rumble of the four MC-130H Combat Talon II engines, and then a voice in his earpiece. He stood slowly, scanned his surroundings, and removed the silencers from his weapons. He secured the 9mm but left the assault rifle at his front, attached to the vest. Steve buckled his harness, bringing the Tavor outside to return fire if necessary. He inflated and released the balloon with its tether line, and readied himself for the jarring impact as the aircraft flew overhead. Dim blinking lights came into sight. He saw the nose hook jutting forward from the aircraft like some big bug's proboscis. One last scan of his surroundings. All clear. Roar—snap—whoosh—he soared up, trailing the C130 until he was hooked and brought into to the loading bay.

Once on board, Steve shed his pack and gear and went to a secure communications line to call his boss, the Undersecretary of Defense for Special Operations. He debriefed the Undersecretary on the events and outcome of the mission.

"Nice job, Steve," said Undersecretary Vic Alfonse. "Those two women are very lucky to be alive. I'll note in the report the risk you took, without jeopardizing the success of the mission, in order to avoid civilian casualties. Also, I'll call my friends in SIS, the British Secret Intelligence Service, and let them know that the last four terrorists of the 2005 London Metro bombing no longer need to be extradited. Today is a very good day."

"Thank you, Vic," Steve said, gulping Gatorade. "I was able to visually confirm all four identities."

"I'll make a note to that effect as well. Again, well done." Vic paused for a moment as if to let the two of them celebrate the outcome. "I want you to get some rest when you get back to Ramstein. Take a few weeks off. Enjoy the holidays. The week after New Years, I want you to come to DC for a briefing on your next assignment."

"Looking forward to it. What can you tell me now?"

"You're going to Israel. I'm seeing some problems with our intelligence collection in the Middle East. It's making me irritable. More than that, I fear what I don't know, and when it comes to the Middle East, not knowing is *very* dangerous. I know *that* from experience. I want you to look into it. Neither CENTCOM[1] nor EUCOM[2] are attuned to the situation—yet—but I want to have the answers before they start asking questions."

"Great, sir, I mean Vic. Sorry, I'm still not used to calling you by your first name."

"I understand, Steve. It's actually an endearing quality about you. See you in January."

"Goodbye, Vic."

"Mr. Barber?" the pilot broke in on the internal communications set.

"Yes, captain."

"Anything we can get for you until Ramstein?"

"No, thanks. Just some quiet time for now and a long hot shower in K-town."

"Great to have you on board, sir."

"Thanks for the lift, captain. Good night." Steve pulled off the headset and settled against his seat's canvas, wishing he had a martini. He would like to get some sleep, but the adrenaline was still pumping and he expected to be awake until touchdown at Ramstein. *No wounds this trip*, he thought, as he pressed his arms, legs and torso, searching for the sharp pain of bruising or the sign of broken bone. *Not a scratch. That's a first.*

Steve closed his eyes; put the night behind him. To his surprise, he started to drift off, exhausted. *Israel. A harsh, yet beautiful, place.* Something tugged at his mind. *Masada.* About 30 miles from Jerusalem, a place called Masada, which means fortress in Hebrew. *Where did I hear that? Did I read it? I remember. That's where the elite Israeli military units induct their members.* A steep rocky hill rising over 1400 feet above the Judean desert on the southwestern shore of the Dead Sea. *Vic seemed very on edge for a warhorse with his experience. Wonder why. Wonder why he's chosen me.*

---

[1] Acronym for (US) Central Command, the unified military command for the Middle East (excluding Israel), Egypt and Central Asia.
[2] Acronym for (US) European Command, the unified military command for Europe, Iceland, Greenland, and Israel.

Chapter Two
Friday, January 10, 2014; New York, New York, USA

"Bombay Sapphire martini, straight up, sir?"

"Sorry," Brian Kendrick replied. "What was that?"

The bartender repeated, "Bombay Sapphire martini, straight up, sir?"

"Thank you," said Brian. *Why do all these guys want to meet at the Bull and Bear?* He left the drink on the bar. It was more of a prop for the meeting he was about to have than something he wanted to drink, at least for now.

Brian thought the place was a tourist trap and overpriced. He then answered his own question: the massive mahogany bar where you could stand and watch people pass by outside, the heavy tables and chairs with starched linen tablecloths, and the lack of fussiness in the ambiance provided a very masculine air, so men were drawn to it. So were expensive women, another male attraction. *Rich people playing rich people for their own amusement. Not impressed.* Still, its location within the Waldorf Astoria at Lexington and 50th Street was a plus when meeting with visitors to New York—hard to get lost in mid-town and very close to Grand Central Station.

He also thought that fifteen-dollar drinks were a bit much, not that he couldn't afford them. He was one of five Managing Directors at Chandler Hines Kendrick LLP, the premier oil industry investment bank. Even Goldman Sachs was no match in merger/acquisition, M&A as it was called, and nobody outdid CHK for general financial advisory and underwriting work within the oil industry. CHK was it.

Brian had established the firm just after the tumultuous times of the market meltdown of late 2008 and early 2009. He seethed at the government's heavy-handed, unimaginative approach to dealing with the crisis. Brian, then a Morgan banker, had banded together with a few friends at other investment banks and authored a comprehensive proposal for dealing with GM, Chrysler, AIG, and the stacks of toxic bank assets. Bernanke and Geithner took the time to listen, but members of Congress, none of whom knew shit about the capital markets or finance, were intent on passing half-baked legislation that protected special interests and campaign coffers.

In working with the highly intelligent people he'd assembled, however, Brian discovered that they refreshed him. Chandler Hines Kendrick was the result. Over the last five years, CHK had catapulted from among the great unwashed investment firms and was now ranked ninth overall in value of M&A work, taking the number one spot in oil industry M&A.

The bartender wiped the polished mahogany counter with a towel much too white and then glanced at Brian, making eye contact in the way that bartenders expecting big tips do. *Everybody's out for a buck.* The bartender offered a packaged hand sanitizer to Brian, sliding it on the counter near his still-full martini glass. Brian chuckled; raised his glass in a mock toast. A new approach, at least. He'd leave a decent tip.

The reason Brian was here made him think about his firm. Much of CHK's success had to do with the firm's willingness to try new approaches. They knew that larger banks with huge M&A groups and billions in capital would adopt every good idea. So the answer was to leave the competition working old ideas. Every member of the firm took every client's needs personally and beating the competition was a gift each gave the other. They also gave each other about $50 million a year in earnings. These profits were distributed every year only after the principals approved an eight-figure donation to the CHK Foundation, which teamed with local non-profits to improve the lives of children everywhere, principally through improved education, health care, and security for them and their families. *It was brilliant and it was good.*

Brian had a personal foundation as well, through which he took on politicians who pissed him off with their avarice and stupidity. Several powerful members of Congress hated him, but he didn't much care. He was loved by people working to make America a better country.

Soon Brian's guest arrived, a small man, even for an Iranian, with Chia Pet facial hair and dark, intense eyes. Brian thought he looked somewhat crazed and wondered why the Assistant Director General for Strategic Alliances of the National Iranian Oil Company, politically, if not really, a devout Muslim, had chosen to meet in a bar, a very public one to boot.

"Hello Mr. Kendrick," boomed Sa'ad-Oddin Rezvani as he approached Brian. Both had done their homework, so each knew what the other looked like. "I suppose you are wondering why I chose the Bull and

Bear for our meeting," he continued, as if reading Brian's mind. "Well, I love to observe the decadence of Western cultures for it assures me of the glory of Allah."

Small man, big voice Brian noted, taking just a quick moment to inventory Rezvani. Black, no, dark olive, custom tailored suit; British cut. Heavily starched white shirt with a royal purple Hermes tie and matching silk hankie in the breast pocket. No briefcase, no folio, not even a pen. *This guy travels light.*

"Hello, Mr. Rezvani, and welcome to New York," offered Brian congenially, thrusting his hand forward for a hearty shake. Rezvani ignored the gesture. Brian smoothly withdrew his hand by bringing his arm around to point to a table he had reserved for them. *That's one*, Brian thought to himself allowing a little inner smile as his thought triggered the memory of an old, bad joke.

"Oh, Mr. Kendrick, I have been to this wonderful city many times. It is a pity that all here shall perish in the fires of eternity," said Rezvani, without emotion. He preceded Brian to the booth, which was away from the other customers, ordered hot tea and, checking his surroundings and Piaget watch, got to the point.

"We have carefully researched your firm, Mr. Kendrick. We did not choose you by accident," said Rezvani, unfolding his napkin and laying it in his lap as if he were a British schoolmarm out for tea and gossip. "The Islamic Republic of Iran, now joined by our Shi'ite brothers in Iraq, seeks refining assets to vertically integrate our oil holdings. Our goal is to be refining fifty percent of our own crude within five years. We wish to retain your firm to assist us in this matter. Of course, we must insist on total confidentiality."

Another patron walking by the table bumped it accidentally, spilling Rezvani's tea. He shot the person a murderous look, frowned, and snatched a napkin off a neighboring table to soak up the tea in his saucer. As if catching himself in an expression truer to his nature, Rezvani slapped on a smile, tugged on his gold cufflinks to straighten his suit jacket and shirt, and nodded toward Brian.

"On behalf of Chandler Hines Kendrick, thank you for the honor to assist in this important purchase," Brian said effortlessly. He'd rehearsed these words and wondered how long it would take Iran to make this move once the "limited" political integration with Iraq had been announced. CHK had already conducted an in-depth analysis of the compatibility of Iraqi and Iranian crudes with known refineries worldwide. Brian had a list tucked neatly inside his coat pocket. He did not take it out.

"Mr. Rezvani, may I offer some observations and propose the next steps?" Brian asked. A waiter hovered. Brian waved him away.

Rezvani took a sip of tea and dabbed his lips with a corner of his napkin. He momentarily let a scowl cross his face as he gingerly placed the teacup on the borrowed wet napkin. "Of course. We assumed that you would wish to do so," he said.

"In a few moments, we'll discuss a contract, but I want to make sure that you understand our view of the complexities of what you seek to do," Brian began. "In addition to the sheer intricacies of matching refining assets with the chemical makeup of your crude oil outputs, there are a host of political considerations. Why have you decided not to build refining capacity in Iran or Iraq?"

The waiter returned with a fresh teacup and pot of tea, removed the old, and placed a clean linen napkin over the offending tea stain on the tablecloth, removing any wrinkles by drawing his hands across the napkin. *Too bad,* Brian thought. *I was enjoying this guy's irritation with little things. Observant waiter, though.*

"An excellent question, Mr. Kendrick, which has a geo-political answer. We have considered doing as you suggest, but with the Zionist usurpers of Palestine having current military advantage with missile and air assets superior to ours, we have decided to hedge our bets, as you Americans say. We see great advantage in owning important refinery assets in other countries, especially in Europe and North America."

"Western governments have not been pleased with Iran in the past. Why does having assets in those countries give you comfort?" Brian inquired pointedly. It was important to know Rezvani's answer and more importantly, Brian needed to show he wasn't afraid to seek the truth, even at the risk of offending a potential client. He would respect, but not defer.

"Because those governments have been very vocal, but not actual, shall I say, in the prosecution of their complaints against us," Rezvani shot back. "We care nothing about Security Council resolutions. I am sure you know that. We care about being economically integrated with the rest of the world, for reasons that I will not share, but which you will probably surmise."

Brian knew what Rezvani didn't share. Being "economically integrated" with the rest of the world meant that no country could expropriate Iranian assets without harming its own economy. If you are "integrated" in the right way, should one country take something from you, you could take something of equal or greater value in return. *I don't want Iran to have this competitive advantage within the global oil industry or anywhere else.* Brian struggled to keep a poker face that would mask his thoughts.

"Owning assets in other countries requires accepting sovereign dominion over those assets. Don't you find that uncomfortable?" Brian finally took a sip of his drink, eyeing his companion over the rim of the martini glass to gauge his reaction to the question.

"If that is all that we intended to do, such might be the case, Mr. Kendrick, but we have other elements to our strategy. We intend to borrow the funds for purchasing these assets in the international bond market. Through cross-collateralization, those same refining assets in multiple countries will secure the bonds."

"So, you intend to access the Eurobond market. That will not shield you from expropriation." Brian pushed his still nearly full martini to the side.

"You are correct. That is why one of the conditions of purchase will be that the seller invest no less than twenty-five percent of the net sale proceeds within either Iran or Iraq through infrastructure bonds or investment in exploration and production assets. So, should a government wish to take some action against us by seizing refining assets, then we, the Iranian National Oil Company, would claim 'force majeure' on the international bonds, an action that would ripple through the international credit markets." Rezvani glanced again at his watch, but sipped his tea and placed his cup on the saucer slowly, as though he had all the time in the world for this conversation.

"What you're saying is that if any one country expropriates your refinery assets, then you will default on the Eurobonds and let the bondholders deal with the country that took over your assets."

"Precisely, Mr. Kendrick. The consequences would be born principally by the bondholders, not by either Iran or Iraq. Further, history, as written by Mexico, Argentina, and other countries that have abrogated their foreign debt obligations in the past, tells us that credit markets have short memories and even the worst offenders eventually are able to return for additional funding. And, of course, with foreign oil companies having invested billions in our country, we would also have recourse to substantial internal assets to offset against assets expropriated by any country." Rezvani took another sip of tea, draining the cup, and placed the small china vessel back down smartly as though he had just declared checkmate.

"My compliments," Brian said with earnest admiration. "You obviously are fully aware of the complexities of this transaction. My apologies for not assuming that you would be."

"I do not take your questions as an insult. Your firm has a reputation for being direct and truly focused on serving its clients. I accept your inquiries as a means of understanding our strategy so that your work will benefit from that context."

"Very good, Mr. Rezvani," said Brian. *And I do thank you for telling me all about your strategy.* "We have some details to work out such as forming the transaction team within our two organizations. I'll have a draft engagement contract to your office here by end of day tomorrow. I will personally manage this effort, if that's agreeable." *I'm not about to let Iran, or you, get this political leverage.*

"Of course," said Rezvani, nodding. "You will not be surprised to know that we have allocated a twenty-five basis point co-management fee to a consulting firm in Zurich."

Brian responded blandly, hiding his true feelings for those who jam their snouts into the public trough. "Mr. Rezvani, we're very familiar with the common courtesies extended to important contributors to these intricate transactions. So, in answer to your question, we're not surprised."

Brian waved for the check and told the waiter to leave his drink. After paying the bill and watching Rezvani meticulously fold his napkin and place it on the table, Brian escorted him to the Lexington Avenue door where his limousine awaited.

If this guy weren't such a goddamn fanatic, Islamic chauvinist, and dirt bag, he might make a great banker. He went back to the table and thought about the deal as he finished his martini. He would normally be ecstatic at having such a transaction for the firm, but, instead, Brian was deeply troubled.

Chapter Three
Sunday, January 12, 2014; Chicago, Illinois, USA

Rezvani placed the call at eight in the morning from the Prince Charles Suite. His room was considered one of the best at the Drake Hotel and was named in honor of HRH's visit back in the 70's. Room service had been slow and the meal lukewarm, so he had sent it back with a brief tongue lashing for the hapless server. *Imbecile Americans*, he raged inwardly. *How could they have acquired such power?*

He looked out of the suite's windows into the cold foggy nothingness on the other side. *I cannot wait to get out of this place and back to the French Riviera. The French are stupid, but at least they know how to live.* He habitually tidied the room, picking a thread off a silk throw pillow and tossing a tissue into the wastebasket, as he waited for the other party to answer. He had visited over a long lunch in New York with some important international banking friends on Saturday and then flown to Chicago to meet with several petroleum exploration and chemical processing engineering firms. Rezvani was recruiting a set of unaffiliated advisors upon which to draw and counter-check the advice given by others, even CHK.

"Hello," said Rezvani when he heard someone pick up. He punched the speakerphone button. Rezvani did not call his counterpart by name, a standard operating procedure between the two. By not using names in any communication, it would be much harder to identify the participants sharing the transaction fees to be paid to the co-manager. Theft was harshly punished in Iran under the Quran, so precautions were in order. They were about to pick their government's pocket for $500 million and, if they were caught, they might get more than a hand cut off for theft of this size. *I wish this were over and I had my money,* he thought. *But wishing, like associating with Americans, is a useless pastime.*

"Salam, doost. Hello, my friend," came the somewhat hollow-sounding reply over the long-distance connection. "What news do you have to share? And remember, we may not be alone."

"We have successfully concluded the arrangements, and now we must set up the facilities in Switzerland so that the co-manager can be paid and proceeds distributed to the faithful," informed Rezvani.

"I will see to that. Khoda haafez," came the reply.

"God protect you. Khoda haafez," responded Rezvani and hung up. He felt satisfied as he watched ice that had formed on the windowsill crack away and fall to the pavement below. He could see nothing through the mist of the thick clouds, but imagined the frozen missile hitting the sidewalk, sending shards of ice toward a mother and child hurrying through the streets, heads bent against the harsh January wind. Rezvani smiled. *Such is what should happen to all infidels*, he mused.

Rezvani thought about his share of the money that would be distributed to the faithful—those few in power in Iran who would receive tens of millions of dollars into accounts in Switzerland as their cut of the money to be raised and spent by the National Iranian Oil Company. *Faithful to whom? Faithful to what?* He thought about his own answers, smirked, and calculated his share one more time. *I am doing all the work and receiving the least share.* He frowned and began packing. *Time to play among the beautiful infidel women.* He placed a call to the front desk for a limousine that would take him to O'Hare, then to the south of France.

Sunday, January 12, 2014; Beirut, Lebanon

The street, more of a large alley, was dimly lit, normal for so late at night. The man leaning against the ancient brick building felt his lip quiver with distaste, almost contempt. He could see that the woman walking on the other side of the street did not have her head covered, as she must. He would deal with this strumpet; a good beating would help her to remember her place. Perhaps he would do more. He adjusted the sling on his AK-47 so that he could push it behind his back and started across the street.

"Stop, woman!" he shouted loudly in Arabic.

Neena Shahud stopped and turned toward the voice. She smiled, demurely, as she had practiced many times. The man reached her in a few steps and admonished her, "Woman, you must always cover your head in public," he shouted, spraying Neena with spittle. "To do otherwise is an insult to Allah!"

"I have no wish to insult Allah," said Neena. She adjusted her stance ever so slightly.

"Good. Then I shall beat you and you will submit."

"You may *try* to beat me, but I will *not* submit." *Bet that pisses him off*, she mused.

The man, a beefy two-twenty or more, raised his left hand as if to slap Neena across the face. She sprang to his right, bringing her left fist against his neck with a force that cracked his larynx. The surprise on his face delighted Neena, but he managed to bellow through his crushed vocal cords and reach for his weapon. As he did so, Neena's foot flew into his right knee, snapping it like a twig. His corpulent body folded instantly. In one fluid movement, her body followed his to the ground. As she fell upon him, she drew two nine-inch Japanese Tanto knives from behind her back and crossed them under his throat.

"Go to your Allah, pig," she breathed into his ear. Neena quickly drew the two knives together across this throat, drawing the blades up so that they scraped across the vertebrae in his neck. She rolled him over and sliced his stomach from sternum to bellybutton and then over to his left side. She cut out his stomach and intestines and threw them in the gutter. Neena stood up, wiped her hands with a small towel and pulled off her outer layer of clothing, which she stuffed along with the towel into a small bag. *One more. Good!* With a final sneer, she spit on his body, pulled her *hijab* over her head, and walked calmly into the dark night unable to shed the despair that haunted her in this godforsaken city. *Eema, Abba, I am nearly finished. Only a few more.*

Chapter Four
Monday, January 13, 2014; Washington, DC, USA

Undersecretary Vic Alfonse felt gloomy, not unlike the Washington morning. Gray as squirrel fur out there and yet another storm blowing in from Canada. Vic listened to the disembodied droning of Senior Strategic Analyst Jeff McAdams over the speakerphone. *McAdams wouldn't know good intel if it fell on him.*

"I don't give a good goddamn what your challenges are," Vic fumed. "I want you to find out what the hell is going on in the Middle East and stop saying you can't tell me. American taxpayers don't pay you a salary to say you can't do your job, and if you don't do that job, that salary is going to stop. And soon." Vic stared out the window imagining he had just thrown McAdams through it. *I would, too, if it weren't for his uncle.*

"Yes, sir!" replied the incompetent McAdams.

Vic heard the click signaling the end of the phone conversation. *Impertinent asshole.* He circled his wood and leather office as though he could find the answer to his question among the oriental carpets and neat stacks of file folders. He still preferred paper to electronic files, the feel and reality of paper. Comforting. You could rely on it. Like a revolver—load and fire. Simple. Or good, smart, dedicated intelligence officers in the field who could tell you what a mullah had for dinner last night by smelling his shit. *God, I wish I had more of those.*

"What the hell is happening?" Vic said out loud, exasperated. The President of the United States had taken the extraordinary step only last year of elevating Vic's former position as Assistant Secretary for Special Operations and Low Intensity Conflict to that of a full Undersecretary. Vic had come to know well the man in the Oval Office, who had already told the Secretary of Defense that he wanted direct and unrestricted access to Vic. Undersecretary Alfonse might report to the Secretary, but he knew it was the president he had to please.

For the past six months, data and intelligence from the field and his assessment groups had gaping holes. No one was pointing out those gaps, but he saw them. Less data on weapons movements and nuclear developments, some information about communications between Iraq and Iran. He was convinced his people in the field were first rate, but reports for the last several weeks had been sterile, devoid of nuance and scenarios; that is, useless. It was as though some were sharing what data they had or what they were thinking, but not everyone was sharing and not all was revealed. He could tell. Something didn't smell right. Even the other western agencies—England's SIS, the official name of what most people think of as MI6, and the French Direction Générale de la Sécurité Extérieure or DGSE—seemed to have lost deep contact. *Time to find out.*

Vic hit the intercom button. "George, please ask Steve Barber to come in. Thank you." Vic was always polite, even to subordinates. It did not do to be impolite just because you could be or because you wanted to save time. And George was a damn fine secretary. Kept his mouth shut, his opinions to himself. A fine soldier, too.

Vic stood up to greet his visitor, a man who had been part of his organization for only a few months, but one he already admired. Steve Barber had a knack for overcoming obstacles—the ones intel never spotted but which can mean life and death, literally. In his role as the president's go-to military specialist, the man the president looked to when he needed something done quietly and quickly, Vic had his pick among America's armed forces, including those in USSOCOM, the country's unified Special Operations Command made up of the elite units from each of the military services. Vic knew that working for him was the ultimate for any warrior; the pay and benefits were outstanding. But more than that was the knowledge that what you did was goddamn important to your country. And Vic never asked anyone to do something that a warrior—as he was, or had been—would not want to do. That was part of the attraction, too. Vic played fair.

Steve walked through the large mahogany door held open by George, who closed it softly, respectfully, after Steve was inside the office. George had been with Vic from the beginning, through the terms of five presidents, and could be counted on. George was also Vic's personal bodyguard, a job George had asked for after serving under Vic in Vietnam.

"Nice to see you again, Steve," Vic said, and offered his hand. "Did you have a good time in Europe over the holidays?" Steve had a solid grip, no hesitation. An honest, straightforward kind of guy. Vic could always tell from a handshake.

"It's a pleasure to see you again, Vic," said Steve. "As for the holidays, I spent them back home in upstate New York."

"But you don't have family up there. What did you do?"

"You're right about the family; only my sister left and she's in California. I got back early from Ramstein so I could work on the local 'Toys for Tots' program that the Corp runs every year. It's a treat to be near those kids—they don't ask for much and they light up when you give them a simple gift. It's sometimes hard to leave them."

"You seem fond of children, Steve." Vic picked one of his tattered manila folders and walked over to his favorite leather easy chair, motioning for Steve to join him.

"Yes, I am. I'd like to settle down and have a family, but I haven't met anyone who would tolerate what I do for a living. Coming back from these assignments is never guaranteed. I've had a few serious relationships, but they haven't lasted when I leave in the middle of the night and won't tell them where I'm going, what I'm doing, or when I'll be back. Frankly, I don't blame them. Perhaps I'll have to settle for being a good uncle." Steve sat down on the brown leather sofa and Vic noticed his gaze didn't waver.

"You surprise me, Steve," said Vic. "Pretty serious thinking for someone I thought was gallivanting around Europe and having a wild time." *It was like that for me until I met Laura. God, I miss her.*

"I get all the wild times I need working for you, Vic," Steve said with a smile.

"Well I hope to disappoint you with this next assignment." Vic paused for a moment to allow the discussion to turn serious. "Steve, I'm concerned that we're not getting proper intelligence in the Middle East. There's some kind of void, someone shutting down communications. Gaps in what we're hearing and seeing. There seems to be a structural barrier to collecting intelligence and I don't know if that barrier is accidental or intentional. Either way, we need to find out what it is. This is your next assignment." Vic pushed the manila folder across the coffee table to Steve.

"Sounds like a vacation, Vic. If I may ask, why don't you get CENTCOM or EUCOM to assign an intelligence asset to this?"

"It may not be as dangerous as most of your other assignments, but I can tell you that it's equally important, if not more so. An intelligence void in this part of the world is a disaster waiting to happen. I am assigning you because, while most of our intel guys are combat trained, the Middle East is extremely dangerous. If shit is going to happen, I want someone there that can deal with it. That means I want *you* there." Vic stood up to pick a small envelope off his desk.

"You'll start in Israel," Vic said as he handed Steve the envelope containing an airline ticket. "The Israelis are the smartest and best in the Middle East. I know I haven't given you much to go on, but there isn't much. That's the problem. How do you want to get started?" *I hope he's as smart as I think he is. This job needs brains as much as anything.*

"I'd like to see some of the reports that you're getting, if I have proper clearance. They'd give me a better sense of what you're seeing. Or not seeing, in this case." Steve moved to the door, his hand on the knob.

Smart kid. Knows the meeting is over, Vic observed. "Consider it done. And, yes, you do have the clearance." Vic pressed the intercom button. He knew that intercoms were a technological anachronism, but he enjoyed them anyway. As long as it was his office, he would use whatever technology he damn well pleased. "George, would you please pull together a set of the last six months' Middle East Intelligence Reviews for Mr. Barber? And find him a comfortable place to read them, would you?"

"Of course, Mr. Alfonse. Right away."

"As you know, the reports cannot leave my offices."

"Yes, I'm aware of that security protocol. When I'm finished, I'll return them directly to George."

"Fine. Now let's go see George and get you those reports." Vic put his arm around Steve's shoulders. Vic was pleased. *Just the man for the job. He had better be. This feels like the '67 war all over again. Too many secrets.*

Monday, January 13, 2014; New York, New York, USA

The offices of Chandler Hines Kendrick LLP were located on the 25th floor of 101 Park Avenue, just south of Grand Central Station. Inside, with walls of glass and the thickest carpet money could buy, in the corner overlooking Park Avenue and E. 40th Street, was the Founders' Conference

Room. The room, dedicated to the signers of the Declaration of Independence, was home to memorabilia of those who had set the country on a course of freedom and power. The seven partners of CHK always met there, comfortable in their leather chairs, but humbled by an authentic copy of the Declaration—purchased after the firm's first year in business—framed in carved antique gilt. The document was a reminder to keep egos in check and work for the common good of the firm and America. The Founder's Room was intended for important decisions and one weighed heavily on Brian Kendrick's mind now. Snow was falling and the late afternoon sun was a mere glow through the heavy clouds. Small piles of wet flakes were accumulating on the windowsills. *Heavy snow for heavy thoughts*, Brian mused.

Brian leaned forward, placing his elbows on the polished walnut table. He'd briefed his partners on the previous Friday's discussion with Sa'ad-Oddin Rezvani. Now, there were assignments to be made to complete major tasks. Those tasks involved both finding companies who wanted to sell assets and arranging all the financing. Easy in principle, demanding and complex in execution. This transaction would overwhelm all but the best in the business. CHK would knock it out of the ballpark.

The partners were energized about the deal, both because of its size and revenue potential for the firm, and its impact on the global structure of the oil industry. This transaction would be the talk of the financial world for months, if not years. Just as everyone was beginning to enjoy the party, however, Brian threw a very large turd into the partners' punchbowl.

"I've shared with you my discussions with Sa'ad-Oddin Rezvani because, as your partner, I have an obligation to do so," Brian began. "But I have very serious concerns about this deal." The sidebars among the partners halted abruptly. Fingers stopped tapping on the Blackberries.

Harold Chandler, or Hal, as he was known, was the oldest partner at sixty-three years of age. Humble in every way except for his obsession with his full head of silver hair, Hal took pride in the way he looked—"presence' he called it. He was dressed, as always, in a tailored pinstriped navy blue suit with a folded white kerchief in the breast pocket, starched white shirt, and subtly patterned yellow tie. While his experience was more deeply rooted in the more common aspects of M&A and underwriting work, every partner, and most others on Wall Street, listened when Hal had something to say. Brian gave Hal his full attention as he raised his hand to speak, as Brian knew he had learned to do at boarding school. Hal fixed his gaze on Brian and did not wait to be given the floor.

"Brian, if you have serious concerns about this deal, I would like to know what they are. Before you begin, though, I think we all recognize that a transaction of this kind comes along only once in a lifetime, and mine is almost over," said Hal, inserting a little humor to take the sudden tension out of the air.

"Let me explain my position," said Brian, smiling at Hal and pouring water from a crystal pitcher into his glass, trying to get the last ice cube to slip over the spout. He wished he had aspirin for the headache he knew he was going to give everyone. The ice cube plopped into his glass, and Brian took a long drink of water.

"I believe that this set of transactions can be structured in ways that appeal to all parties, and I also believe that the Iranians are counting on us to make that happen," said Brian. "The oil companies are very capital-intensive and the prospect of reducing the capital employed in refining assets will be very attractive. Even the requirement to reinvest twenty-five percent of the net proceeds in Iraq or Iran will not be a deterrent because they will have either the infrastructure bonds or exploration assets on their balance sheet. They might see the long-term danger that I will outline in a moment, but they will succumb because (a) Iran will be willing to pay top dollar and (b) they will presume that the other oil companies will go along and will not want to be left behind."

Brian paused and glanced out the window. The snow had turned to a hard, icy rain. It was dark now, light from the conference room dancing on the raindrops as they hurled themselves at the windows.

"You've got that right, Brian," Hal interjected. "We all have industry clients trying to shrink their balance sheets."

"And, of course," Brian went on, "were the oil companies to discuss among themselves their common interests in declining to participate and jointly decide to forego the sale of refining assets to Iran, the Antitrust Division of the Justice Department would get all kinds of hot and steamy." The partners chuckled at this. Hal winked at Brian in a familiar expression that Brian knew meant "good show."

"The international bond buyers will have the same dilemma," said Brian, feeling this was going fairly well. Perhaps he wouldn't need that aspirin after all. "The yield on the bonds will be attractive because Iran will make the yield whatever it takes to place the debt. The fact that the bonds will be secured by physical assets in Western countries will make it even more difficult to resist. What mutual fund or public pension fund would be able to say 'no' when the others say 'yes'?"

"At least until the issuer defaults," put in one of the partners. "We get it, Brian," he continued. "This train is going to leave the station, with or without us. All I have heard so far, though, is good news. What's the bad news?"

Brian shifted in his seat. Damn knee was acting up but he didn't want to stand and pace the room, as he would normally do. He needed the partners' undivided attention. "This deal will not just leave the Iranians holding significant assets in a strategic global industry. They will be further insulated from any economic sanctions that the world community might wish to impose on them because of their ability to create bottlenecks in the supply of fuels and other petrochemicals."

"So, if I get where you are coming from," Hal said, a touch of his Boston accent still obvious in his voice, "Iran would feel virtually unrestrained in its avowed objective of total hegemony in the Middle East and the literal destruction of Israel."

"That's it exactly, Hal. I don't think this world needs a fanatical Islamic regime the size of Iran, enlarged further by its annexation of Iraq, with few checks on its power." The rain was louder against the windows now. Brian felt a chill and glanced at the thermostat behind him on the paneled wall. Seventy degrees. *Twenty-one degrees Celsius. Feels colder.*

The room was quiet for several moments, the impact of what Brian said being distilled by bright minds. Brian rose to stretch his knee. *Give them a few minutes.* The rain swirled in wild patterns, and it was difficult to see the taxis lined up on 40th Street below. The commute tonight would be a nightmare and Grand Central would be a crowd of wet and angry travelers. Brian lived alone uptown, so the commute was not much of an issue for him, but he knew his partners would have a tough time of it. After a while, before the murmurs between neighboring partners could become a din, Hal stood up.

He waited for the silence and attention each partner expected of the others. Brian returned to his chair.

"I share Brian's concerns," Hal began. "We can all agree that the free market system is amoral—it does not judge our efforts in its name and has no defense against actions that we would consider wrong. The free market system leaves to us, its participants, the task of judging whether the actions we might be *free* to take are actions that we *ought* to take."

"Hal, get to the point. It's getting late and I want to get to the Knicks game," another partner moaned.

Hal shot the partner a lift of his patrician jaw and continued. "I also know that were we to abandon this project, the Iranians would simply find another firm—one certainly of lesser moral balance—to achieve their objectives. As I've thought about what Brian has discussed, I have concluded that, for the good of our firm and our world, we cannot enable the Iranians to achieve their goals. So, I think the challenge is doing this deal in a way that will be acceptable to the Iranians yet remove or substantively mitigate Brian's concerns. No easy task, but we pride ourselves on creativity, do we not?" Hal finished, sat down and was silent as his words, like Brian's, poured over the partners.

The next to speak was Joe Burstein. Although his name was not on the door, Joe was a partner in every respect. He was also a sartorial contrast with Hal—wearing slacks and a button-down shirt to the office except when meeting clients, on which occasions he consented, in deference to his partners, to wearing a sport coat.

"I think Brian and Hal have done a great job at crystallizing what we have here," said Joe, leaning back in his chair, one leg crossed casually over the other. "This room reminds me to think about this deal like our country's founders might and act in the best interests of our country, our clients, our industry, each other and our families. If I hear Brian and Hal correctly, then we need to own and control this transaction so that, at worst, we have done no harm and, at best, we have submarined the ayatollahs in a major way. I am pleased to report," he grinned, "I already have a few ideas about how to go about this."

The other four partners, two men and two women, also had something to say, so the meeting lasted past six o'clock. At the end, the partners decided easily and unanimously to, as Joe said, own and control the transaction. Brian then took charge of the deal and added Joe as the second partner. The two of them would run the deal team. The other partners would be brought up to date occasionally and, as needed, brought in to brainstorm or assess ideas. Later, the seven partners would review and approve the final transaction in full detail. There was a lot to do, however, before that would happen. Brian's headache came on full force.

Brian stayed in the office long after the other partners had left. He went back into the conference room, turned off the lights and stood in front of the windows, so close that his breath condensed in foggy patches on the glass. He felt like he had when he had been a Marine going into Iraq the first time. He relished the challenge, but he could always see, or foresee, more than others. *This could get nasty. I hope my partners can handle it. Some precautions for all of us are in order.*

Chapter Five
Thursday, April 17, 2014; Gat, Israel

Steve Barber looked at the white concrete block wall across from the gray metal table and shook his head. He was not disagreeing. He was focusing. No one in the room with him—good. Noise in the hallway—bad. Where *was* he? Didn't matter much. He knew he was in deep shit.

Steve knew a lot about shit because he kept landing in it. Part of the job. At least he was well trained—an eight-year veteran of force reconnaissance in the Marine Corp, he inhaled combat and weapons training and exhaled a particular skill at stealth maneuvers. Although he didn't find the statistic attractive, Steve knew that Vic Alfonse kept Top Secret files on Steve's thirty-two confirmed kills, including the four in Egypt last December. He did not work hard at what he did for the pleasure of killing, but because it was his way of making a difference—hopefully a positive one.

He was groggy—not the good kind from a long workout and a full day's work—the chemically induced kind. He guessed they'd probably used sodium thiopental. He was almost a connoisseur of these things by now and sometimes created tasting notes in his head just to focus on something and get his mind under control. Control was always key.

The hallway noise was getting louder and Steve could distinguish words. Hebrew. *Hebrew? Israel is a goddamn ally. What the hell am I doing tied up and drugged by Israelis?*

"Mr. Barber, I am pleased that you are alert," said Major Ari Lapid as he stepped into the room. Steve had heard the jingle of keys in the door lock and brought his mind into clear focus so that he could greet his visitor properly. He felt the handcuffs pinch as he pulled himself erect in the metal chair. He took a moment to catalog his environment. The door was steel with a twelve-inch, mesh-reinforced window; the room, not more than ten feet square, but very clean and well lit. No openings beside the door, except for a small ventilation duct covered with mesh wire. "I am sure you know that we do not normally treat our American colleagues this way, but you have been under surveillance for a few days. Frankly, your recent behavior is discomforting, very discomforting."

Discomforting? Who is tied up and fighting a hangover? Not you, shithead. Steve kept these thoughts to himself. *Control. Find out what you can.*

"What are you talking about?" Steve managed to say calmly.

"Three days ago you entered our country ostensibly for the purpose of attending a symposium at the Weizmann Institute. Not only have you not attended any portion of that symposium, but you have also been observed near sensitive military installations where you have taken photographs. Wouldn't you agree that such behavior should be discomforting to us?"

Steve knew that Lapid meant the Symposium on the Changing Middle East. He'd intended to make some of the presentations. Countless minds sorting out what the virtual absorption of Iraq by Iran less than six months ago meant—some experts were stunned. Most were trying to put on a good face, but the truth was that a combined Iraq/Iran was a scary thought in most western and Sunni capitals. *Well, say what you will about the Israelis, they're not fools*, thought Steve.

"Come on, Ari, you know damn well I am with US military intelligence," Steve lied. Steve had an authentic US military identity card, but he worked directly for Vic Alfonse, Undersecretary of Defense for Special Operations. "And you also know that those installations have been photographed by every intelligence agent with as little as a digitally enhanced iPhone. Besides, those photographs aren't of the installations. They're photos of the valleys and towns around them. Israel is a very beautiful place, if you haven't noticed."

"I have noticed, Mr. Barber. Why have you not attended the Symposium?" Lapid walked around the table and stood close to Steve.

"I decided that the Symposium was going to be boring—a lot of people who don't know anything trying to sound like they do. I assume you didn't want to go either. By the way, where are we? And why am I tied up?" Steve pulled his arms to the side and wiggled his fingers, reminding the major that he was handcuffed.

"I am not going to answer those questions, at least for now. Do you remember how you got here?" asked Major Lapid.

One of those dumb little teasers some asshole interrogators like to dangle in front of you. "Last I knew, I was having a drink at a bar near the Sea

Executive Suites Hotel," answered Steve. "Now that you mention it, I do recall an unusual tang in that martini. So, no, I don't know how I got here." He thought for a minute about the various intelligence services and their preferences for drugs. He might put a game together—match the agency with the type of drug. "Are you going to tell me?"

"Certainly not," said Major Lapid. "Besides, it is of no significance to our current situation. Mr. Barber, I am not here to get information from you, but to deliver a message. Go to the closing of the Symposium and then leave Israel. Then your behavior will no longer be discomforting to us." Major Lapid turned toward the door.

Steve decided to push a little, if only because he was pissed. "Shall we discuss the consequences should I not do as you suggest?" asked Steve, already knowing the answer.

"I do not think that such a discussion is necessary," Major Lapid responded mechanically. "We both know the range of possible outcomes, but let me offer that we see America as a less valuable ally than in the past and so we are becoming much less deferential to people like you. Goodbye, Mr. Barber. Shalom." He left the room.

Steve sat motionless in his chair despite having to take a leak. *This is very strange. Why was Lapid—Israel?—trying to give an American the boot?*

One of the Major's minions came back with a hypodermic. It made no sense to struggle. "I prefer the left arm," Steve said in flawless Hebrew. The Israeli did a double take. *Damn right, chaver, friend, I speak your language.*

Steve recognized his hotel room. *Damn, they couldn't just let me leave, they had to pump more crap into me and dump me here.* His body was stiff so apparently he'd been out for hours. Even his eyelids felt taut. His throat was dry and he could feel carpet burn on his cheek. *Nice of them to drag me.* Steve rubbed his bruised wrists, something he was used to doing, and clumsily dialed room service—coffee, eggs, toast, and grapefruit juice. Orange juice didn't have enough bite.

Thursday, April 17, 2014; Qom, Iran

Ayatollah Mohammed Khoemi thought the day was going to be brilliant. Today's forecast was just like yesterday's 12 to 14 degrees Celsius and, at least today, no chance of rain. *A beautiful April day and a good day for doing Allah's work*, he thought, hypocritically. Khoemi enjoyed the spine-tingling sensation that his false virtue spurred. The recent defense and foreign affairs pacts with Iraq were manifestations of growing Shi'ite strength, and Iran's influence in the Middle East had leapt as a result. Next on the agenda was a cooperation agreement between the Iraq National Oil Company and the National Iranian Oil Company. This agreement would assure crude oil supplies and provide currencies for building or buying additional refining capacity. Soon Iran would be virtually independent of the international markets for oil and refined products and Khoemi planned on using this success for furthering his own.

Khoemi put down his Quran once he saw the servant had left the room and picked up the "Financial Times". *I am getting tired of pretending. Soon I will not have to.* He checked the spot and futures prices for crude oil and smiled quietly in the solitude of his small garden. He checked real estate listings in London and mentally circled a couple of manors in Surrey. *Lovely country. I will buy one house there.* He needed to leave for a meeting soon, but took several moments to review what he had accomplished toward securing his new future.

After the phone call from Sa'ad-Oddin Rezvani on January 12, Khoemi had contacted private banks in Switzerland and established numbered bank accounts. These types of accounts were not as impenetrable by foreign governments as they once were. Over the years, Switzerland had signed a number of treaties under which the Swiss were obligated to provide information regarding those accounts. But the primary impetus behind the treaties on the parts of the counterparty governments was to uncover tax evasion and that was not the objective of Khoemi or his partners within the Guardian Council, which ruled Iran. He, and they, just wanted the money to be safely outside Iran.

Khoemi and the partners had also set up a small "door plate" consulting firm in Zurich, to which a twenty-five basis point transaction fee on the deal would be paid at the closing of each individual transaction. The trick was that they would be paid the points both on the M&A purchase amounts as a "finder" and on the principal amount of the Eurobonds as a co-manager of the deal. Double dipping this way would result in total fees upon the full $100 billion investment equaling $500 million. A woefully corrupt and incompetent government is only a problem to the taxpayer. *It is all coming together rather well.*

Khoemi left his home dressed in a combination *pirahan, shalvar,* and *jameh* with a wide belt called a *kamarband* wrapped around the *jameh*, which draped to just below his knees. He also wore the traditional headdress, known as the *sarband*. Khoemi, on the outside at least, was a true believer.

He walked the few blocks to a small café on Lavasani Street, and on his way, he could see the deferential smiles and nods of the faithful who recognized him. He was not a well-known figure outside of Qom and he preferred it that way. *Harder to find me afterward.*

He liked the fact that Qom, known best as a center of Shi'ite Islam and a place of pilgrimage, was about ninety-seven miles from Tehran in north-central Iran. He had studied long and hard, and after years of stern effort, mostly at the large madrasah or theological college in Qom, he had been rewarded with the title of Ayatollah. With that, he had catapulted to a level of power and influence that shook him mightily and fatefully. Within only a few years, Khoemi had capitulated to the evil side, and with exceptional cunning, had successfully masked his complete abandonment of Mohammed. *The evil side. It is only evil if you believe. I do not.*

Crossing the doorway of the café, he hailed Danesh Mahdavi, one of the Ayatollah's direct reports within the Qods Force. Khoemi chuckled as he thought of the irony of the name Qods, which meant Jerusalem. *The Jews will never let the Jerusalem Force into Jerusalem.* Although technically a part of Iran's Islamic Revolutionary Guard Corp (the "IRGC"), the Qods Force operated under the direct control of Supreme Leader Ayatollah Ali Khamenei.

"Allah's blessings be upon you," he said to his subordinate.

"And upon you," replied Mahdavi.

The two moved to a large booth in the back and as they did so, others moved from nearby tables to give them greater privacy. Khoemi smiled at the people as they did so. *The faithful are such sheep.*

Khoemi ordered a cup of tea and, as Mahdavi did also, Khoemi looked around at the bare, but clean surroundings. He took pride in what the Iranian people were capable of doing with few resources. The mud brick walls of the café had been lined with the wood from discarded pallets and painted white. Small curtains, fashioned from old robes, were held in place by paper clips twisted into intricate designs. *The West often overlooked this strength,* he mused.

"How are things going with the merger of the defense forces?" Khoemi asked, referring to the integration of the Iraqi and Iranian armed forces. Of course, the IRGC was exempt from this activity and would retain their separate powers, forces, and weapons.

"All proceeds as anticipated. We are maintaining the illusion of offering open arms to the Sunni contingents. At the same time under the guise of integrating forces, we are re-distributing the Sunnis in small numbers within larger Shi'ite units. Soon, we will be able to remove all Sunni armed forces in a single night, as you have instructed." A waiter skittered by, obviously not wanting to disturb the Ayatollah and his guest.

"Good. Praise be to Allah," Khoemi stated, emotionless. "I have something else for you to do for me," he said, handing Mahdavi a large sealed envelope. "In there," Khoemi said, pointing to the envelope, "You will find the transcription of an intercepted message. I don't know the source, but I sense a group within Israel sent it. What intrigues me is the message's inclusion of large number arrays. I want you to find out who sent the message and what the message is about, especially the number arrays. What kind of resources do you need?" Khoemi took a sip of his tea and scoured the café for important faces. *None. Good.*

"Let me work on this alone for now," Mahdavi said. "What level of security do you wish to keep on this?"

"Keep this between us for now," Khoemi said. "If you need to bring someone into this, do so only to find out what those numbers mean. As you find out more, let me know immediately." Khoemi drained his teacup, stood up and left. He expected Mahdavi, as always, to pay.

Mahdavi remained seated as Khoemi left. He had become inured to Khoemi's brusque manner and rudeness. *No matter,* he thought. *I will get mine. Perhaps Khoemi will get his.* He took advantage of being alone in the booth, opened the sealed envelope, and read the message to himself.

"The data in the matrix below are to be substituted in the relevant systems upon receipt. Destroy message and contents in accordance with the Masada Protocol."

That was it. That and a string of numbers in an array as Khoemi had said. *In accordance with the Masada Protocol. Hmm. Masada is the name of a hill near the Dead Sea that was the scene of a mass suicide by Jews back in Herod's day. They wouldn't surrender to the Romans. That makes it Israeli, as Khoemi thinks. "Protocol" means it is probably military in origin. What systems are they talking about?* He paused to reflect, deciding that people were beginning to take too much notice of both him and the envelope. He paid and walked out of the café. *I know who can help with this.*

Thursday, April 17, 2014; Beirut, Lebanon

The late spring sun baked the tourists on the beach just outside the InterContinental Le Vendome, Beirut Hotel, conveniently located on the coast road. Gabir Haddad sat in the Lobby Lounge and sipped on his strong coffee, enjoying some of the beauty before him. He told himself that caressing the bodies of infidel women with his eyes was not adultery and dismissed the harpy in his head imitating his father's gravelly voice.

Guests and servers, bellboys, and an aroma of the best perfumes mingled around him. He was dressed like a wealthy westerner—an off-white Armani suit, open tan silk shirt, and light brown Ferragamo shoes. Perfect for today's weather, the fabric of the suit smooth and lightweight; not a hint of sweat under his arms. Gabir wore a customized Tag Heuer watch with an array of built-in special electronics. His face, in defiance of Islamic preferences, was clean-shaven, what his mama would call a "sweet baby face". His hair was cropped to above his ears and combed with a part on the left side. He was a long way from the slums of Beirut, but only in some ways.

Gabir Haddad had grown up in a strict Islamic family. His father was a mix of gentleness and brutality, both of which he applied with little consistency. Avowedly Muslim, his father drove religion home, and Gabir and his siblings were schooled thoroughly and ruthlessly in the Quran. In his youth, Gabir claimed to have passed from the Islam level of faith through Iman to the highest level, Ihsan. His weapons training was equally, if not more, thorough, thanks to dedicated teachers in Qom, and he had demonstrated this talent during the 2006 incursion by Israel. The Glock model 17C semi-automatic 9mm strapped to his side was easily accessible and a deadly tool in his twenty-nine-year-old hands, as was his Gerber Touché belt buckle knife. Gabir was thankful that his duties required him to dress this way and consume alcohol upon occasion. So thankful was he that he often created those occasions.

Gabir was at the InterContinental to observe and report on foreign agents whose presence annoyed Hezbollah, but not to the extent that he was ordered to threaten or harm them. The Americans were everywhere and so obvious as to arouse Gabir's curiosity—were they so poorly trained or were they flawlessly executing some operation? Either way, it was not his problem, at least not today.

He liked the French and had adopted their lifestyle. The Brits, Americans and German were cogs in bureaucratic wheels and generally uninteresting. One Brit, Sir Joshua Bennett, was an exception in a way that Gabir found somewhat endearing and very entertaining. Sir Joshua often would have a couple of gins and take over the Yamaha grand piano in the Lobby Lounge. He could carry a tune and would spend an effortless hour sharing a repertoire that included show tunes and ballads popular during the last fifty years.

As Gabir was completing the visual examination of a young woman from Germany, the corner of his eye caught another beauty entering the Lobby Lounge from Le Petit Bar off the main foyer. He quickly noted that she was a Prada buyer and wore it very well. *I have to meet this woman,* thought Gabir. As he was planning to do so, she walked straight up to him with a smile that was all business.

"You miserable son-of-a-bitch," she said in a hiss, teeth bared. "Who the fuck do you think you are?"

Her tone was so aggressive that Gabir moved his hand instinctively to the 9mm under his coat. "I am sorry, miss, but I don't even know you," responded Gabir with professional control, his thumb around the weapon's grip. "Perhaps you confuse me with another," he offered courteously.

She looked sharply at him and then, with a warm, glowing smile laughed, "Oh, rfiki," she said, using an Arabic word for friend. "You don't remember me! I was in training with you at the Fateh Qani-Hosseini Garrison. You called me your little Basmah, your little smile."

"Basmah," Gabir erupted in happiness as he pulled his hand from under his coat. "I never imagined you would become such a stunningly beautiful woman! What has happened to that little girl? I can see the smile remains. I left you so long ago. Tell me everything that has happened." Respectfully touching the fringe of the tan cashmere shawl she wore over her black Prada sleeveless dress with its incredibly low-cut neckline and cinched waist, he observed, "You appear none the worse for your devotion to our cause."

"And I see that you have been able to adapt to the needs of martyrdom, as well," she laughed softly, fingering the sleeve of his Armani suit, spilling her long, raven-colored hair over his arm.

She suggested that they have a drink by the pool, to which Gabir could only blurt out, "Brilliant." He spent the next forty-five minutes hearing the tale of her last eight years.

She had left the Hezbollah training camp three years ago and had been working in Jerusalem and Europe. Her facility with languages and excellent counterfeit documents allowed her to function as native-born in six countries, including France, Germany, Italy, Lebanon, and Iraq. Her physical prowess, honed by years of training and discipline, was legend within Hezbollah. Gabir recalled one story that had her taking out two heavyweight martial artists in a seedy part of Marseilles, where the two thought that Basmah might enjoy an involuntary ménage à trois. Instead, they ended up hanging, gutted, from the rafters of an abandoned warehouse.

"Basmah, you have come very far from the little girl I knew," Gabir said. He took a moment to run his eyes over her, pretending to be the uncle who is gesturing in surprise at how big she has become. *Had I known,* was all that came to his mind.

Basmah could see in Gabir's eyes that he was enamored and intensely impressed with her accomplishments although he could never admit so openly. What Basmah did not share with Gabir or any other Hezbollah was that she was born Pnina Shahud and traced her family's roots to a small Jewish community in Lebanon. The Jewish community had all but disappeared with the hostilities that followed the establishment of Israel in 1948. What Neena, as she was nicknamed, also did not share, was that she was a top agent of the Mossad, and only five people in that organization knew of her existence. She had been embedded in Lebanon and Hezbollah when she was seventeen years old, a third of her lifetime ago. She was a deft assassin with an individual and oh-so-effective twist of sadism for enemies of Israel. She would flirt now and slit his throat later. *We'll soon be up close and personal in a way he isn't expecting,* she thought.

Thursday, April 17, 2014; Pädäh, Jerusalem, Israel

The grounds of the house, covering about five and one-half acres, were exquisite, from the square stone fence topped with short, thick cedar-paneled walls that ran the circumference of the property to the fine collection of rare rose trees forming the center of an elegant, small garden in the back on the north side. The cedar walls were mounted on top of a set of hinged metal panels. At the order of the watch commander, armored plates capable of stopping .50-caliber rounds would rise through the panels and surface to a height of ten feet.

There was a basement, strengthened with ultra-dense, reinforced concrete and steel, and the entire interior of the house had been retrofitted with thin layers of laminated graphite sheets to absorb both ordnance and van Eck emanations, which could be intercepted and reconstituted by parties unfriendly to Israel. A few floors had been added under the basement and they were similarly hardened and reinforced.

The house was built in the early 1950's by an elderly relative of David Ben-Gurion, who gave it the name Pädäh, meaning "to deliver" in Hebrew, to commemorate the most recent formation of the state of Israel. Pädäh had passed from the man's estate to the Mossad as a gift in remembrance of those who had died during the Holocaust. Colonel David Alon knew the house well. His uncle was the builder.

David was meticulous about his craft and the design of Pädäh's security carried his touch everywhere. Electronic intelligence tracked the inhabitants and scanned the exterior for hostile movements. The instruments even scanned the environment, projecting observed images against stored digital files and running algorithms for abnormalities. Seismic sensors detected subterranean aberrations, compared them instantaneously to documented tremors, and deduced potential attack via the underground. Forty highly trained members of the Mossad comprised the full-time guard; four 12-hour shifts of five members on site, with another five in reserve, and the last fifteen off premises. In addition, roaming randomly, there were two cars with two heavily armed agents; each within ten kilometers of Pädäh. David Alon personally picked every man and woman on the security team. Each was a patriot. Each was a superb weapon. Each was dedicated to David.

David oversaw every security element mainly because he lived at Pädäh without interference from anyone and wanted to keep it that way. Pädäh housed an ultra-high secret group and only a few people outside of the house and its security team knew of it. The Israeli Defense Minister, Simon Luegner, was one of those few.

"Sergeant Shachar, get your ass in here!" David bellowed. Zadok Shachar, known as "Zee", jumped at the command, as David knew he would, and was in the Colonel's office in less than ten seconds.

"Yes, sir," replied Zee as he rushed through the doorway to David's office.

"You did not encrypt this message before you sent it. Why the hell not?" David demanded, waving a printed sheet of paper as if it were a white flag.

"Sorry, sir, but your orders were to send it immediately and the encryption software had not been updated with the new keys. Is there a problem, sir?"

"I don't know. But there could be," David said firmly. He paused for a moment, a trick he often used to drive home his irritation and remind a subordinate how bad an idea it was to piss him off. It always worked and he watched Zee, a battle-hardened veteran, squirm, just a little, under his professional exterior. "Standing orders are now that everything, repeat, everything is sent encrypted. If you have a technical issue with executing any such transmission, you are to bring the communication to me for action. Is that understood, Zee?" he said, lapsing into his informal way with the men and women he respected so highly and needed in order to protect Israel.

"Yes, Colonel. Understood," Zee replied. "Sir, if I may ask, what do you think someone could do with the information? The coordinates have been re-adjusted per the Masada Protocol so that they are gibberish to anyone reading them."

David picked up a couple of walnuts from a porcelain bowl on his desk and cracked them in his large calloused hands. He picked the nutmeat out of his palms as though lifting lint off a jacket, and tossed the pieces into his mouth. "They *may* be gibberish," corrected David when he had finished chewing. "The mere existence of a communication with what appear to be geographical coordinates would interest most of our enemies. If someone has intercepted this, he will try to determine the context and meaning. Have no doubt. Put out a silent message to our networks to listen for these kinds of queries. Take no action and do not be proactive with this one—just listen!" He tossed the shattered walnut shells into a brass wastebasket under his gray metal desk and slapped his hands together several times to knock off any walnut detritus.

"Yes, sir. Will do," Zee left the office, the heels of his boots clicking on the wooden floor in a pattern that pleased David. *So methodical that sound. If someone has intercepted this, we may have a problem to eliminate,* David thought. *Nothing worse than disorder.*

David entered a 256-bit encrypted password into a laptop computer sitting on the low metal credenza behind his chair. The laptop had been strengthened with a special hard drive and crush-proof casing so that he could literally throw it against the wall if need be and still be able to use it afterward. He pulled up a folder labeled "Masada" and opened the Timeline.xls file. May 4, 2014 was marked with a Star of David for the 66th anniversary of the founding of modern Israel—Independence Day. The day before, May 3, had its column marked with a series of encrypted notes. *The day before Independence Day*, mused David, leaning back in his chair and wrapping his hands over his head of dark, cropped hair. He absentmindedly found the two-inch scar in his scalp, which had enriched his hairline since the '73 Yom Kippur War, and rubbed it like a talisman. *The day we remember those who have lost their lives in making and keeping Israel free. This Memorial Day will truly be a day to remember.*

"Colonel," croaked the speaker on the security monitor screen on his desk.

"Yes, lieutenant," David responded, seeing the face of the watch commander.

"Colonel, we have company."

"Friendly?" David queried, even though he assumed so because he saw no alarm in the man's face.

"I believe so, Colonel. They are broadcasting over our secure channel seeking permission to enter Pädäh. They responded with the proper pass codes," the officer replied.

"Thank you," said David as he closed out all the files and logged off his computer. "Observe our security protocol. I will meet them in the courtyard. Have a light security detail ready and look for shadowing vehicles and movements." David grabbed his Jericho 941, chambered a round, slipped the weapon, nicknamed the "Baby Eagle", into his shoulder holster, and snatched his jacket.

Thursday, April 17, 2014; Tel Aviv, Israel

"That felt good, especially after that last shot of sodium thiopental," Steve Barber said aloud to no one. He'd had breakfast on his balcony overlooking the Mediterranean Sea, and felt pride at his rapid recovery from his drug therapy, as he liked to call it. Fully alert back in his room at the Sea Executive Suites Hotel in Tel Aviv, he contemplated the events of the last twenty-four hours over espresso, so strong it crept from the cup.

He had detected the listening device upon first checking in, thirty minutes after arriving in Tel Aviv three days ago. The large flat screen LCD HDTV was now on at medium volume, showing one of the almost-constant soccer games. Although the TV didn't drown out every sound, Steve had not talked on the phone and he was alone. That and the fact that he'd been whisked away for questioning by the Israelis for nearly 24 hours, so the eavesdroppers must have been bored to tears. Steve was not annoyed. *Hell, we do it, too.* What he had not liked was the micro camera in the bathroom, so during his first night, he'd spread a thick layer of Vaseline on the lens. Steve enjoyed the nuance of using petroleum jelly.

He lounged for a while in the hotel's cotton robe and poured over his coded notes of the past few days. *Strange behavior, even for these guys*, Steve concluded. *There is nothing I've done that should've resulted in this high-intensity response.* Steve dressed in khaki pants and a short-sleeved shirt called a *chultzah im sharvulim k'tzarim* so that he would blend in with the locals. He "accessorized" with a Walther PPK/S 380CP that he slipped into the back of his pants. *Luckily, I did not take that with me to the hotel bar last night. Tough to explain losing a weapon to a friendly.*

He strode out of the hotel and continued along Herbert Samuel, turning up Trumpeldor past the Metropoliten. The day was bright and clear, the exact opposite of how he felt this assignment was going. Although not concerned about being followed, he still went through the steps to keep his skill level high. He stopped occasionally using store windows to reflect the people and events around him. Steve noted people with caps pulled over their eyes and those reading newspapers. He mentally inventoried everyone walking in the same direction, and compared these inventories block by block to identify those who were consistently with him. He doubled back on a block once or twice and re-ran the inventory. He did many things the hard way—like memorizing the descriptions of every person walking alone on his block—so that his skills would keep their edge.

As he walked down Shalom Aleichem and came to Ha-Yarkon Street, he saw the US Embassy at Number 71. Despite passage of the United States Jerusalem Embassy Act on October 23, 1995, under which the Embassy was to be moved to Jerusalem by May 31, 1999, the United States still maintained its Embassy in Tel Aviv. Steve knew many of his Israeli friends bristled when the topic arose because the highly symbolic move was to be a clear demonstration of America's firm support and, if necessary, military defense of its small, yet highly respected ally.

Walking into the compound, he showed his DoD identity card and US passport to the Marine guard and asked for Bill Elsberry. He entered the embassy foyer and noted the white marble floor and walls forming an octagon about twenty feet across. In the middle, under a massive crystal chandelier, a large mahogany table matched the room with its octagonal shape. The table was intricately adorned with inlaid yew and rosewood in the form of the Great Seal of the United States of America. On the table, an immense dried flower arrangement displaying the many flowers of Israel rested on a starched white lace runner. *My tax dollars at work*, Steve admired.

"Good afternoon, Mr. Barber," greeted Philip Palun, the Embassy Secretary and a career diplomat within the State Department. "How may I be of service?" Steve generally liked the career people. It was the political appointee that occasionally pissed Steve off.

"Hi Phil," said Steve in response. "I would like some time with Bill Elsberry if he's in." Steve wanted to bounce ideas off of someone with brains and experience. Bill Elsberry was one of those people and Steve had already cleared bringing Bill into the assignment with Vic.

"Let me check," Phil responded pleasantly and disappeared down the eastern wing. He returned after a moment with Bill by his side. Bill greeted Steve with a bear hug and a wide, toothy smile.

"Great to see you again, Steve," said Bill, motioning Steve to walk with him down the hallway. "Have you given up trunkbunking for honest spy work?"

The two men walked down a narrow side corridor, talking about friends, and stepped into a small, but well-appointed office. A secure fax machine and telephone were visible as was a set of electronic panels that flashed digitized numbers on LCD screens. A large American flag stood in a brass holder in the corner by a well-worn leather couch. A silver tray with an ornate hand-hammered silver samovar and two china cups sat ready on a mahogany coffee table. Loose-leaf teas in a divided wooden box were beside the cups, the scents of orange and cinnamon permeating the office. Strong, fresh smells. Bill was a coffee drinker, but, as a courtesy, he kept a wide selection of Middle Eastern teas for his guests. Small porcelain bowls held hunks of raw sugar and slices of lemon. The office was clearly a man's, in spite of the tea service. *Elegant, but not too fussy. And it projects power.* Steve considered that perhaps embassy duty was not without its good points. Bill poured piping hot strong black coffee into two cups. The two talked for a few more minutes as friends, reminiscing on past cooperative operations before Steve decided it was time to get to the point.

"So, Bill, other than wanting a free cup of coffee, want to know what brings me here?" questioned Steve.

"Now you've hurt my feelings, Marine. I thought you just wanted to spend the afternoon with me." Bill got up, closed his office door and returned to his seat. "What's up?"

Steve briefed Bill on his assignment and filled him in on his encounter with Major Lapid. Then Steve leaned forward as he habitually did when he expected undivided attention from a listener. "Bill, you and I know that what Lapid did was bullshit." Steve put his cup down on the saucer. "I can't imagine he was acting under official IDF orders, so I'm convinced someone is pulling his chain. How does what I've said strike you?"

Steve sat silent for a minute to let Bill think. Some people process information by talking about it; others, like Bill, needed some quiet time to absorb the data and let the brain turn it over and over until patterns emerged. As he waited for Bill's mind to finish percolating, Steve recalled how the two met on a special operations team in late 2002.

The operation had been in preparation for the eventual invasion of Iraq in March of 2003. The team's objective was to enter Iraq unobserved, re-supply a friendly contingent of sheiks, provide weapons training to their forces, track down and eliminate some local Baathist operatives, and leave the same way. The team was a little over three kilometers inside Iraq when they came under fierce assault by heavy weapons and RPGs, the acronym for rocket-propelled grenades. A few sheiks had given up the plan to the Baathists, who, with their own paramilitary force, had lain in wait for the Americans. Bill, a colonel in the Army Rangers at the time, had been the operation's leader, and as the attack strengthened, he assessed the situation and executed a withdrawal. Steve still bristled when he thought of it. He was not a man who retreated. He knew, though, that Bill had made the right decision under the circumstances and admired the skill with which he had led the team.

Steve saw that Bill was still thinking and stood up just to move. Steve could command his body to be still for long periods of time, but he preferred frequent physical movement. He fought the urge to pace knowing that might distract Bill and, instead, pulled aside the light linen drapes and stood looking out the large bulletproof window into the embassy's garden, thinking about that night in Iraq.

The team made it out of Iraq with minor casualties, helped greatly with fearsome pinpoint nighttime air support, which had swept into the tiny valley within minutes of the "mayday" call. Steve and Bill were not back across the border ten minutes when each looked at the other and made the same decision. Back at base, the two formulated a mission based on critical intelligence collecting as a primary objective to obtain approval to reinsert.

Three days later, the two men went back across the border and secretly trekked the twenty-three kilometers to the original team's meeting point. They interrogated several Iraqis, all of whom were left alive to bear witness to their actions, and killed each of the betraying sheiks and their eldest sons in their own homes. So fast and so quiet were the two that the Sunnis of the area still called them "silent doom". They were reassigned when the true nature of the mission had become known, but no one in general command wanted these two reprimanded for the action taken. They had kept in touch and took the time to see each other when in the area. Very different men, but Steve and Bill respected each other greatly. Steve knew that Bill was not a man who retreated, either.

"No question about it, Steve," Bill began, snapping Steve out of his reminiscence. "Something is up and even before you came in today, it was clear that Washington is hot to find out what it is. Your boss, Vic, is all over me and the other intelligence guys out here. He sees a void in the reports. Things *are* too quiet, too uneventful. It's as though everyone is on vacation, and we know damn well they aren't. I have checked with our British friends in SIS and some French DGSE colleagues. I even contacted some of our old sheik friends in Iraq," he said exchanging a look and a smile with Steve. "Nothing. It's eerie."

"What about Lapid?" Steve asked, turning from the window. "Abducting me and giving me that kind of message in that way is not something I would have expected in Israel. Iran, yes; Israel, no."

"Well, Steve," Bill responded, "I've spent a lot of time here and I can detect a growing dissatisfaction with America among Israelis. There's an increasing fear that we are not the stable and dependable ally that we were under Bush Two, Reagan and earlier administrations. Frankly, I share that opinion."

"How so?"

"We have let the greatest detractors of Israel hold high positions in the UN and its commissions. We slap Israel and its leaders around publicly in some wacky attempt to placate our temporally friendly Shi'ite and Sunni governments. We hold Israel to the highest human rights standards and yet let the countries surrounding them oppress and torture their own people. And when it came to opposing Iranian and North Korean efforts to develop nuclear arms, all we could muster was a series of worthless Security Council resolutions."

Steve let the drapes fall back into place and walked back to his seat. It was hard to swallow, but Bill was speaking the truth. "Well, Bill, I share your views. The Israelis must be asking themselves who their friends are."

"I might add that Iran is a country that has an official foreign policy position stating that Israel is illegitimate and should be, and I quote, 'wiped from the face of the earth.' Then, we have the gall to ask the Israeli military to do the dirty work of bombing the bad guys and their nuclear weapons facilities. Worse, we pretend as if we were not at all involved in the planning and execution of the attacks and let the Israelis take shit from everyone. If I were an Israeli, I would be really pissed off. In fact, as an American I *am* pissed off!"

Steve saw Bill's temperature rising—along with his own—and knew that he needed to channel his and Bill's thinking to something positive. "I think it's a good idea to team up on this one," Steve offered. "Someone is behind the lack of information. I think we can agree that what we are seeing, or more to the point, not seeing, is intentional. We need to know who that someone is and his motives."

Phil Palun opened the door as he knocked on it and reminded Bill of a meeting in ten minutes. Bill nodded and Palun left, closing the door behind him. "Agreed," said Bill. "I hadn't focused on this until our conversation, but now that I have, I am concerned because intentional actions like this are usually the result of something very bad. It takes effort to create vacuums in nature and this is a big vacuum here. I have friends in the IDF and Mossad. Let me see what they can tell me. What are you going to do next?" Bill stood up and went over to his desk. He pulled out a small well-worn leather address book from a locked drawer.

"I could give Major Lapid a thrill and leave Tel Aviv for a while." Steve chuckled to lighten the mood. "Yes, why not? Think I'll go up to Lebanon and poke around. Do we still have resources there that I can work with?"

"We do," Bill replied, thumbing through the address book. "Not as many as we used to, and I'm sure some of them are doubles. What I don't know is which of them are. You might want to start with Christian Meureze. He's retired DGSE and has never learned English, but he's been in Beirut for over thirty years and worked the Middle East when he was in the Directorate. Charming guy. How's your French?"

"*Je parle Français assez bien, mais pas couramment.* I took it in college and brushed up when I was assigned to NATO for a couple of years. *Je vais voir si Christian peut nous aider*," Steve said with a slight shrug of his shoulders.

"If you need to speak with me, use this number, which I will answer at any hour," Bill said, writing it on a small card. "If I need to contact you, I will get word through Christian. Also, I don't want to make this overly dramatic, but I think we should operate under a code for this." He thought for a minute. "How about 'Masada'?"

"Okay, I know the story and its significance, but why *that* word?" asked Steve.

Bill responded, "I was the guest last week at IDF induction ceremonies on top of Masada and was quite impressed. Those men and women are serious—I mean *serious*—about their country. I guess it just popped into my head."

"'Masada' it is," affirmed Steve. "Could I use one of your secure lines to call my boss and bring him up to date?"

"Of course."

Steve placed the call to Vic Alfonse from a small conference room. Vic told him that he would contact Simon Luegner, the Israeli Defense Minister, and ask him to offer any assistance possible. Steve returned to Bill's office and the two quickly embraced. Bill walked Steve to the embassy's entrance and waved as Steve crossed over Ha-Yarkon Street.

As Bill disappeared into the embassy compound for his meeting, the hair on the back of Steve's neck prickled. He accepted this call from his sixth sense. He kept walking at a steady, strong pace and used shop windows to observe behind him and to his side. *Don't see him, but I know he's there.*

Across the street, the man on the rooftop squeezed the trigger of the unloaded weapon and admired the imagined shot he would make, instantly killing the target on the street below. "Colonel's orders," the man muttered to himself in Hebrew, "but I'll have my day." He collapsed his Heckler & Koch PSG-1 sniper rifle, disassembled it, and placed it respectfully in its carrying case. He then pulled out his cell phone, placed a call, and left down a rear stairwell.

Later Thursday, April 17, 2014; Pädäh, Jerusalem, Israel

The decorated metal gates opened slowly, betraying their purpose, as the abatis, a three-foot high metal collision wall, disappeared into the driveway. The watch commander observed the incoming caravan. The lead car, a GM Suburban that had been armored and the engine modified for greater power, with run-flat heavy-duty tires—"hardened" in security speak—had stopped at a small guardhouse outside the compound and offered a password that matched the correct phrase for the day. Had the password been incorrect, the watch commander who monitored all vehicular entries to the compound would have hit a button resulting in the instantaneous implosion of the ground under the car. The result would be the vehicle dropping into a reinforced concrete pit six feet deep.

The other two cars had remained on the street beyond the driveway to allow greater maneuverability for evasion and escape. When the lead car was fully inside the compound, the other two cars sped into the courtyard. An armed security detail that had been standing along the interior wall ran to surround the vehicles and a second detail stood watch over the scene, weapons at the ready.

David Alon emerged from the house and Simon Luegner, Israeli Defense Minister, stepped out of the second car, also a "hardened" Suburban. The two men embraced. The security detail was dismissed and the drivers of

he vehicles followed the detail into a small, but comfortable waiting room off
he courtyard. Out of courtesy, Simon Luegner's personal bodyguard was
allowed to remain with him. Two members of David's command were
assigned to kill the bodyguard upon David's order, a pre-determined gesture.
David hoped he would never have to make that gesture.

"Shalom, Simon," David said. "How is Israel's distinguished Defense
Minister today?"

"Shalom, David. I am well, thank you." Simon replied. The two men
strode into the house. They passed through a side door and into the butler's
pantry, then out to the main hall and into a small parlor. The windows were
translucent, allowing light into the room, but not transparent and were
impenetrable by anyone outside, even with the aid of electronic listening gear.
David closed the door behind them and pressed a command on his cell phone
disabling all surveillance of the room.

"How are preparations coming, David?" asked Simon, settling on a
plushy armchair opposite David's chair. He straightened out a lace doily.

"We are on schedule," said David. The room was eerily quiet. No
beeping of surveillance monitors, no hum of the computer, no chatter over the
tactical, or "tac", security channel. David pushed another command on his cell
phone and a large flat-panel screen came from behind the wall. The words
"Masada Protocol" ran across the screen. "Let's go through the major points
of the Protocol."

"I don't know why you can't just call our plan a plan. Why do you
have to use the term 'protocol'?" Simon took out a nail clipper from his pants
pocket and chipped away at an offending cuticle.

"Simon, the Masada Protocol is more than a plan. It sets forth our
established code of procedure in executing every task we must complete. It
tells everyone what the tasks are and who is accountable, just like a plan, but it
also describes how we handle information, maintain security, and issue orders.
The term protocol is well understood here. I don't care if it is not understood
elsewhere." David snatched a couple of walnuts from a porcelain bowl and
demolished them between his hands. *What a pompous ass!* He picked out four
large pieces, ate them and dumped the remainder in a trash can. *I need our
distinguished Defense Minister for only a few more days.*

Simon took a break from commanding his personal hygiene battle and said, "Very well."

David entered another command on his cell phone, which brought up a detailed timeline on the screen, and continued, "We have modified all of the guidance software as outlined in the Masada Protocol and we have entered 167 coordinate sets. We have scheduled our people to be on duty and we have checked and re-checked every person's background. Our psychologists have affirmed each individual's ability to operate as instructed. We are currently placing a virus in the launch control software to disable all self-destruct and re-targeting commands." He came from behind his desk and walked up to the screen.

"What about security?" Simon asked.

David responded crisply, "We have surveillance on each launch team and we are scanning all traffic for key words and analyzing random communications phrases for possible connection with us. We have restricted information flows with all allied agencies as well as with some domestic security agencies. We are getting some flack for that, but I have explained to our domestic friends that we are upgrading and hardening our systems against cyber-attacks, which is taking us offline from many standard communications and data sharing protocols. We did have one communication that was sent unencrypted and have taken precautionary measures to look for an intercept."

"Damn. How did that happen? I thought your almighty Protocol covered that," asked Simon, turning his fingers over and back, inspecting his polished nails.

"We were upgrading our encryption software at the same time that I sent a message to our launch teams," David replied, not willing to reveal the person responsible. *Damn you, Zee, for being so careless.* "We have taken steps to ensure that no future communication is unencrypted. Luckily, the coordinates were in straight data arrays and were re-calculated based on the Masada Protocol, so it will be very difficult to understand the message. Someone intercepting the message may assume, incorrectly of course, that it is actually encrypted."

"What was that last bit about data arrays?" Simon asked. He snapped the clipper back into the closed position, placed it back in his pocket, and stared blankly at David.

What a dumb sonovabitch. "The coordinates are expressed as longitude and latitude. Those numbers were in the message as one long column, what we call an array. If you didn't know what the numbers represent, you'd have a very difficult time figuring out what they mean. In addition, the presence of so many numbers in the message might lead whoever might intercept it into believing that the message is in code; that is, encrypted." David turned toward the screen to hide the scowl he felt crawling over his face.

"All right," Simon said, sounding somewhat hesitant. "I need to tell you about a conversation that I had earlier with Vic Alfonse of the US Defense Department."

"I know Vic," said David. He turned and beamed a pleasant face at his soon-to-be-expendable co-conspirator. "He's a good man. What did he have to say?"

"He was inquiring about what he senses is a void in intelligence information flows over here and wanted to know if I knew anything," Simon said.

"What did you tell him?" David asked.

"That we sensed it, too, and would like to work with his people on it," answered Simon. "He has sent Steve Barber, one of his best, over here. I thought it would be better for us to know what they know. Do you have anyone who is credible, but who is not part of our plan, to assign to this?" Simon stood up and walked over to a bottle of scotch in the butler's pantry. He pulled a glass out of a cabinet and helped himself to a short drink.

David thought for a moment and said, "Yes, a remarkable young woman. I have her assassinating Hezbollah to keep her and them occupied. We run the risk of her finding out what we are up to, but I think I can manage that. I will re-assign her to working with the Americans. Too bad, though, she doing a superb job eliminating the enemies of Israel."

"Well, we will take care of all of that soon," Simon said, throwing back the scotch. "Vic Alfonse also complained about the treatment given by Uri Lapid to the operative, Barber, the man he has working on the intelligence void."

"Lapid acted on my instructions. Mr. Barber has been doing a lot of probing and we would be at less risk if he were to leave Israel. I have had an agent tracking Mr. Barber as a precaution. Don't worry. I have given the agent strict orders to observe and report only. No harm will come to him at our hands, at least for now." David felt the scowl returning and fought it.

"Perhaps the new agent you will assign to work with Mr. Barber can control him."

"If anyone can, she will."

"Keep me posted. There is no room for error and no going back."

No shit. "Understood," David said, clenching his large fists. The two men left the room as David re-enabled internal surveillance. Security did a sweep of the area surrounding the compound and issued an "all-clear" signal, upon which the small caravan rushed out of the gate. David returned to his office in the house to issue an encoded message to Neena Shahud. *I hope she's causing someone trouble.*

Chapter Six
Early Friday, April 18, 2014; Beirut, Lebanon

Steve flew from Tel Aviv to Athens on Sun D'or International Airlines and from there to Beirut. *Better to have my passport with a Greek stamp in it than Israeli,* he noted to himself. Now traveling as Stephan Butterhändler, a senior sales representative for a German manufacturer of numerically controlled three-axis machine tools, he was wearing squarish glasses and his hair was slicked back. The NC machine company was the parent of the company he was in Lebanon to represent—an armaments dealer. He liked playing parts. This was one of several in his repertoire—the Teutonic merchant of death.

Steve enjoyed adding a sense of irony to his adopted persona. "Butterhändler" in German means butter dealer. So, he trades in both guns and butter. *Clever, if I do say so myself.* He had similar twists to his other aliases. Steve believed it helped to have a sense of humor, however bizarre.

In flawless German, Steve told the taxi driver to take him to the InterContinental Le Vendome, Beirut. Then, professing a lapse of memory and in a flurry of German profanity, he re-directed the driver in accented French. The trip took only twenty-five minutes as the driver raced through the bumpy, narrow streets of Beirut as if he could not endure someone speaking French badly. It's possible they were airborne at one point. Steve rather enjoyed it. But, in spite of the wild ride, Steve had ample time to go over his plan.

He would spend some time at the hotel, noted for its wealthy international guests and great views of the Mediterranean, and see who was keeping the hotel under surveillance. After lunch, he would call Christian Meureze and set up a meeting. Bill Elsberry had agreed to contact Christian and provide background. From there it was a matter of discreet inquiries among known traffickers in intelligence and number-ten envelopes filled with dollars. Assess and redirect, as necessary, afterward.

"Welcome to the InterContinental Le Vendome, Beirut." The doorman spoke cheerily in French, interrupting Steve's thoughts and opening the taxi door. The doorman did not bother to ask if Steve needed help with his luggage, but immediately summoned a bellman to take the large leather suitcase around which a thin, lightweight, two-inch wide chain mail belt was drawn so tight that the leather bulged. There was only clothing in the suitcase, but Steve liked playing with people's impressions so he made it look like it held diamonds. Christian would provide an untraceable 9mm when they met.

The hotel was very accommodating because, with the election of Hezbollah to a majority of the 128 seats in the Lebanese Assembly, tourism had fallen by over thirty percent. So although it was morning, Steve checked in and went to his room, tipping the bellman a 10,000 Lebanese Pound note worth about six dollars and fifty cents. *Bet his income's been hit hard.*

He had not been to this hotel before and took several minutes to examine the suite. The newer hotels were contemporary in design and furnishings, almost minimalist. Tiled floors in neutral colors, lots of glass and reflective surfaces, halogen lighting, and electronic everything. Steve thought the décor was cold, functional, yes, but lacking Grandma's welcoming warmth. Taking a small iPod from his briefcase, Steve selected a special application and swept the suite for electronic emanations, finding only a small transmitter in the living area. He left it operational. *They'd just replace it with a different one.*

He freshened up, buttoning a new casual shirt and rolling up the sleeves, donning slacks, and changing his shoes for sandals. He put his favorite Maui Jim sunglasses in his shirt pocket and took the elevator to the lobby where he bought a paper and sat watching the movements of people. He noticed a man noticing him and internalized the fact, including a complete mental picture of the individual, from his high-priced shoes to his dark close-cropped hair. The morning and lunch were uneventful, so he made the call to Christian Maureze.

"Hello, Christian," Steve spoke effortlessly in French. "Are we all set for two o'clock this afternoon?" Christian confirmed the time. They would meet at Bakawat for coffee.

Steve chose to walk the several blocks to the restaurant, which was located in the Beirut Central District near the Place d'Etoile. He thought he saw the man from the hotel in a car, but with so many vehicles having tinted glass, it was difficult to be sure and it might have been someone else. Nonetheless, Steve took a couple of quick detours and entered the restaurant through the employees' entrance at the rear. The kitchen clattered with activity s he slipped through, heading toward the swinging doors he assumed led to ne main dining room. A couple of prep cooks looked up with bland xpressions but continued chopping onions as though strangers wandered rough the kitchen daily.

"Welcome to Beirut, Steven," offered Christian with sincerity but also ome surprise at Steve's entrance. *Like me, he's done his homework*, Steve lmired. *Knew me on sight.*

"Hello, Christian," said Steve, "It's a pleasure meeting you." They ound a small table near the front windows, which were full-length and pushed an open position on their pivoting hinges to allow the fresh air to swirl out the café. A sparrow flew in and landed on a busboy's tray, pecking at ftover crumbs. The street was crammed with vendors hawking clothes, tchenware, and the latest in counterfeit electronics of all kinds. Stalls filled ith green, red, yellow, and purple vegetables jammed up against tables with olts of fabrics in every color. Voices of the vendors, raising and lowering in tensity as they haggled, blended in a cacophony of commerce. The street mmered with bodies weaving in and out, sandals clacking up and down rrow stone steps in between stalls, the pungent scents of sweat and spices d incense wafting through the open window of the restaurant. Expressions weathered faces were passionate as each engaged in the serious task of eryday buying and selling.

Steve and Christian each ordered a cup of the aromatic, strong presso for which Beirut was known, and both men scanned the room, specting the surroundings. Steve searched for anything out of place, a chair ainst a door or the barrel of a gun peaking from under a waiter's towel, or dividuals who showed too great an interest in them. Steve was satisfied.

"It's kind of you to meet with me," Steve began, again speaking in ench. "Bill Elsberry told me much about you, and I'm very pleased that u've agreed to help us." Steve leaned forward. "As Bill explained to you, e're very concerned that a group with great power in the Middle East is eating an information vacuum. We have nothing concrete—just a void in the nds of information that normally flow among intelligence societies. Vic lfonse, whom you know, has detected this and wants to know what's going . We can't tell him yet because we don't know. I've come to Beirut to see hat can be learned here. Have you noticed anything similar?"

"Yes, I have," replied Christian, "but before we get further into this matter, I have the book that you wanted." Christian reached into a canvas bag and brought out a large French/English dictionary.

"Thank you, Christian," said Steve. He knew the book had been hollowed out for a 9mm semi-automatic. "Hopefully, I won't need it, but it's nice to have with me." He placed the book on the table next to his left arm.

"Now about the intelligence void," Christian began, "I think I might have something for you. We have noticed such a void here as well, but I would say that the principal missing information is what normally swirls around and through the Israeli intelligence community. For example, we are still receiving and exchanging data around Iranian and Iraqi movements, including their push to buy refining assets in America and Europe, but the flow is to and from non-Israeli conduits. I think you are seeing the Israeli intelligence community cutting off normal contacts and information flow with the western agencies."

Steve turned from searching the street to face Christian. "That's interesting. Do you know why?"

"No, I do not, but such behavior suggests that either they are focused on something of great importance to them or they are purposely disengaging from their western allies. Do you have a sense of which it might be?"

Steve didn't answer because movements outside momentarily distracted him. He now surely saw the man from the hotel diagonally across the street, and a few steps away was a very attractive woman whose attention was not on Steve and Christian, but the man. Steve noticed that the man did seem to notice the woman and that he was trying very much to blend in as just another person visiting vendors on the street. *Fat chance looking like a regular Joe when you're wearing Armani.*

"I see it as well," said Christian, as he raised an eyebrow and followed Steve's gaze.

"Do you recognize them?" asked Steve.

"The man is Gabir Haddad, but the woman is unfamiliar. She is clearly trained in such things because Haddad is no amateur and he's totally unaware of her presence."

"I saw him at the InterContinental this morning," said Steve, sipping his espresso, keeping his eyes on Christian while using peripheral vision to watch for movement from the man across the street. "What do you know about him?"

"Gabir Haddad is currently acting as eyes and ears for Hezbollah among the international visitor set," Christian replied. "He may seem like a dandy, but he was well trained in Iran and has a history of assassinations, including several Jewish families that had remained in Lebanon up until about 2000. He has a reputation for extreme brutality. Now, there are no Jewish families here, and he is one reason why."

"She is tailing him," said Steve. "Do you know of any factions in Lebanon so bold as to get in the face of one of Hezbollah's assassins?"

A group of uniformed school children passed in front of the restaurant, momentarily blocking their view of the street. *Damn!* Steve fought the impulse to stand and look over the heads of the school children. Christian seemed to understand the question in Steve's mind. Christian nodded twice. He could still see Haddad.

"No." Christian responded, "There are various opposition groups and they are armed, of course, but it is not the style of any of them to operate in such a manner." The street cleared in front and Steve again saw Haddad out of the corner of his eye.

At that moment, it seemed as if Haddad realized that they were talking about him. He swung to look in a shop window and, with a casual air, turned again and walked out of sight down the street. The unknown woman followed, first striking up a brief conversation with a passerby and then, after a few steps, crossing the street to the side of Bakawat, but down the block fifty feet or so. Then, she, too, disappeared.

"Well, our meeting is now known to the bad guys," Steve observed. "Is that going to be a problem for you, Christian?"

"They are aware of my background, and they know that I have many friends from many places," said Christian. "Our meeting will be noted, but without further data, they will assume that we are either just friends or exchanging information. They are too busy trying to dominate Lebanon and please their Iranian masters to make trouble for one or two foreigners. Thank you for your concern, but don't worry about me." The waiter returned, removed their empty cups, and waited long enough for Steve to pay.

"Is there some way we can follow up on your view that the Israelis are behind the lack of intel?" asked Steve. With one last look up and down the street, Steve stood up.

"I have some contacts in the Mossad from long ago," Christian said as he got up as well. "As long as I do not ask for specifics, I will be able to find out. I will only be able to determine whether the Israeli intelligence groups have gone quiet, but not why they have done so."

"Fair enough," Steve said. "So, I'll call you tomorrow afternoon?" The two headed away from the table and through the restaurant, filled now with a noisy lunch crowd.

"Yes," Christian answered. "That should allow me sufficient time. Good day, Steven. Kindly give my regards to Bill."

"Of course," said Steve, shaking hands with Christian and then leaving the same way as he'd entered. As he left, Steve heard the dissonant sound of a police siren wailing nearby. *Can't be me. I paid the bill.*

Neena had tailed Haddad since daylight. As he was absorbed in watching two men drinking coffee at Bakawat, Neena waited for her moment, blending in with female shoppers in the outdoor market across the street. Although she preferred the darkness for her work, she worried that Haddad would be more difficult to locate and isolate later. *Why did I have to feed my ego by getting in his face yesterday?"* Neena bitched at herself. She knew the answer—she would enjoy the shocked look, the wide-eyed terror, his overwhelming confusion at being so betrayed—a perfect moment.

Haddad had continued down Maarad Street for a few blocks. He was clearly unaware of Neena and was taking no standard precautions. *The mistake of taking comfort at being on your home turf,* thought Neena. *A fatal mistake.* Haddad had stopped on occasion to speak with someone or to go inside a shop. At these times, Neena would pull up her *hijab* and engage a market vendor in conversation, pretending to haggle over the price of figs or avocados. She was alert, hypersensitive to movement or a shift in Haddad's body language, and none of the sellers seemed at all confused or offended when she abruptly moved on, picking up the tail.

Ten minutes after she stopped across from Bakawat, Haddad took a turn into an alley. Neena moved liked a cheetah. As she pulled back her *hijab*, she scanned windows, doorways, and rooftops—all were clear. She pulled out twin nine-inch Tanto knives—her favorites—and called out his name. "Gabir," Neena said, just loud enough for him to hear.

Haddad stopped in his tracks, spinning with a broad smile and hands outstretched to greet his Basmah. Just as he did so, Neena lunged forward and swept her right foot under his left, causing him to crash backwards onto the pavement. In one effortless move, Neena pivoted and came down full force with her left knee on Haddad's chest, her right leg stretched to the side for balance. In an instant, she had jammed one knife under his chin against the jugular and the other blade point ripped through fabric to the bones of his ribcage. Haddad tried to say something, to ask why, to beg for his life, but his voice failed and Neena just pushed the knives harder—they were drawing blood now. She smiled.

"You piece of shit!" she spit, small flecks of moisture shooting onto his face. "You will know who has cut your throat. I am Pnina Shahud. Ten years ago, you and your small band of murderers butchered my mother, my father, my brothers." His eyes told her that he remembered. The terror in them was a beautiful sight. She continued in a whisper laced with brutal bitterness, "I have been an Israeli agent from the time you called me Basmah. And you thought you were training an assassin for Hezbollah." Neena sneered, and pressed harder with the knives as Haddad's blood flowed. "Well, this assassin is going to slit your belly open and rip out your insides as you did to my family. I will say a prayer of thanks as I watch you die in the same agony."

As Neena moved her right hand to bring the blade of the Tanto across his stomach, movement nearby made her flinch, and offered Haddad an opportunity. He jammed his right thumb up between the blade and his throat, forcing the knife away though it cut deeply into his thumb. At the same time, he spun his body to his left. Again, he spun to his left, pushing her off.

Neena reacted instantly, jumping back and to her right as Haddad, despite his deeply lacerated thumb, managed to draw his weapon from under his coat. He fired several times, but the deepness of the wound kept him from holding the weapon firmly. The bullets shattered against the alley walls, missing Neena.

Neena thought of thrusting herself headlong into him with knives ready to carve, but realized that she would face his 9mm at point blank range.

Instead, she threw one knife, seeing it strike him in the chest, but knowing it sank too far from the heart to kill instantly. As Haddad staggered from his wounds and the impact of the Tanto, Neena pulled her hijab about her head and whorled from the alley as it filled with people attracted by the gunfire. She saw the fear in their eyes and knew that was an advantage. They would stare at the wounded beast and ignore her. Cloaked in the fog offered by their terror, Neena slipped through the stunned spectators and eased into the street amid the enveloping crowd.

Steve dismissed the commotion outside Bakawat as just another moment of chaos in Beirut and returned to his hotel room through streets crowded with shoppers, honking cars, goats and children. He entered the hotel room, while his mind connected dots. Was Mossad behind this? Was there a link with Major Lapid? He placed a call to a special number and left a coded message for Bill Elsberry. He would give Bill a fuller briefing when he got back to Tel Aviv.

Steve had a few contacts of his own in Beirut and would speak with them to validate the information he had received from Christian. Not that Steve doubted him, but it was always wise to corroborate information from other sources.

Steve showered and donned clean clothes, tucking the 9mm from Christian's dictionary in the back of his pants—not his favorite location, but it was less obtrusive there because the small of the back provided room for the weapon.

He sat in the lobby for an hour or so, enjoying the informal fashion show provided by the women guests of the hotel for those inquiring, and occasionally naughty, male minds stuffed in the lobby chairs. He thought about a scotch, but decided to keep his mind clear. A couple of attractive French women passed by talking about their spa appointments. *Ah, perfume, that will get the heart pumping*, Steve thought. He felt a pang. *She wore that fragrance.* The perfume was 24 Faubourg, named for Hermes' street address in Paris. His mind erupted, filled with a turbulent mix of the lingering subtle sweetness of the perfume and bitterness of his memories.

Steve thought back five years, to a woman in Minnesota, whom he'd tried to forget. She was an exceptionally gifted writer and great outdoorswoman, a hunter of deer and elk and an expert with a rod and reel, a combination that various sporting magazine markets found fascinating. She shared his bizarre and ironic sense of humor. She, too, was a Monty Python fan. She was physical and handled her rifle well—something that Steve liked in women—yet very feminine. He liked that, too. She had wanted the life that he could not give her. One night as he was leaving once more to do what he could not tell her in a place she could not know of, she had wept. The stream of tears fell from her chin like sweat from her pounding, breaking heart, as she threw his belongings in the street. She was gone by the time he returned—some of the neighbors said she had moved to Montana. He thought of tracking her down—he could do that in his sleep—but something told him to let it go. She was not the one. But, oh, he had *so* wanted her to be the woman in his life. *Will there ever be someone?*

A loud group of Italians passed nearby, chattering and gesturing, flinging him from Minnesota to the hotel lobby. *Must be almost time*, Steve thought. He would meet his contacts one by one in the late afternoon and evening as people gathered to drink in the bars and cafes. *By the way, where's Haddad? He should be here at this time of day. Not a very competent spy.*

Curious, Steve rose and strolled through the plush lobby with its thick purple carpet, noting the people at the newsstand, the barbershop, and the upscale ladies' jewelry boutique. He scanned the patio where late lunch patrons lingered over dessert at ornate iron tables, date palms casting shadows on the red tile floor. He ambled through the dark cozy bar, a few travelers washing the dust of the day down their throats. Looking at his watch, Steve decided that Haddad would be seen soon enough and left the hotel.

The streets bustled with late afternoon activity and Steve dodged a scooter, the rider shaking a fist at him as he zoomed past. *Up yours, buddy.* Steve's first contact was a former colonel in the Lebanese army during the times of armed conflict with Hezbollah. The fighting had been bitter and the feelings more so. Despite that, the colonel had adapted to the Hezbollah political regime, ingratiating himself because of his skill and experience in subtly playing one person against another. Although never truly trusted by Hezbollah, the colonel nonetheless had ways of learning secrets and selling them discretely to others willing to pay. *Over here, even the good guys sell. It's the way.*

"Rfiki!" Steve said with genuine affection. "It is a delight to see you again." Steve used only the word "friend" to refer to his contact in any communication, written or spoken. No need to give listeners more information.

"Hello," the colonel said warmly, taking a seat at the bar. "How have you been these past few years?"

The Centrale Restaurant Bar, located on a small street off Avenue Georges Haddad, was very chic—contemporary with teak tables atop chrome legs and sleek chairs with burnt orange cushions. The bar, all glass and chrome, overlooked a series of small gardens wedged into a neighborhood slipping into high-rise development. It was still early for the evening set and only two other people were at the bar, several stylish stools away.

The bartender arrived as they sat and attempted to engage them in small talk. They deflected his chatter by ordering and for several minutes discussed old friends and what were once better times for Lebanon. The bartender returned with Steve's Johnny Walker Red and an Absolut on the rocks for the colonel. They drank to mutual health and good fortune.

Steve got to the point: lack of information. He gave the colonel a two-minute summary and asked him what he had seen. The bartender brought a plate of olives and small slices of bread. He stood nearby until Steve's look convinced him to check the levels of alcohol in the bottles at the other end of the bar.

Steve's contact thought for a few minutes and then said, "There is something amiss here. You are correct about that. I cannot quite say what it is, but it has to do more with the amount of information, rather than what the information entails. The 'chatter' as you say is lower, but I am still hearing things."

"Such as?"

"The Iranians have retained an American investment bank to help buy oil refineries in America, Europe and Asia. Ayatollah Mohammed Khoemi is the person in charge of the operation for the National Iranian Oil Company."

"How big is this?"

"I am told that they have one hundred billion dollars to invest."

"That gets my attention."

"The fact is that information is flowing, but not as much as usual. The problem is that it is hard to know why."

"How so?" Steve noticed that the colonel had thrown down his Absolut and waved for the bartender to bring another.

"Well, information has an original source and then gets passed around. Sometimes I know the source, but most of the times I do not. So if the amount of information has slowed down, it is either because original sources are not providing it or intermediaries are taking the information off the market, so to speak."

"Do you have a sense of which sources are particularly quiet?"

"Easily—the Israelis. I used to swap information regularly. Sometimes I would call them. Sometimes they would call me. I have not had a call from them in at least four or five weeks. When I call them, they don't have time to talk and say they will get back to me. They never do." The bartender brought the colonel's drink, removed the empty glass and nodded toward Steve's glass. Steve shook his head.

"Do you have any idea why they've shut down?"

"None at all, but it cannot be for any good reason. As you know, that's not how these things work." *Yes, I know*, Steve thought. *My bones tell me shit is about to happen. But where?*

The conversation came to an end, and Steve paid the check. As they shook hands, Steve handed the colonel an envelope filled with American currency. The colonel smiled and left, weaving through the patrons who were gathering.

Steve continued meeting with contacts at various Beirut locations and finally, his long day was nearly finished. Others had confirmed what the colonel said; some also knew of the NIOC deal, which was beginning to interest Steve almost as much as the lack of information. He chose Al Balad, a restaurant on Ahdab Street near Nijmeh Square, to meet with someone in the Finance Ministry and settled in with his second Johnny Walker of the evening to wait for the contact. Because the restaurant was known for great Lebanese food, he decided to have a small dinner there after his contact left. *This spy stuff can be harder than ops. Well, at least I'll get a good night's sleep after this.*

Friday, April 18, 2014; Qom, Iran

Assistant Director General Sa'ad-Oddin Rezvani hated Qom as much as Khoemi loved it. A man accustomed to traveling a style befitting his position was not used to the relatively harsh conditions of places like Qom that lack Ritz-Carlton hotels and Four Seasons restaurants. Despite his sober behavior with Brian Kendrick in New York, Rezvani was a seasoned epicure of world delights—he just kept his private life *very* private. *Luckily*, he thought, *If events work out as planned, I will never see this horrid place again.*

As Rezvani waited, he imagined what he would do with his share of the transaction fees to be deposited in his numbered account in Switzerland. He had calculated his share of the $500 million transaction fee at $75 million. He felt a little underappreciated as he thought about his meager fifteen percent share of the fees, but several members of the Guardian Council were part of the scheme, and they were key to approving the transaction. *Perhaps I can skim a little more off the fees of other advisors—a 'finder's fee' for making them rich. Just as I hope to do with the insurance company.*

Khoemi walked to the table wearing a scowl and offered Rezvani a moribund greeting. "Allah's blessings be upon you," Khoemi said.

"And upon you," replied Rezvani. *He is such a curmudgeon.*

"How are the plans for the transactions coming?" Khoemi asked.

"They are proceeding very well," Rezvani answered. "Chandler Hines Kendrick is very efficient and knowledgeable. They understand each company's motivation and every refining asset in the world. In three months, CHK has secured four letters of intent with three of the major oil companies, and another is pending with an independent refiner that has fallen on hard times." A waiter, attired in a clean but worn smock, arrived, and the men each ordered a pot of tea. *I hope he doesn't touch the tea* Rezvani wished, sweeping the table with the back of his hand for crumbs, and then continued speaking.

"Brian Kendrick tells me that we should see four or five more agreements this week and another ten by the offering date. The refineries are located in seventeen countries: eight in the US, six in the Caribbean, four in the United Kingdom, ten in Asia, and the other twelve or thirteen in

Scandinavia and Europe. If all are signed, we will have commitments for about $96 billion in asset sales. He and I have agreed that if we reach at least $80 billion in commitments, we will proceed with the Eurobond offering. We can continue the Eurobond offering while we work to get the full $100 billion in commitments." Rezvani stopped briefing Khoemi as the waiter approached with the tea. He glared at the waiter's dirty fingernails, stifling a slight shiver of displeasure. He was silent until the waiter had served them and left.

"Timing for that offering is set for April 28, a Monday," Rezvani went on. "We want to have a couple of days of trading support for the underwriting before the weekend. There are no major holidays for the weekend of May 3 and 4, so trading should be strong after settlement day, up to the market close on Friday the 2nd."

"How are the deal terms shaping up?" inquired Khoemi watching his tea steep.

"The key terms are very acceptable," Rezvani responded. "We are paying a five to ten percent premium above the CHK valuation model numbers for the assets, which is well within our guidelines. It seems the oil companies are more anxious to raise cash than we had assumed. The projected interest rate to be paid on the Eurobonds is only fifty basis points higher than a GE Eurobond with a comparable maturity. Lastly, we are looking at paying fifty basis points less than the Eurobonds on our infrastructure bonds, or on par with the GE Eurobond." He paused for effect, knowing full well he was delivering very positive news.

Not seeing a sign of appreciation on Khoemi's face, he added, "This rate is exceptional given that our government is not guaranteeing the infrastructure bonds, while the refinery assets secure the Eurobonds. This will make our friends in the Finance Ministry very pleased. I have already discussed this with them, and the documents to authorize the issuance of the infrastructure bonds are ready to be approved by the Guardian Council. One issue is that the oil companies balked a little at the interest rate on the infrastructure bonds, so Brian Kendrick and I have come up with an idea that will need your approval."

"All that you have declared is very good news," said Khoemi. "Now tell me your idea."

At last he sees what I have done, Rezvani thought, recognizing an expression of greed in Khoemi. *He must be running his hands through his $150 million share of the fees.* "The idea is for us to set up an insurance company in Switzerland to insure the infrastructure bonds," answered Rezvani. "Then the yield on those bonds would be more attractive to the oil companies. We would capitalize the insurance company with $50 million and insure the infrastructure bonds above a twenty percent loss in principal value. This means that, in the event of a default by the Interior Ministry, which is issuing the bonds, the insurance company would pay up to eighty percent of the principal plus accrued but unpaid interest on the bonds."

The waiter started to approach the table, but Rezvani held up his left index finger and glowered at the man. He turned and walked away.

"I do not understand. How do we insure eighty percent of $25 *billion* with $50 million in capital?" Khoemi asked.

"It *is* complicated," Rezvani said, a little exasperated partly because he did not fully understand the answer himself. "Let me explain. The capital requirements are based on statistical probability of loss. Through CHK, we have hired a firm that performs analysis of probabilities of losses, such as those involving bond defaults. The firm is very specialized and must be chartered in Switzerland for its report to be acceptable to the Swiss insurance authority. That firm's analysis shows that we need approximately $47.85 million in capital. If we will put in $50 million, the Swiss insurance regulator will see more capital at the insurance company than is required. That will please the regulator. Do you understand so far?" While Rezvani waited for Khoemi to answer, he thought of drinking some tea, but he could not bring himself to touch the cup. *Filthy wretch.*

"Yes," Khoemi said at last. "Go on."

"I have saved the good news for last. The Interior Ministry has agreed to pay the insurance company twenty-five basis points for the guarantee so that the infrastructure bonds would carry the low interest rate—that means we will get paid an additional $62.5 million for providing insurance on the $25 billion in infrastructure bonds. So the capital to set up the insurance company comes from the Interior Ministry, not us, and we pocket another $12.5 million between you and me!"

Rezvani found that, in his excitement, he had lifted the teacup to his lips. He gracefully spit the tea back into the cup and dabbed his lips with a scented handkerchief.

"Sa'ad-Oddin, my friend," Khoemi glowed, a smile creasing his lips, "You are a genius. This is all great news, but I must leave. I have meetings with our Guardian friends to inform them of our progress. They will be well pleased, but, of course, I will keep the matter of the insurance company between us."

They said their goodbyes, with Rezvani feigning disappointment at not being able to spend more time in Qom. *I hope that I have not caught some disease from that waiter*, Rezvani thought, paying for the tea and enjoying the thought of his first-class flight back to the French Riviera.

Friday, April 18, 2014; Al-Rassoul Al-Aazam Hospital, Beirut, Lebanon

The doctors finished with Gabir Haddad and let his visitors see him briefly. He lost his right thumb, which had been sliced so deeply that it dangled from the base knuckle. He had also needed one hundred, twenty-five stitches from his left ribcage around his torso through the middle of his back. The cuts were cavernous and the knife had lacerated deep muscle tissue, nicking internal organs. Only swift action by the emergency team had kept him from bleeding out. Haddad, groggy from anesthetics, thought he was a very lucky man. His father's nagging voice reached through the mental fog and warned him to repent of his licentious ways. *Fuck you. Can you never just comfort me?*

Three Hezbollah security men, learning of the incident, rushed to the hospital. Haddad surmised they cared less about him than the fact that someone had attacked one of their own.

"Brother Haddad, what can you tell us about your attacker?" asked one.

"The bitch Basmah did this. She is an Israeli agent!" he tried to scream the words out, but the bandages and damage to his throat prevented him. Gabir sounded like a sick crow. His head fell back on the pillow and the room spun.

"How do you know this?" inquired another, leaning close to hear Haddad's raw, whispered words.

"She told me as she was about to stick her knives in me. I killed her pig Jewish family and she wanted vengeance, but *I* will kill *her*." Gabir was now spent and fell back into the bed, gasping and spitting into the metal dish next to him. The three men left.

Watching the three Hezbollah leave the hospital, Neena realized that she was now the hunted. Her momentary carelessness had left her cover blown—David Alon would not be happy. Mossad had invested many years and precious sums in her penetration of Hezbollah. David had looked to many years of return on that investment. *I will face David when I get to Israel. Right now, I have to carve a pig.*

She entered the hospital through the employees' entrance and, with a rapid intake of the surroundings, sprinted into a supply closet. She dressed in the uniform of a floor nurse, tightly wrapping her own clothes into a roll, which she tucked into the small bag she carried. She still had one Tanto knife and she would make excellent use of it.

There were only two areas in the hospital that Gabir would be found and as she approached the first and checked the patient listing, she realized she had chosen well. There were no guards outside his room—who would be brash enough to attack a member of Hezbollah in a Beirut hospital? *He was lucky once, but he will pay this time.*

She thought for a minute about how to enter the room without allowing Gabir to raise an alarm. As she did, a hospital nurse came toward her. *Remain calm. She might be useful.*

"Who are you? Why are you here?" the nurse asked.

"I have been sent by Hezbollah to provide full-time care to our wounded martyr," Neena invented. "Why are no doctors attending him?" she questioned.

The nurse seemed startled by Neena's question. *It always works. Turn the challenge back on them.* "Never mind. I will call one of ours." She started toward Gabir's room as the nurse stood speechless. Neena stopped, turned and asked, "Where can I find a syringe and fentanyl to ease our warrior's pain?"

The nurse pointed to a small room where medications were stored, and without being asked, walked over and unlocked it. "Thank you, sister," Neena approved. "Now, please carry on about your business." *I will take good care of him.*

As the nurse left the meds room and disappeared down the hallway, Neena picked up a tray and found a syringe. She took a handful of gauze pads and a roll of wide adhesive tape, placing them on the tray. She strode directly into Gabir's room, inching the door shut behind her.

Gabir Haddad lay in a half-stupor and as Neena entered his room in her white uniform, she saw relief in his eyes as he blinked and the corners of his mouth twitched in a weak smile. She knew he welcomed the nurse who would alleviate his pain with one of her magical injections. Gabir's eyes closed.

With breathtakingly swiftness and grace, Neena stunned him with a chop to his temple—not to kill, but to silence him. In seconds, she strapped Gabir to his bed and muffled him with gauze and tape. He twisted and lurched in a frenzied attempt to get free, gurgling, trying to make any sound that would attract others. His effort was futile. Neena went straight to work without a word. *He knows what is happening. He is pissing his bed now.*

She threw a pile of towels on his stomach and made a deep incision with her Tanto knife from under his sternum down through his bellybutton and then at a right angle over to his right side, ripping through the new stitches. The towels quickly turned deep red as the blood gushed from his arteries. She cut out his stomach and intestines and threw them on the floor. Gabir was falling into hypovolemic shock, but Neena knew she had a few seconds to taunt him.

"Die painfully, pig." She whispered into his right ear. "Your Allah cannot protect you. You are Humpty Dumpty now, and no one can put you back together." She spit on his face, used another towel to wipe her hands and the Tanto, then left, turning the sign on the door to "Patient Sleeping" as she stepped briskly, but calmly, down the corridor.

Gabir Haddad, flooded by the excruciating pain of his wounds, lived the eternity of a few minutes. In his torment he could not even pray to the Allah for whom he had slaughtered so many families for a place in paradise.

Neena had not stayed to watch because she knew what he would feel. Later, in a safer place, she would be silent and savor his terror and pain. In minutes, she had cleaned the remaining blood off her hands and arms and had changed back into her street clothes. *Now I have to survive.* She felt no emotion, only satisfaction for another task complete. She took a moment to chamber a cartridge in her Walther PPK and return it to its place under her long *abaya* where it remained concealed, much as the women of ancient times once hid prized possessions under the folds of their cloaks.

Friday Evening, April 18, 2014; Beirut, Lebanon

Steve chose the Al Balad, a restaurant near Nijmeh Square and well known for its casual atmosphere and genuinely good, inexpensive, food. His last meeting of the day, thank God, would soon be over. He had an hour before his contact arrived at nine thirty and Steve intended to stay for dinner. Steve surveyed the restaurant, noting details.

The kitchen connected to the restaurant by a wide, waist-high, service bar with a mahogany top trimmed in ogee bullnose edging that extended over a short wall of rustic, mottled-brown ceramic tiles. A trapezoidal structure of metal framing and glass covered the kitchen area like a squashed chef's toque. The ceramic tiles ran throughout the interior of the restaurant and seemed very much at home with the simple wooden tables and chairs. A portion of the sidewalk offered seating, which was shielded from the evening air by a canvas awning tilting at 45 degrees from the building.

Steve chose to have dinner outside where the light from the restaurant, neighboring cafes and lampposts bathed the street and he could watch the entire block. *What a beautiful night!* Steve took a moment to enjoy it.

Then his cell phone rang. Christian. "Allo," said Steve into the phone, using the typical French telephone greeting. "I have been seeing other friends in Beirut and I'm waiting for another to have coffee with me. What's up?" Christian asked to see Steve and said he could be at the Al Balad in five minutes.

Steve hung up the phone and had the waiter provide service for two. *Shit, I was enjoying that moment of peace. Should have known.*

Christian walked straight to Steve's table. Without waiting for a welcome, he said in French, "Steve, there are some important developments following our lunch today." Christian sat down and picked up his napkin, placing it on his lap. He leaned forward. "Do you remember the woman across from Bakawat?"

"Of course I do," replied Steve.

"You will remember that we thought she was following Gabir Haddad." Steve nodded. "I have heard from sources that she attempted to kill him in an alley just after we saw her and later finished the job while he was recovering at the Al-Rassoul Al-Aazam Hospital."

"Amazing," Steve said, looking up and down the street as though he was expecting more company. "Where is she now?"

"Vanished," said Christian. "But the *real* buzz is that she is a Mossad agent who had been undercover for years in Hezbollah and that she *gutted* Haddad in his hospital bed. They say that she cut him wide and deep and ripped out several internal organs and left him to scream into a gauze and tape muzzle. That is one hard woman, my friend."

"Well, if she is Mossad and was deep in Hezbollah, there is no doubt she knows how to kill," said Steve. "But that kind of kill is personal, so there must be some history between the two."

"I have nothing to offer on that, Steve. But there is something I find interesting about this."

"What's that?" Steve asked. He looked at his watch. *I have time. My contact isn't due here for a while, but I don't want one to see the other, at least in my company.*

"The news came from some old NGSE friends and a Lebanese contact. I called two local Mossad contacts and they claimed to know nothing about the events and even questioned the accuracy of the reports. What I told you *did* happen. I have independently checked."

"Why would Mossad deny it?"

"It follows their recent behavior, as I told you this afternoon at Bakawat. The Israeli agency has shut down all contacts with the outside." A waiter came, but both men waved him off. "There are reports that Hezbollah has sent several two-man teams out to the streets to find 'Basmah' as she apparently is called."

"I would not want to be in her shoes" Steve said, thinking about her standing across from the restaurant. *So attractive. I wonder why she hates so much.*

"Also, as I promised, I have called a couple of old Mossad friends and, unofficially, they told me that traffic within Mossad has been much reduced in recent weeks and external contacts have been also curtailed by order of David Alon. Do you know him?"

"Yes," replied Steve. "I have not met him. All I know about him is that he reports directly to Simon Luegner and runs a tight, highly trained and loyal special operations group. That about right?" *I'll have to meet David.*

"Yes," said Christian. "I have met David a few times, and mark my words, he is the most important man in the Israeli defense community. Bar none. If this Basmah is a Mossad agent and she has been undercover in Hezbollah for several years, I will bet everything I own that she is one of his agents. I no longer feel that Mossad is the source of silence in Middle East information. I *know* that is the case."

"Sounds like you're convinced," said Steve. "Frankly, that is what my contacts have been confirming to me all afternoon. Let me talk with my next friend and get back to you later this evening. Would that be okay? Not too late?"

"Steve, I am retired, but I am not dead," Christian chuckled as he stood up. "I am going out to dinner with a lovely lady and will return around eleven o'clock. We will talk later. Goodbye."

"Goodbye," Steve said. *It's funny how Christian reminds me a bit of Vic Alfonse. Same kind of humor.* Steve watched Christian disappear and picked up the menu. He made a note to try the batata harrah, a cubed potato dish with garlic, coriander and hot pepper. He also wanted the minced eggplant dish, motabbal batenjan. *Decisions, decisions.*

Friday, April 18, 2014; Washington, DC, USA

"Mr. Undersecretary, I am very pleased to meet you," Brian Kendrick offered his hand in genuine warmth and received a strong handshake in return. Getting into the office had been more complicated than Brian imagined. He had spent days working through political and business contacts to arrange the meeting. Finally, the CEO of a major oil company gained Brian access to a man that most people outside the very powerful could not reach: Vic Alfonse.

Brian knew security would be tight, but he was not prepared for a visit by agents from the Department of Defense or DoD—he had been on the Hill often and was permitted open access in those halls. Fortunately, Brian's military record helped. He had enlisted in the Marine Corp after college, mainly because he was not sure what he wanted to do and knew that becoming a Marine had no downside, at least to him. He became an intelligence expert and served in both Panama in 1989 and Desert Storm in 1991. He was especially good at interrogation and turning enemy combatants to the American side. When his enlistment was up, he chose Columbia Business School and received his MBA in 1995. From there, he joined Morgan. His Marine Corp training and combat experience prepared him well for the eighty-hour weeks that investment banking associates normally worked.

The DoD poured over his private life as well. While Brian had done some of those things that all young people do, there was nothing that the DoD thought would endanger the Undersecretary or national security. His clearance came only two days before his appointment with Alfonse. Now here he was in the guy's office, shaking his hand.

Vic made a dismissing motion with his left hand and his aides and security personnel left the room, leaving Vic and Brian in private. They discussed mutual acquaintances, discovered when Brian had completed his own research on the Undersecretary. One could not be too careful. Brian knew several sons and daughters of Vic's friends and also a few industry leaders who were close to the Undersecretary.

"Brian," Vic said as the pleasantries ended, "Before we get to the purpose of your visit today, I want to thank you for your generosity and that of your partners in helping the youth of America. As you might expect, my people are very thorough, and I must say that I have been looking forward to meeting you. How can I be of assistance?" Vic moved to a corner of his office where he had a small sitting area. Brian followed, leaving the chair for Vic. *That's his chair*, Brian guessed. Sure enough, Vic settled into the chair.

"Sir, er, Vic," Brian corrected himself. "I'm here today to tell you of a large transaction that my firm is managing for the National Iranian Oil Company. That alone might be of interest, but my partners and I have strong misgivings about the transaction and have decided to take some actions that will require your help."

Vic served his guest as he always did, pouring Brian's coffee first and placing the cup and saucer in front of him on the coffee table. "I know of many of the contacts you have been making throughout the oil industry and, frankly, I didn't know if I should be curious, concerned, or both," Vic offered, as he poured himself a cup of coffee. "Why don't you tell me the details?"

For the next forty-five minutes Brian systematically went over the various elements of the transactions. He then outlined the concerns of his firm and asked Vic for his reaction. Vic took a cloth napkin from the service cart and rubbed the dark patina that had built up on the coffee table over many years. Brian had the feeling that much had been discussed over that antique table and that Vic liked things worn and comfortable.

"Brian, I'm very impressed by your investment banking skills," Vic began. "I'm even more impressed by your political insights and, frankly, the values you and your partners have demonstrated in taking on the Iranians and in meeting with me. I know that I'm not an easy man to reach, for reasons I'm sure you understand." Vic stood as though contemplating what he was about to say. "You mentioned needing my help. What do you need?"

"Vic," said Brian, "The insurance company is key to controlling the Iranians and unhinging their plans. I have a friendly actuarial firm in Zurich, which has authored a report that will support capitalizing the insurance company at $50 million. The real capital requirement is more like $500 million, but I doubt Rezvani would put up that kind of money, which is roughly equal to the fees they will be paid as co-managers."

Brian got up from the sofa and stood facing Vic. He hoped his expression showed the sincerity he felt. "It's critical that the Swiss insurance regulators accept the insurance company application and allow them to guarantee the Iranian infrastructure bonds, at least initially."

"But how does that help?" Vic asked. "Do we want an undercapitalized insurance company guaranteeing $25 billion in bonds that American and other oil companies will have to purchase?"

"No, you are absolutely correct," said Brian. *I need Vic to understand this very clearly.* "The real trap is found deep in Swiss insurance law, which holds that *any affiliated entity* of an undercapitalized insurance company will have its assets attached until such time as the risk of loss has diminished to a level that the capital base would support." Brian waited, examining Vic's reaction for comprehension or confusion. *The lights are coming on!*

"I think I'm about to learn something," Vic said. "That does not happen every day. Please go on."

"There are two critical points here." Brian held out his left hand, touching its pinkie finger with his right index finger. "The first is that under Swiss law anyone receiving fees from the issuance of infrastructure bonds insured by a company based in Switzerland is considered an *affiliated entity*. The consulting firm that Rezvani has set up in Zurich to receive fees will be an affiliated entity."

Brian waited and got the nodding head from Vic that he wanted. He touched his left ring finger with the right index finger. "Second, we have calculated that it will take twenty years before the Swiss would release the affiliated entity assets. This means that these guys will have no access to the money in their numbered bank accounts until 2034, unless, of course the Iranian Interior Ministry buys back the bonds." Brian dropped his hands and stood almost at attention waiting for a response from Vic.

"Would they do that?" Vic returned to his chair next to the sofa. Brian followed and sat down on the sofa, drawing himself up close to the coffee table so that he was balancing on the edge of the sofa's cushion.

"The Ministry is unlikely to do so because (a) they will have spent or siphoned off much of the proceeds from the bond sales, and (b) the bonds are structured with a sliding three-point prepayment penalty during the first seven years. But it doesn't matter for our purposes."

"Why not?" Vic leaned toward Brian, attentive, eyebrows raised.

"Because, once the Ministry buys the bonds back, the oil companies get repaid and the political leverage for Iran in this deal falls apart. Why? Because, in the event the Iranian government then chooses to default on the

Eurobonds, the Iranians will end up losing their refining assets as the holders of the Eurobonds foreclose. They will have spent a lot of money to achieve nothing, which will require our Iranian deal buddies to do a lot of explaining to some very stern guardians of the Quran."

Brian waited for Vic to say something. *This is it*, he thought.

"Very complex and *most* brilliant," Vic said after a moment. "I understand why you need the Swiss insurance regulators to accept the insurance application, but how will you get the assets attached?" Vic stood up and circled his desk. He pulled out a hand-carved humidor from the bottom left drawer. A large sterling silver escutcheon decorated the lid of the humidor. It bore the Latin inscription "Acta non Verba" meaning "actions not words". He rubbed the escutcheon, smiled, and opened the humidor, saying, "They are Honduran. Wish they were Cuban, but that's not possible with the embargo. Would you care to join me? I feel in the mood."

"No thanks, Vic, but please go ahead and enjoy it." *It looks like we have a deal.* Brian got up to join Vic, standing across from him in front of his desk. *I think he's celebrating.*

"Now tell me about how you intend to attach those assets." Vic pulled a cigar clipper out of a compartment in the humidor and carefully prepared his smoke by nipping a piece off the closed end of the cigar. He placed the cigar in his mouth, twirling it a few times as if to get a taste first before he smoked it.

Brian nodded, "I have a friend in the Swiss banking department who will keep them from taking money out of the bank for a few days."

Vic nodded his understanding of how such things can happen if need be and held the flame from an old Zippo lighter against the dry end of the cigar. He stopped, frowning. "Damn. I keep forgetting that I can't smoke these here anymore." He closed the lighter, putting the unlit cigar back in his mouth.

Brian went on. "The Iranians are not likely to want to move their money, but we'll make sure that they don't. During that time, which will be after the various transactions have closed, my friendly actuarial firm will discover an error in their calculations—an error that my firm will allow them to attribute to us. The report with the corrected calculations will show that the insurance company is woefully undercapitalized."

Vic stood listening, his mouth clamped on the cigar. "What liability does your firm face for making such an error?" he asked.

"Our standard contract language states that our liability is limited to the lesser of actual damages or $50 million. We will reserve the fifty million and buy U.S. Treasury Bills upon closing of the transaction."

"That is a generous contribution to the welfare of our country," Vic said as he looked at the unlit end of the cigar. "Thank you. How will you go about finding the Iranian assets?"

"The Swiss insurance regulators are lawfully permitted to subpoena all Swiss banking records, and my Swiss banking friend will make sure he complies fully and quickly so that the Swiss insurance regulators know who is an affiliated entity and where the assets are."

"If I understand this correctly, the Swiss insurance department will need to act quickly on reviewing the new actuarial report and attaching assets. I assume you will need my help in that, too." Vic was smiling.

"Yes, very much—once the Iranians get word of this, they'll want to transfer their money out to other international banking centers. If they do, we will not be able to tie up their money, at least not this way." *He understands and he's in!*

"All right," Vic responded. "I see how the pieces fit, and I understand what I need to do. Please make a note of this telephone number," he said as he wrote and then handed a post-it to Brian. "But don't associate my name with it. Doing so might put you in danger. I usually tell people to mark the record in their cell phones as 'plumber'—why not, I do get people out of hot water—and yes, a pun is intended," Vic smiled as he said this and Brian grinned in return.

He is certainly enjoying this, Brian thought and remained still allowing Vic to savor the moment.

"My experience tells me," Vic continued after a while, "That you may need a friend like me in the future. The Iranians may not be forgiving of your honest actuarial error and may want to cause trouble. I have also found that events like this have a life of their own and we sometimes go where the event takes us, not the other way around. You might find that you need a lot of help sometime soon."

"Thank you, Vic," Brian said earnestly, "My firm has considered possible retaliation and we have retained AAD, Inc. as our risk manager. They are very qualified. However, it's nice to know that we can come to you if we need help."

"You need not thank me, Brian," Vic responded. "You and your partners deserve the thanks. I know that risk management firm. Do you know what AAD stands for?"

"No, I don't."

"Well, most of the senior guys there are former officers of the 82nd Airborne Division. AAD stands for the nickname of the Division—All American Division—that was derived from the back-to-back A's on their shoulder patches. They are very good at what they do."

Brian glanced at the American flag on its polished brass pole, and turned to Vic as he once again chomped on his unlit Honduran. *And only my partners will know I was here*, he thought. *Can't wait to tell Hal!*

"A word of warning—if any of my people, or anyone else for that matter, contact you in regards to our conversation this afternoon, they will use the code word 'Ulysses'. He was the brains behind the Trojan horse, and I think you are at least as smart as he was." Brian knew that this was a great compliment. He nodded to Vic in simple appreciation.

"If anyone contacts you without first using this code word," Vic continued, "Presume the worst and take any action you believe appropriate to protect yourself, your partners, and your families. You will certainly want to call me then, and we'll give you all the help at my disposal and, rest assured, I have a lot of help at my disposal." Vic gently placed the cigar on the edge of a glass ashtray in the shape of the Liberty Bell, which would amuse Brian if it were on the desk of someone less significant.

"Now, please excuse, me Brian. I have a few telephone calls to make to the Swiss. I also must bring the Ambassador into this, but without the details, and I'll need to speak with the secretary of defense and the president during our standard briefings."

As Brian left his office, Vic thought to himself, *I'm glad that young man is a Marine. He may damn well need that training.* He was about to pick up the telephone when another thought came to him. *I wonder if this is at all connected to the Middle East intelligence vacuum? Can't see how, but you never know. I'll call Steve Barber and bring him up to speed on this.*

Later Friday, April 18, 2014; Beirut, Lebanon

After leaving the hospital, the three Hezbollah security men contacted their superiors who sent a general alert throughout Lebanon. Within Beirut, two-man teams were put on the streets to find and kill Basmah, the only name by which they knew their prey. Gabir Haddad died without disclosing Neena's real name. Only a few hours had passed when the word of Basmah's savage revenge on Haddad jarred those looking for her.

Neena imagined that terror mingled with anger in the minds of the Hezbollah hunters, their bold swagger crippled by the reports of Gabir's agonizing last few minutes.

Neena, knowing her cover was blown, hurried to her apartment after seeing Gabir off to his blessed Allah and packed a few important belongings in a large shoulder bag. She burned papers that she would not risk holding should she be captured or killed or her apartment discovered. She packed three passports, a silencer for her Walther, and a spare Tanto knife to replace the one thrown at Haddad in the alley. *So great to have that balanced feeling again!* She added three ammo clips, a couple changes of clothes, a blonde wig, a small first-aid kit, and some makeup items, including a hairbrush, to the bag. She did not need much. If she were not out of Lebanon within twenty-four hours, she would not need anything.

Neena took a quick shower, dressed, took her apartment telephone off the hook and left by the back stairway. As she reached the mezzanine level, she scanned the streets for watchful eyes and hostile movements. There were none. She squared her shoulders and strode out, blending into the crowds mingling in the late afternoon sun.

She had two locations available to her within Beirut, both safe houses run by Mossad. Unfortunately, she was not known either by identity or visually to anyone in the Mossad organization in Beirut. She decided, based solely on proximity, to go to the house located on Gregorius Haddad. *Haddad, that's ironic.* From there, she would have transportation—a car to a boat, which would deliver her to a friendly ship outside the port, and back to Israel. David Alon would be notified and Neena would have to face him, but that would be later—David would selfishly want his valuable Mossad asset safely in Israel.

It took Neena nearly thirty minutes to reach the Mossad safe house. Her calm demeanor belied her intense scanning of her environment as she searched and evaluated every gaze, every movement, for the telltale sign of discovery. Nothing. A block later, she took several breaks in her pace to look slowly in shop windows, and then, about one hundred feet away, she made a direct line for the building as though she had lived there for years.

She made it to the exterior doorway of the building, which looked like an apartment house, but which was occupied entirely by Mossad personnel. She followed the prescribed protocol by buzzing apartment 3A and asking for Mohammed. The correct response issued from the speaker on the wall, "What do you want with my son?"

"I have flour and tea from his uncle, Simon," was Neena's answer. The buzzer sounded, unlocking the second door and Neena entered. Instantly, the door was slammed behind her and two agents grabbed her in vice-grip holds, pressing 9mm automatics against her head and chest.

"Who are you and why are you here?" demanded the first agent.

"My name is Pnina Shahud and I work directly for David Alon. I need help in leaving Lebanon." At the mention of David Alon, the grips relaxed only a bit to tie her hands behind her with plastic bands. The agents relieved her of her weapons and shoulder bag. By this time, a man who introduced himself as Samuel Rapp had come down from a floor above. After exchanging a few words in Hebrew, he placed a call to David Alon on a secure line. David had already heard of the Hezbollah hunt for the bitch traitor Basmah and told Samuel Rapp that he wanted to speak with Neena. Rapp unbound her.

"What the hell have you done, Neena?" barked David over the telephone, on speaker for the benefit of Samuel Rapp who, Neena learned, was the agent in charge. She had intruded on his operation and he needed to know the details. The others had been dismissed. Neena knew this was classified. "Do you have any idea of what you have done to our Lebanese operation? On whose orders were you acting?"

"David, I can explain it all when I get back to Tel Aviv, but right now I am being hunted by most of Hezbollah, and I would rather leave quietly than hack my way through a bunch of hit teams. I think you would prefer that as well," Neena said, firmly. "Will you help me?"

"Of course I will," replied David, static obscuring the tension in his voice but Neena detected it anyway. "The worst Jew is worth a million Hezbollah. And you are certainly worth more than that. Turn off the speaker and let me talk to Samuel."

Neena handed the telephone to the agent. As he and David spoke, she noticed another agent standing at the top of the stairs, seemingly reading documents, but very intent on the events below. *How much has she heard?* Neena noticed the woman was missing her left pinkie finger. *Wonder how that happened?*

Her extraction from Lebanon would take only a few hours to arrange. Mossad had a constant stream of personnel entering and exiting the country, none of which was through border crossings and customs. Neena did not engage in conversation with the Mossad agents. There were rules to be followed by both them and her, and those rules meant that neither party was to know anything about the other. The best way to make sure that the rules were followed was not to talk.

The agent at the top of the stairs tried to engage Neena in small talk, but she graciously reminded her of the rules and said no more. *She's missing* both *pinkies!* Neena spent the remaining few hours cleaning her weapons, which along with her shoulder bag had been returned to her. It was a meticulous task but one she performed automatically. The routine allowed her time to review what she would say to David Alon when they met.

Neena was briefed on the extraction only five minutes before she left. Two cars had been sent ahead and stationed in different locations. She would be taken in one car from the safe house and she would transfer to the other two cars in sequence. She would travel with only the driver because a heavily armed group or convoy would only attract attention. The third and last car would take her to Le Petite Mer, a small seaside inn near the port, where she would board a small, but powerful, motorboat. From there, she would be taken three and one-half kilometers off the coast where a Mossad attack boat would rendezvous with them and bring Neena back to Israel. She was to disguise herself as a male hospitality worker at Le Petite Mer. The first car left at 2105 hours.

Neena allowed herself a small sense of security in the vehicle, knowing of no similar extraction that had failed in the last three years. She tightened instinctively, though, as the tumblers in her mind opened the lock on a door of unease. The agent at the top of the stairs. *Why was she there? Shouldn't she have been at a duty station? Why did she initiate conversation when she should have known the rules, the protocols that helped keep everyone safe?* Perhaps it was a series of innocent coincidences, but, regardless, Neena jumped mentally to high alert. She knew that it would be useless to try to include the driver in her conjectures and doing so would only distract him. Besides, the rules forbade conversation. *How did she lose those fingers?*

The telephone rang in a secret room on a special line signaling an important incoming call. The connection was automatically transferred as a text message on a screen with audio. The caller spoke as the words formed in a text box, black on the blue flat screen monitor, the system scrambling the voice so it was unrecognizable.

"Allahu akbar," the caller began, "Code zulu delta five five oscar." Even with the scrambling, it was obviously a female voice, high pitched, peaking and dipping on the graph in the corner of the screen.

"Code accepted. Response code six nine sierra bravo victor," said the answering voice into a voice-activated microphone. The answer, too, was transmitted to the screen so that the sender could read and make sure the software had converted the message to text accurately.

"Response code accepted. Basmah is in transit to the coast in a Mossad car. She will transfer to a green Fiat on Ahdab Street near Al Balad. The arriving car will be a black Polo. Both cars will have only the driver and passenger. The driver of the green Fiat is very inexperienced. Basmah will be dressed as a male hospitality worker. Approximate time of transfer is 2130 hours."

The caller disconnected without confirming receipt of message. Anyone answering that line knew that the message would be given only once and the second the connection was broken, the words disappeared from the screen, the conversation erased from the hard drive.

The receiver went to a different telephone set, dialed, and repeated the message to the person answering.

Friday Evening, April 18, 2014; Beirut, Lebanon

The first car stopped at the pre-arranged location. Neena got out of the black Ford and into a black VW Polo. She had only thrown a scarf over her head during the transfer—she would tie up her hair and put her server's cap on in the third car. She was alert for trouble, but did not find it there.

The black Polo surged as Neena jumped into the back seat. The car traveled fast but not recklessly. She would transfer for the last time to a green Fiat in about five minutes near Al Balad.

After his short meeting with Christian, Steve continued to wait at Al Balad for his nine thirty meeting, knowing that his contact was likely to show up sometime between then and ten o'clock—that was just the way things worked here. Lights twinkled on and Steve could see the entire block. As he waited, he thought about the news Christian relayed and what this person Basmah must be like.

His musings were interrupted by a sharp snap of clarity, telling him to pay attention to his surroundings, which he immediately scanned. His focus moved to two, no, three sets of men about fifty feet from where he sat. The three two-man teams were set in roughly a right triangle around a green Fiat with a man in the driver's seat. *Hezbollah?* Steve wondered. *Not sure who they are, but it's definitely a hit. What weapons do they have?* Steve felt like calling out to the driver, but he knew it would be no use—his shout would only alert the men and get the driver and him killed.

Calmly, he called the waiter over, gave him a slip of paper with writing on it and some money. He got up slowly, wiped his lips with the napkin and placed it on the table. As he was leaving the café, he stepped behind a curtain and removed his 9mm from the small of his back, chambered a round and tucked the gun under his left armpit. He walked with his arms folded, strolling down the street, keeping the three teams in sight.

The teams, obviously confident whatever their purpose, were not vigilant. They chatted among themselves, looking first at the green Fiat and then down the street as if waiting for something. Steve took advantage of their amateurish demeanor and moved to a position close to Team Two as he had labeled them, getting within about five meters.

Team One was closest to the driver of the Fiat, who had parked on the left side of the street. They stood about ten meters away, next to an abandoned building. Team Three was directly across the street from Team One, and Team Two was on the same side as Team One but twenty meters behind the Fiat. Steve caught sight of indiscreet flashes of automatic weapons and decided that whoever the target was, he was in grave danger. *These guys are packing.* He scanned the street, crowded as always. Two barefoot boys played on the sidewalk, kicking a bottle back and forth, giggling as it rolled off the curb and shattered in the gutter. *They, too, are in danger.*

Steve wedged himself between a dumpster and a doorway. After several minutes of watching, he saw the faces of Team Two tighten, and he looked in the same direction that they were looking—a black Polo with someone in the back seat. His mind was calculating, connecting dots, and analyzing patterns as years of experience had taught him. *I bet that's Basmah. Who else would get three teams assigned to the hit? Somehow, I hope I'm wrong.* Steve knew instinctively that he would have to help whoever that was—*Basmah?* —survive this ambush. *I'm not wrong, not about these things.* The adrenaline kicked in hard.

Damn, no silencer. This is going to sound like a fucking cannon! The good news is that Basmah and her driver will be alerted. He brought out his 9mm and, with three lightning shots, dropped both men of Team Two. He knew by the way they fell that both were either dead or incapacitated. He raced for their weapons as Team One opened fire on him and Team Three sprayed the driver of the Fiat. The young man in the Fiat never knew what killed him. His newspaper spit flakes of shredded newsprint and nailed itself firmly across his chest, instantly turning red. A woman screamed, people scattering.

Luckily, Team One was firing blindly in his direction because they had not yet spotted who had fired the weapon. They soon saw him running toward Team Two, though, and aimed. Steve dived between two cars where one of the bodies lay. He ripped an AK-47 along with part of a jacket off the shoulder of one of the dead Team Two men, released the safety, and cocked it for firing. By now, the street was deserted as if the city was used to this kind of bloodshed. *Where's that car?*

The black Polo driver stomped on the brake pedal, jammed the gearshift into reverse and attempted to back down the street. A hail of automatic fire ripped across the windshield. The driver lurched backward and then slumped onto the steering wheel as the car careened backwards, smashed into a parked van and came to rest on the right side of the street. Steve gave covering fire against Team Three as a wiry girl dressed as a male hospitality worker jumped from the car. *It's got to be Basmah and that's no man, not with that ass.* Basmah yanked open the front passenger door and snatching an Uzi, took cover behind the vehicle. She saw Steve and acknowledged his covering fire with a wave of her left hand. *So, perhaps I have a friend.*

Basmah zigzagged to a construction debris bin up the street while Steve peppered the night with gunfire, the sound reverberating off the stone buildings in the narrow street. As she ran, a member of Team Three stepped from shadows to fire his weapon. Basmah saw the opening and let loose a burst of fire. Pieces of his smashed weapon stuck to his face and jacket as he exploded against a shop window and slumped to the ground. Steve saw that Basmah's aim was off a bit—she was hit in the right shoulder. He recognized the expression on her face, one of pain, a grimace he'd seen many times. *In the mirror, in fact.* The grimace was fleeting, though, as she fought off the pain. Steve knew that in moments, her firing arm would be useless.

Team One was silent for several seconds and Steve knew they were calling for more men. One of them had a Beretta CX4 carbine rifle with a 15-cartridge magazine, and he fired at the car that hid Steve, shattering the windshield, pulverizing the hood and bumper. The Beretta had to be taken out or he would die from shrapnel wounds as it ate his cover bit by bit. *So, he wants to play cute.* He motioned to Basmah that he was going to run up the street, his left side shielded by parked cars. This would leave him exposed to the remaining Team Three man so she would have to keep him down.

Basmah nodded, jammed her Uzi under her chin, and fired a series of short bursts. The recoil kick against her shoulder made her want to shout with pain, but she was silent. She knew that giving the Team Three survivor a clean shot would mean the death of her new friend and her. *Whoever he is.* She fired again.

Steve jumped just as Basmah opened fire. As he ran forward, he heard the Beretta's .45 caliber rounds smash into the parked cars and saw shards of metal and glass fly by. He felt fragments hit his left cheek and right hand. No time to see how badly he was wounded—he wasn't blinded and could move his hand without difficulty. He kept running toward Team One.

He neared an open parking space and sped up to throw his opponents' firing timing off just enough. In the open, Steve raised the AK-47 and let loose at the Beretta man, catching him in the head. The man spun from the force, his rifle firing a round that ricocheted off the pavement, hitting Steve in the left thigh. He staggered past the space and fell between two cars. There was little cover for him there. Both Team One and Team Three survivors had direct lines of fire at him.

As the two men closed in, they raised their weapons, grinning as they walked toward Steve. The grinning ceased, their heads and torsos exploding in a fusillade of heavy gunfire. Blood and pieces of flesh erupted from blossoming holes in their bodies. *What the hell*, thought Steve, sure that the next burst of fire would kill him. *Must be the cavalry!*

Just then, Christian yelled in French, "Stay down. My men will come to you while I make sure our murderous friends are finished."

Steve shouted the message across the street to Basmah in Hebrew, not knowing she spoke fluent French. Three of Christian's men picked the two of them up and placed them, swiftly, if not gently, in the back of a VW van. The van lurched forward with one guard riding up front and another in the back with Steve and Basmah. The man with them checked their wounds and set up IVs. Through the back window of the van, Steve saw Christian and his remaining men checking to make sure the Hezbollah were dead, then they jumped into separate vehicles and sped away. Both Steve and Basmah still clutched their weapons. They smiled wearily at each other, silently acknowledging a mutual joy at being alive.

"I'd say that worked out pretty well," Steve joked in Hebrew.

Basmah tried to stifle a laugh to save herself a shot of pain, but couldn't.

Chapter Seven
Saturday, April 19, 2014; Beirut, Lebanon

Just after midnight the VW van raced into a small compound on the outskirts of Beirut, the compound's security detail on full alert. As the van entered, the main gate clanged shut and the perimeter sealed. The van sped, spewing gravel, and pulled into a bay on the east side of the compound. Metal doors closed. A crew wearing white lab coats sprang into action, shoving gurneys forward and swinging doors open as the van lurched to a halt. Steve and Basmah were offloaded, IVs and all, then whisked to the anteroom of a fully equipped operating room next to the loading bay.

Steve's wound threatened an artery, so he was treated first. Luckily, the large round had lost energy during its ricochet, so the wound was gaping but not deep—great scar material. He would be walking in twenty-four hours and fully ambulatory in a week. He heard a doctor say that Basmah's wound could have been very serious had it been a half-inch to either side. The bullet had passed through her upper shoulder, barely missing the scapula. Her recovery would be complete, but she would need physical therapy for several weeks. Steve strained to hear every word. *Why do I care? I don't even know her.*

Both slept until noon the following day in the same windowless room. Steve waking and drifting off again, glancing to Basmah's bed each time he woke. He noticed she slept curled into a fetal position, her blankets pulled tightly up to her chin. She looked so young and vulnerable. He knew she was not.

Later, Christian visited. He brought red wine, a welcome diversion.

"How are my patients doing today?" asked Christian in French, pulling a cork key from his breast pocket. He jammed the silver spiral into the cork, removed it, and poured three glasses.

Basmah smiled but didn't answer. Steve answered in French, taking a sip of his wine. It went down well, the deep, fruity aroma an improvement over the eucalyptus liniment smell of the room. "I'm a lot better than I thought I would be at this time. I sent the message a whole fifteen minutes before you got there. What took you so long?"

"I also speak English if you prefer," said Basmah in flawless French, her accent Parisian.

Steve was impressed. Christian turned slightly to speak directly to Basmah and said in French, "I am sorry, Basmah, but I have never mastered the English language. Please forgive me." Then he turned back. "It wasn't much of a message, Steve," said Christian, chuckling. "'Come to café quickly. Be well prepared. Major shit about to hit the fan. Seconds will make a difference.'"

Christian held the wine bottle aloft to invite a refill. No takers. He continued. "I will tell you the details of last night, but first I need some information." Christian turned to Basmah. "What is your real name, Basmah? Why did you murder Gabir Haddad?"

Basmah kept silent for a few seconds, stalling. *How much should I say?* She weighed the consequences of an unauthorized disclosure of information against the proven bravery of Steve and Christian's actions in saving her life. *What can David do about this that he won't do already about my killing Gabir?*

"I am Pnina Shahud. I prefer to be called Neena," she said, speaking in French. "I am, or rather was, a deep cover Mossad asset within Hezbollah. I have been operating directly for David Alon for the past eight years, of which the first five were spent in Hezbollah training camps uninhibited by any Mossad protocols."

Christian wheeled an examination stool over and sat down. "Why did you kill Gabir?" he asked.

"I have been working occasionally outside of David's control for the past ninety days tracking and killing Hezbollah who were members of the team that tortured and killed my family in 2004. Gabir Haddad led that team." Neena stopped. She had answered the question and now took a small sip of wine. *Merci bien, Christian.*

The pieces fit and Steve now understood the furious effort being put forth by Hezbollah to find and kill her. Christian looked at Steve and raised his eyebrows. Steve nodded that he was in agreement to tell Neena the details behind last night.

"To answer your question, Steve, about what took me so long, all I can say is that you could have picked a better time for your adventure. Luckily for you and this lovely lady," Christian nodded toward Neena with a smile, "I always answer that particular cell phone. Luckily, also, I have a group of friends who jump at a moment's notice." Christian pointed to the hospital room's double doors, behind which the noise and bustle of activity was constant. "They happily joined me in killing Hezbollah. And, while we are on the topic, you owe me a dinner."

"Where did you get all this?" asked Steve, pointing to the double doors the way Christian had done.

Christian poured a little more wine in everyone's glass. "As Bill told you, I retired from the NSGE. What Bill has now authorized me to tell you—and Neena—is that I now work for EUCOM, the US unified military command for Europe and Israel. I report to Bill." Christian's smile filled his face.

"That sonovabitch!" Steve laughed and grabbed the stitches on his leg.

Christian went on to provide additional background. Christian's group, operating as Strike Force Abraham, was constantly prepared to perform critical tactical operations within Lebanon, so a unit was armed and ready to go at Christian's command. The immediacy of the need for the assault team, however, meant that certain precautions were not taken, so preparations were already underway to temporarily disband the Strike Force within Lebanon and re-constitute it later in a new location. A high price to pay, but Bill told Christian that he believed it worthwhile under the circumstances.

What Christian did not tell them was that as he answered Steve's call for help, he had ordered the assault team into action without getting Bill's prior approval as he was supposed to do. Bill later approved the operation and briefing Basmah, the only name he knew her by, subject to her providing background information on herself.

After Christian completed his briefing, Steve shifted in the hospital bed to look directly at Neena. "You were on the run after killing Haddad at the hospital," he said. "And I assume Mossad used standard methods during your extraction from Beirut. How do you imagine, then, that Hezbollah was so confident in their knowledge of both your transfer point and timetable?"

Christian glanced at Steve and Neena's glasses. Each had an inch or two of wine, so he poured the rest of the wine into his glass. Christian held the glass to his nose, inhaling. Steve almost laughed; he looked so absorbed in the wine's aroma.

"I believe that the safe house I visited has a double agent," Neena answered. "One of the female agents who was missing both pinkie fingers. She should have been at her duty station, but took the trouble of listening to what was going on. She also tried to engage me in conversation, which is strictly against our rules. The rules are well understood by all Mossad agents, however inexperienced. I had a premonition in the first car, but I dismissed it as an innocent coincidence. I won't do that again."

"I assume you will let David Alon know so he can take a hard look at her," Christian commented.

"I intend to do just that," Neena said nodding.

Christian had arranged for lunch, a favorite of his: an assortment of cheeses, grapes, hummus with lots of garlic, flat bread still warm from the oven, various crackers, and a rabbit pâté. He also served a slightly chilled Crozes Hermitage. It was as if locusts had descended upon this small, well-equipped medical facility. Steve was ravenous. *No wonder I'm so hungry. I haven't eaten in twenty-four hours!*

To avoid discussing matters off-limits, they talked about Middle Eastern history. Neena told of the virtual elimination of Jews from Lebanon and the increasing pressure on the Maronite Christian minority there. After half an hour, the three people of distinctive backgrounds understood that the Middle East was becoming more intolerant of people of different cultural heritages, especially religious. Neena agreed that, within Israel, even Arabs who had not left the country in 1948 and Christians, many of whom were Israeli citizens, were increasingly being squeezed out economically and legally.

At one thirty in the afternoon, two men, with automatic weapons strapped over their shoulders, brought clean glasses and bottled water. They removed the food tray, plates, used wine glasses and wine bottles. Christian poured water for everyone as the armed men left. The conversation quickly returned to the topic.

"It is not right," Neena admitted. "But we believe that external pressures are forcing us to be more homogeneous in order to improve internal security. If you are not Jewish, you are much less likely to be sympathetic to our survival and more likely to be a terrorist. That is how we see it. We do not see many friends in the world, at least any whom we believe will be standing at our side when we are eventually attacked."

I agree with her. I'm not happy about it, but she's right, Steve thought. Then he asked, "What makes you so sure that Israel will be attacked?"

"It is simple," said Neena. "The radicalization of Islam over the last twenty years combined with fanatical regimes in control of three major countries—four if you include Iraq—plus Gaza. Add to that the acquisition by Iran of nuclear capabilities and the stage is set."

Steve stood up and winced. "Sorry, but I have to try this leg. Please go on." He took a few cautious steps, each one sending a snap of pain to his spine.

"These Islamist governments and other Islamic elements in the Middle East, Africa, and even within Western countries have neglected the economic and social development of their peoples. Instead, they feed them hatred of Israel and Jews. No moderate Muslim element is tolerated within any of these Islamic societies."

"That's certain," Christian said. "I have seen this intolerance grow over the forty years that I have lived and worked here. You can *taste* it now." He went over to a supply closet, pulled out a pair of crutches and gave them to Steve.

Neena continued. "I, and many others inside the Israeli defense ministries, believe that within two years some unforeseen event will unleash Hezbollah, Hamas, and the Iranians in a quest to annihilate Israel. There will be, of course, tragic consequences for Israel. However, the Islamists will find that the destruction of Israel will leave all these millions of people looking to hate something new—my bet is that it will be their own governments and officials who lead them into the apocalypse, which such a war will loose upon all."

"So the child of hate will eat its parents," Steve said. *She is right on.* Steve took a couple of steps to try out the crutches.

"Yes!" Neena agreed. "The irony is that what they have begun, they cannot stop."

"Yet, you hate as well, don't you?" Steve asked.

"Yes," Neena agreed and said no more.

Steve, thinking Neena took his question in a way he did not intend, said, "Neena, I am on *your* side *and* the side of Israel. But, hatred exists on both sides, or should I say, all sides—Christian, Jew, and Muslim. I have no idea where all this hatred is going to lead, and I wonder if time is running out."

Christian interrupted. "This seems to be a good time for me to leave you two. I must make final arrangements to close this facility, disband the Strike Force and cache our equipment and weapons. It is only a matter of time before Hezbollah identifies me and finds this location. And, I have to get the two of you out of here. Very soon!"

Christian had orders to avoid a fixed battle. He could no longer count on the help of the Lebanese army against Hezbollah, which although still commanded mainly by Maronite Christians, was ordered to remain in its barracks. He left for a moment and returned with a large leather suitcase around which a thin, lightweight, two-inch wide chain mail belt was attached. Christian saw the surprise in Steve's face. "I had one of my men check you out of the hotel. No sense giving them any more information about you than they already have." He brought his right hand to his forehead and gave an informal salute to the two. "Rest now. I will get you up when we need to leave."

After Christian had left, Neena swiveled on her cot to face Steve and said, "Thank you for saying you are on my side. Not many people are. I have lived among my enemies, killing them, for a long time. It's a lonely feeling."

Steve, standing by his bed, took a long look at Neena, her dark hair unbound and lying about her shoulders, and said, "I understand hate, Neena. I understand rage. Loneliness is what you have after hatred eats everything else."

Neena was watching his blue eyes, looking for lies, hoping to see truth. "What do you have in *your* life?"

Steve smiled, barely parting his lips. "Not much more than you. Peace, I guess. Because, what I do now, I do for love."

"Of whom?" Neena turned her head slightly to one side.

"Not whom, Neena. What." He sat next to her. "I love my country, and what it stands for." He stopped for a moment. "I love to watch children playing, knowing they will have choices in their lives. I love to see old couples, who have been through all kinds of shit together, still holding hands like teenagers. I do what I do so that I can see those things. For freedom."

"Yet, like me, you are alone. You have no one to go home to."

"Yes, that seems to go with the job. I don't have a home, just an apartment I visit when I am in the States." Steve stood, walked to his cot, and sat, propping the crutches against the wall. "How about some shut-eye?" *So hard. So soft,* he thought as he looked over to find her hazel eyes still probing his.

Neena nodded. As she pulled up her covers and eased herself onto her healthy side, she thought, *He's very different, this one.*

Saturday Afternoon, April 19, 2014; Washington, DC, USA

"Sorry it took a while to get back to you, Bill," Vic Alfonse apologized, flipping the button on his desk phone to speaker so that Bill's voice rang out. No one was in the vicinity. Even George had the day off. Vic didn't mind coming in on the weekends. He'd been doing it since Laura died. "I had to leave a horrid game of golf with the Russian military attaché and find a secure line. What's up?"

"Steve Barber intervened in an attempted assassination of a highly prized Mossad agent in Beirut," Bill reported. "He was successful, although I had to commit Strike Force Abraham to assist. He and the agent were wounded, though not seriously. I had to temporarily disband the Strike Force because we believe the HQ will be compromised."

"How big a mess was there in Beirut?" Vic didn't need this. He took a deep breath and reminded himself that Steve was the right man for the job. If Steve made a mess, it was a mess thought through.

"Seven Hezbollah killed including one that was gutted by the Mossad agent while he was in a hospital bed. Beirut's a hornet's nest right now."

Vic sat down on the edge of his desk, near the phone. "What do you know about the Mossad agent?"

"She is a woman, Pnina Shahud, who was orphaned by Hezbollah when she was seventeen. David Alon had her in deep in Hezbollah until yesterday, when her first attempt on the person she killed in the hospital blew her cover."

"Are we tagged with any of this?" Vic grabbed a pen from its stand on his desk. It was a gift from Ronald Reagan and he liked the way it fit his grip. *This is a man's pen. Dutch is someone else I miss. He was a man's man. He'd have liked Steve, too.* He pulled a small note pad from next to the pen set and began making notes.

"We're not linked to this—at least not yet. The Mossad are, though, and Christian Meureze is likely to be—he rode to the rescue just in time, but it's likely that witnesses will identify him. That's the reason I decided to disband the Strike Force—as a precaution."

"How are you getting them out?" Vic stood up and walked a few steps, but stayed within earshot of the phone. He liked to pace when discussing operational matters. It made him seem to be more physically involved somehow.

"I'm working with David Alon to extract them from Lebanon. The extraction is scheduled for about seven hours from now across the Israeli border. Alon is heading the operation."

So, Alon, personally, Vic thought. *This Shahud must be important to him.* "Do you think this has anything to do with the intelligence void you're looking into?"

"Not directly, Vic, but both Steve and I have reports that Mossad is the source of the vacuum. If they are, our getting close to David Alon will help. It's an opportunity for Steve to learn a lot more than we know now."

"Okay, Bill. How long will the Strike Force be out of commission?"

"It'll be three months until we secure a new suitable facility. The assets are there and we can still project force, but not as rapidly until we get a new facility."

"Thanks, Bill. Keep me posted on Steve. When he gets back to Tel Aviv, please have him call me when you can both be on the speakerphone. I want to bring you up to date on some news of the Iranians. Not urgent. Goodbye."

Vic made a few more notes. He had file folders filled with them. He never made these kinds of entries in a computer. He thought about Steve and made a note to find out why he'd intervened to save Shahud's life. *Steve's a good man. He had a good reason.* Vic looked up as though touched by something and noticed how empty his office felt. *No, not the office,* he corrected himself. *My life. Without Laura.*

Late Saturday, April 19, 2014; Beirut, Lebanon

It was dark. Strike Force Abraham's facility was mostly empty. Christian and his team had spent the day uploading encrypted files to safe locales via satellite, making hash of hard drives, and otherwise preparing computers and other electronic gear for secure travel. Two heavily guarded trucks filled with electronics and ordnance had left. They would remain in a safe location until the Strike Force was regrouped. Staggered departures of smaller vehicles had taken members of the Strike Force in twos and threes to temporary posts in and around Lebanon, leaving a small detail to extract Steve and Neena out of Beirut. Afterward, the detail would also disband.

Hezbollah had set up roadblocks along key routes, but they did not have the manpower to cover all the streets. As the trucks and smaller vehicles traveled to their destinations, the drivers relayed information back to Christian about the specific locations of the roadblocks. What disturbed Christian more than the existence of roadblocks was the fact that Hezbollah was moving the location of the roadblocks about every two hours. That meant that the window for extracting Steve and Neena through a specific route was at most two hours, unless he wanted to risk running a roadblock. He did not.

He thought about the Lebanon of his early career with its grand mix of peoples peacefully coexisting, a growing economy, and a subtle, warm blending of cultures. Beirut then was the Paris of the Middle East, and Christian savored its cosmopolitan status, tastes, money, and, oh, the women. Now, a deadly hatred and intolerance corrupted much of the land and its people like leprosy. A bitter, murderous hag now wore the dress of the sensual Venus that had seduced him in his youth. Christian loved that goddess still. He would fight the hag as long as he had breath.

Christian finished packing the few papers and items he would take. The rest he would destroy. He left his near-empty office and walked the compound, which was returning to the simple concrete block structure of just a few years ago when the Strike Force had set up operations. As Christian's boots crunched on the gravel path, even the Cyprus trees at the edge of the compound looked forlorn, abandoned, the leaves dusty and gray.

He turned toward the infirmary to wake his sleeping patients. Shouts from his men and women told him that the last of the equipment was almost loaded. Bursts of temper told him they were nervous that Hezbollah might close in soon. He knew his people were not afraid to fight, but now, packed and dispersed, they were vulnerable to attack. *Allez! Allez! Let's be off!* Christian urged himself.

"Time to go," Christian said, as he entered the room, turned on the light, and tapped their feet to rouse Steve and Neena, "We must depart soon." He had learned to wake warriors like this by tapping their feet after he once shook someone's shoulder and found himself on the floor with a knife in his face. *Tap the feet and stand away*, he told himself after that.

Steve and Neena reacted reflexively, demonstrating the depth of their respective training, and, despite stiff muscles and painful places, were on their feet immediately. "Can you give us some briefing?" Steve asked alertly, stretching and rubbing his leg.

"Of course," Christian responded. "We are going overland to the Israeli border. The harbor is much too active now and they will not expect us to take the harder way. Bill Elsberry has contacted David Alon and, for obvious reasons, this is now a joint operation between EUCOM and David's unit. My Strike Force is to get you to Labboune, about one hundred, twenty-five kilometers from here and three kilometers from the Mediterranean. David

Alon and his people will meet you across the border and take you from there to Pädäh. Bill will rendezvous with you there, Steve, and get you back to Tel Aviv."

"How are we going to get across the border?" Steve asked. "It's typically sealed tight." Steve took three steps with his new crutches. He tossed them onto his bed and took a couple more steps, flexing the wounded leg.

"A good question," responded Christian. "A Mossad agent will fire a series of missiles from inside Lebanon near our extraction point into Kibbutz Kabri. This will give the IDF the excuse to retaliate with covering artillery. Anyone around the area will go to cover and this will allow us to get you to the extraction point. Of course, we will be prepared for the possibility that a lone guard spots us, but the main guard force will be underground waiting for the artillery to stop." Christian opened the door and admitted two of his men. They started packing up the beds and medical equipment.

"Isn't it possible that the missiles will kill or injure some Israelis?" Steve asked.

"Yes," Neena interjected, answering for Christian. "No one at the kibbutz will be warned because that communication might be intercepted by Hezbollah and put the mission at risk. That is how David thinks, and, frankly, that is how I think."

"Don't they get a vote?" Steve asked. The men finished packing and left the room. All that remained was Neena's bag taken from the bullet-ridden black Polo outside of Al Balad.

"Most Israelis accept that their lives are at risk, even at the hands of other Israelis for a greater purpose. Those who have protested this kind of thing in the past have been immigrants from America and other Western countries. Although often persecuted and discriminated against, they have never fully comprehended the price Israelis pay to remain independent. We Israelis have the good fortune to be constantly reminded that freedom is not free—something most Americans have no inkling about."

"That's a hard line." Steve said as he grabbed some extra dressings for his thigh and put them in a small pack.

"Sometimes a hard line, as you put it, is needed for Israel to be free. It is a price most Israelis are very willing to pay. Israelis have a motto, 'Masada will never fall again', and we very much mean that—at *any* price." Neena examined the bag that Christian's men had retrieved and, turning away from Steve for modesty, changed into traveling clothes. She eased her Tanto knives into sheaths on her back and strapped her Walther on her right side so that she could reach it with her good left hand. Steve noticed that Neena, agile, physically powerful, and of moderate build projected a much larger presence. *It's her intensity*, he concluded.

"I've heard about Masada and that elite units of the Israeli Defense Forces are inducted on top of Masada." Steve said, now mimicking Neena by turning his back and changing. Before pulling up his trousers, he wrapped additional gauze and adhesive tape around his thigh. Welcoming the sight of the 9mm that Christian retrieved for him after the firefight, he slipped it into his shoulder holster.

"Not only elite units of the IDF," Neena rejoined, "But every Mossad agent as well, including me. Masada is a spiritual place." The two, fully dressed, turned toward each other.

Christian brought the discussion to a close as he entered the room, saying, "Okay, we have ten minutes to mop up here and leave. You will want time to pick out and check whatever weapons you need. See my men for that. Pack whatever you want to take and can carry. What you don't take will be destroyed. I've got two cars waiting, Fiats, tres rapide." Christian mimicked the zoom of a sports car and Steve chuckled.

Christian gave Steve and Neena additional details of the operation. After departure, the two Fiats would separate and then regroup for the sprint to a location just north of the extraction point. There, at a prearranged time, they would transmit a 24-digit alphanumeric code—a blind transmission broadcast—twice on a specified frequency. If they heard a corresponding pre-assigned 24-digit code in response, the missiles would be launched into Israel within fifteen minutes.

A no-fire corridor would be maintained by IDF artillery through which they would proceed to the extraction point and join up with David Alon's forces. David would take them to Jerusalem.

Christian and the Strike Force members would accompany Steve and Neena to within one kilometer of the border. They would then return to Beirut and disband until Bill Elsberry issued them new orders. Ten minutes later, the two Fiats left the compound. Nothing but bare walls remained, Cyprus trees bending in the breeze as if waving goodbye.

Steve and Neena were originally assigned to different vehicles for security reasons, but the two wanted to ride together. As they left the compound, Neena spoke to Steve in German, predicting he could speak it, so that the driver might hear but not understand, "Why did you help me escape that ambush?"

Steve, not at all surprised she, too, spoke German fluently, said, "Part of the answer is that the enemy of my enemy is my friend. But most of the answer is that it wasn't a fair fight. From what I know of you now, you're as good as two or three of those guys, but you couldn't have taken on that ambush by yourself. Also, I'd heard that you went to the hospital and took Haddad apart. That took either immense stupidity or great passion, and I wanted to find out which it was." Steve finished with a small laugh.

"So, have you decided that I am immensely stupid?" Neena asked, turning her head.

"No," answered Steve, first with a smile and then, in a serious tone, continued, "Everything I've learned about you tells me that you're a person of great passion. You miss your family terribly and you will do anything to avenge them. You have a sense of justice, and you do as you say you will do. Most people have neither passion nor personal integrity. Most don't even understand how important those are in life."

Steve noticed the driver craning his neck as though he was trying to understand what they were saying. *Viel glück, freund! Good luck, friend.*

The car sped down a paved, two-lane road. It was almost midnight and lights were few as they approached the rural border area. Oncoming traffic was light. The cool night air painted a fog on the windows and the car's defroster labored to clear the windshield. The driver sped on, seeming to enjoy not seeing where he was going, relying on the taillights of Christian's lead car to keep him on the road.

"I am surprised to find you so thoughtful," Neena responded. "Most men, and women for that matter, that I know are too self-absorbed to think about what is truly important in life. Most people are totally unaware of others around them, merely doing or saying what they want in absolute disregard for the impact on others. I have used that behavioral tendency often during my assignments, although professionals tend to be very aware of their surroundings."

"Haddad was not aware of you when you were following him across from Bakawat," Steve observed.

"That is true, and it cost him," was Neena's unemotional response.

The two cars hurtled toward the blind transmission broadcast point. Christian and the Strike Force members were connected by satellite communication—SATCOM—radio so that they could communicate between the vehicles. Steve and Neena could hear snippets of orders from Christian in the first Fiat. They were about ten minutes from the broadcast point.

"You are a very attractive woman," Steve blurted out, surprising himself. *Idiot, you sound like a high school kid with a crush.* Then, in a rush to distract her from his remark, he asked, "Why did you choose to be a Mossad agent? You could have served Israel in the IDF and gone on to have a normal life, if there is one anymore. Why Mossad?" *Talk about blowing your cover, dude!*

Neena answered, "I was working on a kibbutz during the summer that my family was butchered by Haddad and his gang. One afternoon, I came in from the fields. David Alon was waiting for me, alone. I did not know him at the time, but he told me who he was and, then, he told me the news of my family." She turned away for a moment, her breathing audible, and Steve felt his stomach tighten with sympathy.

"I don't know what else to say," she continued, ducking her head and pinching the bridge of her nose with her thumb and index finger. "At that moment, for some reason, David became my family. David stayed at the kibbutz for a few days as he waited for his agents and others to retrieve the bodies of my family. So that we could bury them properly. During that time, he started to recruit me—not directly, but by speaking about Israel, its enemies, and what Jews are called to do to keep Israel free."

The Fiat, traveling at 100 kilometers per hour flew off paved road onto gravel, and skidded sideways a little. "Sorry," the driver said over his shoulder in Hebrew, correcting his steering but not slowing down. "We're getting close, judging by the road."

"Thank you," Steve said to the driver in his language and gripped the door handle for balance while focusing on Neena's story. "Go on," he encouraged.

Neena sighed but then the corners of her mouth turned up in a slight smile and she leaned closer. "He told me the story of Masada and how every Jew should remember that the price of Israel's freedom would always be Jewish blood. By the time the bodies of my family arrived, I had all but signed up and when they showed the photos—detailed, grizzly photos—of the slaughter, I wanted to kill every enemy of Israel. David sensed that, and he used my emotions very effectively."

Steve studied Neena as she spoke, watching her expressions, making mental notes. The raven hair, her deep, expressive brown eyes, a slight scar above her right eyebrow. Her skin was clear and had a slight olive cast. Neither she nor he had showered since the firefight outside Al Balad, yet she had the faintest scent of oranges and cinnamon. *She is* very *beautiful*, he concluded, surprised how strongly affected he was by her nearness.

As Steve drank her in, Neena continued, "Now I know that David was manipulating me, but I do not blame him—in fact, I would do the same thing if a seventeen-year old showed up on my doorstep. But I miss the love of my family, and while I call David, and the Mossad, my family, it is not a family based on love. It is based more on a shared sense of history, pain and calling. At times I feel very hollow and I fear one day that I will have killed all the enemies of Israel and have nothing left to live for."

"Quite a story," Steve said, not exactly sure how to respond. *Should I comfort her or keep casual?* "Mine is unremarkable compared to yours.

"You know, I don't know why I'm telling you all this," Neena said. "Maybe I feel I owe you because you saved my life."

"Maybe because I'm willing to listen." They were quiet for a few minutes, listening to the whiny hum of the small Fiat running flat out in sixth gear, gravel pinging the undercarriage.

"I'm very sorry about your family," Steve whispered. In a firmer voice, he continued, "I don't think you have to worry about running out of enemies of Israel to kill, but I wish you could get back some sense of love. I've had the same feelings and I have the same wish for myself. I'm always mentally engaged in what I do, but I wish my heart had a soft place to land."

Neena and Steve locked eyes, neither one speaking. "Two minutes to the broadcast point," barked the driver, who then spoke into his transmitter. "It's show time," said Steve. They both smiled briefly then reached for their weapons and packs.

Chapter Eight
Early Sunday, April 20, 2014; On the Road to the Israeli/Lebanese Border

"Zee!" shouted David Alon over his hand-held radio, called a "brick" because of its shape and weight. "Can you confirm that the 2nd Artillery Brigade knows what it's supposed to do?"

"Yes, Colonel Alon," Sgt. Shachar barked back from another vehicle. "I had Colonel Ehud repeat the instructions back to me. By zero two hundred hours, the Brigade and we will be in position and ready. Our principals will signal us at zero two seventeen and we will respond. Missile launch commences at zero, two thirty. Artillery fire commences at zero two fifty-one and ends at zero three hundred. Colonel Ehud repeated the zigzag no-fire corridor coordinates. I have rechecked them against what we have from the principals. They are scheduled for receipt at zero three oh five."

"Very well, Zee," said David. "Over and out."

The convoy of three vehicles had been on the road for about an hour. Operating within Israel as an elite military unit, they rocketed over the roads. They were armed to the teeth. *If there's going to be a fight at the border*, thought David, *we will kill a shitload of Hezbollah*. Then, he thought, *I prefer this kind of fighting, but the politicians have taken that away, too.*

As they approached the Lebanese border, the pace of the convoy slowed to pass through security checkpoints. David made a stop at 2nd Brigade HQ to pay a courtesy call on Colonel Ehud thanking him for his assistance but also to let him know that if he fucked up, he had better fall on a grenade.

The Mossad convoy continued for about five more kilometers. They got out of the vehicles and left them to be guarded by an IDF platoon patrolling the border. No one asked what this special party was up to. It was nobody's business.

The Mossad welcoming committee, "Qibbus B'ruchim Haba'im", as David called it, numbering twelve, jogged to the meeting point fifty meters inside Israel. The area of the operation, code-named Shoov, "to return" in Hebrew, was a one-hundred-meter corridor to the border. All IDF personnel were ordered *in situ*, meaning to stay in place, until their commanders lifted the order. The Mossad team would not worry about whether someone was supposed to be there—anyone moving in that corridor would be considered armed and unfriendly. After the successful pickup of the principals, the people being supported by the operation, David would relay a coded message to Colonel Ehud who would lift the *in situ* order.

Three Mossad, including David, would take cover around the meeting point and greet Steve and Neena. Another six would split into two teams of three, taking the right and left flanks, and the remaining three would set up at an elevated location. These last men were to provide surveillance over the operation and long-range heavy covering fire as the principals were retrieved and brought back. The last group was also armed with high-powered sniper rifles and infrared scopes to track and protect the principals. They would take out any unfriendlies intent on dying this particular morning. David felt he had been as thorough as possible.

The Mossad team was in position for less than twenty minutes when they heard an AK-47 and Uzi open up near their front. Then, three or four more AK-47s joined the music of the night. David's heart pounded at the sound.

Early Sunday, April 20, 2014; Near Labboune, Lebanon, and the Israeli/Lebanese Border

The two Fiats, engines whining under the lead feet of their pilots, reached the outskirts of Labboune and slid to a stop. The occupants got out of the vehicles and set up a defensive perimeter. Christian looked at his watch and joked, "We had another three minutes to get here, so why did we risk killing ourselves at those speeds?"

Someone farted lustily and another said, "So that we could escape from that toxic gas!" *Good*, Christian thought, *A little humor to take the edge off.*

At 0217 hours, Christian sent the 24-digit alphanumeric code twice and then waited. The correct response code came back in forty-five seconds. "Time to move," said Christian. He, Steve, Neena, and two members of the

Strike Force started out, leaving the vehicles with the remaining two Strike Force members.

Around them, small rolling hills thick with forty-foot pines comprised the terrain. The area near the border was much flatter, less forested, a valley of undergrowth and shrubbery. In the wet season, a small river would take over a wandering path between the countries, but the landscape was dry this night. The whole area was crisscrossed with small dirt paths, gullies, and slight etched ravines that told of erosion during the rains.

They followed a path for one and one-half kilometers. As the group moved, silent and focused, they heard the distant whoosh of rockets heading into Kibbutz Kabri. The sounds of the night, hoots and chirps, the flutter of a breeze, stopped, and the valley lie still. Tension settled on the group as collectively, thoughts turned to the threat to the innocent kibbutzniks and for a moment, everyone stopped walking. Steve broke the silence. "We can do nothing to help them," he said. "Let's go."

A few minutes further, Christian stopped. "This is where we leave you, my new friends," he said softly. "Here is the map. You have about ten minutes until the barrage begins. Don't push yourselves too fast. Be alert to Hezbollah patrols. Use the artillery cover. If you can, stay well within the corridor that brackets this path and the ravine it shadows. It will take you across the border to David."

Neena hugged Christian and planted a kiss on each of his cheeks in the French style. Steve gave him a slap on the back and a handshake. Christian had been good to them. Steve would not forget that.

The three were silent for a couple of moments. "We will wait here for about sixty seconds," Christian said, breaking the stillness, "If you run into trouble after that, your best bet will be to reach the border. You will have much more fire support over there. Please give my regards to David and Bill. Godspeed."

Steve and Neena slipped quickly into the night. The two continued along the path that paralleled the ravine for two hundred meters and then paused with the map to mark the proximity of the upcoming artillery barrage. They hastened the pace and Steve's thigh throbbed, but the stitches were holding well. They were well within the no-fire corridor, so the only way out was either forward or back. Both moved in silence, intently observing with their eyes and ears through shrubbery that pawed at them in the late night darkness.

"Neena," Steve whispered over his shoulder, "There's something going on." He shifted his backpack slightly to distribute the weight to his good leg. They had packed light, some extra clothing, granola bars, and ammo, but every ounce on his left thigh made movement more painful. The path was fairly even, but it periodically dipped a few feet into the ravine and wound back up the bank. Steve glanced back at Neena, barely visible in the dark although he caught a trace of her scent. "I'd like your help finding out what it is."

"What are you talking about?" Neena whispered back.

"A few intelligence agencies have noted a dramatic slowdown in information flow in the Middle East, a partial void of the kinds of information that would normally be intercepted by human intelligence collecting. It's as though someone or some group has purposely put up barriers to information flow. Am I making sense to you?"

"Yes. There is always a background of information flowing in and out of any area. Troop movements, technology updates, back channel discussions of political changes and proposals. Nothing of top secret importance; just the usual chatter." Neena carried her backpack on her left to keep her wounded shoulder free. She held her Uzi in her right hand; barrel up. Steve admired her tenacity and suddenly realized that it bothered him she was in pain.

"Exactly," said Steve. "We, and others who operate in Middle East intelligence, have noticed that the usual chatter has virtually stopped. We also believe that the Mossad is behind whatever is happening." A rabbit jumped from under cover a few feet in front of them, causing them to raise their weapons and halting the whispered conversation for a few moments.

"I don't know anything about Mossad's involvement," said Neena, lowering her weapon. "But David Alon sent me a coded message last Thursday that sounds like it has something to do with what you are asking about. He didn't give me any details, but he did mention working with the U.S. Defense Department, looking into a void in information flows."

"I think that means working with me." Steve smiled to himself in the darkness.

"Not as much fun as killing Hezbollah, but I might learn something."
Neena's voice had a lilt to it and Steve pictured her smile. The underbrush was
thinning out as they neared the floor of the valley between the two countries.
Steve knew cover would be scarcer from this point on.

"Before we get thrown into a crowd where we cannot talk alone for a
while, you should know that we are using the code word 'Masada' for this
project."

"Okay, Masada. What made you pick that word?"

"Bill Elsberry, the American military attaché in Tel Aviv picked it.
He'd just been to an induction ceremony and was very impressed by the old
fortress."

"He should be. Masada is an important symbol to all Israelis." As they
progressed into open terrain, they became even more vigilant. The path now
led across the small ravine, which had widened and was deeper as it neared
the dry riverbed in the center of the valley.

Steve realized that he was anxious to spend much more time with
Neena. He was beginning to have a better feeling about this assignment.
Whoa, boy, he thought. *Assignments are never this good. Something always
comes along to spoil the moment.*

Neena saw them first. She elbowed Steve and he glanced up, peering
into the shadows cast by a cluster of large shrubs in the faint moonlight. It was
a Hezbollah patrol of seven men advancing single file about four meters apart
in the ravine.

Steve motioned with his chin that they should move forward and then
pointed to the right. Neena understood and moved off. He headed left.
Silently, the two clambered onto opposite banks, crawling to the crest of the
ravine and along the ridge twenty meters. Neena held up first one finger, then
a second, barely visible in the moonlight. Steve knew she meant that she
would take out the first member of the patrol, for Steve to get the second and
so on.

The rhythmic thump of boots on dirt, thirty meters, twenty-five,
twenty, fifteen—Neena's Uzi spit, ripping through the first and third
Hezbollah with one burst and then another. She had not lifted the weapon to
her wounded shoulder, but had fired by jamming the stock up against her

pack, which she had brought around in front of her prone body. "Not bad," Steve said out loud. He'd not expected her to be that accurate so soon after her injury.

Steve had taken an AK-47 from the Strike Force compound, and he fired his weapon just as the Uzi spoke. Three down, four to go, but the remaining Hezbollah returned fire wildly, retreated twenty or so meters, and jumped out of the ravine onto the west—Neena's—side. *They're trying to flank her, take her out, and then come after me.* Knowing time was short, he jumped to a crouch, ran across the ravine and up to Neena's side. His left thigh roared in pain, but he shut it out of his mind. She put her finger to her lips, put down her Uzi, and pulled out a Tanto knife. Steve nodded, and Neena slipped to the right.

The four Hezbollah separated and advanced in parallel, leaving several meters between each gunman so they could fire at the presumed location of their target from more angles. Neena crawled out in an arc to a point passed which the outermost Hezbollah would come. She half-buried herself in the scrub brush and waited like a stone. Steve, his weapon on semi-automatic, sent small bursts at the advancing Hezbollah.

On the other side of the border, the Mossad sniper squad, which had taken up position one hundred, ten meters above the valley, relayed its observations to David, who waited with impatience. He would rip apart southern Lebanon to save Neena and he was looking forward to doing so, if need be.

Even at two in the morning, the snipers could see well into the valley. The ultra-sensitive and high-powered infrared scopes brought the scene clearly to the squad. The situation was not new to these veterans, who had years of training in all conditions. They knew how to triangulate themselves to offer an array of shots at targets in the valley. The hill on which they lay concealed was wooded like the hills on the far side of the valley, but they had selected a clearing and removed underbrush so that they could observe, target, and kill at a distance well over one kilometer. They took advantage of their knowledge of the terrain. The valley floor was nearly devoid of large vegetation, so David's snipers could identify a human target with ease.

"Colonel Alon," one sniper said, "Our principals have eliminated three enemy and the remaining four are advancing on them. One principal has moved to a flanking position on the far left side of the enemy." He continued to track the distant objects illuminated in his infrared scope, finger alongside the trigger guard.

Principals, David mentally repeated the word. *Hard to think of Neena as a "principal", when she and I have been through so much.* "Do you have a clear shot on any of the four remaining enemy, Sergeant?" David asked.

"Yes, sir," was the prompt reply. The three snipers repositioned for a clear shot, eyes brought closer to the scope, fingers ready to press against the trigger.

"All right, Sergeant, make the shots as you see them," came David's command. *I hate waiting!*

Only thirty meters now separated Steve from the four Hezbollah. One of the four, the second from Steve's left, stopped. He was now standing, an obvious target for Neena. The standing Hezbollah began firing in Steve's direction as his companions continued to crawl forward. Neena struck like a cobra. She slit the throat of the bold and foolish man in one motion—almost decapitating him with the nine-inch blade. She rolled his body onto its side for cover, grabbed the idiot's weapon, and fired. The three Hezbollah broke off their assault, seemingly confused by their comrade firing at them.

At that moment, the artillery barrage from across the border began with a series of kabooms as thirty projectiles left their barrels, pushed into the starlit sky, and landed all around the corridor, blowing brush, rock and dirt in fury at the night. The explosive concussions and ear piercing detonations did the job.

As the Hezbollah hit the dirt, protecting their faces with their hands, Steve crawled to Neena's side, motioning that they should return to the ravine. She nodded and they began to inch their way. Turning to the ravine, Steve and Neena exposed their right flank. Steve made sure he was between Neena and the enemy. *I'm not going to let* anyone *hurt her.*

Two Hezbollah, glancing over to where their dead comrade lie with his head tethered to his body by a slab of skin, stood to fire. As they raised their weapons, their heads exploded as armor-piercing shells completed their graceful arcs through the night air and slammed into them. Steve watched the last Hezbollah sit up reflexively and stare until his head, too, blew apart. *Yes,* Steve thought. *More cavalry!*

Steve imagined the Mossad snipers grinning and giving each other a "thumbs up" all around. *Three night kills at over 500 meters, at least,* Steve thought. He knew they would celebrate this in warrior style.

"Colonel, three targets engaged and eliminated. Looks like one of the principals took out the fourth by hand."

"That would be Neena," replied David to no one in particular.

"The principals are now advancing up the ravine. No pursuit observed."

"Thank you, Sergeant. Good shooting."

Steve and Neena reached the ravine and ran forward as the shelling continued, now more sporadically—in salvos of two and three—on both sides of the ravine outside the extraction corridor. Steve knew that the shelling would continue long enough for them to cross the border. That would keep any other Hezbollah pinned down. *I could do without the noise, although it does keep me from thinking about my leg.* Steve was running now with a pronounced limp.

They reached the border minutes later. David wanted to jump up and greet them the second he spotted the running figures, but he knew the orders he had given and he, too, would follow those orders. David's team was to remain in place until the principals were within Israeli territory and identities confirmed. He would give other, harsher, orders during the next few days and he wanted those followed as well. "Colonel, the principals have arrived," David's earpiece crackled.

Steve and Neena sprinted through the ravine until David called out in Hebrew, "Neena, stop! Welcome home!" Neena and Steve stopped where they were, and slumped onto the bank, smiling in celebration of having survived once more. Their smiles became grimaces as their wounds pulsated and each realized they were bleeding again.

"Let's get you home," David said, lifting Neena to her feet and hugging her gingerly. "Mr. Barber, thank you for helping Neena. We welcome you to Israel. Bill Elsberry will be at Pädäh to greet you and take you back to Tel Aviv."

"Pleased to meet you, Colonel Alon," Steve responded. Steve met David's eyes and in them, Steve thought he saw a shadow of disdain. He could be wrong. *Just a flicker.* Steve struggled to his feet and tried his left leg to see if it would hold up. It did, but the pain burned to the bone. He winced, stretching out his hand to shake David's in an unspoken challenge of strength. David's grip was crushing. "I am especially thankful to a few of your colleagues with sharp eyes and steady hands," said Steve.

"Yes, we all are," said David, turning and placing a hand on Neena's elbow to guide her up the slight incline. "You will meet them at the vehicles. Come. Let's go. It has been a long twenty-four hours."

"Amen to that!" Steve followed, suddenly troubled by David's hand on Neena's elbow. *Stupid. I have no reason to care. So why do I?*

Early Sunday, April 20, 2014; Pädäh, Jerusalem, Israel

Steve rode in a vehicle with the three Mossad snipers. Neena rode with David. Although Steve would have preferred to be with Neena, he took advantage of this time to find out more about David. He learned that David was a veteran of every Israeli war from the six-day1967 pre-emptive attack onward. David was respected and feared. Those that crossed him regretted it deeply. As Steve had judged, the men talked of David being a man of great physical strength. "I've heard that he has crushed an Arab's balls with his bare hands, the way he crushes walnuts," one of the men jested.

The three men, all members of David's elite team at Pädäh, knew of Neena and her history. They added pieces of her story to what Steve had gleaned in Beirut. Neena was prized by Mossad for her abilities and adored by David. The men would not venture an opinion as to whether or not David was more than an adopted uncle to Neena. They saw no reason to meddle and suggested the same to Steve. *I know what it is I see in him. Control, not command, but control. Everything and everybody is his. Well, we'll see about that,* he found himself thinking.

Headlights shone eerily on the landscape, the road twisting and turning as the car sped, the grasses that bordered the road blurring and Cyprus branches arching like probing fingers. Finally, one of the Mossad snipers gestured out the windshield toward a foreboding series of walls barely visible ahead in the early dawn and said, "There is Pädäh. Colonel Alon's uncle built it in 1951, after Israel was reestablished."

Steve saw a guardhouse outside a gate and through the iron slats of the gate, an old, but spotless, cut stone building on the inside. Trees and flowering shrubs flourished, making the fortress appear softer. *It's camouflage for the hardness of the compound. Just like David's gracious manner.*

The vehicles rolled into the compound at seven fifteen in the morning. Pädäh remained in the shadows of the eastern hills as the sun shone on the distant landscape. Bill Elsberry was already there, beaming as he saw Steve, and then Neena and David step from the cars. Bill rushed to shake David's hand. David, in turn, introduced Bill to Neena, and pleasantries took place as the sun tipped the tops of the hills to the west.

The Mossad teams unpacked gear and weapons and then headed for a small conference room to debrief the operation. Bill, Steve and Neena attended the meeting at David's request and provided additional details: the timely arrival of Christian Meureze's Strike Force Abraham, how they took on the Hezbollah patrol, and the deadly accuracy of the Mossad snipers. David then invited Bill, Steve and Neena to breakfast.

He showed them to a small dining room where a table had been set for four. The table was dressed in a starched white linen tablecloth and matching napkins. A large bowl of fruit commanded the middle of the table. Mugs of steaming coffee and orange juice, fresh squeezed, judging by the pulp floating in the glass, had been poured. A basket of breads on a tray with butter, jellies and jams occupied the remaining space on the table. Steve had a feeling of being processed, like a set of papers in the Pentagon. He was already beginning to dislike spending time in David's presence.

"I have some good news to report," David offered, after they found seats and began eating. "I checked with the IDF during the return trip and there were no casualties at Kibbutz Kabri. The missiles fired by the Mossad agent from Lebanon as a pretext for the covering artillery fire landed in fallow land." David smiled and looked clockwise around the table at each person. *Does he want us to give him a medal?* Steve wondered.

"How will the artillery barrage be explained?" Bill asked.

David picked up two walnuts from the fruit bowl and crushed them in his palms. As he ate the nut meat, he said, "Simon Luegner—Steve, Simon is Israel's Defense Minister," *I know who Simon Luegner is, asshole,* Steve shot back in his mind. David stared at Steve and Steve adjusted his expression to one of undivided attention.

"Simon will have his office issue a press release in about an hour condemning the unprovoked missile attack," continued David. "The press release will contain the standard language about confirming the IDF's artillery response to this blatant violation of Israel's right to exist peacefully. The deaths of the seven Hezbollah will be attributed to their unlawful incursion into Israel, thereby precipitating hot pursuit by the IDF and a resulting firefight, in which the seven Hezbollah were killed with no IDF casualties. Something to that effect." David dumped the shattered, empty walnut shells on his plate and wiped his lips with a napkin.

"David, after breakfast, I would like to show Steve around the compound," Bill began. "May I?"

"Of course," David responded, with a wave of his hand toward the door. "Be my guest. The rose garden is lovely now."

Soon, breakfast ended and Steve and Bill, after a few parting words, left. David turned to Neena and said, "Neena, I need to speak with you about the events of the last few days." He stood up and walked out of the room, Neena following. He walked to the surveillance-proof parlor where he had met with Simon Luegner just three days before and locked the door after Neena had joined him inside. David invited Neena to sit, taking a place next to her.

"What were you thinking, Neena?" David said in a hushed, but very edgy tone. "There are critical projects underway that you don't know about and which your behavior could very well put at risk. The reason that we have rules of engagement is to prevent that sort of thing. Your personal vendetta has no place in Mossad. When I assigned you to assassinate Hezbollah randomly, I meant *randomly.* Now, by killing Gabir Haddad, you have exposed yourself as a Mossad agent, and I no longer have an asset deep inside that organization."

"You had me inserted into the Hezbollah camps and they trained me well," Neena said defiantly. "So punish me as you will. I will survive. The memory of my family haunts my every night and day. I see the photos that *you* showed me. I see the horror and the disemboweled bodies. I will not rest until every last one of those scum has experienced unbearable pain and terror—as my parents did—in their last minutes alive."

"Neena," David attempted to interject.

Neena ignored his interruption. "You and Mossad have used me as chattel property—I have killed and been a whore for the good of Israel—and I have accepted that. Do not think, however, that my following your orders comes without its price. That price is the death of enemies of Israel that *I*, not *you*, choose."

David was silent for a few minutes. He looked directly into Neena's eyes. "Whatever harm has been done, has been done," David responded, his voice calm, but stern. "Frankly, we are now at a moment in time that whatever else you might have accomplished in Lebanon is unimportant."

He reached over and placed his hand on Neena's, completely enshrouding her hand. Neena left her hand under his.

"Israel is in crisis," David continued, "And we must take action. So, you and I will leave this for now and deal with our crisis. Then, we will sort out your future in Mossad." He patted her hand, removed his, and smiled.

"I know that smile, David," Neena said. "You have something planned for me. What is it?" She crossed her arms.

"Steve Barber. What do you know about him? What does he know about you?"

"I have picked up bits and pieces over the last day or so. He has a lot of military training and handles himself well in battle. I had to tell him and Christian who I am and why Hezbollah was hunting for me—I did not divulge any Mossad operational details or secret information other than my personal history that led to my joining Mossad. Beyond that, we avoided talking about our professional backgrounds because we both knew that we should not go there."

"Steve Barber is a highly trained, former amphibious reconnaissance Marine—one of the best ever by all reports," said David, standing and pacing the room as was his habit when agitated. And he was very agitated. Neena had put Mossad at risk at a critical moment in Israel's history. She also seemed to like this American. She may not know it, but David saw it. He didn't like it, but he definitely saw it. *I didn't create this woman for the likes of Steve Barber,* he thought.

"Those guys are tough as nails," David went on, "And his dossier is very, very impressive. He is also bright—summa cum laude from Cornell University—in mechanical engineering. He now works for Vic Alfonse, the American Undersecretary of Defense for Special Operations—Vic runs black operations and is personally very close to the President of the United States."

"Is Barber married?"

"No, but why do you ask?" *I knew she liked him. Damn!*

Neena realized that she had asked a very personal question about Steve. She looked around the room as though she would find the answer to David's question in one of the tidy bookshelves. She felt stifled by David, a feeling she had the last time she saw him a few months ago. Maybe he'd always stifled her. Yet she owed him. *Do I?* David was so *consuming* compared to Steve. It was like he sucked the air out of a room, at least any room she was in with him. She rushed to cover her indiscretion and move on. "I need to know these things. I don't want to be working with someone who might compromise me because of a wife and family."

"I see," said David. "Let me get to my point. Vic Alfonse called Simon Luegner about a void in information flow in the Middle East, and Simon offered our help. Your assignment is to work with Steve and keep me in the loop."

"Seems straightforward enough," Neena said, uncrossing her arms and sitting back in one of the stuffed armchairs. She grabbed a pen and pad from a shelf to take notes. *Yes, let's talk about work and not Steve.*

"Normally, yes, this would be a straightforward assignment. However, we have some key projects under way to upgrade and harden our systems against cyber-attack, and I have cut back on our communications with other domestic agencies to keep this information under wraps. This may be what is troubling Vic Alfonse, but I don't know. I do not, repeat *do not*, want the fact that we have instituted communications restrictions revealed to anyone outside of Mossad. This information in the wrong hands could precipitate military action by our enemies, who might think we are momentarily vulnerable."

"Understood," said Neena. "Am I to use the code word 'Masada' when communicating with you about this?" David instantly flinched, visibly, but for just a moment. Neena caught his response to the word. "Is there something wrong, David?'

"No, it's just . . ." David hesitated for a few moments. "It's just that the word 'Masada' has great personal meaning for me, especially in these unstable days. You may know that my grandparents died in Auschwitz and that my uncle died in the '67 war. My only sister died in that war also, and when I hear the word 'Masada', memories of my family's struggle and sacrifices consume my mind. I am always shocked somehow by that word because it personifies the centuries of Jewish suffering just to have a homeland."

"I see," Neena said softly, admitting to herself that she did not. "Steve said the Americans are using that code word. I assumed we would as well."

"Yes, of course," David agreed as he cracked his knuckles repeatedly. "Let's use 'Masada'. We have too many code words in use as it is. Using the American code word will simplify things. Now, tell me about the ambush in Beirut."

Neena told the story of the ambush—her misgivings about the female Mossad agent at the safe house, how Steve had jumped in to help her, and how Christian had shown up in the nick of time. She also told David of the conversations she'd had with Steve at Christian's compound about the current state of Middle East tension and growing cultural and religious intolerance.

"Well, we have a lot to thank Steve and Christian for, don't we? You are here and you are *safe*," David said, smiling. Neena noticed a note of sarcasm in David's voice. *Or had she imagined it?* "Let me look into that agent in Beirut," continued David. "If she is a double agent, we may be able to make use of her in a special way. When you have lemons, make lemonade they say. Yes?"

"Yes. When do I start work with Steve?" Neena felt a stab of pain from yesterday's wound and intentionally dropped the pen she was holding. Bending to the floor to pick it up, she masked a wince, knowing David would judge her weak.

"Immediately. Before he leaves the compound, you should discuss the operation and put together a plan."

"David, you know that you have been like an uncle to me and that I respect you greatly."

"Yes, I do."

"I must kill those Hezbollah," Neena said as she put the pen and paper down.

"I know that is in your heart, but you must let that go until after Memorial Day."

"So after Memorial Day, my assignment will be to kill the few remaining Hezbollah who butchered my family. Correct?"

"I promise to give you that assignment—at that time." David was smiling, but Neena saw that he did not want to.

Neena smiled as the two left the meeting room and Neena went to look for Steve.

David went to his office and called Samuel Rapp, the agent in charge of the Beirut safe house. That night, the woman agent at the safe house died quickly and silently in her barren and bleach-cleaned apartment. Her body, unidentifiable except for hands missing pinkie fingers, would not be returned to Israel for burial, but dumped at a known Hezbollah gathering place. As David told Rapp, the agent *was* to be used in a special way—as a warning to Hezbollah not to fuck with him.

Sunday, April 20, 2014; The Gardens at Pädäh, Jerusalem, Israel

Bill and Steve strolled through Pädäh's gardens. The morning was warm and Steve was glad for the cotton shirt and lightweight khaki slacks that David had provided. *Too bad I didn't have room to bring my clothes back from Christian's compound after he took so much trouble to have me checked out of my hotel and retrieve my suitcase.* Steve's stitches had been re-sewn earlier during the trip from the border, but his leg was beginning to throb. He hoped it wouldn't start bleeding again. *What a damn nuisance.*

They sat on a bench in the shade facing the bright morning sun that was now marching toward them, down the western hills. A light breeze brought a mix of soft fragrances from the rose garden. Steve relayed a few more details of his conversations with contacts, describing the ambush in Beirut and the extraction from Lebanon.

"You've had an exciting couple of days," Bill chuckled.

"Yes, it wasn't the trip I had expected, but it was useful," Steve replied with a smile.

"How so?"

"Well, Christian and I pretty much confirmed that Mossad is behind the information void, the lack of the 'usual chatter', as Neena puts it. What I don't know is why. But I don't think Neena knows either."

"What's your take on her?" Bill inquired.

"She's quite a woman. A warrior of the first order. I've never seen a woman of her slight stature project such physical power," said Steve. *She fills those petite sizes very well, too.* "She's also fearless. I saw that in Beirut and in the ravine coming over the border. She would fight to her last breath, spitting on her enemy as she died."

"She has obvious strengths. Any Achilles' heels?" Bill asked, raising his eyebrows.

"You know the story of her vendetta. That obsession could be a chink in her armor. She could be made vulnerable by offering her the chance to complete her quest, but I like the idea of working with her. I know my back will be covered."

"Is that all?" Bill stood and looked down at Steve. He knew that standing was a show of intimidation, one of Bill's interrogation techniques to dominate the conversation, convince him to talk about things he might be reluctant to disclose. *Fine, Bill, but you're not fooling me. I would've told you anyway,* Steve thought.

"Well, since you ask, I think she is very, *very* attractive. I'm aware of those feelings and I'm alert to them preventing what needs to be done. I don't think it will be a problem."

"As usual, you are very self-aware," Bill said with a little smile. He sat back down. "Neena is key to finding out what's behind Mossad's information restrictions. Do you think she will tell us if she finds anything?"

Two of David's men walked through the garden and stopped a few meters away. They examined the blooms on a rose bush, exchanged some words, and left. Steve memorized the faces.

"That is very problematic," said Steve after the men moved out of earshot. "First, she's a loyal Israeli and a loyal Mossad agent. Second, she has an emotional attachment to David, so any information that might compromise him is not likely to come from her. I think what we have to do is let her help us discover information and watch how she reacts. If she remains open, then we don't yet have the answer. If she closes up or becomes vague, then we'll know she's learned something we need. The trick then will be finding out what she knows. I know that we won't get it from her involuntarily. She would jump on one of those Tanto knives of hers before she would do that." Steve got up and walked back and forth, gently rubbing his left thigh.

"Are you bringing her back to Tel Aviv with us today?" Bill's question was the same one on Steve's mind all morning. As much as he looked forward to Neena's company, this was business, important business.

"No," said Steve. "I'll ask her to join me in Tel Aviv in a few days. She needs to rest and give her shoulder a chance to heal. I also want her near David for a while to see what she can learn just hanging around. I don't want her to stay here beyond a few days because I think David would get suspicious. He would expect her to be working with me, and he might start to think that she has doubts about him if she stays longer. I *do* think, however, that David is the senior official who has put the kibosh on information flows. It has his fingerprints all over it."

"Well, let's get you both working on this," said Bill. "I believe your instincts and assessments are correct. Let's watch her behavior and, when we think she knows something, we'll have to figure out how to get the information from her voluntarily." Bill stopped speaking, distracted by something in the distance. "Wait, I think I see her coming this way." Bill waved to attract her attention. "Over here, Neena."

When Neena arrived at the bench, Bill rose. "You two have some planning to do. Steve has the details of what we're looking for, so I'll leave the two of you to get on with it." Bill turned to Steve. "I'll give you a lift back to Tel Aviv, Steve, when you're ready. Nice meeting you, Neena, and I look forward to working with you. Goodbye. Shalom"

"Shalom," Neena replied, settling onto the bench next to Steve.

Steve noticed that she leaned back carefully on the wooden bench, her movements stiff as if her shoulder hurt more than she would say and she were hoping no one noticed. *She's not going to admit the pain to anyone, any more than I would.*

Chapter Nine
Wednesday, April 23, 2014; Qom, Iran

Mahdavi entered the small, non-descript, white-washed building in which Ayatollah Khoemi kept his private office. The building consisted of two anterooms, Khoemi's office, and a bathroom for men. Women did not need a bathroom because they were not permitted in his office.

The anterooms were sparsely furnished; a couple of wooden benches lined the walls, and two of Khoemi's staff roamed the anterooms, making notes and questioning the men waiting to see him. The entrance to the building was a large alcove in which two burly guards with AK-47's kept watch. A third guard stood across the street. Women did not bother to attempt to see Khoemi because he would never see them, at least not at his office. Women had petty issues, nothing of importance to the Ayatollah.

After passing through the alcove, Mahdavi did not bother stopping in the anterooms, but went directly to Khoemi's office door, which was always closed and guarded by a fourth armed man. The guard acknowledged Mahdavi and stepped inside for a brief moment, after which he held the door for Mahdavi to enter. The guard stepped outside as Mahdavi stepped past him. The office, about twenty feet square, had a desk and chair on which Khoemi sat and two straight-backed wooden chairs in front of the desk on which visitors could sit if allowed to do so by the Ayatollah.

As Mahdavi entered the room, Khoemi waved a hand as an invitation to sit. "Allah's blessings be upon you," offered Khoemi.

"And upon you," replied Mahdavi. "I have received a message from one of our cryptologists. He states that he has solved one riddle in the message you intercepted, but has discovered a second. I decoded his message, which was sent in the C-AZF-287 configuration."

"Let me see the message."

Mahdavi unsealed an envelope and pulled out a single piece of paper. It was from Dr. Nahid Samimi, a respected senior mathematician in Tehran who advised the Iranian government regarding advanced mathematics and encryption techniques. He handed the paper to Khoemi, who read:

"Greetings to you and Allah's peace be upon your house.

The message you asked me to examine has two parts. The first is a paragraph to the intended recipient that requests him to review the data and either confirm or modify the data as presented. The paragraph was written in simple code, and I presume it was to be encrypted as well. Without being encrypted, the coded message itself was relatively simple to interpret.

The second part constitutes the majority of the message and is a data array. That is obvious, even to one not schooled in mathematics. However, determining the nature of the array required developing several hypotheses and testing each rigorously. In my humble assessment, it represents a set of 167 geographic coordinates. I have examined many other hypotheses and none is as satisfying to me.

While I am fully convinced that my conclusion is valid, another mystery has emerged with regard to the data array. I attempted to plot the geographic coordinates using standard longitudes and latitudes, but the locations so determined all lie within 750 miles of the equator and in the vicinity of the Atlantic Ocean and West and Southwest Africa. These seem inappropriate for this message, which you have assured me originated within Israel.

I remain steadfast in my conclusion that the data array represents a set of geographic locations determined by longitudes and latitudes. I am equally convinced, however, that the data reflect a modified location of either zero degrees latitude and/or zero degrees longitude.

I am running various hypotheses, but this will take time because the computer on which I am running these analyses has been assigned to the nuclear weapons agency for running some large programs. Please be assured that I will relay the results of my analyses as soon as they demonstrate suitable application in real space.

Your humble servant,
Dr. Nahid Samimi"

Khoemi wore a frown in danger of becoming permanent. Mahdavi would not want to be within reach if his temper exploded. He unconsciously moved his chair back a few inches.

"What do you make of this, Mahdavi?" asked Khoemi.

"I believe the doctor. Although I am not a mathematician, the data array can be plotted as geographic coordinates. Were this information part of a war plan, such coordinates would make sense. I just don't see the Israelis launching a war."

"How do you reach that conclusion?" Khoemi said putting his elbows on his desk and bringing the tips of his fingers and thumbs together.

"Their last large-scale incursion into Lebanon in 2006 was disastrous from both a military and public relations standpoint, and their several incursions into Gaza have been, in reality, police actions. The Americans have been an unreliable ally of Israel for over two decades, and the Europeans have shown a remarkable cowardice in several international confrontations over many years, including a few with us. Israel's circumstances today are not those of 1967 or 1973. They might still have the element of surprise, but they were not fighting Iran in those wars. They would quickly lose such a war without support from the United States or Europe."

Mahdavi shifted in his seat waiting for Khoemi's reaction. He hoped he had guessed Khoemi's views accurately.

"What you say makes sense," Khoemi said, "But the Jews have a history of doing what cannot be done. Ask the good doctor to complete his analysis with all speed. Do not promise him that I will intercede with the nuclear agency to provide him with a priority on the computer. I do not have enough information to take that political risk, at least not yet."

"Very well. I am traveling to Tehran tomorrow and will tell him then."

"Our friends in Baghdad may be able to help us understand this message, so send it when you request an update on the status of the merger of our armed forces."

"Of course," Mahdavi said wanting to end the conversation. *The longer I stay here the more likely he'll find something to be angry with me about.*

"Ask them to provide a date by which the elimination of all Sunni contingents in the armed forces in a single night will be achievable. In the not too distant future, our Shi'ite colleagues on the Supreme Council will want to end Sunni influence in Iraq forever."

"I understand, Holy One," Mahdavi said, waiting for an opportune moment to leave.

"I do not want that to be interpreted as an order to do so. I only want to know when I will be able to issue that command without so much as a single shot being fired in opposition. Done quickly, we will be successful. Done poorly, we will face the prospect of massed Sunni opposition across the Middle East. This is a lesson learned from Hitler. That is the reason that I have called this Operation Kristallnacht."

"I will do as you ask," Mahdavi said as he placed the message back in the envelope and turned to leave the room.

"Allah is with us," Khoemi offered perfunctorily as Mahdavi turned and bowed slightly before closing the office door behind him.

Chapter Ten
Friday, April 25, 2014; Tel Aviv, Israel

Just before three o'clock in the afternoon, a black Fiat, the driver having shown the proper credentials to the Marine guards, drove into the American Embassy compound. Neena emerged from the passenger side feeling strong again after her few days at Pädäh. She took note of the Marines' subtle gazes as they rolled over her body, straightened her slacks and blouse, and stepped toward the entrance. The driver remained with the car while Neena went inside and was greeted by Philip Palun, whom Neena recognized from his dossier, one of many that Mossad kept on foreigners in Israel.

"Welcome, Ms. Shahud," Philip said warmly, stepping forward to shake Neena's hand. "Mr. Elsberry and Mr. Barber are expecting you. Did you have a pleasant trip from Jerusalem?"

"You must be Philip Palun," said Neena. "I have heard from Mr. Barber that you are very gracious. Yes, I did have a comfortable trip, thank you."

"You are too kind, Ms. Shahud." With a sweeping gesture, Philip motioned for Neena to proceed down a long, wide hallway where portraits of past Ambassadors and the current American Secretary of State hung, their faces solemn as though the job was a difficult one. To Neena, it seemed as if the artists had captured them on a particularly trying day. She recognized a few faces, among them Ambassador Pickering, whom David Alon knew. She noted that many of the ambassadors were career foreign-service officers rather than non-career appointees. Neena thought the latter were dilettantes and neither serious people nor useful to Israel.

At the end of the corridor, Neena saw the brass and mother-of-pearl nameplate marking Bill Elsberry's office. Philip knocked twice and opened the heavy cedar door. Bill and Steve stood up as Neena entered. Her heart skipped a beat when she saw Steve and she felt foolish, like a schoolgirl with a crush.

"Please let me know if you need anything," said Philip, and closed the door behind him.

Neena surveyed the office. The usual electronics and American flag. Leather couch and upholstered chairs, old but elegant. A tray and samovar were sitting on a mahogany coffee table. She could smell the slices of lemon in a dish by the samovar and the mix of loose teas in a large wooden box. *So the former US Army Ranger colonel enjoys some amenities in his harsh post in Israel*, Neena mused.

Steve failed to stifle a broad grin. Neena smiled back and he beamed brighter. *Is he flirting? Careful. Nice guy, but it's not good to get involved.*

"Welcome, Neena. Please have a seat," said Bill, as he pointed to one of four teak armchairs upholstered in deep red silk with black pinstripes the width of a hair woven into the fabric. "What have you learned so far as part of our small band?" Bill asked.

"I do not have much to report," said Neena, settling into one of the chairs and marveling at the luxury and softness. She ran her hand along the carved armrest. Hand-hewn. Expensive. "If I did," she continued, "I am afraid I could not tell you as most of the activities at Pädäh are not within the scope of our joint operation. I do not mean to be unfriendly. It is just that I need to follow our protocol, as do you. David, of course, sends his regards."

"Well delivered, Neena. I expected you to be professional and that you are," Bill said. "I'm sure that Steve and I have not taken offense. Have you uncovered anything that would be helpful to us in understanding the information void?"

Bill got up to answer a knock on his door and returned with a tray of small sandwiches and fresh vegetables. He placed the tray next to the samovar and said, "Sorry for the interruption. I thought you and Steve might still be building your strength after Beirut," Bill said. "Please go on."

"I can confirm to you that Mossad has instituted restrictions on internal communications, but I cannot tell you what is behind those restrictions. That information is highly classified. To the best of my knowledge Mossad is not attempting to prevent Israel's allies from its standard intelligence collecting operations. It makes sense, though, that if Mossad has instituted communications restrictions for whatever reason, there would be a major void in intelligence-based information flows in Israel. Mossad honors its close relationships with allies and has historically shared information freely under normal circumstances."

"That does make sense and, naturally, we're not asking you to divulge privileged information, " said Steve, leaning on the arm of his chair, his chin resting lightly on his hand. Neena thought he looked young and vulnerable. She knew he was anything but vulnerable, though, and she brought her mind back to his words and away from the shape of his nose.

Steve continued, "Let's leave that for now. We want to discuss a message we intercepted yesterday as it was being sent from Qom to Baghdad. You'll see the message has two main topics. The first, based on its code name, appears to be a plan to eliminate Sunni members of the Iraqi armed forces. The second has something to do with a data array that a mathematician believes contains geographic coordinates. This is by far the biggest piece of information we have seen in the Middle East in several months and the sender believes Israel is involved somehow."

Steve handed Neena a typewritten message and said, "We've sent a copy to David and other friends to get their response." Neena thought she caught a hint of sarcasm in Steve's voice and listened for it as Steve went on, "We would like your opinion."

Neena read the message.

"Greetings and may Allah's blessings be upon you. AK wishes to know when Sunni armed forces contingents will be fully integrated into Shiite units and by what date he should expect to be able to execute Operation Kristallnacht. This is not such an order, but only an inquiry for information. Take no action at this time. Repeat. Take no action at this time. Respond directly to me.

Further, we have intercepted a message believed sent from a group within Israel. The message has two parts according to a respected Iranian mathematician. The first part is a paragraph to the intended recipient that requests him to review the data and either confirm or modify the data as presented.

The second part, which constitutes the majority of the message, is a data array. The mathematician believes that the array represents a set of 167 geographic coordinates, but he has identified another mystery with regard to the array. As he attempted to plot the geographic coordinates using standard longitudes and latitudes, the locations so designated all lie within 750 miles of the equator and in the vicinity of the Atlantic Ocean and West and Southwest Africa. These do not make sense if the message originated in Israel.

Consequently, he is convinced that the data reflect a modification of either zero degrees latitude and/or zero degrees longitude. He is continuing his work to identify the specific modifications.

AK requests any information or analysis you may have regarding this message and its contents be sent to me as soon as practical.

Allah be praised."

Neena held the document for a few minutes as she considered the implications. She nibbled on one of the sandwiches, placing the remainder on a linen napkin on the coffee table. "Yes, I see your point on the first topic. Operation Kristallnacht, if its name has anything to do with the Nazi 'night of broken glass', it sounds as if they are planning to arrest or murder all Sunni members of the armed forces. This is highly inflammatory if its authenticity can be validated." Steve leaned forward as though he were hanging on her every word. Neena smelled his cologne, something light and musky. "The second topic regarding geographic coordinates is a mystery to me as well," she continued. "The number 167 is intriguing because . . ." She stopped in mid-sentence, looking at Steve and then Bill. "Sorry, I cannot tell you why that number is intriguing—it is classified and, technically, not associated with this joint operation."

Steve frowned and said, "Neena, we agree with your assessment of the meaning of Operation Kristallnacht. As you know so well, that event was precipitated by the assassination of a German diplomat by a Jew in November 1938. Hitler used this as an excuse to send his Gestapo, Hitler Youth and SS to arrest over 25,000 Jews, who were then sent to concentration camps."

Neena waited for Steve to finish his sentence, although the mere mention of Hitler turned her stomach. She fought to keep her expression impassive. "As you say, I am well versed in that part of history," she said. "Almost one hundred Jews were murdered during this night of horror. Also, 177 synagogues were destroyed and over 7,000 Jewish homes and businesses were ransacked. That is where the phrase 'night of broken glass' comes from."

Steve continued, nodding, "That part of the message, if validated as you point out, is dynamite. Whoever this AK is, he's planning something very nasty for Sunnis in Iraq. The other part of the message—the part about the geographic coordinates—can you tell us *anything* about that?"

Steve stood up, walked around his chair, and leaned on its back. He looked directly into Neena's eyes. *I would like to help,* Neena told herself, looking back at Steve, *but what that number represents is off limits.*

"Let me answer this with a series of questions," Neena said at last, "So that I am not disclosing classified information. I will neither confirm nor deny any conclusions you may reach in response to my questions. Acceptable?"

"Yes," Steve said, returning to his seat.

"To your knowledge, does the United States have a data array of strategic geographic coordinates?" Neena chose her words carefully and watched Steve's face. She saw neither disappointment nor malice, although she knew he sensed she was holding back.

"Yes," Bill responded, "We have several such data arrays. Coordinates for all top-priority secure locations; a separate set for all major permanent military installations both in the U.S. and overseas; another dynamic set, updated every fifteen minutes, for all U.S. Navy ships at sea, high profile government officials, and military units deployed overseas. We also maintain the targeting coordinates for our land-based ICBMs, both land and submarine based."

"Do you suspect that another country might have similar sets of coordinates?" Neena asked next.

"Why, of course," Steve said, snapping his fingers. "All major countries have these data arrays for the very same purposes. Now which set would most likely be associated with a number like 167, the number mentioned in the intercepted message?"

"I can't help you with that," Neena said. "I have done all I can. Sorry." *I may have done too much.*

"You have helped quite a bit," Bill affirmed as he stood up. "Why don't the two of you take the rest of the afternoon off and enjoy the day? I'll have my people work on the message from Qom. I think I know how to approach the meaning of the number 167. Now, go!" Bill said ushering the two to his door.

As Steve and Neena left the embassy, Steve held the door for Neena, who nodded at the gesture as she walked through. "Neena, I have a couple of things I need to do back at my hotel room. Would you like to have dinner with me this evening?"

Neena cocked her head to one side and then answered, "Yes, that would be very nice. I have some friends in Tel Aviv and I will visit with them and freshen up. What time? Where?" *I wonder if this is such a good idea.*

"Let's go to Carmella Ba'Nachala on Ha-Tavor. It has a wonderful veranda and great food. The wine list is exceptional."

"Fine. Why don't I meet you there? I have a car and it would be very convenient for me to join you at the restaurant."

"Do we need a third chair for your driver?"

"No," Neena answered with a smile. "I will let him have the evening off. You are a much better bodyguard, anyway."

"I'll make sure you get home safely. Eight o'clock?"

"Eight is perfect." Neena climbed into the back of the waiting Fiat, leaned forward to say something to the driver, and left the embassy compound. *Maybe this is a good idea.*

Friday Evening, April 25, 2014; Tel Aviv, Israel

Steve went back to his hotel—as usual, he was staying at the Sea Executive Suites on Herbert Samuel. He sent a coded message to Vic Alfonse assuring the Undersecretary that Mossad had been identified as the cause of reduced information flows in Israel and elsewhere in the Middle East. He also told Vic that he remained concerned about Mossad's actions and was continuing to seek information regarding what was behind the communication restrictions imposed by Mossad. He had earlier forwarded the intercepted message and discussed the implications of Operation Kristallnacht. He now outlined what actions were being taken to identify the meaning of the number 167.

After completing his message, he showered and changed the dressing on his wound. "Looks good," he said to himself as he peeled off the old bandage. Meeting Neena was worth the pain. He decided that he was very excited about the evening ahead.

Steve dressed in black slacks with an off-white long-sleeve shirt and brown houndstooth sport coat. He remembered his dad buying him his first good sport coat when he was twelve years old. It, too, was houndstooth. *Where did the past twenty-two years go?* He thought about a tie, but the restaurant described its atmosphere as 'elegant casual' and he thought a tie would be a bit much. Besides, he wanted the evening to be informal.

Although he was back in Israel, he had started carrying his 9mm Walther wherever he went and so he cleared the chamber, checked the safety, and slid the weapon into his shoulder holster. A touch of Armani Acqua Di Gio and he was out the door.

He took a taxi to the restaurant rather than walking the mile or so—his leg was much better, but he didn't want to take the chance of it aching during dinner. *I feel like a damn teenager!* At the restaurant, Steve checked in with the maitre d' and, because the table was available, decided to sit down and enjoy the view from the veranda while waiting for Neena.

The building, one of the oldest in Tel Aviv, had a beckoning charm, like an older woman who has lived lustfully unafraid of the opinions of others. The veranda, in need of some paint in places, was warmly welcoming in its imperfection and had been transformed into a cozy garden. Large potted palms, a forest of them, were strategically placed to provide diners privacy, and each table was adorned with a small centerpiece of fresh cut flowers to fill the moments of romantic gazes with hints of fragrant intimacies. Steve sensed a funny feeling and he realized that sentiments he'd left behind were stirring. *Maybe it's time*, he thought.

Neena had no friends in Tel Aviv. She had told Steve that she did so that he would not feel obligated to be with her in the afternoon. She did not like having people feel obligated in any way toward her. Instead she went to a Mossad office where she was well known so that she could conduct some research on the number 167. *Yes,* she said to herself after about thirty minutes, *I knew that was the number!* She logged off the computer in the secure room and joined some agents in the staff break room. She got herself a bottle of Neviot water from the small fridge in the corner.

"Hello, Moshe," she said to one of the agents, recognized from a former shared assignment.

"Hello, Neena. I heard that you caused a lot of excitement in Beirut recently. I also heard that you were reducing the Hezbollah population with prejudice," Moshe grinned.

"Well, I did have some help."

"I heard. An American."

"Yes. Nice guy and very experienced," said Neena. "We had the pleasure of sending more than a few on to Allah."

"Heard that as well. Also heard that our snipers proved their stuff."

"You heard that correctly. They were superb." Neena untwisted the water bottle cap and took a deep drink. "Moshe, I am in Tel Aviv on orders from David Alon working with the American on a project. What can you tell me about a communications restriction order?"

"Well, I heard there is one, but it does not seem to affect most Mossad operations. It seems centered mainly within David Alon's organization, but, like all things associated with David, I have not heard much."

"Are we upgrading and hardening our systems against cyber-attack?" She took another swig.

"Not that I know of," said Moshe. "We have had no outages of the kind that you would expect if programs were being modified and upgraded. Where did you hear that?" Moshe wiped the Formica table in front of him with a small paper napkin, scooping some crumbs into the palm of his left hand.

"I thought I overheard some agents talking about that in Jerusalem," Neena lied. She did not want to link David Alon to this conversation. "How are Rebecca and the children?" she asked, changing the subject.

"They are fine. Thank you for asking. You ever find that special someone?" Moshe stood up and walked over to a trash receptacle and dusted the crumbs from his palm into it.

"Not yet. I haven't had the time. Nor the inclination."

"Life is too short, Neena."

"I know. Shalom, Moshe." She excused herself and went to the women's room to freshen up. She had a small shoulder bag with her in which she carried a couple of changes of clothes—a field agent's habit. She was glad she had it.

She put on a black Versace dress and took a cashmere pashmina for the cool night air. She thought of Steve and his big smile. *He is a very good looking man,* she thought. *And he understands what I do and why I do it—very uncommon trait.* She realized she was smiling and had a growing peaceful feeling about the evening ahead.

Neena applied a touch of pale pink lipstick on the way to the restaurant. She said farewell to her driver and told him to go have some fun and not tell David Alon about it. The driver smiled and drove off. As she entered the restaurant, she caught the eye of the maitre d', who cheerfully escorted her to her table, swerving in and around the potted plants. As she walked up, Steve rose and gave a slight bow. *Quaint,* she thought. *And very nice.*

The maitre d' helped Neena with her chair. As Steve had promised, the veranda was delightful. Twinkle lights were strung from the overhang and lamplight on the quiet street cast a soft yellow glow over the sidewalks. It was a balmy night and the temperature was about 23 degrees Celsius—the pashmina would be perfect. *This is lovely,* she thought, admiring the peaceful setting.

Candles on the table threw gentle shadows on Neena's face and made her eyes sparkle. Steve became aware that she was much more beautiful than he had realized, even this afternoon when she had looked particularly attractive. He knew he was staring.

"Pleasant afternoon with your friends?" Steve inquired, trying to distract Neena in case she had noticed his staring.

"Yes," she lied. "Friends of my family from before the horror of 2004. We had a nice chat and got reacquainted."

"Do they have any idea what you do?" Steve noticed that her head dipped when she answered. Perhaps she was lying. He decided to pass it off as unimportant.

"None. They think I work for the foreign affairs department. That seems to explain my behavior for them. Thankfully, we are not that close, so I do not have to tell them much about my activities."

Steve had looked over the wine list before Neena arrived and now offered his suggestions. "I thought we might start with a glass of Cristal and then have a bottle of 1961 Trotanoy with our entrée. How do these sound to you?"

"I am leaving myself in your hands. Are you an expert in wine?" A waiter approached, but Steve waved him off with a slight movement of his hand.

"When I attended Cornell, I managed to take the 'Introduction to Wines and Spirits' course at the Hotel School. I discovered that finding and drinking good wine is a lot of fun. I also have several friends in the wine business in the U.S. and they give me a reason to keep on top of the subject. I don't consider myself an expert, though. I think of myself as someone who appreciates the subtleties of fine wine. When I have the chance, I like to share the experience with friends." Steve smiled, hoping he didn't sound pompous.

"Well, Mr. Barber, oenologist exemplar, I accept your thoughtful suggestions."

"Terrific!" Steve motioned to the waiter, who had moved away just enough not to be obtrusive, and discussed the wine selections. The waiter made notes, voiced the usual "excellent selections, sir", and disappeared.

"If you will allow me," Steve started, "You are lovely this evening. I'm proud of myself for having the courage to ask you to dinner." *Easy boy. Slow it down.*

"Thank you for that wonderful compliment. It has been a long time since I have heard such a nice thing from someone that I was not about to kill." They both laughed.

"Well, the night is young. You could kill me yet." Steve opened the leather-bound menu. "What looks good to you?"

"I think I will start with the foie gras. Will that go well with the champagne?"

"Yes, it should be a good pairing. What about your entrée?" Steve closed his menu and placed it on the table.

"The duck looks good and I believe that the Bordeaux you ordered should complement that very well." Neena put her menu down, too.

"Absolutely! Are you a wine expert?"

"Let's just say that I've had the opportunity to learn many things in the course of my assignments."

"So you *are* a wine expert. Please let me know what you think as we taste them." *Hope she likes them, Mr. Wine Guy,* Steve chastised himself.

They ordered. The champagne followed shortly and was judged "very nice, with a hint of apples and nuts." They laughed as they pretended to be wine columnists for *The New York Times*. In the charm of the moment, Steve reached across the table and gently touched Neena's hand. She held on. Steve reflexively started to move his hand away, but quickly accepted the gesture. It was both strange and welcome.

"Thank you," was all he could think of saying.

The waiter came to freshen the champagne in their flute glasses and took the empty appetizer plates with him. Steve made sure he did not pull his hand back as he started to do when the waiter appeared.

"I have been thinking a lot about you lately," Neena said softly. "I never thought about having the opportunity to care about someone—it never seemed to go with what I—or we—do. After you jumped into my life in Beirut, I began wondering whether it might be possible."

"It's funny," Steve began, leaning closer. "I've thought about you in the same way. It has been a wonderful, crazy feeling, and like you, I wonder how it fits with what we do. I can tell you that I'm not yet ready to set aside these feelings. They're very new. And wonderful."

"Now that we have confessed without being tortured," she quipped, "Why don't we just enjoy our time together and this beautiful evening?" They instinctively removed their hands from each other's touch, although slowly, so that the moment would last.

"I like that idea very much. I'm already having the best time I can remember."

"Likewise."

They talked about places they had been and activities they enjoyed. They covered fond childhood memories, the most important books they had read, and songs they knew by heart. Steve skirted the topic of family, not wanting Neena to feel sadness on this night.

While they were talking, the waiter brought the Trotanoy. They both agreed that the bottle was corked—the bane of fine wines everywhere—and after a short discussion with the sommelier, a substitute bottle arrived minutes later. In the middle of decanting the Bordeaux, which proved to be spectacular, the entrées arrived.

Steve felt the night air swirl around his head. It served a strong cocktail of scents from the wine, the flowers, the aroma of the red wine reduction gracing his entrée, and, most wonderfully, Neena. He could hear the sprinkling patter of other hushed conversations and the faint song of a thrush nightingale. He closed his eyes for a moment to memorize how alive he felt at that moment. *Not too long. Just enough to always remember.*

"Why do you continue to put your life at risk?" Neena asked, swirling her large wine glass with an effortless twist of her wrist. "You could do so many other things, and well, I believe."

"What I am called to do is to make a difference." Steve revealed. "I choose to do that by helping my government achieve specific objectives through clandestine activities. And, I'm really good at what I do. Sometimes I feel that whatever I do and however well I do it, the world seems to become more evil, less just, and a more frightening place. That frustrates me, but I can't just turn my back on what I feel I'm called to do." Neena nodded as if she, too, felt exactly that way.

"Why can't you?" Neena took a bite of her duck.

"Because then I'd become just like the many people who have abdicated responsibility for themselves and want to avoid the consequences of their actions. Life is not good to them, so they imagine villainy in others and demand compensation from someone, from everyone. And there are those who use their leadership positions to encourage this behavior for their own purposes, money and political power being chief among them."

"Leaders can only take people where they want to go," said Neena.

Steve noticed a fleeting expression of concern on her face as if she were remembering someone from her past. "That's true," said Steve, swirling his glass of Bordeaux as Neena had done and inhaling the aromas of chocolate and berries. The wine was doing its work, and he felt relaxed, comfortable, even talking about something so close to his soul. Or maybe it was Neena's presence. Either way, he had not felt this at ease with anyone in years. Not since just after graduating from Cornell. Allison would listen and he knew she cared, but she never understood why he chose to be a Marine, a warrior. She had wanted what Steve called the Ozzie and Harriet life—home, children, two cars, and a country club. Allison would never have understood his work as Neena did. They were two of a kind.

"All societies are complicit in their own destruction," Steve continued, his thoughts focusing again on their conversation. "By not demanding that all its members bear the consequences of their actions, a society gets wrapped around self-inflicted guilt for failing to adequately tend to the wants, not just needs, of everyone. The outcome is predictably ineffective and misguided legislation to regulate life. Worse yet is a society's expectation that such legislation will correct life's ills and eliminate the risk of living." Steve realized he was getting a little overzealous and then thought, *no, I am who I am and she either gets it or not.*

They were quiet for a few moments. Steve couldn't remember the last time he had entered into such a deep discussion.

"That does sound like the world we live in," Neena offered as she lifted her glass to her lips.

"Yes, it sure does." Steve couldn't help but feel that she was a lot like him, and went on. "When society allows the individual to avoid the responsibility and consequences for his or her actions and abets their behavior with the establishment of a large welfare state, then the only possible outcome is the society's eventual collapse under the weight of the indolent." *Indolent, where did I get* that *word?*

"So, what is the answer to my question? Why do you continue to put your life at risk?"

"It's less complicated than you might think. I continue to do my job because I will not allow myself to be a victim. If I can't do enough to turn the tide somehow, well then I'll just have to accept that outcome. But I will not sit on the sidelines, doing nothing to change it. This is more than you wanted to know, perhaps, but that is my answer." *Time to turn the tables.* "What about you?" He took a bite of asparagus.

Neena finished chewing, placed her hands palms down on the edge of the table, and answered, "I am very much like you, except that I sense that my goal is much more focused—I am not looking to deliver the world from evil, just keep Israel in existence. I am frustrated by the behavior of our allies who want Israel to comply with the demands of its enemies without so much as insisting that those enemies accept our right to exist as a state. But like you, I will not be a victim. Nor will Israel. We have been through almost 5800 years of history, and we only re-established our promised homeland some sixty-five years ago. You know the story of Masada—the Israeli people will not let Masada fall again. I continue to do what I do to see Israel survive. That is my duty. That is my life."

Steve waved off the waiter once again. *She's wonderful!* He poured each of them a little more wine.

"My observations hold here, Neena." Steve was into it now, excitement pumping through his veins. Never had he had someone to talk to like this. "Israel is threatened by fanatical Islamist regimes because Muslim societies and Western governments have been complicit in abetting the alleged victimization of Muslims. It's the same cycle that I talked about just a few minutes ago—fanatics have declared themselves victims and have demanded compensation in many forms. Many Muslims have been all too eager to jump on that bandwagon. Moderate Islamists have acquiesced to this charade, either out of fear or ignorance, and now the fanatics are in control of what those societies do. This is what happens when individuals, and governments, fail to take responsibility for doing what's right, what's just."

Steve shot the waiter a look to indicate he would call him when he was ready and the waiter moved off to tend other customers.

"I see what you mean," said Neena. She was turning the stem of her wine glass on the table like a safe's tumbler to unlock her thoughts. "Our aggressive neighbors and the Palestinians are self-named victims. The Arabs, not the Israelis, rejected UN General Assembly Resolution 181 and created the Palestinian problem. Before they—Jordan, Syria, Iraq, Lebanon, and Egypt—invaded us and tried to blot out our country in 1948, Jews and Palestinians lived side by side here. We had hoped to live peacefully with our neighbors, but those countries chose otherwise."

They were both leaning forward as though they were exchanging state secrets. Steve was totally engrossed in Neena, the conversation, her eyes, her lips. The neckline of her black dress that dipped just enough to reveal a hint of cleavage when she leaned toward him. He snapped back to attention in order to keep his train of thought.

"And during the war," Steve began, clearing his throat and sipping his wine, "The Palestinians, at the *urging* of the aggressor countries, fled Israel. With the exception of Jordan, however, those countries failed to integrate or otherwise care for them." He sliced a thin strip of veal. "Those countries have kept them in refugee camps, not even acknowledging their own role in making the Palestinians homeless. Now, for political purposes, they continue to claim that they are the victims, but it is a victimization by Arabs, not Israelis."

"They are not victims." Neena interjected placing her knife and fork on her plate. "They want the world to portray them as victims so that they can justify the elimination of Israel as just compensation or retribution." She used her right index finger to jab the table for emphasis. "And the world community, including the United States, fails to accept its responsibility—it was under the auspices of the United Nations that Israel was established—and now we have well over three hundred UN General Assembly resolutions condemning Israel's actions in protecting itself from its neighbors and *not one* resolution condemning an Arab country for any of their aggressions against us. Israel may fall, but, first, hell will open up and swallow the world."

Steve marveled at her passion, the fire in her eyes. Her courage made his heart thump. They were kindred spirits. *A once in a lifetime occurrence, if you're lucky.* "I, for one, do not wish either to happen," Steve said, putting down his knife and fork, too.

They were silent for a few moments, thinking about what had been said. After a minute, Neena signaled that she was done with her entrée by placing her fork and knife together across her plate in the European style. She brought her right hand up and extended her palm upward toward Steve, touching his face. *She is so graceful,* Steve thought.

"Steve, there are many in Israel who believe that Israel will be destroyed within just a few years by an axis of Lebanon, Iran, Iraq, Syria, and other countries. With Iran in the picture, their combined forces have the nuclear weapons and conventional forces to threaten, even destroy, Israel. Not many Israelis believe that the United States or any other Western country will come to our aid. We see ourselves alone and vulnerable, a feeling that we have not felt before."

"Judging by our actions of the last thirty years, I can understand why you feel that way," said Steve, placing his hand over hers where it now rested on the table. His face tingled from her touch. "But, I know many people in our military and the federal government are frustrated by our acquiescence to Middle Eastern regimes. I would count on help."

"If you were Israeli, perhaps you would not. I do not." Her glass clinked as she pushed her plate into it and placed her hands on the arms of her chair.

"Then, would you at least accept that I would help?"

"Yes, I know I could count on you. You have proven to me that you are a man of truth and conscience."

"I do not want you to feel alone."

"Thank you. When I am with you, I do not feel alone. Now," she said, waving a hand as if to brush away the conversation. "Let us talk of other things."

Neena told Steve about her family and its history. Steve knew a barrier had fallen if she trusted him enough to share her story. Steve talked about his family and how much, as a boy and then later, a man in the military, he had admired his father. How much he tried to be like him. When the waiter reappeared, Steve waved him over to order dessert. The entrées had been exceptional, and the wine helped them move past the world's problems, at least for the night. They regained the lighter side of the conversation. They discovered a mutual love of history and historical novels.

The crème brûlées were accompanied by 1988 Chateau d'Yquem. The golden liquid shimmered in the candlelight and the reflection bathed Neena's face. Steve was grateful for the interlude of peace that being with her brought. Espressos, served in dainty demitasse cups, followed, accompanied by *mignardise*, a French term for small sweets, set in a star pattern on a tiny bone china plate.

Steve was in no hurry for this to end and he sensed Neena felt the same. Sometimes they spoke. Other times they just held hands. At eleven o'clock, Steve noticed that the restaurant was empty, save for them. *Don't want to overstay our welcome and spoil the moment.*

Steve called for the check and as he waited, he said, "Neena, I'm very happy that you do not feel alone when you are with me. I feel the same way when I'm with you."

Neena started to speak and then stopped. Then, softly, she began again, "I would not like to be alone tonight."

"Nor would I."

Steve reached across the table and held her hand quietly until the waiter returned with the credit card receipt. He signed it, and they left arm in arm.

Chapter Eleven
Saturday, April 26, 2014; Pädäh, Jerusalem, Israel

Neena's driver picked her up at ten o'clock in the morning at a prearranged location and drove her back to Pädäh. David was finishing a senior staff meeting and, upon seeing her enter the compound, immediately invited her to go for a run. After changing into the proper clothes and packing some water, they set out of the main gate. A chase car with two armed agents followed fifty meters behind.

They started out at a light jog and after about five minutes, David pushed the pace up to ten-minute miles. After two kilometers, Neena pushed the pace to eight-minute miles as they started up a fire road on one of the hills to the east. *If you push me, I'll push back,* Neena thought. She kept two strides ahead of David. When he sped up, so did she.

After a good eleven kilometers and about 230 feet of elevation gain over five switchbacks, they reached the top of a hill where there was a cluster of stone walls, part of an Israeli lookout post in 1948. Neena had led them to a six-minute pace by the top of the hill. They stopped and walked along the walls, both breathing hard. They were alone. The chase car had stayed below on the paved road.

"How was Tel Aviv?" David asked as they sat catching their breath on one of the walls, Pädäh sprawled below. Mountain blue Galilee lupines and golden chamomiles were in wondrous bloom under the noonday sun, carpeting the hills and crawling over the walls. Waves of bending blossoms, driven by a light breeze, seemed to be bidding hello to David and Neena and inviting them to rest in the private hillside garden.

"You know of the message intercepted from the Iranians," said Neena, clearing her throat and taking a sip of water from a bottle attached to her waist. "Bill and Steve think there may be some way of using the information about Operation Kristallnacht if they can find out who is behind the message."

"Yes," David agreed, "That could work to the advantage of Israel if we could validate that the Shiites intend to annihilate the Sunni armed forces cadre. What about the part regarding the data array?"

"They are very focused on the number 167," Neena said, looking for a reaction in David's eyes, "And they have deduced that all advanced countries have more or less similar sets of data arrays."

"Such as coordinates for all top-priority secure locations, military installations, high profile government officials, and the like." David stood up and stretched by placing one leg and then the other on the stone wall and bending down, touching and holding his toes.

"Yes, they are convinced that if they look at the same kinds of data arrays that the U.S. maintains, then they will be able to identify what kind of data would match a number like 167." She watched David for another moment and then turned to look over the Israel she loved, rooftops popping like mushrooms peacefully in the distance. *How precious this place is.*

"How close are they to figuring that out?" David was now stretching his arms and shoulders.

"I do not know, but I imagine they will soon figure out that 167 is the number of targets for Israel's land-based ballistic missiles." Then, Neena stood up facing David and asked pointedly, "You know who sent that message from Israel. Don't you, David?"

David stopped his stretching and wiped his brow with the hem of his shirt. "Yes, we sent that message. It was sent accidentally un-encrypted by Sergeant Shachar—he will not do that again."

Poor Zee. He must be in such anguish over this, thought Neena. "What does the message mean? Why are you involved with geographic coordinates for ballistic missiles? That has never been the business of Mossad—IDF Strategic Command is accountable for that."

"We are running a top-secret counterintelligence probe to see if we can break into the missile command software and re-target the missiles," said David. "This project is being conducted for Simon Luegner."

"Why? What can Mossad do for the Defense Minister that is so special? Do you have information that the systems have been or could be compromised?" Neena started to stretch and felt David's eyes watching her body as she twisted and pulled to loosen her muscles and tendons. *Funny, I didn't use to mind so much.*

"We have no hard evidence, but Simon wants to know if it is possible. That message was sent to one of my agents who had gained access to some areas of the command facility. He will attempt to reprogram the target coordinates. If he is successful, then we will know that Simon's fears are real—our enemy *could* penetrate our strategic systems." David looked at his watch and took a long drink from his water bottle. "Let's start back."

Neena finished stretching, keeping herself facing David. When she finished, she asked, "If that agent is successful, won't that leave us vulnerable to an attack?"

"No, the 167 targets will still be loaded." David started a slow jog. Neena kept alongside. "Can we agree to jog, not run, down the hill?" David asked. Neena nodded. *Getting old are we?* Neena mused.

"Then how will you know—or how will you prove—the agent was successful?" Neena probed. She looked over at the expanse of wildflowers as if David's answer did not matter.

"Because the geographic coordinates will be calculated using substituted zero degrees latitude and longitude—not the Prime Meridian or the Equator. We can identify that change even though the targets remain unchanged."

"So, the Iranian mathematician is correct," said Neena. "He just needs to figure out the adjustment to the geographic coordinates. When he does, and I believe he will, he will know how many and which targets we have programmed into our land-based missiles."

David stepped on a large stone and twisted his ankle. He grimaced, but kept jogging without a break in the rhythm, but with a noticeable limp. "Yes, but that should not be a surprise to them." David breathed. "I believe they already have an accurate picture of our nuclear missile capabilities."

"What do you think they will conclude after they have solved the geographic coordinate puzzle?" Neena pressed.

"That we have gone through an exercise of testing the flexibility of our targeting software."

"For what purpose?" Neena said, knowing she was badgering David.

"In some ways, I don't care," he answered with a hint of annoyance. *Good,* Neena thought. *He's uncomfortable.*

David went on. "I think they will assume that we may want to be able to re-target on short notice, perhaps to concentrate our defensive response toward any aggression. As I said though, I don't really care. Let it be a mystery to them."

"Does this exercise have anything to do with the internal communications restrictions?" Neena asked bringing the discussion back to her assignment.

"Yes, the exercise is what we are trying to hide," David answered and stopped jogging. Neena held up, too. David raised his foot up and rotated his twisted ankle a few times. He put it down and rotated it again. They slowed to a walk.

Two birds, one much smaller than the other, zoomed by. The smaller was relentlessly attacking the larger, which tried to evade the assault with tight twists and turns. Neena recognized the birds. The smaller was a red-rumped swallow, with blue top feathers, and a reddish rump. It was a fast bird, marked by a forked tail, which fed mostly on insects. The larger bird was a Levant sparrow hawk, which hunted smaller birds. She identified it by the blue grey upper, dark wingtips, and barred reddish belly. She watched the swallow repeatedly gain altitude and dive at the hawk, avoiding its talons with ease and grace. *That sparrow has turned the tables on the hawk. Give 'em hell little guy!* Neena cheered inwardly.

As she watched the birds fly into the distance, with the swallow still in hot pursuit of the would-be predator, she parried, "But you told me that first day back at Pädäh that you were hardening systems against cyber-attack."

"Well, the exercise will determine how hard our missile targeting systems are and how vulnerable they are to cyber-attack." By this time they had reached the paved road and turned toward the compound.

"But the agent is not trying to hack into the systems," Neena said, knowingly squeezing David, taking her chances with his patience. "He has access and is altering the source code in the targeting program, if I understand what you told me."

"It's a matter of semantics, Neena. We are testing the system's vulnerability. What does it matter *how*?" David asked through clenched teeth as he turned to face Neena.

"David, you have not been telling me the truth. I know enough about systems and security probes to tell the difference between simulating cyber-attacks and the full re-programming of missile targeting systems. It doesn't add up and that frightens me."

"You should not be frightened," David almost whispered as he took a step toward Neena. "I would never do anything to harm you or Israel. You know that."

Neena started walking toward the compound and David kept pace at her side. "Yes, I know that," she said. "It's just that all the pieces don't fit right. And you taught me never to accept any information unless all the pieces fit, and perfectly."

"Yes, and you learned well, much to my chagrin," David said with a small laugh. "Tell you what. Stay here tonight and go back to Tel Aviv tomorrow and spend time with Steve. Your driver tells me that you dismissed him last night as you went to meet Steve for dinner."

"My driver should remember what I do for a living," said Neena, only half in jest. *I'll have to be more careful with him.* "All right. Tomorrow I will return to Tel Aviv. How much can I tell Steve and Bill?" They were just outside the compound gate. They stopped walking and turned toward each other. The chase car pulled into the compound.

"You can tell them that you have found out that we are testing our land-based nuclear missile targeting systems. That will explain the number 167 and the communications restrictions. Tell them that we are concluding the test soon and that I would have told everything earlier, but we had to keep our security protocol—no offense intended to our erstwhile allies and all that. I do not want you to disclose to them that I was the source of that intercepted message. They don't need to know that to understand why we have instituted communications restrictions."

"Okay," Neena said. "They will appreciate being brought in on what you and Simon are up to." She turned to walk through the gate. "I am going to the gym to work out on the weights a bit. My shoulder needs some exercise and I want to get back to the range to check out how much the recoil hurts."

"Fine. Dinner?" David yelled after her.

"Of course," Neena said loudly over her shoulder. "See you around eight?"

"Perfect."

After Neena had disappeared, David walked through the gate and over to his office. He had Zee meet him in the rose garden.

"Zee, I have an assignment for you. It will not be pleasant, but our mission requires it."

"What is it, Colonel?"

David brought Zee up to speed on his conversation with Neena. Then he said, "Steve Barber. He is too close to discovering our mission. He and Bill are very smart and they will want to validate the information that Neena will give them. They have enough contacts in high places to find out eventually that no such exercise exists." David began to pace and clench his fists.

"When they find that out," David continued, "Things will become very difficult for us to control because IDF Strategic Command will go through every system and retest them. We can't have that happen. Not now. We have only seven days left."

"What is my assignment, Colonel?"

"You are to kill Steve," David said standing directly in front of Zee and watching for his reaction. *Zee had better not flinch.* "And if Bill gets in the way, take him out, too. Make it look like a Hezbollah attack. After Steve helped Neena in Beirut, a hit on him would not seem improbable. Use a back channel and make sure that Hezbollah knows that Steve was the person who crashed the party they wanted to throw for Neena. Any questions?"

"What if Neena gets in the way?"

"Your job, Sergeant, is to make sure she doesn't. She is not to be harmed. Is that understood?"

"Yes, sir."

"Good. If you can, make the hit before Neena gets back to Tel Aviv late morning tomorrow. That is one way of keeping her out of it."

"Colonel, may I speak?"

"Of course, Zee. What is it?"

"Steve Barber is a good man and a warrior—like us. I . . ."

"Zee," David interrupted, knowing what was on Zee's mind. "I, too, do not like the idea of killing him, but Israel has always come first to us. Her sons and daughters pray every day for peace and pay every day for the lack of it." David turned to the rose garden for a moment and then turned back to Zee.

"You may remember, Zee, that we called a missile strike on Kibbutz Kabri as cover for Steve and Neena to cross the border. We were willing to accept the deaths of kibbutzim—Jews and Israelis—to have Steve and Neena back with us. Steve's death, while regrettable, will enable us to execute our plans on May 3. I admire your concern, but this order is to be carried out. Is that understood, Zee?"

"Understood, Colonel," Zee said, throwing his shoulders back and standing at attention. He saluted, turned with a crisp snap and walked away. *He doesn't like the order, but he'll carry it out. He will or he'll be dead,* David thought as he watched Zee disappear.

David walked back to his office and put in a call to Simon Luegner to discuss recent developments. David would not tell him about the order he gave to Sergeant Zadok Shachar, as the Defense Minister knew him.

Saturday, April 26, 2014; Washington, DC, USA

Vic Alfonse was in the secure multi-media communications room across from his office. It was a windowless room, paneled in fir and a little stuffy because there was no money for rebalancing the HVAC when the electronics were upgraded a year ago. No matter. Vic would not be there long. A thick burgundy carpet muffled his footsteps as he wheeled an office chair toward a long counter in front of a high-definition flat screen mounted to the wall. Vic punched the power button and Defense Minister Simon Luegner's face filled the screen. He was in his office in Jerusalem. Vic recognized the painting of David Ben-Gurion behind him and the Israeli flag that always stood to the left near the window. *This is a modern feature I actually appreciate,* thought Vic. *I can see the mole on Simon's jawbone the picture is so clear.* Vic saw, too, an absence of humor in his friend Simon this afternoon. *He probably doesn't like the fact that I called him on the Sabbath.*

"Good afternoon, Simon," Vic Alfonse began. It amused Vic that his first instinct was to speak loudly as though the distance were too great for the signal to reach the other person without yelling. He had only done that the first time he had used this sensitive equipment, which was guaranteed impenetrable by enemies. Now he spoke at a normal tone, knowing the microphone would pick up every inflection. "You are looking well. I trust that the fine April weather continues for you."

"Thank you, Vic. The weather is spectacular today. How may I help you, my friend?"

"I have it on good authority that the communications gap that we and others have noticed within the Middle East intelligence community is the child of Mossad." With the word "Mossad", Vic saw Simon's jaw clench. *Hmm.*

"It is quite possible . . ."

"And," Vic continued without waiting for Simon to finish speaking, "That the reason for the restrictions was to cover a covert internal exercise aimed at infiltrating the IDF Strategic Command for the purpose of determining whether and to what extent your missile targeting systems are vulnerable. Is that correct, *my friend*?" Vic asked, accentuating the phrase "my friend" that Simon had used earlier in the conversation. He had just the wisp of an edge in his voice, exactly how he wanted to sound at this particular moment.

Simon did not answer for a few seconds and then said, "Yes, Vic. That exercise is being conducted under my personal order. We have placed restrictions on all internal communications to reduce the probability of our enemies discovering it."

Simon picked up a pen that had been lying on a tablet in front of him. He held it clutched between the fingers of both hands like someone holds small twigs they are about to break.

"Simon, I am disappointed that you lacked the confidence in me and the United States to have informed us of the communications restrictions. I would not have expected to know the specifics of the exercise, of course, but you knew of my concerns regarding the lack of information flows in the Middle East." Vic folded his hands together and placed them on the desk in front of him. He felt relaxed and could tell that his friend was not. "You could have relieved me of those concerns with a secure call, like this one. Because you did not, I almost lost Steve Barber and I have had to disband Strike Force Abraham for a few months."

"Steve Barber made his own decision to intervene in Beirut, as did Christian. We did not ask for the help." Vic saw the twitch begin in Simon's lower eyelid and noticed him reach behind his ear, scratching three strokes, a sure sign of discomfort. Or lying. *Good. I'm getting to him.*

"Friends do not need to *ask* for help, Simon. That is what being friends means. It was help freely given, as you said. But friends also have trust in each other. I am sensing that you do not trust me. I don't like to think about the implications of Israel no longer trusting its closest ally."

"The world, at least for Israel, is no longer a place of trust." Simon placed the pen back down on the tablet. He looked at the pen for a moment then raised his eyes toward the camera and continued, "You know as well as I that our strategic position has deteriorated over the last twenty-five years, not in small measure to a lack of consistent, forceful support from the United States. If we felt that we had friends, we might ask for help. If, indeed, we had friends, then, as you say, we would not *have* to ask. Instead, today we feel very much that we have been abandoned by the world and that we can look only to ourselves to protect our freedom."

Vic scanned Simon for every detail. Simon was sitting with his hands clasped so tightly the knuckles turned white, but his face showed calm. *What he would like to say is go fuck yourself. I wonder why he doesn't. He knows me well enough.*

"As a consequence, Vic, I do not share information outside of Israeli defense and security agencies. You may not like it, but that is the way it is and the way it will be until we once again sense the might of America next to us."

"You and I have known each other for many years, Simon. Israel cannot exist, let alone prosper, by severing defense and intelligence ties with the West," said Vic. "What can I do to bring our countries closer?"

"The time has passed for Israel to rely on the United States and Europe. In a few days, we will . . ." Simon abruptly stopped for a few seconds and, then, went on, "We will be through with our vulnerability exercise and I will have more time to discuss how we can rebuild our alliance. For now, I must say 'goodbye' and attend to other matters. Shalom, Vic."

"Shalom, Simon."

After he clicked off the power and the screen went black, Vic pushed a button and said, "George, would you please get Steve Barber on a secure line and connect me in the my conference room? Thank you." *This is worse than I feared, whatever it is.*

Chapter Twelve
Sunday, April 27, 2014; Tel Aviv, Israel

Neena arose very early and drove herself to Tel Aviv to allow her driver a day off with his family. Besides, she disliked being chauffeured, as David had ordered. She sensed that he wanted her to have a driver more to control than protect her. Before she left the compound, she called Steve. She would meet him at The Morning Glory for brunch. The eggs Florentine there (she was amused as she recalled that The Morning Glory was on Florentin Street) were her favorite and she was anxious to see Steve again. Their night together had been one she found herself happy to remember.

Zee left Jerusalem for Tel Aviv the night before. He wanted to have time in the early morning to scout Steve's hotel and its environs before the place was crawling with tourists. He also needed to contact a Mossad sniper who had been tracking Steve on David Alon's orders. Zee did not like the sniper, a ten-year veteran by the name of Ariel Sharett. Zee felt that the sniper enjoyed his job a little too much and that worried Zee. People like that became careless because they were touched with a sense of invincibility. Nonetheless, David had assigned Sharett to Zee, and he would deal with it.

David had ordered a tap, through a friend in the IDF, on Steve's hotel telephone. When Neena called Steve, David was able to forward the restaurant's name to Zee. David had also taken the opportunity to remind Zee that Neena was not to be harmed.

Zee knew the restaurant and, with Sharett, drove to the site. The restaurant was just down Florentin from another coffee shop, City Coffee Break, at the corner of Hertzl, and, like that place, had full-length doors along the front, retracted in good weather to allow patrons to sit in a small patio area on the sidewalk. It was a glorious April morning, so the restaurant's doors would be open. The entrance to the restaurant was relatively narrow, just wide enough to allow one person to leave while another was entering.

Zee decided he had two opportunities. The first was to make the shot as Steve sat at a table on the patio—Neena would prefer the patio, and she had a way of getting what she wanted. Steve might have his back turned to the street, but the ability to identify Neena would also identify the target. The second was to take the shot as Steve left the restaurant through the doorway, when his face would be fully visible, so, again, there would be no chance of misidentification.

Zee preferred the patio shot because Neena would be physically separated from Steve. The doorway shot was riskier because the bullet might penetrate Steve and hit Neena were she close behind him—so that shot would have to be perfect.

Across the street was a three-story office building. Although normally it would be open for the beginning of the workweek in Israel, it was closed. A water main that serviced that building and several others had broken yesterday, on the Sabbath. *I'll take being lucky anytime*, Zee admitted to himself.

Zee found a way in, and soon he and Sharett were in Suite 320, a set of offices leased by an accounting firm. Zee had hoped that one location would have clear visibility for either shot, but a set of potted palms shielded the restaurant entrance from the patio. If he could not take the patio shot, Zee would have to move and set up his rifle again in time to take the doorway shot. He decided that he would assign the easier patio shot to Sharett. If that shot could not be taken for some reason, he would take the doorway shot. *Sharett better not screw this up*, Zee warned himself. He did not like the prospect of relying on Sharett in an operation so important to David. *The colonel doesn't accept failure well.*

Zee estimated that Neena would be at the restaurant in about forty-five minutes. He hoped that Steve would arrive first and select a patio table, banking on the idea that Neena would mention her seating preference to Steve prior to meeting him. That way, Neena would not be there for the shot; not be there to see Steve murdered in front of her eyes. She had been through too much already. But orders were orders. If blood spilled in front of her, she'd get over it. She had always managed to before.

Steve got the telephone call from Neena and called the restaurant to make reservations, which, he learned, they did not take for workday brunch. He then decided to get there early so that they would have a table on the patio. She had mentioned how much she'd enjoyed the outdoor atmosphere at the Carmella Ba'Nachala where they had dinner. He wanted this time with Neena to be special. He felt like a schoolboy and his heart was racing. He couldn't wait to finish showering and shaving. *What is going on with me?* he asked himself. He put on tan slacks, a light-yellow shirt, and a dark brown cotton sweater, hoping he didn't look too collegiate. He decided to leave the Walther PPK in the hotel room and placed it in its hiding place. With a big smile and a newly found spring in his step, he set out on foot for the restaurant.

The morning was brisk and sunny. He enjoyed the walk, thinking about Neena and paying less than usual attention to his surroundings. He waited inside a small coffee bar toward the back of the restaurant and ordered an espresso while he waited for the table. The wait was only about ten minutes, so he paid and walked to the table—it was perfect!—in a corner of the patio where they would be a little away from the crowd and the annoyance of people bumping the backs of their chairs.

He waited, looking anxiously up and down the street for Neena. He tried reading the newspaper he had brought, but found he could not concentrate. Instead, he watched the street bustle with activity. Sunday was the chaotic beginning of the workweek, so the crowds were normal, but something was amiss.

People seemed confused. They tried to get into the building across the street, but for some reason, it was closed. Swirls of baffled workers mingled and spoke, then went away. He placed himself on alert. *Damn, why didn't I bring my Walther?*

Finally he overheard a waiter tell someone that a water main servicing the building was broken so the water company had ordered the building closed. *Well, they're in luck! I hope they are enjoying the extra day off,* he mused as he relaxed and sat back in his chair. *I sure am.*

As he saw Steve approach the restaurant, Sharett took his position by his rifle. He had set it up, affixing the silencer last, on a credenza next to a window, which opened easily, overlooking the restaurant patio. Zee stood to his rear two meters away. They waited in silence and, in a few minutes, saw Steve step onto the patio. He sat down at a table in a corner and opened a newspaper. Sharett positioned himself for the shot, fine-tuning the sight. Zee told him to take the shot as soon as he was ready.

Sharett adjusted his body slightly and placed his eye behind the sight. *Wait. Take your time,* Sharett thought. *You've been waiting for this since that day across from the US Embassy.* Barber looked like he saw something. He had tensed up. But he had not looked up. Sharett watched Steve relax and sit back in his seat. *Perfect. Now.*

Placing his index finger first against the trigger guard, he slowly brought it in and up and began to squeeze. Just then, a swallow flew onto the windowsill, distracting him at the moment the trigger released the firing pin. The shot hit the metal table in front of Steve and ricocheted off, lodging itself in the top of one of the large retracted full-length doors.

A second shot hit immediately and burst through his chair. Steve dived through the large opening into the restaurant and pulled up against the wall four or five feet inside to look across the street.

With Steve's leap into the restaurant, the patio erupted in terror as the realization struck the patrons that shots had been fired. One couple jumped under their table, causing it to topple onto three other people running from the patio. As shocked diners fought their way to safety inside, they smashed service trays, chairs, dishes, and each other, and the resulting din added to the terror. Shouts and desperate screaming overcame waiters' pleas for calm and order. Death was stalking Florentin Street.

Steve's instincts were alive. He calculated the direction of the shot based on the trajectory of the first shot's ricochet off the table. *The closed building. Third floor.* He searched for another exit as his fellow patrons panicked. They were pushing and shoving, scrambling over the low wrought iron fence outlining the patio, jamming through the narrow doorway to the main restaurant. *There's another door! In the back!* Steve sprinted out before people began seeking the man who had been sitting at the bullet-shattered table.

Zee slammed a fist into the wall, leaving a round pockmark in the paint. He instinctively knew that Sharett, in his overconfidence, had not concentrated fully on the shot. Letting a bird's movement take his mind off the shot—amateur hour. He should have had his mind *fully* on the target. *Nothing should have diverted his attention from the target!*

Zee ordered Sharett to pack quickly and said no more. He would deal with him later. The two stuffed their weapons into large canvas bags and left the building in less than two minutes. Zee had a van and driver parked two blocks away, and they sprinted out the back, exiting through a delivery entrance on the southwest corner. Once they reached the street, they slowed to a brisk walk, rounded a corner, walked another block, and turned into Benbenishti Street where the van was stationed.

"I'm sorry, Serg . . ." Sharett tried to say.

Interrupting him, Zee could only spit the words out, "If you say one more thing without my permission, I will beat the living shit out of you. Your arrogance and lack of *total* concentration have ruined a mission of the *greatest* strategic importance to Israel. God help us. Do not say a word! Not if you want to live."

"Corporal," Zee said to the driver, as he clambered into the back seat of the van. "Take us to Pädäh. Don't you speak either!"

The van, decorated to look like a Bezeq telecommunications vehicle, turned out of the side street and just under the speed limit, drove north to Florentin and then turned left onto the one-way street.

Neena arrived to find the restaurant almost empty. A couple of waiters peered through the open doors toward the patio where policemen were taking notes and examining a table, chair, and the full-length door. Glass shards were strewn across the tiles. Remnants of cups and saucers, plates, and food littered the entire patio as though someone had tossed it into a blender. Neena flashed her ID card at a police sergeant and asked what had happened. He told her that as much as they could piece together, someone had taken two shots at a man sitting at the corner patio table. They were not sure whether he had been hit and were looking for him. He was last seen running out the back door and then crossing the street to the building across from the restaurant.

Neena hopped the low fence and raced to the office building without saying another word to the policeman. She took out her Walther and chambered a round. She quickly calculated the trajectory of the bullets and headed for the third floor. As she edged her way down the hallway, she heard men talking loudly in Hebrew, but in calm tones. She headed toward the voices and cautiously entered an office. She saw Steve in the custody of two policemen. Steve was trying to convince them that he would go to their police station the following day, but he needed time *now* to look over the room for evidence. They were telling him that looking for evidence was their job. As Neena slipped into the room with her weapon drawn, the police reached for theirs. Neena flipped her Walther up in her hand and flashed her Mossad ID.

"I'm taking control of this crime scene," Neena stated authoritatively. "This man will remain in my custody and will report to your sergeant tomorrow morning at ten o'clock. Please un-cuff him now." As they did, she said, "Return to the restaurant and continue your investigation there. I will be there in fifteen minutes. Thank you."

When she was sure the police were well on their way back to the restaurant, Neena grabbed Steve and hugged him hard. "What happened?" she asked.

As he hugged her back, he answered, "Someone took two shots at me from here," and pointed to the open window. "I suspect he, or she, used a rifle and it definitely had a silencer. I didn't find any brass casings, so looks like a professional hit. I'd like to see the shell fragments that the police take out of the door. I don't know where the second shot ended up."

"I agree with your assessment," said Neena. "The office is untouched. They must have gotten out within minutes of taking the second shot. That is not amateur work."

"I was here within four minutes of the second shot. I saw no one. Let's go back to the restaurant."

They discovered that they had been holding each other while they talked. Somewhat awkwardly, they parted and smiled at each other. At the restaurant, Neena found the police sergeant, whose last name was Harel, and asked for an update. The sergeant told them that there were no witnesses who saw the shooter—not a surprise to Neena or Steve—and that no one had seen anyone entering or leaving the building across the street.

Sergeant Harel held up a small plastic bag with several shell fragments. "Some pieces were in the upper frame of that door," the sergeant said as he pointed. "Other fragments were found in the chair and the outside of the building—must have ricocheted off the tiles on the patio. One person got a small piece lodged in her calf, but she will be fine—it was a very shallow wound. The paramedics treated her and she left."

"Thank you, Sergeant," Neena said and turned to leave, but Steve stopped her.

"Sergeant," Steve said, "Are you familiar with ammunition of the type you found?"

"Yes. Judging by the fragments we found and what I believe to be the nature of the shots taken, I would say that this is a standard sniper rifle round—perhaps an H&K, if I had to guess."

"Thank you, Sergeant."

"More than welcome, sir. Glad to see that you were not hurt. You must be special—Mossad agents don't normally get involved in criminal investigations unless they have a reason to. Shalom."

"Let's go somewhere else and talk," Steve suggested. "This place is too noisy." Neena laughed. As they headed for the door, Steve stopped and pulled Neena to him and kissed her passionately. She kissed him back with a warmness that filled her body. Then he suggested that they leave by the back door.

Steve and Neena walked just north several blocks from The Morning Glory and reached Herbert Samuel Dock, a couple of blocks south of Steve's hotel. They found a street vendor and bought two coffees, sipping while surveying the area, eyes darting left, right, over the rim of their cups. They headed toward a wall by the water where they could watch the crowds and the sound of the sea would muffle their conversation.

Standing by the low wall, Neena watched waves roll in to the beach, the stretch of sand occupied by sunbathers and children flying kites, the colorful shapes dipping and diving against blue sky. Steve looked inland, the streets bustling as usual. "Not the morning I was looking forward to," Steve said. "I need to call Bill Elsberry and Vic, but I want to sort things out before I report what happened." Steve saw Neena was deep in thought. "What's on your mind?"

"I've been turning what we know over in my head and I can't link the obvious suspect, Hezbollah, to how the hit was attempted," Neena began.

"Why is that?"

"Hezbollah are essentially thugs. They approach most assassinations with little caution and a lot of brutality," she said, leaning closer to Steve to be heard over the roar of the waves and the clamor of passersby. "We saw that in

Beirut. The shooter this morning was highly trained—he scouted the area and identified a safe location from which to take the shot." She blew on her coffee, took a sip.

"I noticed that the office had another window that offered a shot toward the doorway," said Steve. "If the shooter chose the location for that reason, then he or she is very well trained. The shooter used a silencer and, it seems, a sniper rifle. I agree with you. It wasn't Hezbollah." Steve was scanning Herbert Samuel Dock, raising his gaze to include the tops of buildings. "How did the shooter know I would be there?" he continued.

"Good question," Neena affirmed. "That information is very hard for Hezbollah to get in Israel, especially when they only had ninety minutes to get it—I called you at eight thirty this morning from a secure line."

A man on a bicycle approached. He had a package wrapped in brown paper in a basket on the handlebars, so they couldn't see his hands. Steve took a step forward, putting himself between Neena and the man. Neena put her hand on her Walther, leaving it there until the man was thirty meters past, his bicycle weaving in and out in traffic. *Nerves,* thought Steve. *This is unlike me.* It occurred to him that Neena's safety was partly his responsibility. Not that she couldn't take care of herself.

"I know I have a bug in my room," Steve said, "but I've neutralized that by entertaining the listeners with soccer games on the TV. Can the police find out if my hotel telephone has been tapped?"

"Yes, I already asked the sergeant at the restaurant to check that out." Neena took another sip of her coffee and brushed a stray strand of hair away from her eyes. The wind was picking up and the kites over the beach zigzagged, reaching for the sky.

"Will they be able to find out who ordered the tap?"

"That depends on who ordered it," Neena answered, turning her back to the beach to focus on the facts. "If the tap was illegal, that will tell us something—and perhaps we will have to revisit Hezbollah as a suspect. If the tap was legal and the sergeant cannot find out, then the only feasible answer would be high level Israeli security—Shin Bet, IDF's Directorate of Military Intelligence, or Mossad."

"Hezbollah I understand, but why would an Israeli security agency want me killed?" Steve watched the man on the bicycle stop and sit on a bench fifty yards away. He took the package out of the basket, opened it up and started eating something. It reminded Steve that he and Neena hadn't eaten yet. His stomach growled. *Looks like a pita sandwich.*

"I don't know, but they would need a reason. They are not indiscriminate in such matters, especially within Israel itself."

"Let's give Bill Elsberry a call. I'll also have to call Vic Alfonse and update him. Rain check on your eggs Florentine?"

"You're on. Let's go to the hotel," Neena said. "We can take apart the morning step by step and look at the details." She cast a little smile at Steve. "I remember the room well. We might need some time in bed to recover from this traumatic morning"

"Now *you're* on!" *Where has this woman been all my life?*

Sunday, April 27, 2014; New York, NY, USA

Brian Kendrick finished his version of breakfast—two cups of coffee, some strawberries, and a bran muffin—and looked out his office window at 101 Park Avenue in Manhattan. It was one of those glorious early spring days in New York, 72 degrees Fahrenheit, sunny, with a mild breeze. He knew his partners would be antsy to enjoy what remained of their short weekends, but this meeting was critical to the Iranian deal. He looked over the meeting agenda and his notes.

A voice popped out of the Polycom conference telephone announcing that Joe Burstein had joined the call. They would all wait on the line until the last partner joined. As if on cue, the telephone announced the last partner's name. *Show time,* he thought. He hit the mute button again so that his partners could hear him speak. Next he smiled, not for the others to see, but to create a positive mental state.

"Thank you all for taking the time on a Sunday morning to participate in this telephonic partners' meeting," Brian said. "The only agenda item we have is to review the National Iranian Oil Company transaction. Are there any additions to the agenda?" He paused and, hearing no additions, said, "Then let the minutes show that the agenda has been approved as presented. Also, let the minutes show that this meeting is being electronically recorded, as is our standard business practice for these kinds of meetings." He despised spending his and his partners' precious time this way, but the firm's attorneys insisted on firm governance meetings and proper documentation.

Brian brought them up to date on the details of the transaction. The firm now had $98 billion in commitments from integrated oil companies and two independent refiners to sell assets. The sellers and the National Iranian Oil Company (known as "NIOC") had executed legal documents to operate the assets under separate corporate entities and had also signed tolling agreements for those entities to process crude oils for the selling company. "Those documents will be effective upon (a) closing of the asset sales agreements, which are being written and signed as negotiations are concluded, and (b) receipt of payment," said Brian. He leaned back in his chair, stretching his knee to ease the stiffness that was with him most days now. He referred to his notes.

As Brian continued to brief the partners, he thought about the dinner he had the night before with an old friend from college, a renowned chemist. Brian had told him the public parts of the deal and he found that his friend, intelligent as he was, had trouble following the transaction. *Well, I guess if he were telling me about his work with hydrogenated phenols, my eyes would glaze over, too.*

He heard himself telling his partners that the indications of interest in the Eurobond offering by NIOC were strong, in part because of the good collateral value of the refinery assets. He reported that the syndicate expected that the offering would be down to tag ends by the end of day tomorrow, Monday, April 28. Settlement day, the day on which payment for the bonds was due, would be Thursday, May 1, at which time the funds would be transferred by CHK to an escrow account with Swiss Bank in London.

There was more. *Even I'm bored!* he found himself thinking. The remainder of the transaction would close through the escrow account that same day. NIOC would buy the refining assets with the proceeds of the Eurobonds. The sellers of the refining assets would purchase the infrastructure bonds offered by the Iranian Ministry of the Interior, which would be guaranteed by an insurance company based in Zurich. *Joe Burstein, you are brilliant!* Wire transfers would be sent in payment of fees to the managers, underwriters and selling group members as well as to the various advisors, including CHK and a new consulting firm in Zurich.

"Are there any questions?" Brian asked. There were no questions. *Of course there are no questions. Everyone wants to get back to enjoying Sunday.* "Thank you all. Would someone move to adjourn this meeting?" Hal moved to adjourn, seconded by another partner. The meeting ended and each partner then went to a different telephone—a secure line installed by AAD, the risk management firm retained by CHK. *This is the meeting that matters.*

"Welcome to the *unofficial* partners' meeting," Brian began. "For our security, this meeting is not being recorded. Kindly remember not to discuss the content of this meeting with anyone else—even your spouses." Brian leaned forward, staring at his hands as though he held his partners' lives in them. He took a moment to collect his thoughts. *This is important. Everyone has to understand that they are putting themselves and their families at risk.*

"Let me bring you up to date on the discussions with Vic Alfonse and the Swiss insurance authorities," Brian began. He went on to outline the details of the arrangements with the actuarial firm in Zurich, the timetable for informing the Swiss insurance regulators about the actuarial "error", and working with the Swiss banking regulators to attach the assets of the Iranians who were parties to the deal. Brian explained once more how attaching the Iranians' assets was the key to trapping them and ensuring that their political goals were blocked. He polled his partners to make sure they understood how everything worked. They did.

"You are all aware that we have hired AAD, the best security firm in the business, and you understand our reasons for doing so," Brian said. *Now, the moment of truth.* "Once we have informed the Iranians that their assets have been attached because of the actuarial error in calculating the amount of capital required in their insurance company, we expect that all hell may break loose." Brian wished he could see their faces. "This is our last chance at backing out of this deal. If any partner wants out, the firm is out, too. That's what partnership, at least ours, means. Anyone want out?"

Brian waited for a full thirty seconds. *God bless them.* "It's settled. The transaction proceeds. This also means that AAD will be contacting each of you to execute our security plans. I am very proud to be one of you.

Goodbye." There was a round of goodbyes over the telephone, clicks and silence.

Brian walked over to the window and stood for a few moments searching the sky for a sign of the God he had invoked just moments before. He walked over to the large firm portrait on the wall behind his desk. He stood very close and studied each partner's face as they smiled brightly at him through the non-glare glass. He walked back to the window and inspected the blue and white sky. *God protect them.*

Chapter Thirteen
Monday, April 28, 2014; Tel Aviv, Israel

Morning came too fast for Steve and Neena. They were beginning to like waking up next to each other, starting the day by holding one another. The hotel Breakfast Bar was open; they had coffee, fresh fruit, a few croissants, and juice. Following breakfast, they showered together, taking time to make love while the sun shone into the bathroom and through the shower stall.

The first order of business was to visit the Central Division Israel Police. The station was located at the intersection of Jacob Wasserman and Shlomo Way, about five blocks from The Morning Glory. They took a taxi from the rear entrance of the hotel and had the driver make a couple of detours so that they could observe whether they were being followed. They were not.

As they entered the police station, they encountered one of the policemen they'd met yesterday. He told them that Sergeant Harel was on the second floor and would see them immediately.

They took the stairs and, through an open office door, saw the sergeant on the telephone in his office. He waved them in and pointed at two straight-backed oak chairs. Just as they did, he finished his call and placed the old fashioned handset in its cradle.

Steve noticed that the sergeant's office was highly organized, almost sterile. The credenza was clear and his desk held just a blotter, telephone and a few papers. The windows were washed and metal blinds were dust-free. And it *smelled* clean. *Different kind of cop,* Steve observed to himself.

"Good morning," Sergeant Harel said pleasantly. "I have some information—the information, Ms. Shahud, that you asked me for yesterday."

"Good morning, sergeant," Neena replied. "What have you found out?"

"The telephone in Mr. Barber's hotel was tapped under a properly executed judicial order, and the tap remains in place."

"Who requested the tap?" Steve asked.

"A Major Ari Lapid. I spoke with him this morning. Mr. Barber, the major has expressed some concern about your activities in Israel, including your taking unauthorized photographs of Israeli military installations."

"As I explained to Major Lapid," Steve began, "The photographs were of the valleys and farms around the installations." He had to hand it to Major Lapid. It was exactly what Steve would do. "Apparently, he remains unconvinced."

"Apparently so," said the sergeant. "He also asked many questions about evidence we have collected regarding yesterday's attempt on your life."

"What did you tell him?" Neena asked.

"I told him that all of that would be in my report." *Great response, sergeant*, Steve thought. The sergeant continued, "Ms. Shahud, do you know of a reason that Major Lipid would be interested in this matter other than curiosity with respect to Mr. Barber?"

"No, I don't. But it is curious."

"Yes, very curious because he was specifically asking about any evidence we had regarding the *shooters*. Curious, I say, because we have not yet determined how many were involved." A police officer appeared at the sergeant's door with some papers. The sergeant held up his right index finger and the officer turned away without speaking.

"Perhaps Lapid was just making an assumption," Steve said. *Not something I would do, though. Assumptions have a way of biting you in the ass.*

"Perhaps, but why assume more than one shooter for a single assassination? Aren't these kinds of things solo affairs?" the sergeant asked, looking directly at Neena.

"Yes, in an urban area where spotters are not needed, and where one person attracts less attention, especially carrying a large case, a solo operation would be normal."

"The major also took the trouble to inform me that you, Mr. Barber, had been involved with a firefight with Hezbollah in Beirut. He suggested that Hezbollah might be a good place to look for answers. What do you think, Mr. Barber?"

"I think the major has received classified information and has shared it with you in violation of our protocol," Neena interjected.

Steve looked at the sergeant, "I think the major knows who is behind this."

"So do I," said the sergeant. "That is why I have shared this with you even though Major Lapid suggested strongly that I not do so." *I like this sergeant,* thought Steve.

Neena looked at Steve and said, "Sergeant, you have been very helpful. Is there anything further you need of Steve at this time?"

"No. If there is, I know how to contact you both. Mr. Barber, I assume you are in the same line of work as Ms. Shahud. So, even though you may be well trained and experienced, I would be very careful. Someone in great power wants you dead. Good luck. Shalom." By this time, the sergeant had reached the door to his office. As Steve and Neena left, he bowed slightly and returned to his desk.

Steve and Neena walked over to The Morning Glory. *The scene of the crime,* Steve thought. They agreed to sit at the same table where Steve waited for Neena yesterday. As they walked, they scoured the area, looking at gardens, small buildings wedged between the newer multi-story giants taking their places. *Have we missed anything?* Steve asked himself.

The restaurant was tidy, yesterday's glass swept and the patio neatly organized, tables and chairs in place. Steve and Neena ordered espressos. A small crowd of patrons chattered in a variety of accents, coffee cups clinking on saucers, spoons ringing against porcelain. It was as if there had been no sniper and Steve had not had to dive through the open doors to save his life. A breeze blew in from the sea a few blocks away and with it came the scent of new blossoms on jasmine. Steve scanned the boulevard and glanced at the window on the third floor of the building across the street. If he hadn't been alert, he'd be dead. *Just as I'm falling in love with Neena,* he thought. *Luck is with me. So far.*

Glancing over her shoulder and then leaning toward Steve, Neena said, "The major, what's his name? Oh yes, Major Lapid. The major could have received the information about the Beirut assault only from David or one of your people. No one in David's organization would dare share classified data without David's direct authority. Who would have told the major from your side?"

"I can think of a couple of people—Bill Elsberry and Christian Meureze, to name two—who could have told Lapid. But, I don't see how Bill and Christian could be behind this. I keep coming back to someone high up in Israeli security."

"You think *David* wants you dead?" Neena asked.

Steve noticed an edge in her voice. He placed his hand on hers and ran his thumb over a scar on her wrist. He didn't want her hackles raised. He had no intention of screwing this up. "Neena, I know David means a lot to you. But, who else could it be? Who else has knowledge of what happened in Beirut? Who has access to professional shooters? Who can arrange to have Major Lipid tap my phone? You know your security agencies better than I. Who is a better candidate?"

"You are very logical, Steve. It is just that I cannot imagine David doing such a thing. He knows about us. Why would he want to kill a man that I have feelings for?"

"He knows about us?" Steve was just glad to hear that there was an "us" and he smiled at Neena, hoping she saw sincerity in his expression.

Neena nodded, and then blushed, which ran right through Steve. *An assassin who blushes is right up my alley.*

Steve went on. "I think David would avoid killing someone that you have feelings about if he could. But David is a man who is capable of recruiting a seventeen-year old to infiltrate a vicious group like Hezbollah. David is a man who is capable of ordering missiles into a kibbutz. That makes me think that David is a man who is capable of making a hard decision—one that means a great deal to Israel—regardless of the consequences to himself or the ones he cares about, including you."

Neena was quiet for a few minutes, sipping on her espresso. "Okay, let's assume hypothetically that David is behind the attempt on your life. Why would he give that order? What is he trying to do? What is he trying to prevent?"

"I think we should start by looking at what he knows I am involved with here in Israel. He may be jealous of my relationship with you."

"David may love me, but it is as an uncle. He does not care for me in the way you suggest."

"I'm not saying that David has inappropriate feelings for you, but he may want you to be loyal to him in all things. If you have feelings for another man, then your loyalties to David might weaken. He may not like that." Steve scoured Neena's face and eyes, looking for her emotional response as he waited for her to speak.

"I see what you are saying. I do not think David would take such action, but let's work this hypothesis." She pushed her espresso cup to the side. "You and I are relatively young in our relationship. I think that David would wait for a few more weeks or months to see if our relationship goes somewhere." She waited for a moment. Steve could sense her focus. She continued, "I don't think he would risk his men, his unit, or Israel's relationship with America on ensuring my unchallenged loyalty to him unless he was very sure that my loyalties were in danger of being compromised. To me, even if this hypothesis were correct, he would not have acted this soon. What other hypotheses do you have?"

"My connection to our joint operation on the intelligence information gaps and with the intercepted message containing the data array and mentioning Operation Kristallnacht." Steve looked again for an emotional response that might betray Neena's words. *I hate having to be an American agent when I am talking with her.*

Neena thought for a few minutes. "David *has* acted strangely when I have talked with him about this. He winced noticeably when I used our code word 'Masada' in a conversation with him the day after our extraction. Also, he, shall we say, corrected himself with me about the need for the communications restrictions."

"What did he tell you?" Steve asked. People changed stories to cover lies. *Is David lying about something?*

"First, he told me that we were hardening our systems against cyber-attack, but as he and I were discussing the intercepted message on Saturday, he changed his story and told me that the exercise exists to determine whether someone could infiltrate our Strategic Command. I have already shared this with you." Neena made a decision not to tell Steve the rest—about David being the source of the intercepted message involving geographic coordinates in a data array—because David had told her not to do so. *Let's see where this leads first,* she told herself.

"Yes, and Vic Alfonse has had a firm conversation with Simon Luegner about how friends don't keep each other in the dark." Steve could tell Neena was holding something back.

"The point I am making is that David *lied* to me," said Neena. "He has never done that before. He has either told me the truth or said that he can't tell me anything. He has never *lied*."

"Why do you think he lied?" *I knew it!*

"I don't know. The only conclusion that I can make is that he wants to keep me out of something," Neena answered. The waiter walked up and asked if they wanted anything else. Steve looked at Neena and then told him just to bring the check.

"Then why didn't he just tell you that he couldn't tell you?"

"Good question. Perhaps it is because I already know a piece of it."

"Like the communications restrictions."

"Yes."

"So why didn't he tell you the truth?" Steve asked.

"Because he did not want me to know it."

"What makes you think you know it now?" *I need to get to the bottom of this. I hope Neena takes me there.*

"Another good question," Neena admitted. "If he did not want me to know the truth at first, I guess there is no reason that he has told me the truth now."

"So, how do we find out the truth?"

"Well, we find out if what David told me—that there is a top-secret counterintelligence project with our Strategic Command—is the truth."

"And how do we do that?" Steve saw the waiter returning with the check and reached for the ubiquitous leather folder as the waiter held it out.

"I know top people in Strategic Command's security division. I will speak with a couple of them."

"Neena, you know that this may have severe consequences for David." *There may be consequences for you, too, Neena.*

"Yes, I know. But David is the one who taught me never to let go. If he has lied to me, then maybe what he is up to is not for the good of Israel. I do not *know*. That scares me more than anything, even more than the possibility that he is behind the attempt to assassinate you." A couple walked up and sat at the table next to them. The commotion of dragging chairs and settling quieted Steve and Neena for a moment.

Steve leaned toward Neena and said, "And you understand that your talking with Strategic Command may get back to David."

"Yes, and I am aware that he may see that as being disloyal. We may also find out that he has lied again. If he finds out I have gone around him and discovered that the counterintelligence project is bogus, I may join you on his hit list."

"Misery loves company," Steve attempted to jest. But it wasn't funny and Steve felt a quiver of worry in the pit of his stomach. *If anything happened to Neena...*

Neena smiled to acknowledge Steve's attempt at lightening the moment but inwardly, she cringed. She was thinking of David forbidding her to share the fact that he was the source of the intercepted message. She was uncomfortable keeping that information to herself. "I am less fearful of being on Mossad's hit list than finding out that David is behind something that might harm Israel," she said.

"What do we do now?"

"You pay the check." Now Neena was smiling, as she rose, pushing her chair back and glancing around the patio to ensure that all was as it should be. "Then I will go to a Mossad office and make a couple of calls over a secure line. I will meet you back at the hotel."

"How long will you be?"

"Let's see. It is eleven thirty now. I should be back no later than three o'clock."

"Okay. I will drop you off a couple of blocks from the Mossad office. I'll speak with Bill and Vic—but not on my room phone—and see what they can do to help."

Steve paid the check and they left the restaurant. Steve dropped Neena off at Ezra HaSofer and HaKovshim and continued on.

As she watched the taxi leave, she prayed silently, *Great God, what is David up to?*

Monday, April 28, 2014; A Mossad Office, Tel Aviv, Israel

Neena walked the three blocks to the Mossad office, her senses on overdrive. What was David doing? Although she didn't expect that he would harm her in any way, she continuously looked behind her, scanning side streets, bushes, and doorways as she strode to the office. The building, like others in Tel Aviv, had external security and Neena was allowed to enter after showing her ID and the guard calling a number to verify her identity. As customary for Mossad agents, she was allowed to carry her weapon into the building.

She took the elevator to the sixth floor and checked in with the receptionist. She obtained the keys for an office from which she would make her calls. She checked the windowless room for surveillance electronics and found it clean. *You can never tell,* she reminded herself.

She opened her Blackberry and keyed in a 12-digit alphanumeric code to unlock it. She then went to "Contacts" and called up SC100. She never kept names in the Blackberry even protected by the 12-digit alphanumeric code. She had memorized most of her contacts' codes, so she rarely had to access a small PDA, also code-protected, in a safe at her apartment, a one-room pied-á-terre in Haifa. Lastly the telephone numbers were scrambled according to a code generated by her each day. She input the daily code into a Blackberry app and it would unscramble any number she highlighted. Because she was in a secure room that she personally swept for bugs, she put a call into SC100 on the speakerphone with the volume just above a whisper. *I like my hands free.*

Someone answered the phone, and Neena heard SC100's greeting.

Neena leaned into the microphone saying "Hello, Ethan, this is Neena Shahud calling."

"Hi, Neena, it's great to hear your voice. Where are you?"

"I'm in one of our offices in Tel Aviv. I'll get right to the point. I need your help."

"Glad to give it to you, if I can."

"I need to know if you are aware of a counterintelligence project aimed at testing the vulnerability of the Strategic Command's targeting system." Neena kept watch for people standing by the door too long, looking for shadows at the bottom of the door.

"Can you tell me why you need to know?"

"An attempt has been made on the life of an allied agent. We believe that the attempt is linked to the counterintelligence project. We need to verify whether that project is real. This is highly classified, and I can assure you that it is in the best interests of Israel to find out who made the assassination attempt."

"Give me about thirty minutes. Where can I reach you, Neena?"

"Let me call you back from this secure line. Is the number I called secure?"

"Yes, every line here is."

"Great. Thank you, Ethan."

She pushed the off button on the speakerphone, marked the time to call SC100 back, and called another contact. The conversation was virtually identical and she made a note of the time to call SC215 back. She spent the next twenty minutes going over her conversations with David Alon, trying to glean one more nuance, one more hint at what David was up to. *No,* she thought, *I have remembered it all.* Then she put the return call into SC100.

"Hello," Ethan said.

"Hello, Ethan. Have you found out anything?"

"The first thing I can tell you is that, to the best of my knowledge and that of several people who should know, there is no such counterintelligence project underway." *David, what are you doing?"* thought Neena.

Ethan continued, "The second thing I can tell you is that when I asked Captain Ovadia in Programs Security, I touched a nerve. She wanted to know why I was asking, who else I was working with, and did I know who she was. I thought that a strange response from the good captain because I am a major in Strategic Command Security and have every right to ask anyone, especially a subordinate officer, any question I wish. That is also what I told her. She grunted in a very unfeminine way and was very non-committal in her answer. I have made a note to my commander to consider conducting a security inquiry. Perhaps she was just having a bad day, but we'll find out."

"Thank you, Ethan. You have my word that this is a very important matter. I will not attribute anything to you."

"You are welcome, Neena. I remember the several favors you have done, including saving my brother in Lebanon. Shalom."

"Shalom."

Neena then called SC215, who verified that to her knowledge, there was no counterintelligence project of that nature in progress. SC215 did not have the same experience as Ethan. She also did not call anyone in Programs Security.

Neena packed her things and checked out with the receptionist. It was two-fifteen. She would walk back to the hotel and think things out.

Monday, April 28, 2014; The American Embassy, Tel Aviv, Israel

After Steve left Neena, he decided to go to the American Embassy rather than back to the hotel. *Saves having to find a place to make the telephone call,* he told himself. Steve found Bill Elsberry at the embassy and was escorted to his office by the ever-pleasant Phil Palun. "Glad you're here," Steve said, extending his hand.

"Well, you've kept me busy. There's been lots of chatter about the shooting at The Morning Glory yesterday. How's Neena?"

"She's fine. She's at a Mossad office to check a couple of things. I've come here to run them by you."

"What's on your mind?" Bill motioned for Steve to take a seat. "Want some coffee?"

"Sure. Thanks. Neena and I went back to The Morning Glory to put ourselves back at the attempted hit location, and we spent some time going over who we thought might want to kill me."

Bill made a quick call from his desk. "What did you come up with?" Bill stood up, grabbed a flyswatter from a drawer then stalked a black speck on the wall.

"Before I get into that, I need to tell you that we stopped at the Central District Israel Police station and spoke with Sergeant Harel, who is heading the investigation. He found out that Ari Lapid—you know him, don't you?"

"Yes," Bill said. He closed in on his apparent quarry, flyswatter raised in smacking position. "Please. Go on. This sonovabitch has been buzzing me all day. Damn fly is *now* going to die."

"Well, the sergeant told me that Lapid was the one who authorized the tap on my hotel phone—using the 'photography' incident as a pretext. The sergeant also told us that Lapid was very interested in evidence that the sergeant had regarding the shooters." Steve stood up and began pacing—his thinking habit. *Damn leg still hurts every once in a while.* "Sergeant Harel found it odd, as did Neena and I, that Lapid would ask about shooters, when there's been no mention about how many there were."

"It is also the kind of hit that is typically made in a solo operation," said Bill, whipping the flyswatter against the wall, killing the offending Musca domestica.

"Exactly. The major also took the trouble to inform the police sergeant that I had been involved with a firefight with Hezbollah in Beirut. He suggested to the sergeant that Hezbollah might be a good place to look for answers."

"Looks like Lapid knows a lot about this and is trying to deflect attention from whoever is behind it." With a couple of flourishes of the flyswatter, Bill placed it back in the drawer, reached up to a shelf and grabbed a pad of paper. Snatching a pencil, he scribbled a few notes.

"That's the conclusion that Neena and I reached. We looked at who that might be." Steve looked at Bill with a twinkle in his eye. "We ruled you and Christian out."

"Well, I feel so much better," Bill laughed, slapping his thigh.

He really is a straight-up guy, thought Steve. "No offense intended, but we had to be logically thorough."

"I understand, Steve. Everyone's a suspect until they're not. How did you rule us out?"

"I think the links are the major's authorizing the tap of my hotel telephone with someone having knowledge of the number of shooters and the Beirut incident. You and Christian don't have those links."

Bill opened the door to a sharp rap. It was Philip Palun with a stack of newspapers. Bill tossed the newspapers on his desk. "My daily education," he said. "Hard to keep up. So where did this leave you and Neena?"

"I kept coming back to someone high up in Israeli security."

"David Alon?" Bill looked up from his notepad.

"Yes. We discussed whether he might be questioning Neena's loyalty."

"Why would he do that?" Bill rose to answer the door again. It was Philip, but with coffee this time. He placed a tray on the table and turned to leave. As Bill walked Philip to the door, he told Philip that he did not want to be disturbed. *Yeah, the guy is polite and all, but kind of a pest,* thought Steve.

Steve waited for privacy and continued, "David would do that because of our relationship. He knows that Neena and I are, well, seeing each other. That might lead him to remove me from the picture. Neena agreed that he might have those concerns. She also thought he would've waited to see how far the relationship went."

Bill poured the coffee and placed a ceramic mug bearing the embassy seal on the table in front of Steve's chair. "I agree. So what did you come up with?"

"The connection to our joint operation on the intelligence information gaps and with the intercepted message."

"How so?"

"Neena told me that David acted very strangely when she has talked with him about this." Steve sat down again, picked up his mug. "She told me that he winced when she mentioned our code word 'Masada' in a conversation with him the day after our extraction from Lebanon. 'Wince' was her exact word." Steve sipped some coffee. "He tried to deflect his behavior by reciting his emotional ties to Masada."

"He may very well have, but David does not strike me as a man who would visibly flinch over such."

"Couldn't agree more," Steve agreed. *David is really one cold sonovabitch.* "Also, he corrected himself about the need for the communications restrictions. First, he told her that the project related to hardening Mossad systems against cyber-attack. But, then, as they were discussing the intercepted message on Saturday, David told her that those coordinates were being used as part of an exercise to determine whether someone could infiltrate IDF Strategic Command. You already know about this last piece."

"Yes." Bill leaned back in his chair and looked at the ceiling as though thinking deeply about something.

"The point that Neena made to me is that David *lied to her*." For emphasis, Steve tapped Bill's notepad once with his right index finger. "In the past, he has either told her the truth or nothing. He has never *lied* to her." He tapped the notepad again.

"Why does Neena think he lied?" Bill asked, bringing his gaze back to Steve.

"The only conclusion that we could reach was that he wants to keep her out of something."

"Like the communications restrictions?"

"Yes."

"So you want to work through what David might be up to that would make him lie to Neena—something he has never done before in their, what, eight-year relationship—and cause him to want you killed. Is that it?"

"Yes," Steve said, standing up. "Sorry, Bill, but I have to move around a bit."

"I noticed," Bill said with a smile. He went on, "I would start by saying that the potential consequences of both his lying to Neena and putting a hit on you are very, very grave. Whatever it is, he's risking a very important personal relationship and his career."

"Based upon what I know of the man, he would accept such consequences only to save either someone very dear to him or Israel itself."

"Unless you're a threat to Neena or someone else close to David, then he must be acting to save, or protect, Israel. You agree, Steve?" The telephone rang. Bill looked over to a digital display of the caller's number. He ignored the call. After two more rings, the phone was silent.

"Yes," Steve said, wondering where the pest Philip was if Bill's phone was intruding during a private meeting.

"And the only link we have, at least that we know about, relates to the communications restrictions and whatever is truly going on with that."

"Correct. I'm going to make a jump here, Bill, and say that there's a real link to IDF Strategic Command. This is the group that controls Israel's nuclear weapons, including their ballistic missiles."

"Why do you say that?"

"Because David didn't offer *any* of this information. He's had to be backed into a corner each time he's given more information." Steve leaned on the back of his chair, shifting the weight off his stiff leg. "He tried to control Neena and me by saying that it was internal to Mossad. Then, we intercepted the message from someone called AK in Iran and learned that there was something going on in Israel regarding geographic coordinates."

Bill paused for a minute. Steve knew that Bill was letting information sift through his brain and waited. Bill went on, "So, when presented with this information, David changes his tune, telling Neena that he has an agent trying to hack into the IDF Strategic Command targeting systems to see if they're vulnerable."

"Yes, and Neena right now is working on checking that story out, too."

"Then, we're dealing with two possible outcomes. Either David's story is verified or it is not. I think we ought to focus on the outcome in which the story is not verified."

"Why?" Steve asked.

"Because in the event that the story is verified, then David's behavior is truly irrational. It means he lied for no reason."

"Agree."

"But," Bill continued, "He has a reason to lie if Mossad is *not* running a legitimate counterterrorist systems operation. FYI, such operations are not a core strength, or even within the mandate, of Mossad."

"David also alleges that he's conducting this project for Simon Luegner."

"Also strange." Bill made some notes. "DMI, the IDF's Directorate of Military Intelligence, has superb counterterrorism and counterintelligence capabilities. And certainly, the generals would be pissed if they found out that Simon was running something like this behind their backs."

"So, either Simon does not trust IDF general command, which would explain any lack of verification through normal channels, or he's running some rogue project," Steve concluded.

"That would explain the involvement of David Alon, and, in either case, the project could be critical to the security of Israel. The question now, Steve, is which is it?"

"I want to go back to something we touched on earlier. David only discussed the targeting system after Neena backed him into a corner with the intercepted message and the geographic coordinates. Correct?"

"Yes," Bill agreed.

"Then, let's suppose that the project centers on the targeting system of Israel's nuclear missiles." Someone knocked on the door. Bill rushed to answer and barked something, then slammed the door. *Haven't seen* that *Bill in quite a while*, thought Steve.

"Sorry, we *won't* be interrupted again. Now, where were we? Okay. Then, what purpose would such a project have?"

"Either to re-target the missiles or to take control of them."

"As I say this, I dread it—re-targeting the missiles doesn't make sense."

"Why?" Steve asked.

"Well, we have good information on the targets of those missiles today—mainly Lebanon, Iraq, Iran, Syria, Jordan, and Egypt. Also, let's assume that Simon and David are true patriots—they have not sold out to someone. So why would patriots re-target these missiles away from areas of aggression toward Israel?"

"I see your point. So, they are not re-targeting the missiles, they are . . ." Steve hesitated.

"They're seeking control of the missiles," Bill concluded somberly.

"My God!" Steve exclaimed. "That would explain everything!"

"Everything but 'why'."

"Only two possible reasons. Either Simon and David want to use the missiles or they don't want others to use them." Steve was wearing a path in Bill's expensive rug. He moved some chairs to give him farther to pace without turning around.

"I think that if David wanted to keep others from using the missiles," Bill began, "he would just remove the people involved—assuming those people are not authorized by the Israeli government to take control of the missiles."

Bill walked toward Steve, stopping when they were just inches apart. Bill finished his train of thought in a quiet, controlled voice, "Also, if the purpose was to stop others, then David's undertaking an operation involving gaining control of the targeting systems would run the risk of those others finding out and taking preemptive action. Possibly a first strike with Israel's missiles. Whatever they are doing, it's not to stop others from controlling the missiles. Simon and David would risk catastrophic consequences to themselves, but not Israel."

"Following that logic, which I do, leaves the conclusion that Simon and David want to control the missiles. Again for what purpose?" Steve asked. *I don't want to hear the answer.*

"There's really only one purpose—to *launch* them." Bill looked directly into Steve's eyes.

"My God," Steve said, holding his hand up as a way of asking for a minute to think. After a short time, he walked to the other side of the room and continued, "I've just been reflecting on what Neena said about David's visible reaction to our code word 'Masada'. Masada may have something to do with David's project, either as a code word or something else."

"Well, certainly if he were using the same code word, that would have shaken him a bit," Bill said as he sat on the edge of his desk.

"True. But let's go back to the intercepted message. The Iranian mathematician stated that the coordinates were way out of whack. What if those coordinates were based on places in Israel? The equator being replaced by a parallel through Jerusalem as zero degrees latitude and the prime meridian going through Masada instead of Greenwich, England as zero degrees longitude?"

"But why would they do that?" Bill challenged. "The targeting systems can be manipulated as they are. New targets can be input. The missiles can be launched without changing the whole coordinate system."

"What if we are talking about a first strike scenario, as you noted? Then what they are contemplating is a geo-political statement of historic proportions. Why not launch the missiles with Israel as the geographic center of the world? Puny, *friendless* Israel, the base from which 167 nuclear weapons will be launched, saying 'fuck you' to the whole world. And *damn* the consequences." Steve stopped pacing, threw his arms wide. *God, is this what David is really doing?*

Bill sat on his desk, breathing deeply. "Well, what you say makes as much sense as basing the coordinates on any other schema. I'll forward this to the people working on the data array and have them run it several ways—with Jerusalem and Masada as zero degrees longitude and latitude." He unbuttoned the cuffs on his dress shirt and rolled up his sleeves, a worried look on his face. "Now I think we need to get Vic Alfonse on a secure line and bring him up to date—fast."

They spent next seventy-five minutes relaying the facts, hypotheses, and conclusions to Vic. He reluctantly agreed with the conclusions and decided that he would contact someone he could trust in the Israeli defense establishment. Because Bill's office was secure, Vic would route information through him. He would get back to them tomorrow.

"Bill, I have to get back to the hotel. I'll let you know what Neena has found out."

"I'll walk you out." They walked in silence to the embassy front door. Instead of shaking hands, they embraced the way brothers do.

When Bill returned to his office, he pulled out a bottle of single malt scotch and poured two fingers into a glass. He tossed the scotch down his throat. "Dear God," he said out loud, pinching the bridge of his nose with his thumb and forefinger. A migraine, no doubt. The scotch burned. He poured another.

Monday, April 28, 2014; London, England

Brian Kendrick arrived at Heathrow on the redeye from New York at eight in the morning. He hated those flights, but there was no alternative when schedules were tight, as with the NIOC deal. After the tedium of passport control and customs, Brian looked forward to a little quiet time in the limousine, which would take him first to freshen up at the firm's apartment on Canary Wharf and then to the offices of Chandler Hines Kendrick in The City.

As his body relaxed in the back of the limo, his mind did not. He knew that the sale of the Eurobonds was the key domino for all the transactions—if the Eurobonds did not sell, then the Iranians would have no cash with which to buy the refinery assets and the selling oil companies and refiners would have no cash with which to buy the Iranian and Iraqi infrastructure bonds. He was torn. If the bonds didn't sell, the deal would fall apart but so would the Iranian political goals of having the major western countries by the short and curlies. That would be an acceptable outcome, except that Brian knew that the Iranians would just take the deal elsewhere. And that would be very, very bad. He knew he had to make the deal work so that he could lock in the trap for the Iranians and their new Swiss insurance company. *'Do or do not...there is no try', right Yoda?*

Early indications were very strong, but underwriters never rest until the deal is done—especially for an offering of nearly $100 billion. The limo neared the tony Mayfair district just a couple of blocks off Piccadilly, snaking through the narrow streets as the city woke to a new day. At the apartment he would stop only long enough to shower and change into a dark blue pinstripe suit, white shirt, and a colorful Alexander Julian tie.

He was on his firm's trading floor early to oversee the placement of the Eurobonds. Normally, the process on the day of the offering was straightforward: buyers, who had previously indicated interest in a certain amount or "size" at a price are re-contacted to place actual purchase orders. If interest rates were not too volatile and if there were no material events affecting the issuer or the market, the deal would be easy. Brian knew the risk of underwriting a large deal when the market fell away—fortunes might be, and have been, lost. Fortunately, today was a relatively calm day and, as he watched from the trading floor, the underwriting was proceeding smoothly.

Traditional buyers for these offerings were institutions of various kinds and they bought, as the expression goes, in size. *Size matters, at least in underwriting,* Brian mused. By noon, London time, the entire issue was placed except for a small amount, the "tag ends". Brian left the trading floor and called New York to give his partners a briefing on the deal. He also called Sa'ad-Oddin Rezvani to share the good news.

"Mr. Rezvani," Brian began once he was able to make the telephone connection—Rezvani was in Qom, Iran, with Ayatollah Mohammed Khoemi, "I'm pleased to tell you that the entire Eurobond offering has been sold."

Brian heard Rezvani say, "That is excellent news" and then continued. "On Thursday, settlement day, we'll execute the purchase agreements with the refinery asset sellers and all the other documents and close the transactions with a serial closing and transfer of funds. The consulting firm in Zurich will be paid also on Thursday."

Brian listened to the short and sweet response, "Thank you, Mr. Kendrick. Please keep us appraised of all developments."

"Of course, Mr. Rezvani. I am very confident that events will unfold as designed. Goodbye." *All of them.*

After the conversation, Brian realized that he was quite tired. He felt a lot better now about the money the firm spent on the apartment in Mayfair—no checking in, no checking out. He called for the limo and, entering the apartment, pulled off his tie. *Bedtime for Bonzo.*

Monday Afternoon, April 28, 2014; Tel Aviv, Israel

When Steve got back to his hotel room, he listened at the door before entering. As he stepped fully into the room, he felt cold metal press his neck.

"Steve!" Neena nearly shouted as she withdrew her weapon from his jugular. "I thought something had happened. You said that you were coming back here when you dropped me off," she said, with a tone of reproach.

"You're right. I didn't mean to upset you, but I decided to see Bill Elsberry and go over some things I've been thinking about. Let's get a drink. I know I need one," Steve said, pointing to where the listening device was planted. He then stepped into the hallway, pulling Neena with him. "I'll brief you on my conversation with Bill," he whispered. "I want you to test our logic, because, frankly, I want to be wrong."

Neena saw that he was very upset. "Yes, let's do that," she said out loud as she stepped back into the room and dialed room service. Steve turned on the TV and raised the volume level just enough to cover their voices. There was live footage of a peace demonstration on Herbert Samuel north of the hotel.

When the drink mixings arrived, Steve took them out to the balcony overlooking the street and the water beyond, placing the tray on a small iron table in one of the corners. As Neena leaned on the balcony wall, Steve dragged iron chairs to the corner where a shot from the street below would be impossible, thanks to an enormous date palm and the angle of the building.

The sun was well over the Mediterranean Sea and shadows were lengthening. Police sirens could now be heard as a motorcycle vanguard led the protesting crowd southward. The aroma of someone barbequing lamb was fighting with the spicy tinge of teargas being fired at chaotic fringes of the demonstration. *So much for protesting for peace*, Neena said to herself as she turned away from the balcony wall and joined Steve in one of the iron chairs.

Steve reported the conversation with Bill and summed up the phone call with Vic Alfonse. Neena stopped him once or twice for clarification, but listened attentively as he briefed her. When he told her about the idea that the geographic coordinates were based on zero longitude and latitude originating in Israel, she stopped him.

"Steve, David Alon is the source of the intercepted message and he is using those alternate geographic coordinates. He ordered me not to tell you, but I no longer trust him."

Steve stared for a moment and then said, fire filling his gut, "Are you holding back anything *else*? That would've been very useful information to Bill and me this afternoon. I think it's time for you to decide which side you're on, Neena!"

"I am on the side I have *always* been on—the side of *Israel*," she fired back, "And for me that has meant David's side, but I no longer see it that way. David has lied too much these past few days. He is not the man I thought I knew. I have now told you *everything* I know. I am not withholding any other information, and I can eliminate one part of the logic tree you and Bill constructed." The pop of police teargas launchers echoed up the small concrete canyon beside the hotel. Neena went on, "There is no counterterrorism project within IDF Strategic Command with the objective of assessing the vulnerabilities of the targeting systems!"

Steve waited a minute, looking directly into Neena's eyes, willing his instincts to kick in. *Was she lying?* Steve didn't think so. Something about her expression and the intensity of her gaze. *So David's planning was going on behind her back. Great.* "So, Bill had it correct—it makes the most sense to think of David behaving rationally."

"Yes. I could have told you that David is rational, if he is anything. There is more. I heard back that a captain in Programs Security was very upset at the inquiries being made of her by my contact—a superior officer who has the authority to ask anyone any question he wants. That behavior is very suspect." Neena squeezed the lime in her drink, sucked it for a moment, and put the shriveled citrus segment on a corner of the paper napkin lying under her drink.

"One possibility is that the captain is part of whatever scheme Simon Luegner and David are plotting. Just exactly what does Programs Security do in Strategic Command?"

"They are responsible for the integrity and safety of all systems," said Neena. "They set up and monitor all access controls and continuously run checks and diagnostics on the systems. They have the authority to access the systems, including at the program code level, for purposes of auditing and safeguarding the systems." Neena took a big sip of her drink.

"So, if someone wanted to control the targeting system, having someone in Programs Security would be critical."

"Yes. One person with proper authority, which the captain likely has, could access the system code and make changes. Those changes, however, will show up on access monitoring reports, which are reviewed by senior officers. That makes me think that others in Programs Security, and possibly, Strategic Command itself are involved."

"So David has agents in Strategic Command and let's assume he has control of the missiles. Why would he want to be able to launch the missiles? What's his goal?" Steve stood up, took a slug of his drink, walked over to the potted palm and peered through the fronds to the street below. More protesters hurrying south toward the din. Nothing else unusual, but he was jumpy. Too much going on, so much at stake.

"I don't have the answer to that," Neena replied. She took a deep breath. Steve knew she felt the weight of this on her shoulders, too. She continued, "But whatever it is, he is likely to do it soon. Every year, an independent security team does an audit of the entire system—controls, targeting—the works. The security team conducting the audit is not named until thirty days before they are to start work, so David's controlling that team would be very difficult. Also, the more people that David needs to recruit the more likely he is to have his own security breach. I have no doubt that David will act before the next independent audit."

Shouts from the street were louder now and individual words were breaking through to the balcony. "Murderers!" "Zionist killers!" "Racists!" Steve had heard all this before in other countries. *Why is it that so many free people don't know shit about freedom?* he thought.

"When is the next audit?" Steve asked, as the crowd quieted for a moment.

"The annual audit was completed last July, so it needs to begin soon. Strategic Command general staff does not tolerate slippage of that kind."

"So, does this mean he intends to launch some or all of the missiles between now and July?" Steve walked back to his chair.

"Steve, I don't know, but if he waits until the audit, any changes to the system not vetted through the proper channels will be identified and it is quite possible that the system will be shut down until the system has been restored."

"So, is it possible that what David really wants is to shut the system down?"

Neena thought for a few minutes and answered, "If he wanted the system shut down, he has far easier means at his disposal for doing so. As a very senior and respected officer in Mossad, his merely reporting that the system *may* have been compromised would be sufficient for Strategic Command to take action. No, I don't think that is his objective." Neena jiggled the ice cubes in her glass, took a last sip of her drink. She rubbed the condensation off the tumbler and was quiet for a long moment.

Steve couldn't read her mind but he could read that expression of sorrow. He wanted to reach out to her, keep her safe. Instead, he had a job to do, and figuring out what that bastard, David, had in store for the people of Israel was top priority. "Then, we're back to his being able to launch the missiles," he said. "Perhaps he wants to be able to *threaten* to launch the missiles."

"I cannot think of a reason for him to want to do so, but that is a possibility. I would add, though, that I see that action being contrary to his character. In my memory, David has never *threatened* to do anything. He has just done it."

She has to see where this is going. Steve said to himself. *I do, and I don't like it, not one damn bit.* "Let's follow this for a second, okay, Neena? Who could he threaten and to what purpose? Would he want to threaten the

Israeli government or people? If so, why?" *For you, Neena, we are going to give David every benefit of the doubt.*

Neena looked at Steve. He thought he saw gratitude in her eyes, but sadness, too. "David has very harsh views of our enemies," she answered. "He also sees our government as bending under the pressure of western governments to make concessions along many fronts—Gaza, the West Bank, the Golan Heights, and Lebanon—which David sees as an affront, unjust to Jews in general and Israelis specifically. But, David would not threaten the government this way. He knows they could give in to whatever his demand might be just to buy the time to have the missiles disarmed. Prior to launch, Strategic Command can shut the system down in a matter of seconds."

"Unless David has shorted those controls somehow," Steve countered. He looked at his empty glass and placed it on the table by Neena.

"He probably has or soon will. The other aspect is David's character—he does not have the patience to wait months or years for the government to reassert itself, as David might think of it. No, he is a man of action. If he is to threaten, the outcome must occur within days at the very outside."

"What about his threatening, say, Iran?" *David gets* every *benefit of the doubt.*

"I don't think so, for the same reasons I gave for his not threatening the Israeli government. I am very sure that David is not thinking of *threatening* to launch the missiles. I wish that were a real possibility, but it is not."

The riotous peace demonstration had moved well south of the hotel and the barbequing lamb aroma was again wafting over the balcony. Steve welcomed the silence, the calm after the protesters' storm. Were he and Neena experiencing a calm before another storm right now? A storm of historic proportions? Both were quiet, thinking and trying to make some sense of a senseless situation. *Time to find out if we are on the same wavelength,* Steve thought. "Neena, do you know why David or Simon would want a nuclear holocaust? That's what launching 167 nuclear missiles would be—a nuclear holocaust."

Neena poured an inch of straight Tanqueray into her glass, drained it, and set the glass on the table before she answered. "David and many others believe that the enemies surrounding us will soon attempt to obliterate Israel. You and I discussed this at dinner our first night together. David is not one to stand by and let that happen without a fight. Perhaps he feels that if Masada is to fall a second time, the price will not be paid by Israelis alone, but by the entire world."

"Can you see David doing such a thing?" Steve asked. *Last chance for David.*

"You should not confuse my love for David with my understanding of his capacity to make decisions which are, in his opinion, for the good of Israel. While I believe that David loves me, he has had no compunction about using me to serve his purposes. He has a steely ability to draw lines between love and duty. So, under the circumstances, I *can* see him calling down a holocaust if he sees it serving Israel. It is not what I *wish* to see, but it *is* what I see. David trained me to distinguish between the two."

She must be in agony over David. Steve got on his knees in front of Neena and pulled her hands into his. "I can't imagine what you're feeling right now. I know it must hurt and I'm sorry to have been the one to cause you such pain. I feel like I've killed someone you love."

Neena stroked his hair. After a moment, she said, "My love for David is part of my love for Israel. Yes, I am deeply saddened by all of this, but this is David's doing, not yours." She kissed him on the forehead.

They were silent for a few minutes and then Steve rose from his knees and pulled his chair closer to Neena. Holding her hands once more, he said, "Let me recap where we are. We've concluded that David Alon and Simon Luegner, aided by an unknown number of agents, at least some of whom who hold critical positions in Strategic Command, are plotting to take control of Israel's nuclear missiles. They intend to launch them sometime between now and July with the likely targets being Lebanon, Egypt, Syria, Iraq, Jordan, and Iran. The result will be a nuclear holocaust throughout the Middle East. Further, it's possible that they already have operational and targeting control of those missiles. Did I miss anything?"

"No, Steve, I think we have exhausted the topic," she whispered, eyes downcast.

Steve rose and looked over the balcony rail as the setting sun's glow turned the sea golden. "My God, Neena," he said. "What do we do now?" He reached over and brought Neena to her feet, holding her tenderly.

Steve knew that Neena shared his fear, not for herself, but for the hundreds of millions of people who might die at the hand of David Alon. She spoke at last, "The first thing is to verify what we can."

"We'll first need Vic to find someone we can work with," Steve said. "That might take a day or two. Let me get a coded message to Bill now about the Masada geographic coordinates. If David was telling you the truth, then we will know the targets programmed into the missiles."

Steve went inside and made a telephone call over the tapped line. The listening device captured the conversation about a college hockey game between Cornell and Princeton. "Done," Steve said.

"Now let's get some dinner and rest," said Neena, kissing Steve warmly. "I have had enough of the world for today. I just want you."

David, you have lost more this day than you know, Steve thought. *I pity you.*

Monday Afternoon, April 28, 2014; Pädäh, Jerusalem, Israel

David learned of the failed attempt on Steve's life upon the sniper team's return to Pädäh. His first inclination was to send Sharett on a suicide mission in Lebanon for missing the shot, but realized that in a few days he would achieve the same result by keeping him in the compound. Before he was able to deal with Sharett in a more reasonable fashion, though, he ran ten miles and sparred with an agent in full-contact hand-to-hand combat. The agent would be fine in a day or two.

David had studied the Kapap training techniques of the Pal' mach, the Jewish commando squads formed by the British to fight in Africa during World War II. Kapap training included both British knife and baton training, which David had absorbed very well. David was also an acknowledged expert in Krav Maga as well as several martial arts styles. David was a weapon of great talent.

As he stood in the late afternoon sun, he rubbed some of the welts that the now-recovering agent had caused. As he felt his ribcage, David was reminded of the wounds and scars harvested during the battles he had fought. He smelled the roses in the garden, fondling the petals on fading blooms, reflecting on his life. He had seen Israel blossom even in the midst of well-armed and aggressive enemies, the same enemies facing Israel today. He had won every battle he had joined, although Israel had lost others. While most Israelis might have accepted a future filled with defeat, he had not. He didn't know how to quit and he wasn't about to learn. He saw the lions gathering around the lambs, and he intended to be true to his biblical namesake by slaying them all, every last one.

Zee found David standing outside the pantry door of his uncle's house that now served as Pädäh's offices. He had found his colonel by following the sound of cracking walnut shells. David directed his nervous energy toward the obliteration of walnuts. Eating the nut inside was a matter of "waste not, want not" more than enjoyment of the nutmeat. David heard Zee approach and turned to meet him. He was reporting as ordered.

"Yes, Colonel."

"Zee, we have to set up a diversion with the police investigation of the attempted hit on Barber."

"Why sir?"

"We need time to execute the last element of the Masada Protocol on May 3." *I am of their blood, the Jews who killed themselves at Masada rather than be Roman slaves*, David reminded himself. "If we can distract them from their investigation, that might buy us the time we need."

"Understood, sir. I have a couple of ideas."

"Let's hear them."

"You already had Major Lapid introduce the idea that Hezbollah was behind the attack. Is that correct?"

"Yes." David cracked another walnut between his palms.

"Why not deliver them the Hezbollah shooter? Dead, of course. We could make it look like the price of failure."

"Won't the police think that finding the shooter, dead of course, is awfully convenient?"

"Quite possibly, sir, but you said we're buying time to May 3. I think that they would have to divert some resources to identifying the Hezbollah and determining whether he was the actual shooter."

"Good point, Zee. All right, get on it." David tossed the walnut meat into his mouth and dusted the shell fragments from his hands into a potted palm by the door. *Good for the soil.* "Do you have a body?"

"No, sir, but that will not be an obstacle."

"I suppose not. Dismissed." *I'd like to be the one 'finding' that Hezbollah body.*

Chapter Fourteen
Tuesday, April 29, 2014; Tel Aviv, Israel

As the sun rose and light sneaked across the floor of the suite, the coffee was already brewing. Steve had decided to use the Cuisinart coffee maker that the hotel provided. *Time for Neena to have one of my fabulous home cooked breakfasts.* He'd picked up some fine Arabic coffee the day before for this occasion. He'd scrambled eggs, toasted thick slices of fresh herb bread and smothered them in butter, sliced strawberries, and had two glasses of grapefruit juice on a tray. The Cuisinart sputtered and began to fill, but he coffee could wait. He was starving. As he was about to carry the breakfast back to the bedroom, the telephone rang. He answered it after one ring—Neena was still sleeping.

It was Philip Palun, Bill Elsberry's assistant, and as usual, his voice was pleasant, as though he hadn't a care in the world. The aroma of strong coffee filled the suite as Philip explained that Bill was called away but would return late tonight and expected to speak with Steve tomorrow. Bill had offered Steve a *carpe diem* and told him to enjoy the day off. Steve could think of a thousand ways to enjoy the day with Neena. There was a distinct click as Philip Palun hung up, followed by a second click as the other listener, too, disconnected.

Steve continued into the bedroom. He placed the tray on the table near the bed and just watched Neena breathe—so restful, so beautiful. *Where is this going?* he thought, as he looked at her. His heart skipped a beat. He knelt by the bed, watching Neena's chest rise and fall, her cheekbones high and regal and her eyelashes dark against the deep cream of her skin. Her black curls against the white pillowcase were tousled and damp, as a child's were after dreaming. *I don't care. I just want to be on the journey.* He heard the Cuisinart gurgle, signaling the coffee was done and got up to pour two cups.

"Just where do you think you're going, mister?" Neena was awake. Steve turned and saw this wonderful woman smiling at him. He came back to the bed and climbed in pulling her close. They kissed for a long time. *Well, she'll just have to have one of my fabulous* cold *home cooked breakfasts.* Her lips were soft, but firm and he loved how she felt in his arms. She ran her hand down his back and onto his thigh. He raised her satin pajama top—she did not wear the bottoms—and tenderly caressed her body. Neena wrapped her legs around him and pressed her body against his—he pressed back. The two locked in an embrace and made fireworks, the best lovemaking Steve could remember. Afterward, Steve fell back, pulling her close, her head nestled on his shoulder. He kissed her, trying to communicate with that one kiss all the love he would give her.

"I love you, Neena. I want to say more, but I don't . . ."

"I love you, too. Very, very much," she said, interrupting him and pulling away just enough for Steve to feel the distance. After a moment she continued. "We probably shouldn't love anyone, most especially each other."

"Why do you say that?" Steve whispered, a twinge of fear nagging his stomach. He sat up, punched a pillow and positioned it against the headboard. Neena sat up, too, pulling the sheet up to her chin.

"Because we are both so committed to doing what we do."

"So what? Why does that matter? At least we are committed to *something*," said Steve. He grabbed a piece of toast from the breakfast tray and bit it, aware he sounded petulant.

"It matters because today we are allies, but tomorrow we may not be. I don't know where all of this will end up. The Middle East may soon be a wasteland filled with radiation, broken cities and burned human beings—unrecognizable. Yet, the land will still be Israel and I will have to defend it because I love it. I don't know how you will feel about that." Neena scooted down under the sheets, turned on her side, perched on one elbow. Her gaze was even, probing.

"If you love me, then I will be at your side," Steve assured her. "I can still do good things for my country *and* be with you, *whatever* the outcome. And if Vic feels otherwise, then I'll just get a different job. People, good people, pay for what I—what you and I—do. I just want you to love me and let me be with you." A single tear dawdled over Neena's lower eyelid and slipped slowly over her high cheekbone, falling onto Steve's hand as he caressed her face.

"Steve, I am *so* in love with you. I *do* want you with me—*forever.*" Steve felt the urgency in her grip as she pulled him to her and kissed him, squeezing with so much strength he had to catch his breath.

"Wish granted." Steve held her quietly and wiped away a tear of his own.

The alarm clock announcing eight o'clock shocked them both. Steve punched the offending noise until it stopped. He kissed both of Neena's cheeks.

"Let's eat," Steve urged. "My fabulous breakfast will seal our mutual love pact." He knew he had a satisfied grin on his face.

They ate Steve's breakfast, the eggs now cold, but it didn't seem to matter, and coffee with steamed milk. "Let's take the day off and play!" Steve blurted as he put his juice glass on the tray.

"How can we take a day off to play with all that is going on?"

"Because we are waiting—waiting for Vic, waiting for Bill. We need to wait for them to get back to us before we can take any further action, before we can go over what we discussed last night." Steve stood up to bus the tray. "Sure, we can go see Sergeant Harel, but he won't have anything new—you know that. And we probably should keep a low profile until we can take another step forward in solving this puzzle. Besides, neither one of us has had a break since this started. Come on. Waddaya say?" Steve had a big grin on his face by this time. He felt like a little kid.

Neena at first frowned, but Steve's grin was infectious. "Okay. But let's also do some thinking and planning."

"Spoil sport. Fine, thinking and planning are on the fun agenda. Now, let's shower and get dressed. I have an idea."

"What is that?"

"You're taking me to Masada. I've never been there. I'd like to see the namesake of all these code words," he said.

She turned her head and, grinning herself, said, "That's a brilliant idea. I haven't been there since I was inducted into Mossad. You are full of nice surprises."

They got ready and packed water and food for the trip, occasionally shouting "Road trip! Road trip!" They retrieved Steve's car from a parking garage down the street. He didn't use it much, but he always asked to be supplied with one so that he would have it when he needed it. Today he needed it. He needed to have some fun and he knew that Neena did, too. The weather was perfect, the windows were down, music was blasting, and Steve was smiling so much his face hurt.

Tuesday, April 29, 2014; Pädäh, Jerusalem, Israel

The only people not in the basement conference room were the two members of one of the roaming teams and those assigned to the security detail on duty. David would brief them separately after their shifts. The room, from which the conference table had been removed for these periodic meetings, was jammed with nearly fifty people. David felt their excitement and stress. Each person at Pädäh had been hand picked by David because of their military skills, love of Israel, strength of character, soundness of mind, and emotional stability. This group plus the men and women in Strategic Command would exact a heavy price for the world's subservience to fanatical Islamists intent upon the destruction of Israel.

"At ease," David commanded as he entered the room. "We have a short, but important agenda. As a reminder, this meeting is subject to the Masada Protocol established for this project. No notes, no communications devices present, no discussions of the content of this meeting outside this room. Zee, take roll."

As Zee read off names and noted responses, David reflected on what might happen over the next few, critical days. He examined the faces of the men and women in the room. *God, if I only had 5000 of these warriors*, he thought. He was brought back to the moment by a loud, "All present and accounted for, Colonel."

"Thank you, Zee. First let me tell you that I am very, very proud to be serving with you. You have accomplished so much in a short time, with zero hour now less than five days away." A low murmur spread and died quickly. "This morning, I will update you on recent events and give new orders. I also want to assure you that I am even more convinced that we will be successful in our objectives. Now, let me tell of recent news relevant to us."

David related the major proceedings of the past ten days, some of which were known by a few, but not everyone. These included the successful extraction of Neena and Steve from Lebanon and the interception by Iran of his message to an agent containing the geographic coordinates for Israel's missiles. He also covered the fact that American intelligence had intercepted a message from Iran with those same geographic coordinates. Lastly, he discussed the increasingly problematic probing by American intelligence of the reasons behind Mossad's communications restrictions. He did not discuss the assassination attempt on Steve, nor did he reveal the existence of the Iranian Operation Kristallnacht.

Before he continued, he turned and looked at the Israeli flag behind him on his left. He raised his head and stood fully erect, his arms akimbo with his large hands pressed against his wide leather belt.

"We are taking actions to delay the American intelligence operation. We believe that those actions will be sufficient to allow us to launch all missiles at sundown Saturday, the beginning of Memorial Day. We are taking additional precautions and later today, additional war materiel and armaments will arrive. In the next two days, we will add significant defensive capability to Pädäh." A hand shot up. "Go ahead," David said.

"Sir, could you give us an overview of those additional capabilities?" There was a shuffle of movement as people turned to look at the speaker.

"We will be adding several anti-personnel and anti-tank measures outside the compound wall, including anti-tank mines and barriers and abatises," David said, counting out the components on the fingers of his raised left hand. "We will be receiving four surface-to-air LMLs—Lightweight Multiple Launchers—each outfitted with Starstreak missiles on Pinzgauer 6x6 cross-country vehicles. Each Pinzgauer will have internal storage for an additional six missiles. Also for defense against aircraft, we will have twenty of the latest FIM-92 Stinger personal portable SAMs."

David walked back and forth as he spoke, looking directly into the eyes of his forces. *No fear here.* "For defense against ground assault, we are bringing in thirty Spike-MR anti-tank guided missiles and the same number of Mini-Spike anti-personnel guided missiles."

A massive clap of thunder from the storm that had rolled in from the south rumbled through the room. Heads turned in response, assessing, reacting. David, too, listened. He recalled the sounds of the many battles he had survived. *Soon the thunder will be calling us to our death.*

David waited for the thunder to diminish and went on. "Eight .50-caliber Browning M2 machine guns, old but powerful weapons, are arriving tomorrow along with twenty lighter weight Negev machine guns. We will be hardening our perimeter and internal defenses with additional steel, concrete and carbon fiber structures. Lastly, we are bringing in an additional twenty combat troops."

"Sir, it sounds like you are preparing for an all-out assault on Pädäh," someone stated.

"Very observant," David said, giving a rare compliment. "In the event that our plans—those contained in the Masada Protocol to which you all pledged allegiance—are discovered by the Americans or Israeli security, I expect that we will be assaulted by a large specialized combat force. It is only natural to anticipate such in these circumstances."

"How long can we hold?" another asked.

"Any successful assault on Pädäh will be difficult to plan and execute in the time between now and zero hour. First, although we are in a relatively rural area, it is populated, nonetheless, and the compound is in a slightly elevated position with low hills to our west and east." David felt so at ease. Combat was his calling and he knew this was the last great battle. He could feel energy flowing through his body as he talked about it. *Let it come.*

David was once again counting on his fingers. "Second, because of the terrain, enemy forces will have difficulty massing for an assault outside the range of our weapons. Third, there are only two feasible approaches and the nearby topography will force our opponents directly into the range of fire of our strongest weapons positions. The fall of Pädäh is highly unlikely, at least within the first twenty-four hours even with armor and air support. Any assault on us will cost our opponents greatly in both time and casualties."

The questioner said, "Thank you, sir" just as another volley of thunder rolled through the compound.

"Sir, in the event that Pädäh falls, will we still be able to launch the missiles?" a voice from the back shouted out. Another short-lived murmur passed like a shiver through the room.

"The short answer to that is 'yes' as long as we can protect the computers up to ten hours before launch. That is why we built the communications room with such care. Even one of the newest American bunker-buster bombs would not penetrate to our communications level. We have placed a virus in the Strategic Command system software that will allow our silo crews to launch the missiles, but which will prevent anyone, including us, from ordering the missiles to self-destruct or alter course. Once the missiles are airborne, there will be no stopping them."

"What will happen to Israel?" a woman in the front asked. The room fell dead quiet. David looked at the woman.

"Ah," David began, "*the* question. Thank you for asking it." David took a moment and looked at the warriors crammed into the conference room before he continued. "We have discussed this in detail with each of you as we recruited you to join our team. But because Israel is so dear to each of us in a very profound way, it is worthy to recall will happen to our homeland after next Saturday, whether we live or die."

David paused, in part to wait for absolute silence as a couple of people shifted their stances, but also to build to the moment. He realized that what he was about to say would weigh very heavily on each person assembled, including him.

"We are all here because we believe—no, we are *absolutely certain*—that our enemies will soon—within the next twelve to eighteen months—launch an invasion of Israel, perhaps supported by tactical nuclear weapons. We are also *absolutely certain* that our strong allies of the past—including America—will not stand beside us. The once-mighty democracies of the West will remain non-committal to our survival until the combined Islamist forces have overrun our precious promised land." David could feel the tension and absorbed it like a sponge. He could feel his own calm, the calm of battle.

"In this scenario, which we have examined *tirelessly*, we anticipate the outright slaughter of *every* Jewish male—men, boys, babies—and the wholesale rape and enslavement of Israel's women. The destruction will be total—worse even than that which Scipio Aemilianus leveled upon Carthage in 146 BC during the Third Punic War." He watched his people as they inhaled and exhaled and imagined the vision of desolation filling their minds.

"UN resolutions condemning the invasion may flow unrelentingly, but, like all the others, they will be words on the wind. Between the calm morning General Assembly debates and the late night expense account dinners afterward, Israel will be annihilated." A powerful series of thunderclaps rattled the room as David waited to observe reactions once more. He spoke louder as though to challenge the thunder.

"Our men and women will exact an awful toll upon the enemy, but annihilation is certain. *That* truth—that *absolute truth*—is what has brought each of us here. That *truth* is what leads us to strike first, regardless—let me repeat, *regardless*—of the outcome. We will not accept the alternative. We will *never* go into bondage again! And Masada will *never* fall again—it will be *destroyed*!" David was shouting now and his huge fists were raised, clenched in anger. It was an anger he welcomed, one that had building for decades.

Utter silence filled the room. The faces were stern and focused. No one exchanged looks. No one fidgeted. They looked at him in awe. Each had accepted this truth in swearing allegiance to the Masada Protocol. *Good,* David thought. *They grasp. They accept.*

David continued speaking, his voice calm again. "In the days and weeks following Memorial Day, Israel will be changed forever. Nuclear retaliation is possible, but unlikely because available Iranian launch-ready installations are few and we have targeted them. Also, because of the very short flight duration, they cannot get their missiles off the pads." David was now walking through the group and they parted for him like the Red Sea for Moses.

"Other countries, such as Russia, may contemplate launching a counterstrike, but our analysis concludes that they will avoid the consequences of being seen as an aggressor. There would also be little left for them to gain either politically or militarily."

David stopped in the midst of his people and discovered, to his surprise, a tear on his cheek. He gently wiped the tear, held it out and said, "Yes, let us cry for Israel, for the promised land that continues to elude our desperate grasp. Let us cry for our land that we might destroy so that our enemies cannot." He waited and tears came to the eyes of every person there.

After a few moments, he continued in a strong, full voice, the tears wetting his cheeks, "The greatest threat to our beloved country will be nuclear fallout. While we have a favorable geographic position on the eastern end of the Mediterranean and will benefit from the winds that prevail from west to east, the shear number of detonations will mean that Israel will be subject to at least moderate, and perhaps high, radiation. As you know, Israel has many well equipped underground shelters, but up to half of our civilian brothers and sisters will die." There was an audible gasp.

David went on. "We project that the IDF will remain a viable fighting force because it has its own protective facilities. It is important that the military remain strong because neighboring countries will become lawless wastelands. Israel will need protection from brigands, roving armed gangs and remaining elements of enemy military units. The lands of our enemies will suffer from severe radiation, and the death toll among the current population will be nearly ninety percent within one year."

David took a moment and wiped the tears from his face with the clean handkerchief he always kept in his right rear pants pocket. Others did likewise.

"Israel has the great financial support of Jews in other lands, so we believe that re-building and re-settlement is possible if Israel can survive the first year. As the heroes of Masada died, but were not the last Jew to live in our promised land, we hope that the call of our destiny will bring others, over time, back to our homeland." David walked slowly back to the front of the room.

"We hope, but do not anticipate, that the Western powers will come to comprehend and accept the consequences of their abandonment of Israel to its enemies in exchange for the temporary favor of OPEC and low energy prices. If they do, something like the Marshall Plan of post-World War II is possible."

David stood next to the Israeli flag. People took advantage of the silence to clear their throats of tears. He grabbed the flag's cloth, held it to his breast. The storm was directly above them now and the next clap of thunder was the loudest yet. David raised his hands toward the ceiling. "Listen, my comrades, to the anger of God. He speaks and approves this mission. Like you, like me, his anger is justified." David relished the nods of agreement. "With our action, people of all races and creeds might finally grasp that life is too precious to live it as cowards, without principles, without a sense of the judgment of the eternal God of the universe." He paused. "I close this meeting with words that King Solomon wrote in the book of Proverbs, 'The Lord will not suffer the soul of the righteous to famish; but He casteth away the substance of the wicked.'"[3]

There were no more questions. David released the flag and straightened it. Then he said a blessing. After asking officers to remain for their orders for strengthening Pädäh's defenses, he dismissed the assembly. People left, talking only in whispers, many still crying for Israel and cherished dreams that would never be. David thought of Neena. Was she, too, a dream that would never be?

Tuesday, April 29, 2014; Masada, Israel

Neena and Steve traveled quickly. The dark clouds of a brewing storm hovered over the western hills, but the sun shone through in sporadic bursts, like bright pale yellow klieg lights. The end of wildflower season was near, yet the blooms in the semi-steppe shrub lands stretching nearly to the Dead Sea were still in full force. Patches of yellow aizoons, red amaranthus, agrostemma—purple-pink old maids, white ornithogalum, and one that became Steve's favorite, the purple gladiolus Italicus, greeted and waved at them along their way. It was a beautiful drive.

At every checkpoint, Neena's Mossad ID was all that officials cared to see, but the checkpoint queues and traffic slowed them. They stopped at En Gedi, had lunch, and picked up some water and snacks for the last leg of the trip to Masada. Then the terrain, shrub-steppe at first, became more arid and, eventually, desert. Vegetation remained low, and flowering plants became rare in the sand and stone among the hills and mountains around Masada.

Steve and Neena had taken the 90 Road from the north so they could walk the Snake Path to the top of Masada. They congratulated themselves on a favorable time of year—the temperature would peak around 20 degrees Celsius, perfect weather. They arrived at one o'clock and, after buying the audio tour, were soon on the forty-five minute trek to the top.

The storm, black, brilliant, and brief, was uncommon in April. It had passed shortly before they parked the car, leaving both a rainbow and clean-

---

[3] Proverbs 10:3

smelling air. The path was packed dirt, the dust tamped down by the light rainfall, and, edged by loose stones, it wound uphill in a moderate incline with little vegetation. The plan was to get some exercise, tour the site, and leave when the park closed in order to get the best view possible of the sunset.

They saw it all—the synagogue, northern palace, western palace, the storerooms, commandant's residence, the Byzantine church. Dozens of other visitors swarmed on the small mountaintop, like ants at a picnic expecting sweets. There were busloads of Israeli students, families from Europe and the United States, and the ever-present Japanese tourists armed with Canons.

The history and archeology were impressive, but it was at the breaching point on the west side at the top of the Roman ramp that Neena stood spellbound. There, soldiers of the Roman Tenth Legion broke through the perimeter wall and, the following day, entered to find the nearly one thousand Jews dead by their own hand rather than surrender or be taken prisoner.

Steve, too, felt an emotional response, standing at this special place next to Neena. "It's easy to feel the proud desperation of these people across almost two thousand years," he said at last.

"Yes," Neena said softly. "They had no idea what the future would hold for Israel. They just knew that they would not be slaves. As simple—and as complex—as that."

Steve wrapped his arms around Neena, and leaning toward her, said, "I wonder if Israelis today would make the same choice."

"I think we are about to confirm that at least some would," Neena said, as she rested her head on Steve's shoulder. Her expression was sad, melancholy. Steve knew being here was difficult for her. A lone cloud, trailing behind the storm, blotted the sun for a moment. Although warm in Steve's arms, Neena shivered until the sun returned.

"What about you?" Steve asked.

"I would have stood at this breach and forced them to strike me down," said Neena. "They *never* would have taken me alive. I would not have died by my own hand." Steve felt her whole body tense.

"But what about *today*?"

A breeze whisked Neena's curls into disarray and she pulled a barrette from her pocket, twisting her hair into a knot and clipping the barrette with a sharp snap. Wisps escaped and trickled above her ear. Her profile was strong, her jaw chiseled and her mouth set in a determined line. Steve thought he'd never seen a more beautiful woman.

"They still would have to strike me down and I still would not die by my own hand," said Neena.

"So, if we're correct about David, you disagree with him?"

"You know I do! I *understand* why he might be doing this, but that does not mean I *agree* with him. No, if Israel is to bring on a holocaust, let our enemies strike the first blow and then let hell take them—*and* us, if need be. I want to die with my enemy knowing that I have no fear."

"I have never known a woman like you."

"One so focused on killing?"

"No, one so focused on living the way she wants."

Neena smiled and reached up to touch Steve's face. "And the way I want to live is with you, yakiri, my darling."

Ignoring the crowd of people around them, the two kissed for a long time. Then, they stood, absorbing the history and their moment in it, holding each other. The sun was closing on the horizon, and the shadows, like a Roman phalanx, crept up the western side of Masada, the side on which the Romans tediously built their ramp only to find their quarry dead.

As the darkness grew, Steve imagined the Zealot warriors' tears as they cut the throats of their beloved friends, wives, and children. Almost 1,000. He felt a knife in his hand, the stickiness of the blood. The wind filled his ears with the wailing it had borne for nearly two millennia. He turned to look across Masada and buried his wet face in Neena's hair.

"Let's go now," Neena said, clasping Steve's hand. "I want to make love with you. I want to remember today forever."

Steve cupped her face in his hands and kissed her as if that kiss bound them in a pact with this place, the brave that had died, and those that still remembered. As he would. The ride back was quiet. Neena sat with her head against Steve's shoulder most of the way. The windows were up and the music was off. On the horizon, lightning shattered the night sky over Jordan as the storm surged into the heart of the Middle East. Their love filled the evening and both wanted only to drink of it and savor its joy and peace.

Chapter Fifteen
Wednesday, April 30, 2014; Tel Aviv, Israel

The phone in Steve's hotel room rang incessantly. It was six o'clock in the morning, but Neena and Steve were already up and preparing for what was going to be a tough day. Yesterday—a day of respite—was over. Steve picked up the phone, with one hand holding a thick white towel around his waist. After a moment he hung up, tucking the towel so it would hold but wishing he could jump back in bed with Neena.

"Who was on the phone?" asked Neena.

"Sergeant Harel from the Central Division Israel Police," said Steve. The sergeant said there's an important development. I told him we'd come down to headquarters immediately rather than discuss it on the phone. You never know who's listening, right?"

"Right," said Neena.

Steve quickly got dressed and went down to the Breakfast Bar, loading a tray with coffees, juices, fruit and some croissants and jellies. He was back in the room in ten minutes and they ate everything—no telling when they might have their next full meal. Steve called the concierge to flag a taxi for them and brushed his teeth. In minutes they were off. They walked into the police station at 6:53 and went straight to the sergeant's office.

Sergeant Harel was there with a stack of photos, a manila file, and a sniper rifle on his desk. He also had a pot of hot coffee and three cups, and when he saw Neena and Steve, he poured coffee in all three, saying, "If you are like me, you have not yet had enough coffee."

Neena and Steve both smiled and thanked him for being so thoughtful. "What is the important development? Or am I looking at it?" Steve asked, pointing to the rifle on the sergeant's desk.

"About one o'clock this morning, our Station received an anonymous emergency call about two men shooting a third on the street. By the time we were able to get a patrol to the scene, there was a crowd around a man lying on the pavement. He was already dead, shot at close range. We found identification on him and searched his residence—a one-room apartment not far from the crime scene. In the apartment, we found this rifle—an H&K PSG-1 sniper rifle. We are currently double-checking our records and also with

Israeli security agencies, but we have information that the victim was a member of Hezbollah."

"May I?" Neena asked as she reached for the weapon.

"Of course, Ms. Shahud. Let me answer a question you might have—there are no fingerprints on the weapon."

As Neena was examining the rifle, Steve looked at the sergeant's photos and examined the file. "Do you believe this person has something to do with the attempt on my life?"

"I most certainly do, Mr. Barber. But I believe he, too, is a victim. I do not believe he was the shooter. If you look at his hands, they are not the hands of a practiced sharpshooter. He should have calluses on his palm and finger. No, I think someone is trying to make Major Lapid's hypothesis more accepted."

"What leads you to believe that Major Lapid has something to do with the dead man?" Neena interjected.

"I have no evidence linking the dead man to Major Lapid, Ms. Shahud. What I meant is that he offered the suggestion to me that Hezbollah might be behind the attempt on Mr. Barber's life, and, only two days later, a dead Hezbollah with a sniper rifle shows up in the streets of Tel Aviv. Very convenient—we didn't even have to track him down."

"What else can you tell us about the dead man?" Steve asked. *This is one smart cop. I trust him.*

"Our records show him as a low-level operative," said the sergeant, taking a long drink of coffee and grimacing as though it were either too hot or too bitter. "We have had our eye on him for months but our eyes led us to more important operatives. Seems to have been a courier of sorts. A Palestinian baker employed him as a laborer. We are checking with other agencies to see if they have more on him, but I doubt they will."

"So, whom do you suspect as his killers? Two men were mentioned. Correct?" Steve inquired.

"First, we only have the anonymous telephone call. We have no actual eyewitnesses, so we don't know how many assailants there were or their sex. We also don't know their relationship, if any, to the deceased."

Steve picked up the sniper rifle. He turned it repeatedly, checked the sight, felt the balance, and tested the trigger action. It was very much at home in his hands.

"There are three basic scenarios," Neena offered. "One, he was killed by a stranger for unknown reasons. Two, he was killed by fellow Hezbollah, perhaps for failing to kill Steve, as Major Lapid suggests. Three, he was killed by someone trying to make it look like Hezbollah was behind the assassination attempt."

"I agree, Ms. Shahud. I believe we can eliminate the first because the area in which he was found is a very low-crime area. No violent crime there in over three years. I would eliminate the second due to his soft hands and history—he is not a trained sniper—so he did not make the attempt on Mr. Barber's life. I am drawn by the circumstances, many years of experience, and the hair that is standing up on my neck, to choose your third scenario."

"And I think we can all agree," Steve offered, placing the rifle down and grabbing his coffee cup, "that if the third scenario holds, the person behind this is also behind the assassination attempt. Correct?"

Sergeant Harel and Neena both nodded agreement. "Why have they taken this step?" Neena asked. "Did they think that we were going to be fooled by this?"

"I think the objective is to delay and distract us," said Steve. "Some people know that we are getting very close to them, and anything that distracts us will give them more time. I think we're closer to zero hour than we might have thought."

"Mr. Barber, I do not fully understand what you are saying, but I do know that the people within Israel who can identify and murder a Hezbollah agent and plant an sniper rifle in his residence are *very* powerful people. I must treat this as a real crime, but I don't think that I will solve it—you might—but I will not. I will continue to inform you as I make progress. If possible, I would ask that you return the favor. I do not like important cases going cold on me."

"Of course, Sergeant," Steve affirmed. "You have been very kind and extremely open with us. We'll do what we can to help you close these cases. Now, we have to go. Shalom."

"Shalom."

As they left the station, Steve and Neena decided to call on Bill Elsberry, who would be back at the embassy by now. There were other developments to share with him. Steve hailed a taxi and oddly enough in this city of millions, one screeched to a stop. For a moment, Steve stood looking at the police station. *Nice try, David, but no cigar.* He jumped into the car and gave the driver an address.

Wednesday, April 30, 2014; The American Embassy, Tel Aviv, Israel

As they hurtled through the winding streets at top speed, the driver ignoring them, Neena called Bill Elsberry to make sure he would be available at the embassy. He was already there and had some important news to share, but not over the telephone. Fifteen minutes later, the taxi cut across four lanes of traffic and skid to a halt in the loading zone in front of the embassy. Steve paid the driver. No tip.

Bill met them at the lobby door. His usually pristine desk was a pile of papers and so was the coffee table.

"First, the good news," Bill began as they settled around his coffee table, "I was in Ramstein yesterday. Sorry for the short notice to you about my departure—Philip got in touch with you?"

"Yes, thank you," said Steve.

"Good. Philip is a capable employee." Bill leaned forward in his chair. "I wanted to put some heat on the intercepted message and the geographic coordinates, so I personally went to our computer facility there. We verified that Masada is a key to the data array. When we assumed that Masada represents both zero degrees latitude and longitude, we identified 167 sites. These sites in Lebanon, Syria, Jordan, Iran, Iraq, and Egypt—cities, military installations, dams, the works—make absolute sense from the viewpoint of targeting important locations. There is no doubt."

"So, what's the *bad* news?" Steve asked.

"Vic has not been able—*yet*—to identify someone in whom he has confidence who is also not part of the plot." Steve got up, walked over to look out the garden window as Bill continued. "Unfortunately, the vetting process is time consuming. Each person's dossier needs to be verified and cross-referenced against Alon and Luegner. Initial telephone interviews must be structured in a way that the other party interprets as relating to current events. The calls must be made. Then we run them through voice stress analyzers. That's how we'll identify questionable responses. Those responses must, in turn, be assessed, leading to a plan to research, and remove, any doubt."

"Yes," Neena interjected, "I am very familiar with the process. Mossad agents are trained in the techniques to uncover double agents and to affirm the allegiance of recruited operatives. It is a thorough and time consuming process for good reason—the consequences of being wrong are enormous."

Steve rubbed his thigh and returned to his seat. "Did Vic give you a sense of when he might identify someone?" he asked.

"Fortunately, yes. He told me that he had several candidates. Just a matter of a day or two."

"We may not have much more than that," said Steve.

"Why? What have you discovered?"

Steve summarized his and Neena's suspicions about David Alon leading a rogue operation to take control and launch Israel's nuclear missiles. As usual, Bill asked very good questions, which Steve or Neena answered. After thirty or so minutes, the briefing concluded.

"So," Bill began, "now we believe that David has control of Israel's nuclear missiles, and he's likely neutralized the ability of Strategic Command general staff to order the missiles to self-destruct or to change course. Tell me, Neena, do you know if we can verify this through some kind of system check at general command level?"

"Yes, once Vic has found someone we can trust at very high levels."

"Okay, we can leave that on the table for now. And the timing of annual audit of the control systems suggests a launch time before July. Is that correct?"

"That's correct," Steve answered. "There's more. Sergeant Harel of the Central District Israel Police told us of a murdered Hezbollah. A sniper rifle was found in his apartment. The sergeant, Neena, and I think that the killing was meant to look like retribution for his failure to kill me."

"So you believe he was set up and murdered to distract you and the police from finding out the real perpetrator?"

"Yes, we do," Neena said. "We think they are trying to buy some time—distract us enough to give them the extra time they need. Steve and I are convinced that the launch date is very close, perhaps only days away."

Steve watched Bill's face turn ashen, then red. *We hit a nerve.*

"Oh my God!" Bill yelled as he jumped to his feet, slamming his fist on his desk. A stack of papers tilted, the top two sheets falling to the floor. Steve picked them up and replaced them face down on top of the pile. Bill didn't even seem to notice. "Israel's Independence Day is next *Sunday*! If we've truly reached the right conclusions about a momentous geo-political statement, what better date than Israel's Independence Day?" Bill ran his hand through his short-cropped hair. Steve knew exactly how he felt. Defenseless in a race against time.

"And," Neena added, her voice betraying emotion, "The use of Masada as the zero latitude and longitude coordinates fits right in—it is *the* symbol of our freedom and independence."

Bill's telephone rang. He picked it up and listened for a minute. "Are you sure about that information?" he soberly asked the caller, putting the call on speaker.

"Yes, sir. Several deuce-and-a-half trucks, four Pinzgauer vehicles with rocket launchers, and other materiel arrived yesterday. The entire compound is a beehive of construction. More trucks are arriving as I speak. I would say they are hardening their defenses in a big way, sir."

"Thank you, Captain. Break off surveillance for now. David Alon is no fool. Have Sergeant Powers take a drive through in a few hours. I will have some satellite photos forwarded to us here. Goodbye." Bill hung up the phone, his eyes worried, brow furrowed.

"I've had our Marine guards doing a little informal surveillance of Pädäh for the last twenty-four hours," said Bill. "That report was from one of them. Since late yesterday, they've been reporting frequent deliveries of heavy weapons and building materials. This can't be good news." Bill reached for one of his notepads and started scribbling.

"No," Steve agreed. "It isn't, and it fits with a launch schedule that is days, not weeks, away. If the launch date were weeks away, David would move to another location—one more difficult for us to know about. With a launch date only days away, David knows he can't move his base of operations and is preparing for a possible assault on Pädäh by Israeli forces."

"David is passionate about what he sets his mind to do," said Neena. "He is also very organized. It appears that David is concerned that we have discovered what he and Simon are up to and he will defend that compound, or should I now say fortress, to the last person. If we have to take Pädäh, the casualties are going to be very high."

"This just gets worse," Bill sighed. "I will start collecting whatever information we have here and in DC about Pädäh. In all likelihood, we *will* have to take the compound. Steve, can you get some tactical battle planners on this?"

"Yes, I'll call Vic and get that going. We also have a special unit of small battalion strength—about 300 men and women—headed by Black Jack Trevane. Of course we will need Israeli permission to bring them in. Jack is a great battlefield tactician and commander, and the unit packs the firepower of a standard combat brigade. They are the best we have."

"I know Jack," Bill said. "We'll need him."

"Bill, may I use your secure line?" Steve asked. "I need to bring Vic up to speed on what we're facing and to get some battle planners assembled ASAP."

"Of course. You may use the phone in the small conference room over there," Bill said pointing to a twelve-foot by twelve-foot room connected to his office by glass and walnut pocket doors.

"Pardon my directness, Neena," Bill said as he walked over to his desk, "but where do you stand in all of this? David Alon is very dear to you, is he not?" He rolled one of the doors open and gestured to Steve to enter the conference room.

"I stand, as you put it, Bill, with Israel. That used to mean standing with David, but no longer. As for his being dear to me, yes, he is. But Israel is dearer." Neena stood two feet away from Bill, almost as tall as he and her gaze as intent.

Steve stopped in his tracks and turned toward Bill. He could see the tautness in Neena's body as she confronted Bill. He felt his blood pressure rise, but he knew that Bill was just doing his job. *Question asked and answered.* "Bill, I've asked myself that question repeatedly over the last few days. I believe that Neena is sincere in her answer."

"But you're sleeping with her," Bill said his eyebrows arched, questioning. Maybe even challenging Steve.

"Not a secret. And not clouding my judgment. I trust my life with Neena." *We're done here,* Steve thought, as he and Bill looked at each other. "Any doubts left in your mind?"

"No," Bill said, looking at Neena again. "I never had any. Just had to ask."

Steve tried to read if Neena wanted to be in on the call to Vic. Neena shook her head and said, "If you don't mind, I will stay for a while and write down all that I know about Pädäh—defenses, layout, communications, location of the computer room—so that the battle planners have as much information as possible."

"Terrific idea, Neena," said Steve. *Amazing woman.*

"If you will give me the written reports from the Marine observers, I will try to interpret what David is trying to do. Pädäh was intended to be a secure facility, not a fortress. With the reports, I think I can identify what he is trying to do and how it will improve Pädäh's defensive capabilities."

"Excellent. That will be very helpful. Let me get the current reports." Bill left his office to retrieve the folders.

Steve finished with his call and slid the conference room doors closed behind him as he returned to Bill's office. Neena looked out a window above an internal courtyard where a small garden flourished in early blooms. He held her in his arms, standing behind her, inhaling the scent of her hair. "Is this making sense to you?"

"The idea is unimaginable. I think David's view is that if the world is willing to let Israel be wiped off the map, as Iranian presidents have phrased it, then the world be damned." Neena turned around. "As I look at the world from David's eyes, I see why David would do this. I also know that David has the discipline to do this. So, yes the unimaginable makes sense to me. It also frightens me because *now I care* about the future—about *us.*" As she said those words, she held Steve close and kissed him warmly.

Bill returned a few minutes later with four reports from Marine observers of Pädäh over the past twenty-four hours. "Let's get to work, shall we?"

An hour later, Steve and Neena were still poring over the Marine surveillance reports when Bill excused himself, reappearing before long with a large pot of coffee and some sandwiches.

"I totally forgot the time," Steve said with delight at seeing the food. "Thanks, Bill. Very thoughtful."

"We'll need our energy, I'm afraid." He'd only taken one bite out of his sandwich when the phone rang. "Vic, may I interrupt to put you on speaker? I have Neena and Steve with me. The room is secure."

"Hello everyone," said Vic Alfonse. "I have some good news. I think we have found our man—a woman, actually. Our contact is Abital Zahavi. She is Special Assistant for Internal Affairs for the Israeli Prime Minister."

"What is her background?" Neena asked.

"She is a reserve colonel in the IDF and has combat experience. She has spent the last ten years working on assessing Israel's military capabilities in light of changing enemy political and military strategies."

"Her name is very familiar," Neena interjected. "There are not many women combat officers at that rank in the IDF. She might be just the right person."

"I agree," Vic went on. "She was part of the Winograd Commission that looked into Israel's 2006 campaign against Lebanon and presented the findings to the Knesset. That's where the Prime Minister saw her. Soon thereafter, he added her to his staff. She has many contacts in the military and security agencies, including Strategic Command, DMI, and Shin Bet, Israel's internal security agency."

Things are looking up, Steve thought. "How much does she know about what we've uncovered?" Steve queried.

"Very little. We've vetted her thoroughly, but I'd like you to meet with her, analyze her verbal and physical reactions to your suspicions and known facts regarding David Alon. I trust your instincts and training. As you speak with her, make up your mind and bring her in or shut her out. Today would be ideal. I share your concern that the launch date may be only days away."

"Right, Vic. Neena and I will get on it. What's her contact information?"

"I have her dossier on its way to you by encrypted email. That has all the information you'll need."

"Vic," Bill broke in, "We need about thirty minutes more to assess what David Alon is doing at Pädäh. After that, Neena and Steve can make contact with Ms. Zahavi. I would like to begin working with the battle planners—I think this is going to require twenty-four, seven until we have the plan."

"Agreed. I need a little more time getting the battle planners into the Pentagon and briefed. I have already ordered Jack Trevane to Tel Aviv by military jet, and his unit is en route to Incirlik Air Base in Turkey. Jack should be at your embassy by zero, four hundred tomorrow. Once we have clearance from the Israeli government, we'll have Jack's unit in Israel in less than six hours. I'll be staying in my office until this situation is resolved. Call anytime. I'll touch base when the battle planners are briefed. Use secure email to communicate."

"Will do. Goodbye."

While Vic was talking, Steve retrieved Ms. Zahavi's dossier, which had arrived at Bill's workstation. He and Neena studied the documents in the conference room. Steve dialed one of the contacts for Abi Zahavi, spoke briefly, and hung up. "Abi will be here in less than an hour, Bill," Steve said. *I wish she were here now. We need reinforcements.*

Wednesday, April 30, 2014; London, England

Brian left his London office and went to a special conference room, sparse but functional, set up by AAD, the firm's risk management advisors. Vic Alfonse, calling from Washington, was on hold. *What could Vic want?* He had helped with the Swiss insurance and banking authorities to set the trap for the Iranians and lock up their money, but that part of the deal was all set. Brian activated the special electronic equipment that would alert him if someone were scanning the room for Van Eck emanations or attempting to transmit anything. He flipped the button to speaker.

"Hello. Is this the plumber?" Brian began.

"Yes. I see your humor is in top form."

"I find it helps. Vic, I would like to bring Joe Burstein into the conversation, if you don't mind. We back each other up on the Iranian deal."

"No, I don't mind," said Vic. "I need all the talent I can find right now."

"Let me get Joe on the line, then." Brian dialed one of the secure lines in New York City and connected with Joe, who was in the office early to monitor the aftermarket in the Iranian Eurobond offering.

"Good morning, Joe," Brian said. "Sorry to call you so early, but I have Vic Alfonse on the line. He would like to speak with us."

"Hello, Mr. Burstein," Vic said gregariously. "I'm glad to have you on this call. I'm not sure that the partners of CHK are aware of my gratitude. Your firm cares for the future of our country. As I am sure you're aware, Brian has briefed me on your NIOC deal and how you, Joe, found a way to hang up the Iranians in their own underwear."

There was good-natured chuckling, then the speaker crackled and Joe said, "Thank you, Mr. Alfonse. It brought me a little joy to think of that special moment, which will occur in two days."

"Gentlemen, I'm going to share with you highly classified information, some of which has not yet reached the ears of the president. It's not to be shared, even with your partners. I don't have time to get you clearances, so we'll just have to proceed without them."

Brian understood that Vic was not calling about the Swiss authorities. *Whatever it is, it's big.*

"There is a lot—a *lot*—at stake over the next few days," Vic continued. "No one—not wives, mothers, children, or best friends—is to know what I reveal to you this afternoon. The consequences of your breaching my trust might be catastrophic for the *world*. Am I *clear*?"

"Yes," Brian and Joe said simultaneously.

Vic spent the next hour bringing them up to date on the lack of intelligence flows in the Middle East and the events in Beirut and Tel Aviv. He explained the intercepted message with the geographic coordinates and Operation Kristallnacht, the Iranian plan to kill all Sunnis in the integrated Iraq/ Iran military. He briefed them on Steve, Bill, and Neena, recited the findings, assessments and conclusions reached over the past few days. He described details of the defensive build-up of Pädäh.

"So, gentlemen, we seem to be faced with a plot to launch 167 nuclear missiles at enemies of Israel sometime over the next few days. Bill Elsberry thinks that sundown this Sunday, May 4, which marks the start of Israel's Independence Day, might be the launch date. What questions do you have for me before I tell you why I want you to know these things?"

A silence of a few moments followed as Joe and Brian considered the gravity of Vic's words.

"Not a question, Vic," Joe solemnly said after thinking intensely for a time, "but I think the assessment of Israel's Independence Day as the possible launch date may be wrong. We should also consider Israel's Memorial Day as the possible launch date."

"Why do you think that?"

"I'm Jewish. I've made many trips to Israel. Memorial Day, the day *before* Independence Day, is a day dedicated to the memory of all those who gave their lives to establish Israel as a nation and keep it free. Colonel Alon might be dedicating his actions to the people who kept Israel free. Also, Colonel Alon must know that many Israelis will die either as the result of counterattacks or nuclear radiation and fallout. These people, too, will be dying to keep Israel free, whatever is left of it. Therefore, May 3, Memorial Day, might be the date on which to focus."

"I see your point, Joe. I will let Bill, Steve, and Neena know. That makes the possible launch date only three days away—sundown this Saturday. My *god*."

Brian interjected to keep them focused on pending tasks rather than straying to thoughts about the consequences of Alon's success. "Why have you brought us in on this, Vic?"

"I've been thinking about your series of transactions with the Iranians. I have also been thinking about who has the nuclear weaponry to retaliate—the Iranians. And, Brian, I know that while you were in the Marines, you were an ace at intelligence. So, what I'd like from you are ideas regarding how you, with my support, can use what you're doing to keep the Iranians from retaliating."

"I'm not sure anything will prevent their retaliation in the event that Alon gets the missiles off," Brian said. "Not only will they feel justified, but the Iranian military likely has orders to respond upon the report of incoming missiles. We're not dealing with anyone in the Iranian military, so we'd have to work through others to get to them. We would not have time."

"Of course you're correct, Brian. I'm sorry that I wasn't clear. We're currently working with trusted people in Israeli defense and security agencies. We are also planning to attack, and if necessary, destroy Pädäh to reach the computers that control the missiles."

"You're expecting to prevent the launch?" Joe queried.

"That's the primary objective, but I'm working on a secondary objective—preventing the launch of *most* of the missiles. I've asked the Secretary of Defense to order CENTCOM and EUCOM ships with ballistic missile defense capability to the eastern Mediterranean—as many as we can get there by Sunday—or I should now say, Saturday. I'll be holding a complete briefing with the Secretary, Joint Chiefs of Staff and the president on Friday." Someone knocked on Brian's conference room door. *If they know what's good for them, they'll go away,* Brian thought. The knocking stopped. He rolled his neck out ease a kink and leaned back in his chair, muscles tense, a headache coming on.

Vic went on, "They already have the background that I shared with you, but by Friday, we'll have—and need—proof of Alon's venture. The US Navy does not have enough capacity in terms of ships and missiles today to knock out 167 intermediate range missiles, so we have to be successful in stopping most of them before they're launched."

"So our operating assumption for the task you're giving us is that a few, and perhaps none, of the 167 missiles reach their targets. Is that correct?" Joe asked.

"Precisely. Brian was correct—if the majority of the missiles hit their targets, then all bets are off. Even if we destroy all of the missiles, we still have to deal with the possibility that Iran, and perhaps others, will be goaded into retaliation—either with nuclear weapons or conventional forces. I'm asking you to think about how you could, shall I say, 'appeal' to the Iranians to refrain from any such action. Keep in mind the message intercept and the existence of Operation Kristallnacht. That may offer some options as you think this through."

Brian stood up. He thought more clearly when he stood. He knew also that what he'd just been told was jacking up his blood pressure. He needed physical movement. *Damn, I hate long phone calls.*

"Wow, Vic, that's a tall order," Joe whistled.

"Stopping this is a very tall order for everyone, Joe. Even if we're successful, we're going to lose a lot of good men and women—both American and Israeli—in preventing David Alon from scorching the Middle East and, perhaps, bringing on Armageddon."

"Armageddon," Brian began, "means the 'hill of Megiddo' where the final battle will be fought between good and evil. It's ironic that Megiddo and Masada are both in Israel." He paused. "Vic, we know what you want. Give us until later today."

"Sure, Brian. How about eight hours? Let me know if you have something before then."

"Of course." Brian was already contemplating solutions. He worked best with deadlines.

"Brian, I'd like you to go to Tel Aviv and team up with our people there."

"What good can I do there?'

"I want you to get to know Steve, Neena, and Bill. First, they're very bright and may be able to help you and Joe in the task you just accepted. Second, if we're successful in stopping this, you and your firm are likely to be on Iran's shit list. I'll be assigning Steve to work with AAD to help keep all of you safe. A personal relationship based on working on a tough assignment will help with that."

"Got it. When do you want me there?" *Good thing I'm single. Even if I could tell her about all this, she wouldn't believe it.*

"Yesterday, as the saying goes. I'll have a Navy fighter waiting for you at Gatwick in two hours. The pilot should not ask you anything about why you are on board, and you should not discuss anything with him. You will land aboard the USS *Ronald Reagan* and go by helicopter directly to our embassy in Tel Aviv. I'll email instructions to you."

"Will do, Vic. Unless there's more, Joe and I need to sign off and discuss firm matters—as you mentioned, we're in the middle of that Iranian deal. We close on the purchase of the refinery assets and the rest tomorrow."

"I've been following with interest. We're all square with the Swiss authorities, correct?"

"Yes," Joe interjected. "We have the revised actuarial report ready and will be delivering it to them the first thing on Friday. I wish I could see the Iranian's faces when they find out that...."

"Hold onto that thought," Vic said. "You may yet have the opportunity, but you may not want it. I will alert our friends in Tel Aviv about your thought, Joe, that the launch date might be Saturday. Goodbye, gentlemen."

Joe and Brian remained on the telephone for another thirty minutes, discussing a few adjustments to the deal—it always paid to work in teams so that more than one person knew what was going on. They also discussed what would be told to the other partners and staff. Brian's flight instructions arrived by email. Brian then took the firm's limousine to the airport, stopping for only a few minutes at the CHK apartment in Mayfair to pack.

As the driver approached the security gate to the airfield, a British Royal Navy officer met him and under his authority, certain security procedures, including presenting proper written approval to enter by this gate, were waived. The officer transferred Brian and his luggage to a US Navy vehicle that took him to the waiting F18 Hornet.

As Brian buckled his harness and secured his helmet and communications gear, Brian thought about how he had come to know Vic. *I have to believe in Providence. How else can I explain all this? Hope God is on board this project team, 'cause we are going to need the help.* Brian settled in for the flight. In three hours he'd arrive at the US Embassy in Tel Aviv. *Out of the frying pan, into the fire.*

**Later Wednesday, April 30, 2014; The American Embassy,
Tel Aviv, Israel**

As the car drove through the gates and passed the Marine checkpoint, Bill, Steve, and Neena waited to welcome Abi, the Israeli Special Assistant for Internal Affairs who would assist them with the unfolding plot of David Alon. Expecting her to exhibit a very military bearing, Steve was very surprised as she exited the car with the subtle grace of a runway model. She was even taller than Neena—about five feet, eleven inches, probably fifteen pounds heavier—and blond. Not the peroxide blond hair of an actress, but strawberry blond with a hint of brown—and lots of it pulled back into a barrette that seemed to strain against the effort. She wore a tailored business suit. Her coat opened as she walked confidently toward them, revealing a 9mm holstered at her side. Non-embassy personnel normally are not permitted to carry weapons, but an exception was made for Abi. It was a time for trust, not procedure.

"Welcome, Abi," Bill said cheerfully as he stepped forward to offer a handshake.

"Hello, Bill," Abi returned, accepting the offered hand. She shook first Neena's hand and then Steve's. "I am delighted to meet you both. Shall we get on with the matter at hand?"

As they followed Bill and Abi into the building, Steve and Neena took a moment to scan the buildings surrounding the embassy. Clear. The embassy's security detail would be constantly examining the area, but Steve had a hard time ignoring a habit that had kept him alive. It pleased him that Neena shared the habit.

The ever-present pot of hot coffee waited in Bill's office. "Abi, please give us an overview of what Undersecretary Alfonse has told you about our situation here?" Bill poured coffee for everyone.

"Of course. Vic has explained that you suspect a compromise in Israel's strategic defenses. You also surmise that top security and defense agency officials have a hand in this. Vic Alfonse sought me out because he believes that I can be relied on to offer an objective assessment of your findings. He also understands that, if necessary, I have the power to intercede at the highest levels of our government."

"Do you?" Neena asked.

"Have the power to intercede? Yes, Prime Minister Erez trusts me completely." Abi sat back, erect, in her chair, placing her hands on its arms. *Very confident posture,* Steve observed.

"Abi," Bill began, "we believe that the compromise in Israel's defenses is driven by people considered above reproach. They are heroes to virtually every Israeli. Also, we believe that, because of the intricacies of the operation, they have substantial support at many levels of the IDF, Strategic Command, and Mossad."

"So," Abi cut in, "What you want to know is whether I can be trusted?" She smiled.

"Yes," Neena said. Steve observed Neena's unfaltering gaze into Abi's eyes.

"I think my record of service to Israel and the vetting you no doubt have already done will lead you to conclude that my loyalty to Israel is without question. That should be obvious because I am already in this office. The question, then, that I think you are asking is whether I am more loyal to the individuals to whom you are referring than to Israel." *Sharp and to the point,* Steve thought.

"Logically well presented, Abi, and exactly the question we have," Bill said.

"In the dossier that Vic must have sent you are details of my history. I came prepared to answer your question about my loyalty, so I will share those things that are not in the dossier about which you might want to know."

Steve said, "Abi, we don't have the time to continue vetting you to the point of irrefutable certainty. Events are so close at hand that we must trust you—and accept the consequences of your possible betrayal of us." Steve leaned forward, resting his forearms on legs and looked at Bill. *It's time, Bill.*

Bill nodded and then turned to Abi. "We're faced with the possible nuclear devastation of the Middle East, with unknown consequences for humankind beyond that."

Abi gazed, in turn, at each of them. "Then you had better tell me what the hell is going on," she said.

They consumed the next hour briefing Abi, answering her questions.

"I think your assessment is very good," Abi said as the briefing came to close. "You do not have proof, but you do have a strong, if circumstantial, case. I also agree that among the first tasks is to confirm that no counterterrorist systems project exists and to determine whether someone has neutralized the ability of Strategic Command general staff to order the missiles to self-destruct or to change course. If we can confirm your information and conclusions, then we will have what we need to go to the Prime Minister." She adjusted the barrette that contained her wild hair, tilting her head at an angle. "I have to tell you, though, that I hope you are all insane."_

"We wish we were as well," Neena said. "But, we're not. What do we need to do to get the confirmation you want?"

Steve stood up and started pacing slowly. *Abi is the right person, Vic,* he thought to himself. Now that the problem had been identified, he was ready to do something.

"I have the authority to dig into the counterterrorist project issue and to cause a test of Strategic Command's missile systems."

"In helping us, you might be putting yourself in danger," Steve said.

"I know that. The good news is that my death, in the context of the note I will leave with you, will be sufficient for the Prime Minister to shut down our missile systems until he knows the truth."

"If he *can* shut them down," Neena added. The talking stopped for a moment.

"Abi, would it be all right with you if Steve accompanied you?" Bill asked.

"He is quite good at what he does," interjected Neena. "I can vouch for that."

"I will accept the help on the basis that Steve might be able to get important information back to you in the event that I can't. I am used to fighting my own battles—literally and figuratively."

"We understand, Abi," Steve said. "All of us are used to taking care of ourselves. But, teamwork has its place, too."

"Agreed. Then, let me finish this note and leave it with you, Bill."

Abi took five minutes to write the note in Hebrew. She signed it and took a small inkpad out of her purse. She removed a signet ring from her right hand and stamped the note with the signet ring, leaving the motto of her military unit imprinted next to her signature. She wiped her ring thoroughly with a tissue and put it back on her finger. She then placed the note in an envelope and sealed it, handing the envelope to Bill. "The Prime Minister will have no doubt about the authenticity of this note. Now, Steve, let us get to work."

Steve and Abi left together in her car. Although Israel's capital was Jerusalem, Abi also maintained an office in Tel Aviv. They would be there in a matter of minutes.

After Abi and Steve had disappeared from view, Neena said to Bill, "I am going to see David and push him with a few questions."

"I won't tell you not to, Neena, but be careful. I wouldn't go to Pädäh. You might not be allowed to leave if they have locked down the compound, as it seems they have."

"All right," Neena agreed. "My weekly report is not due for a few days, but I will ask David for a meeting—perhaps lunch to make it seem very social—to review progress made regarding the intelligence gaps. He may already have a sense that we are, at some level, on to his plan."

"That makes him dangerous—even for you, Neena. If David sees you getting in the way of the annihilation he has planned for Israel's enemies, he will swat you like a fly."

"Of course, you are right, Bill. Luckily, David trained me well. He will find it difficult to swat *this* fly."

Neena left the embassy and returned to the Sea Executive Suites Hotel. There, she made a call to David. She was angry in a new way—beyond the hatred for Hezbollah over the slaughter of her family. Beyond avenging the past. The David she had loved as an uncle was threatening Israel, Steve, her future—her wonderful future—a future that she now cared about. If need be, she would do some swatting of her own.

Wednesday Afternoon, April 30, 2014; Tel Aviv, Israel

It was mid-afternoon as Abi and Steve arrived at her office, and she immediately went to a secure telephone, hit the speaker button, and dialed a memorized number. Steve took the opportunity to study her office. It was very neat. A simple pine desk and matching credenza provided the main working spaces. A contemporary, upholstered sofa lined the wall to the right of Abi's desk. An Israeli flag held vigil in one corner of the office by a large window, and a framed display of eleven military awards hung over the credenza. An Uzi leaned against the credenza near the flag. Photographs of Abi and the Prime Minister and other Israeli dignitaries of various political stripes dotted the remaining walls. *She's comfortable playing with the big boys*, Steve mused.

Someone answered. "General Amit, this is Abi Zahavi. I am sorry to skip the small talk, but I am formally requesting an inquiry into an alleged counterterrorism project that might compromise our nuclear missile systems. The project's alleged objective is to test whether a determined and resourceful terrorist group could penetrate our missile control systems."

"Abi, I will look into it," General Gideon Amit, commander of Israel's Strategic Command said calmly, "But off the top of my head, I can't recall such a project. Unless I am being separated from the project for security purposes, I should know of the existence of any such project." Abi and Steve exchanged looks.

"Gideon, I have reliable, but not verified, information that top people in our security agencies have corrupted and now control our missile targeting and abort systems. You know what this can mean and you know that, if confirmed, we have some very determined and dangerous people in key positions."

"Abi, what the hell is happening?" the general said with alarm growing in his voice.

"I am not sure, Gideon, but before I go any farther with this, I need two things from you. First, I need to know—for *certain*—that no such counterterrorist project exists. Second, I need our systems tested to determine—for *certain*—that Strategic Command can abort and destroy any missile that might be launched. And I need to know *now*, Gideon. How long will it take you to get back to me?" Steve was impressed. *No beating around the bush with Abi,* he thought.

"I will have people in Programs Security run those tests today."

"You should know that the information that I have puts Captain Ovadia, who has a key position in Program Security, under suspicion. I would be very selective of the people assigned to this—especially those that are known associates of Captain Ovadia. I also assume that 'today' means by five o'clock this afternoon."

"Abi, I will get this done. Who else knows of this?"

"I won't answer that to protect both you and me." *Smart move,* thought Steve. "Be careful, Gideon," Abi said. "I would not want to lose you."

"Thank you for your concern, Abi. I usually travel with a security detail anyway."

"You should also know that my information implicates high-level individuals in the IDF, Strategic Command, and Mossad. You might want to change your security detail."

After a brief moment of silence, Gideon continued, "Abi, can you tell me what the *fuck* is going on?"

"If what I have seen and been told is accurate, our entire nuclear land-based missile capability will be launched against selected Middle Eastern targets before next Monday. We are looking, potentially, at a nuclear holocaust. Pray I am wrong, but find out either way, Gideon."

"My god, Abi. I will get back to you every hour with a report. Where will you be?"

"In my Tel Aviv office."

"Shalom."

"Let's hope. Shalom." Abi ended the call. She walked over to her credenza and looked at the Uzi.

"What else can we be doing?" Steve asked.

"I would ask a second person to do what I just asked General Amit to do, but I want first to see if I can trust him. If I get a call in a little while asking me to meet someone somewhere, I will know that he has betrayed me."

"Good thinking," Steve said. "That would most likely mean you are being set up. Okay. We wait. I have an idea if you would like to hear it."

"Right now, I will take all the ideas you have."

"In order to launch the missiles, I assume you, like us, have men and women in the silos with launch codes and keys. Is that correct?" Steve had sat on the edge of Abi's desk. She sat down on the couch.

"Yes. They received their training from your Air Force. They are assigned in teams of two and are locked in the silo until their 24-hour shift is up. How can this help?"

"Well, the day of the launch, Alon will need his people to be assigned to the shift so that the missiles can be launched. One of the failsafe design features is to have actual control over the launch in the hands of a human being rather than a computer system that can be compromised." Abi was nodding her head. "After all, we've heard that the targeting system and the abort function have been compromised, but no one has said anything about being able to launch the missiles by computer command."

"I see where you are going—find out who is assigned to the silos on Saturday and Sunday and detain them."

"Exactly." Steve's mind was whirring like a pinwheel.

"But who will man the silos if we pick up all those crews?"

"Perhaps the answer is 'no one', at least for twenty-four hours or so as you vet each crew. Alternatively, you can take the remaining crews and have them staff five or ten silos so that you have some nuclear capability until you can completely vet the Saturday and Sunday crews," said Steve.

"We will find out who is on duty while we wait for Gideon to get back to me." Abi walked to her desk and entered a series of codes into her workstation. After five minutes, she had a list of names. Another ten minutes and she had an address to match each name.

"Now we need a small group of security personnel that we can trust to pick these people up," Abi said. "Do you have any more ideas? If Gideon proves to be clean, he might have some personnel. But we have seventeen silos: sixteen with ten missiles each, and one silo with seven. So two crew members times seventeen, times two days equals sixty-eight people to detain and we have to do it virtually simultaneously."

Steve was pacing now, focused on a solution. "Israel has a great police sergeant in the Central District Israel Police—Sergeant Harel. I'd ask him to pick as many police as he completely trusts."

"I remember his name from your briefing. You trust him?"

"He had many opportunities to dismiss Neena and me. Instead, he went out of his way to help. He strikes me as a straight shooter."

Just then, Abi's telephone rang. "Hello," she said as she hit the speaker button.

"Abi, this is Gideon. I don't have the results of the system tests yet, but I can tell you that no one who *should* know can verify the existence of that counterterrorism project." Steve nodded, but being right didn't make him happy.

"Oh, Gideon," Abi said with despair in her voice, "I had been hoping that my information was wrong. I suspect that the systems test will be bad news as well, but I will wait for your report. Thank you, Gideon."

"One more thing, Abi, regarding the systems test."

"What is it?"

"A number of Strategic Command people, including Captain Ovadia, have been reported as seeking and, in some cases, gaining unauthorized access to Strategic Command programming modules."

"Shit! How did that happen?"

"I don't know *yet*, but I'll find out."

The call was over. Abi walked slowly to the large window in her office overlooking the Mediterranean and hung her head. A few tears ran down her face. Steve called Bill Elsberry. The report was brief. Afterward, Steve stood patiently and watched Abi fully absorb the reality of the peril facing her beloved country.

Wednesday Afternoon, April 30, 2014; The American Embassy, Tel Aviv, Israel

At four o'clock, a US Navy Seahawk helicopter lowered onto the roof of the US Embassy building. Without shutting down the engines, the pilot motioned to Brian Kendrick that he was at his destination. Brian jumped down, ducking to avoid the deadly rotor blades swooshing overhead. A Marine sergeant stepped up. "Let me take your suitcase, sir," said the Marine. "I'm here to escort you to Bill Elsberry's office."

Brian, however, leaned over and said "Semper Fi, sergeant. I tote my own shit." The Marine smiled and offered a salute, which Brian returned. He left the helicopter behind him, carrying his own bags. As he and the sergeant stepped inside a small doorway on the roof, the big Sikorsky lifted off effortlessly and sped directly back to the waiting USS *Ronald Reagan*.

As Brian and the Marine approached Bill's office, Philip Palun appeared from nowhere and opened the door. Brian stepped inside and the Marine turned sharply and left the click of his boot heels echoing in the hallway as Philip gently closed the door.

"Hello, Brian," Bill said, offering his hand as he stood. "I'm very pleased to meet you. Vic Alfonse has briefed me on your plans to ensure that the Iranians don't get all they want in the NIOC deal. Not many people would take that risk, but, then again, you're a Marine."

"Thank you, Mr. Elsberry," Brian said as he vigorously shook Bill's hand. "We're just doing what we think is right. Many others have done the same."

"So, a self-effacing Marine, eh? Please call me Bill. How was your private jet ride?"

"Quite a treat, actually, despite the circumstances. Impressive to see that kind of contemporary military hardware up close and personal." Brian found a corner where he could put his bag down.

"Great. Coffee?" Bill pointed to a tray with cups and a carafe.

"Yes, thank you, Bill. What can you tell me about events since I left London?"

"We met with Abital Zahavi, who works directly for the Prime Minister. She and Steve Barber are at her office looking into whether Strategic Command's missile targeting and abort systems have been compromised." Bill looked over a notepad and completed the briefing.

"Where is Neena Shahud?" Brian asked, looking around Bill's office.

"She's back at her hotel. She arranged a meeting with David Alon. She intends to push for much more information."

"I don't know her, but isn't she putting herself in serious jeopardy by doing that?" Brian was standing, slowly twisting his torso from left to right and back.

"Absolutely. But, Neena does what Neena wants to do, especially when it comes to protecting what she loves. She's quite a formidable woman."

"So it would seem from what Vic Alfonse has told me. What can I do until we get together with Steve and Neena?"

"I would like to go over your ideas on how the NIOC deal can be used to deter Iran's possible retaliation in the event that we can't stop all the missiles from being launched."

"Sure. I did some thinking on the plane ride over. I'd like to bounce ideas off of Joe Burstein. It's about nine o'clock in the morning in New York, and Joe's waiting for my call."

"Let's go into my conference room where we can be comfortable and get him on the speakerphone." Brian dialed.

"Hello, Brian," Joe said alertly. "I've been waiting for your call."

"Sorry we didn't give you the full eight hours, Joe," Brian apologized. "I know you would've liked some more time, but I have some ideas."

"Great. I'm getting tired of carrying your water," Joe said with a laugh.

"I have Bill Elsberry on the speaker with me," said Brian. "Let's start with some premises. First, the Iranians with whom we are working include top civilians and members of the Guardian Council." Brian held out his hand, palm up, counting off the first premise by folding his thumb inward.

"We know of Rezvani, Khoemi, and Mahdavi. The other members of the Iranian deal group have set up individual accounts in Switzerland into which their share of the fees paid to the consulting firm will flow," Joe offered. "My contact will get us names and we can do the research on those names from here."

Brian bent his index finger, tucked it under his thumb. "A second premise is that the consulting fees being paid to these Iranians through their Swiss consulting firm are not being shared with all Guardian Council members or senior military officers."

"I'm on board with that," said Joe.

"So am I," Bill seconded.

"My last premise is if the other members of the Guardian Council and senior military officers knew of the fees being paid to our NIOC deal friends and their Swiss bank accounts, our little group would be in deep shit." Brian had three digits tucked now, which he made into a fist. The thought of anyone attempting to jeopardize his firm or his country, for that matter, struck to his very core.

Bill ran his palms back and forth on the edge of the conference table like he was at a keyboard. "I see where you are going, Brian," he said. "The group working with you, if in sufficiently high positions to influence any decision on retaliation, could be persuaded to do so if they thought their corruption and the money they hold in Swiss accounts would become public information."

"And it won't matter that they can't get at the money for twenty years because the Swiss have attached the accounts to provide equity to the insurance company they formed to guarantee the infrastructure bonds," Joe added.

"That's right—the mere existence of the money will be sufficient to condemn our Iranian deal pals," Bill affirmed. "And they are likely to hope they'll have the money *some* day."

"Then there's the information about Operation Kristallnacht," Brian added. "It's not connected to the deal, but we can probably put it to good use, too."

"I have another idea for that," Bill interjected, as he put his palms down on the conference table like he was closing up the piano. "We release that information into the intelligence pipelines in Iraq. The resulting Sunni reaction will create a major distraction, if not an all-out internal war, that will occupy our friends in Tehran and Qom for quite a while. The added leverage would be that we could connect the release of that information to Mohammed Khoemi, Danesh Mahdavi, and Sa'ad-Oddin Rezvani, all of whom we know hold top spots in your deal."

"We might let the rumor surface that those three sold the information and that money is in Switzerland as well," Joe said with a hint of glee in his tone.

"Gentlemen, you have once again shown the creativity your firm is known for," said Bill, standing up. "Joe, could you get to work on identifying all the holders of the Swiss accounts?"

"Sure thing. I'll place the call to my contact now. We should have the names by close of business in Zurich and we will go from there. Where should I reach you when I have the information?"

"I'll give you my secure line here in the embassy. I pretty much live here full-time now." With that Bill read off a number to Joe, said good-bye and hung up.

"I'm going to need a place to flop," Brian said. "Do you think there's room at the hotel where Neena and Steve are staying? Might as well be close to them."

Bill raised his index finger as though he was balancing something on it. "Philip Palun—the gentleman who met you and the Marine sergeant at my office door—already has booked you there. The Seas Executive Suites Hotel. It's nearby."

"Great. When will I meet Steve and Neena?"

"They'll be returning here around six. You'll also meet Abital Zahavi. The five of us will have dinner here, near our secure telephones. In the meantime, please feel free to stay and use this room to make calls—I want your NIOC deal to succeed at least as much as you and your partners do."

"Thank you, Bill. I'll do that," Brian said, as he opened his briefcase.

"I'll call Neena and Steve and let them know you're here," Bill said.

Later Wednesday, April 30, 2014; Tel Aviv, Israel

Abi waited anxiously by the telephone for General Amit to call with the results of the system test—the test that would prove that David Alon, Israeli hero and Mossad legend, was about to obliterate the Middle East with Israel's land-based nuclear weapons. She could only pretend to work. Her mind was turning, folding, and re-examining all that she had heard earlier in the day. It was devastating, and she kept trying to dismiss the facts. *No*, she thought, *we can't have worked so hard for so many years at such a cost to lose it in a moment of madness.* At last, the reality took hold and she became calm as she always did in tense situations. Abi picked up the phone the second it rang.

"Hello, Abi," came Gideon's voice over the speakerphone.

"Go ahead," said Abi.

"I have news, very bad news about the control and targeting systems, Abi." There was a waver of nervous tension in his voice. "A virus is preventing access to the abort and re-targeting modules. No one can abort or change the course of a missile after launch. *No one* has control over *our* missiles, at least through *our* systems."

There was a minute of silence. "You are *absolutely* sure?" Abi stood at her desk leaning on her palms and staring at the phone. *Can this truly be?*

"*Absolutely* sure, Abi." She shivered once from head to foot as if she had bitten something horribly bitter. Gideon continued, "You should also know that the virus must have been planted because the entire missile system is standalone. We do not exchange data with *any other* system. I am sending Major Navon, who heads our analyst teams in Missile Systems to your office with documentation of the tests and the results. I assume you will be sharing these with the Prime Minister soon."

Abi nodded and realized Gideon could not see her. "Thank you, Gideon. That documentation would be very helpful. I may summon you to testify about this matter."

"Of course, Abi."

Steve looked at Abi; she nodded and Steve spoke. "General, this is Steve Barber. I work for Vic Alfonse in the US Department of Defense. Abi can give you more particulars if you need them."

"No, Mr. Barber, your presence in the same room with Abi is all I need."

"Thank you, General. Abi and I have been working on a plan to neutralize the ballistic missile silos and we need your help." Abi sat down.

"Freely given, Mr. Barber."

"We've identified every silo crew assigned for either Saturday or Sunday, which we believe are the two likely days on which the launch will occur. We need help executing a coordinated action to detain these crews until they can be vetted and released or otherwise dealt with."

"I can help with that, Steve."

"Great. We would execute the detentions on Saturday so that there's no time for the plotters to substitute others with similar loyalties."

"May I ask whom you believe to be plotting this horror?"

Steve looked at Abi, who said, "David Alon and Simon Luegner are the two whom we believe are at the top."

An audible gasp came over the speakerphone. After a moment, Gideon continued, "In some ways I'm shocked. In other ways, I'm not. Both David and Simon have been pretty open about their views on Israel being attacked in the near future. I never thought they would do something as . . . as *ghastly* as this—unleash a *holocaust*."

"We have been fighting this reality, too," Abi said. "I think we need to surrender to it and focus on how to stop it." Abi stood up, her eyes glaring. *We will stop it!*

"Yes, of course, Abi."

"Gideon," Steve began, "How many people do you think you can vet and have ready by early Saturday morning? Also, while you are vetting these people, we have to keep all of this under wraps. I am concerned that David might move up the launch if he sees us close to stopping him."

"I can have at least one hundred trusted and equipped men and women by Saturday morning. We should send teams of at least two. Unless you or Abi object, I would suggest that I authorize deadly force."

"Yes, Gideon. So authorized." Anger boiled in her voice.

"Understood. Do you have other resources? My one hundred will take care of fifty crewmembers, but there are sixty-eight. We need an additional thirty-six security personnel."

"Steve knows of a top-notch sergeant in the Central District Israel Police who might be able to help."

"It's a longer story than we have time for, but I trust Sergeant Harel," said Steve. "He'd need to be brought up to speed, but he's very astute and already figured out something important is swirling around."

"Then let's get the personnel put together and then we can brief them collectively. When should we do that?"

"Early Saturday morning. Leaves less time for leaks to occur."

"Agreed. I will get back to you both as soon as I have all my people."

"Good. Call here or my cell phone—which is not secure—or through Bill Elsberry at the US Embassy."

"Fine. I know Bill. Anything else?"

"No, I think that's it for now. Shalom."

After Abi ended the call, Steve said, "Now, there's no doubt. We must consider this as a substantiated internal threat to your nuclear missile complex."

"I agree. I need to call the Prime Minister. He will want to meet with his key cabinet members, top security people, and some members of the Knesset."

Abi placed a call to Bill Elsberry on the secure line. Bill told them that Brian Kendrick had arrived at the embassy. He also briefed her and Steve on the ideas for convincing Iranian leaders to forego retaliation in the event that some missiles are launched. The next call was to Vic, who told of the potential deployment of US Navy ships and combat unit under General Jack Trevane as well as a briefing of the president, his Cabinet, the Joint Chiefs of Staff, and the Congressional Intelligence and Armed Services committees scheduled for seven in the morning on Friday, two days away. Abi agreed to obtain official authorization for American ships and combat personnel to enter Israeli sovereign territory.

Steve stepped out of Abi's office to let her brief the Prime Minister in private. Bill had arranged a dinner for all of them, including Brian Kendrick. Steve looked forward to meeting the man and to a few hours of relaxation. He poured himself a glass of water from a carafe on the credenza and wished he could turn back time. It was nearing sundown. The streets teemed with people. *They have no idea*, thought Steve as he watched a woman pushing a stroller stop, retrieve a small object from the sidewalk and give it back to the child in the stroller. *There is no way to save these people if David succeeds. There will be no way to save Neena. She'll be in the fight to the end. Maybe that's why I love her so.*

Wednesday Evening, April 30, 2014; The American Embassy, Tel Aviv, Israel

Steve and Abi entered a parlor, just outside a private dining room, where Bill, Brian, and Neena were waiting. The parlor was sparsely furnished, intended for dignitaries to cut mingling short and get down to business. There were only two Mission chairs in the room, each flanking a Craftsman sideboard on which an ornate silver tray, engraved ice bucket and Waterford crystal tumblers had been placed. Steve thought the room suited Bill, functional with only a touch of frill. No expense was spared on the liquor selection, though. A mural depicting life on a farm covered one whole wall and Steve remembered that Bill grew up on a farm in Iowa. Walls were papered in elegant ticking; the doorways, ceiling, and floors were finished in thick, wide, layered moldings rich with paint that looked like vanilla ice cream. The parlor made Steve hungry. He nuzzled Neena's neck instead.

Ice clinked in glasses as Bill served drinks and introduced everyone. "Shall we have dinner?" Bill inquired. "It is a bit early by traditional standards here, but I think we all need some rest. Tomorrow isn't going to be any easier. Let me show you the dining room." Bill opened the doors to the dining room and gestured for them to enter.

The room was set for the five of them with the embassy's best china and crystal. The Ambassador, Bill's nominal boss, was from New York and had a taste for New England antiques, some of which she brought from America to enjoy during her appointment. The Ambassador was back in the United States for a family wedding and would not be in residence for the next week or so.

As they found their places, Bill said, "I hope you don't mind, but I thought that during our appetizer course—a marvelous smoked trout in Belgian endive and zucchini potato pancakes—we might get better acquainted with one of those icebreaker activities."

"Okay," said Steve, "Let's have at it." There was amused enthusiasm all around.

The evening was a welcome break from the stress of the past few days and the pending disaster. Steve thought that Bill's icebreaker questions had been a very clever way of giving each person a couple of items to chat about with the others. The resulting conversations were very diverse and laughs erupted from time to time.

Toward the end of the evening, Steve reminded the group why they gathered.

"I have enjoyed this evening. Thank you, Bill, for your gracious hospitality and thoughtful conversation starter. We have a lot of work to do tomorrow, so I am going to call it a day. Abi and I will follow up with General Amit and, as I understand, you, Bill, are working with Neena and the battle planners in DC. Brian, you have asset purchases closing tomorrow. Bill, can Brian work from here? I only ask because I'm sure he will have the same security issues with his room at the hotel as we have with ours."

"Absolutely. With the Ambassador back in the States, we have less activity here, so it'll be easy to accommodate such a distinguished investment banker," Bill said with a slight bow to Brian. "Jack Trevane will be here early tomorrow morning and he will be helping us plan the assault on Pädäh."

"Steve," Neena began, hesitated and continued, "I am going to meet with David Alon tomorrow."

Steve turned in his chair to look directly at her and said, "That's risky. He must at least *suspect* that we're on to him. You've made inquiries that Captain Ovadia knows about, and Abi has done more of that today with General Amit. David is too good not to have eyes and ears in many places. Not that I don't trust your judgment." Steve knew he was pushing her.

"I agree with you, but I know what I am doing. I want to see what he will say. After all, I am still assigned to work with you to look into the intelligence gaps. He might be more suspicious if I were to avoid reporting to him on our progress, which is how I have positioned our meeting."

"Then, I would like to go with you." As much as he respected her, he couldn't lose her. Alarms blared in his head. *I'm always right about these things.*

"That is not a good idea. I can rely more on my relationship with David if you are not there. Besides, you and Abi have important work to do."

Steve looked at her a long time. The others were silent, observing the two. Finally, he said, "All right, Neena. It's your call." He felt the muscles in his cheeks tighten as he spoke.

"Well, then, why don't we call it a night," Bill put in quickly. "Brian, please feel free to return when it suits you. You need a good night's sleep after your trip." Steve thought Bill looked edgy. *I guess he looks like I feel. Neena shouldn't meet with David.*

"Thank you, Bill," Brian responded. "I'll see you around eight in the morning. Let me add my thanks for a wonderful evening."

The five said their goodbyes and left. Steve, Neena and Brian shared a car back to the hotel. The talk was cordial but Steve could feel the strain between Neena and him. Abi drove herself home, and Bill retired to a small bedroom in the embassy to get some sleep before Black Jack arrived. "After he gets here," Bill announced to no one, "things will *really* start hopping."

Chapter Sixteen
Thursday, May 1, 2014; Tel Aviv, Israel

The second hand on Abi's wall clock clicked to eight as the security guard called to announce Steve in the lobby. She was standing by her desk when he entered and she appeared frightened. "Abi, are you all right?"

"I have been trying to reach Gideon for the last five minutes. I can't get him at his office or on his cell phone."

"Let's get focused. First, call the Prime Minister and make him aware of your concern for Gideon. In the meantime, who can you call to check the General's home and office?"

"I don't know who to trust."

"Then we'll do it. Come on."

Abi raised her right index finger as she made a call to the Prime Minister. He was in a meeting, but his administrative assistant assured Abi that the Prime Minister would return the call soon. They took the elevator to the second parking level and Abi's Alfa Romeo.

Abi drove like a tyrant, passing everything on the road and Steve checked his seatbelt while he called Bill to tell him where they were going. Just as Steve hung up, Abi's cell rang. The conversation with the Prime Minister was brief, Abi veering onto the shoulder, the Alfa Romeo spitting gravel as she talked. Fifteen minutes later, Abi showed her ID to the air base guard, and they entered Strategic Command headquarters.

Abi screeched to a halt into one of the visitor parking spaces. The morning was crisp and clear and jasmine were in bloom around the building. "Interesting contrast with what is happening," she said. "Life goes on."

Steve nodded, distracted by thoughts of Neena. *What does she hope to accomplish with David?* Perhaps, even Neena did not know.

As they entered the building and signed in, a woman captain walked through the lobby, glancing at them for a moment. Steve noticed a scar etched on her right temple. She turned quickly and disappeared behind a fire door. The security guard at the front desk took their weapons, which would be returned as they left. He insisted on calling General Amit's office in advance of their visit. "No answer, Ms. Zahavi," he said.

"That is all right, corporal. I will wait for him in his office."

"I am not authorized to let you do that, Ms. Zahavi."

"But *I* am. If you doubt me, call the Prime Minister." Abi started for the eastern corridor, leaving the guard with a confused expression on his face. Steve stifled a smile and caught up with Abi as she entered the doorway. Five steps into the corridor, paint flakes flew off the walls at them. So did chunks of the concrete wall underneath. Someone was shooting. They lunged for cover in the nearest office.

"Shit," Steve exclaimed, realizing he had no weapon.

As more projectiles missed their mark, Steve peered through the crack of the open office door and saw the security guard racing down the corridor. He became the target, taking a bullet in his leg. He buckled to the floor and Steve reached out and grabbed him by the front of his shirt. With one jerk, the guard was in the office. Steve drew the guard's weapon as Abi checked his wounds.

"Nothing life threatening," she said. The guard was alert and started to say something. Abi whispered to him, and he was quiet. She helped him place his hand over the wound to stem the bleeding.

"The shooter is not an expert. Spent seven rounds by my count. I don't think he will advance on us now, certainly not when he sees we have a weapon. Abi, can you call security from this office? I would rather not have to flush this guy out alone."

"Yes." As she spoke, she gently leaned the wounded guard against a filing cabinet.

Abi called security and Steve shut the office door, moved them to the west wall, where there was a view of the entrance and grounds. Within seconds, guards were everywhere, trampling the very flowers that Abi had admired only minutes earlier. Steve dropped his weapon and raised his hands as the guards arrived, kicking in the door. Abi raised her hands, too, flashing her ID. A sergeant checked the badge and security backed off.

Paramedics took the wounded guard. The base was instantly sealed and placed on full alert. After a few minutes, during which base command staff appeared, a lieutenant came to fetch them. As guards conducted a thorough search of the building, which included the floor they were on and five stories below, the lieutenant led Steve and Abi down the corridor, pointing at 9mm shell casings on the floor.

The lieutenant spoke. "We will gather the casings and bullets for ballistics, but it will be a couple of hours before we can match them with a weapon. Every weapon authorized to be on this base has a ballistics record, so we have a good chance of naming the shooter. Or at least the person to whom the weapon is assigned."

"Great, lieutenant," said Abi. "However, we need to get to General Amit's office *now*." She flashed her ID once more.

"Yes, Ma'am," the lieutenant responded, motioning to follow.

The lieutenant knocked on the general's door. There was no answer, so with his weapon still drawn, he opened the door. They entered the outer office where Gideon's administrative assistant worked. Her body was slumped on the floor behind her desk. The lieutenant started toward the body, but Steve put his finger to his lips and pointed to the General's office. Quietly, the officer opened the inner door only to reveal what was left of the General's head, face down on his desk in a pool of blood. Pieces of skull and flesh had spattered the desk and nearby cabinets.

Steve stepped into the outer office and quickly returned. "Both shot in the back of the head at close range," he said. "About an hour ago."

"I need to call the Prime Minister, lieutenant," said Abi, worry creasing her forehead. She stabbed the lieutenant in the chest with her finger. "And *you* need to get the base commander to this office *immediately*."

As the lieutenant grabbed the transmitter pinned to his left shoulder, Abi was on her cell phone. "Put me through to the Prime Minister. I don't care if he is in a meeting, I must speak with him *now!*"

Abi nodded to the phone as if the Prime Minister were standing in front of them. Steve heard her say, "General Amit and his administrative assistant have been murdered."

The response was so loud, even Steve heard him exclaim "Oh my God!" *Welcome to our world, Mr. Prime Minister*, thought Steve.

Abi briefed the prime minister and hung up. "He is canceling his meetings for the rest of the day," she said. "He wants to keep the murders from the public for as long as possible. Based on the looks of security around here, it will leak in moments." She laughed, cynically. "Chacham," she called to the lieutenant, "never mind calling the base commander. Take us to him, now. The Prime Minister wants to hear from him immediately."

After a quick meeting with the base commander, Abi and Steve headed back to Tel Aviv. On the way, Abi's cell phone rang.

Steve caught bits and pieces of the conversation and Abi filled in the rest. By the time she was off the phone, they were traveling 120 kph in a 70 zone. Lieutenant Chacham from the air base called to tell her that the owner of the weapon fired at her and Steve was Captain Ovadia. *I bet it was the captain who walked through while we were at security reception,* Steve thought. *She looked too interested in visitors.* It was also the weapon used to kill General Amit and his assistant. *Well, doh, lieutenant.*

"The captain is not in custody," said Abi. "While they continue to conduct an exhaustive search, she is presumed to have left the air base. Shin Bet and Israel Police have been alerted."

"My guess is that she's on her way to Pädäh," Steve said. "It's the only place she can go now."

"We will deal with her soon," Abi said calmly, but with a flash of anger in her voice. Her foot pressed down on the pedal.

Abi pulled her car into the US Embassy compound, braking hard from warp speed outside the gate to avoid a violent reception from the Marine guards. Bill and General Jack Trevane, commander of the Black Watch, were huddled in Bill's small conference room. Maps and papers were taped on the walls and spread across the table. Brian was on the phone in an intense discussion with his London office.

When Bill saw Steve and Abi arrive, he stood erect, twisting his back to work out a kink. He sighed, as though the weight of the world was on his shoulders, and Steve thought that it probably was. *It's on all our shoulders.*

"Abi, I'm so sorry to hear the news of Gideon and his assistant," said Bill. "I know that he was dear to you and he's a great loss to Israel."

"Thank you, Bill. It is hard to believe. Harder still to know a member of his staff would do such a thing."

"We've been presented with many harsh facts lately, haven't we," he said rhetorically. "Abi, Steve, I'd like you to meet General Jack Trevane of the United States Army."

"It is a pleasure to meet you, General," Abi said extending her hand. She had done some research after learning that the renowned Black Jack

Trevane would be arriving in Israel. *Even at the age of sixty-one, he is a hunk,* thought Abi. She recalled a few highlights: West Point class of 1974; Airborne; Ranger; Special Forces. *All tough programs.* He had been awarded two silver stars and three purple hearts. *Good thing he has that big chest for all those medals.* Multiple tours in Iraq and Afghanistan; many, many classified assignments; and he is the only currently active duty general to command a combat unit of less than brigade strength. He is a battlefield legend and an expert on assaulting high-value fortified positions in enemy territory and rescuing hostages *anywhere.* He personally leads his men into battle. *Wish the IDF had a bunch of these guys.* Is now heading special combat unit, the Black Watch, part of USSOCOM, America's unified Special Operations Command, but assigned to Vic Alfonse. He was revered among warriors as a modern day Achilles without the benefit of having been dipped in the Styx. He was kind and unassuming, even humble, but no one fucked with Black Jack. All this she knew because she'd done her homework. But nothing had prepared her for his charm.

"Delighted," Jack responded with a great warm smile. "I wish we were meeting under more enjoyable circumstances."

"Thank you, General."

"Jack, please, Abi—if I may."

"Of course." *He's polite, too.*

"Abi," Bill broke in, "Major Navon from Strategic Command dropped off a sealed package for you. It must be the documentation that Gideon wanted you to have. The package is on my desk."

Abi fingered the package, thinking of the price of the documents inside. She tore the seal and examined the papers. Then she said to the group, "Yes, this is the documentation of the missile systems tests. It's very thorough. Gideon said he was absolutely sure, and this proves it. I will tell the Prime Minister. Excuse me for a moment." She walked over by the window and dialed a number on her cell phone and spoke for a few moments.

When she finished her call, Bill said, "Major Navon asked me to have you call him at a number you will find in the package."

She looked through the papers and found a handwritten note with a telephone number.

She picked up a secure handset, almost elbow to elbow with Brian, still on a London call. A man's voice answered. "Hello, Major." The call went on for several minutes and Abi asked him to hold.

"Steve," Abi said, cradling the handset, "Turns out Gideon had a premonition about Captain Ovadia, so he brought Major Navon in on what he was doing. The Major has assembled their teams for detaining the missile silo crews. They are awaiting a briefing tomorrow and are being barracked at a secure location with him until then. I have asked him to work with you to execute the detentions." She thrust the handset toward Steve.

"Thanks, Abi," Steve said, taking the handset. Steve spoke with Major Navon for fifteen minutes. He strolled, deep in thought, to the window with the view of the embassy's garden, absorbed in the fate of General Gideon Amit. *He knew he was a target, but he wouldn't quit. He shouldn't have let Ovadia get that close. Well, you're a dollar short and a day late with that advice, Steve, buddy.* Guilt settled in. It felt as if he couldn't save anyone lately. *Neena,* he thought, fear flooding through his body. *No way anything is happening to you.*

"I have to go to see Sergeant Harel. I'll be back in about two hours." *I can't just sit around.*

Thursday, May 1, 2014; Jaffa, Israel

Neena arrived early at Café Puaa so that she could check it out before David arrived. It was almost noon and the surrounding flea market, called Shuk Hapishpeshim in Hebrew, was in full swing. *Good,* she thought. *A very public place.* She had come up Rabbi Yohanan Street, circled the restaurant and now walked down the same street. She was looking for people who weren't shopping, people on roofs, beggars not collecting money—the out of place. She was satisfied. Finding nothing out of the ordinary fit her hypothesis: if David were going to have her killed, he would do it personally. By his own hand. Neena's pulse quickened at the thought of what she might be up against.

As she approached the restaurant, she saw David at one of the tables on the patio. She was not surprised that he, too, would be early. That was his style. He would also have inspected the area for the same reasons she had, if only out of habit.

"Neena," he called out, waving his left hand.

"Hello, David," she yelled back in acknowledgment, feigning delight. She made her way to the table and David bent down to his right side as if placing something on the floor, and then stood up to hug her. Somehow the hug was artificial, an empty motion that once had been filled with mutual love. They sat down, Neena backing her chair away from the table just enough to allow her arms freedom of movement. A waiter immediately brought menus.

"Would you like to order a beverage while you look over the menu?" he asked.

"Bottled water," Neena announced, before David could answer for her. David smiled and bowed his head slightly toward Neena to signal the waiter that he would have the same.

"What have you—and Steve—been finding out about the communications gaps?" David inquired, wasting no time.

Neena recognized his intent and took him on. "We have found that there are no authorized counterterrorism projects within Strategic Command, so we have been unable to verify what you told me."

"Are you certain?"

"As I assume you know, I made inquiries within Strategic Command. My doing so apparently distressed Captain Ovadia of Programs Security. We have also verified our findings with General Amit, who yesterday told us that no such projects exist."

"I must seem like a liar."

Neena bent slightly forward and, for only his ears, said, "You *are* a liar, David." She would have continued, but the waiter returned to the table with bottles of water, glasses and lemon wedges. The waiter realized that they had not looked at the menus and left. "Why have you lied? Why have you lied to *me*?"

"You ask this question and, yet, you have not been fully forthcoming with me," David said as he bent down again to his right and then straightened, adjusting his napkin on his lap with his left hand. "Someone has been running systems tests at Strategic Command and I believe that you, somehow, are behind that."

"Yes, I am," said Neena.

"And American Marines have been performing surveillance of Pädäh. Are you behind that as well?"

"No, I do not command those Marines," Neena parried.

"You are not answering my question."

"Very well. Yes, I am involved in that."

"And what have you learned?"

"Normally, I would not answer, but you already know the answer—you are engaged in a large defensive buildup at Pädäh." A party of five, led by one of the wait staff, walked passed the table. Neena took a sip of water, grateful for the momentary distraction. *Calm. That's what you need now.*

"And why would I be doing that?" David asked.

"Why don't you tell me?" Neena seethed with anger. *He has betrayed me and he is about to betray Israel. And now he's being* clever *with me?*

"Very well," said David. "I believe that armed forces will assault Pädäh to prevent what they believe is armed aggression toward our neighboring enemies."

"Are you planning such armed aggression?"

"No."

"Then, what *are* you planning? You are fortifying Pädäh for a reason." *How could I have loved him? He is an arrogant traitor.*

"I, or I should say *we* are not planning *aggression*. We are simply taking preemptive defensive action against fanatical regimes with an avowed purpose of annihilating Israel. It is not aggression if one is protecting one's country."

"How? By launching *every* Israeli land-based ballistic missile? By killing *tens of millions* of people, including *Israelis?*" *How dare he play this game with me!*

David leaned forward, bringing his left arm up onto the table. "Should we wait for the Islamists to strike first? We are *alone*, Neena—we have been alone since the time of Abraham. Who will come to our defense? The Americans? They have become fops and fools."

Neena watched the pupils of his eyes widen in anger, the words coming through clenched teeth. She listened as he went on. "The American public is complacent in the memory of their past power. They have deluded themselves about the threat of fanatical Islamists and pretend the world is Disneyland. They will pay dearly—not at my hand—but at the hand of Muslims, for becoming a country of self-indulgence and atrophied morals. And *certainly* the Europeans will not help us," David sneered as he accentuated the "s" sound like the hiss of a snake. "They have sold out as well to lives of least resistance—they avoid problems because they lack the discipline to deal with them. They have lost all sense of moral right. They are OPEC toadies. Do you not see the political reality?" David shot back in his chair, almost tipping it, and rubbed his forehead with his left hand.

"You don't have the right to do what you are planning to do!" Neena edged herself forward in her chair, placing more weight on her feet.

"*Rights?*" David spoke through a slight smile. "You talk of *rights?* Where was the United Nations when the Arabs attempted to overrun our new country in '48? The same United Nations that *created* our country by partitioning Palestine. The United Nations that stood by wringing its hands, watching as we fought with outmoded weapons against mechanized infantry and tanks."

David turned his head and looked at his right arm, hanging at his side. He looked back at Neena. His tone was calmer. "The world waited for the Arabs to win that war and solve the 'Jewish problem' for good. No one has *ever* cared about *our* rights. The UN General Assembly has passed over *three hundred* resolutions condemning Israel. The Security Council has passed over *seventy* similar resolutions. I have stopped counting." Neena saw his jaw clenching again. "And how many UN resolutions have there been condemning other countries for launching tens of thousands of rockets into our kibbutzes and towns, for supplying and supporting suicide bombers who kill our women and children, for kidnapping and killing our citizens and soldiers?"

David did not wait for an answer. "The answer is *one*. No one gives a *shit* about our rights," he spat as he clenched his large left hand so tight that its veins stood out like blue pasta, "so I don't give a *damn* about theirs. I care *only* about *Israel*."

"How can you say you care about Israel," Neena asked, "when you are ready to destroy it?" Neena adjusted the clothing on her right side. *Be ready. It will come soon.*

David relaxed his left hand, putting it in his lap. "What we will do on Saturday *may* destroy Israel—I happen to believe that Israel will survive—but if we take no action, Israel is *certain* to be annihilated, along with its troublesome Jews. Why? Because with every passing day, the fanatical Islamist regimes become stronger with oil revenues and the armed support of outside parties—China and Russia among them. There is no winning a war that *they* launch—there is only the *possibility* of winning a war that *we* launch. As far as I am concerned, this *is* the Armageddon."

Neena did not let her expression change when she heard the word "Saturday". She made a mental note of it. *David is not as guarded because he sees no way for us to stop him. I will let him keep that illusion.*

"David, you are insane. Our God is stronger than what you presume in your plan. We overcame bondage in Egypt and the Babylonian Captivity—even the Holocaust. I cannot condone what you are doing. You are planning another holocaust, and I will do whatever I can to stop you—it may not be enough—but I will try."

"Neena, I am sorry that you cannot see. There is no stopping us. We control the missiles—I know you know that—and you can't stop us in the time left to launch. Even if we lose some missiles, those that we *do* launch will result in full retaliation. I have won. Israel has won."

He grasped the Jaguar 941, its silencer in place, more firmly in his right hand. Still holding it under the table, he tilted it upward to fire. Neena, trained by the best—the man with the gun—had been watching David use only his left hand—an unnatural act—and was ready. Just as he fired, she lunged to the right, twisting her body to extend her right hand, her Tanto gleaming, to slash at David's neck.

His silent bullet blew through Neena's empty chair, smashing into a copper pot in a flea market stall across the street, clanging loudly. With his right hand and forearm under the table, he could not stand fast enough to avoid her blade. He arose just enough for her knife to miss its mark and gash his upper left shoulder. Blood flooded his clothing.

David fumbled bringing his weapon from under the table. Before he could fire again, Neena shoved the table into him, ran into the café and through the kitchen. People screamed at the sudden vicious movements, the sight of blood.

David calmly placed his weapon in his shoulder holster and easily jumped the low hedge outlining the patio, trailing dots of blood like crumbs. Witnesses told the police that a couple had had a violent quarrel and had left. Fifteen minutes later, the café was back to normal.

Neena ran two blocks and caught a taxi back to the hotel. She knew that David would not follow. The hotel was busy and she took the stairs to avoid eye contact in a crowded elevator. Steve wasn't in the room. *That's right, he is with Abi,* she reminded herself. She sat on the couch and pulled out her bloodstained Tanto knife to clean it. She turned and looked out onto the balcony and remembered how Steve looked that afternoon just a few days ago. She thought of how he held her. *I miss you terribly, Steve. You were right about David. And about me.* She stood up to take a shower and wait for her beloved.

Thursday, May 1, 2014; Pädäh, Jerusalem, Israel

David Alon's car stopped abruptly at the guardhouse at the entrance to Pädäh. He had wrapped his jacket around his shoulder wound to stem the loss of blood, but his entire left side was bloody. The guard opened the entrance and called the watch commander, no doubt alarmed by the blood, judging by the guard's fright-filled face. As David pulled into the courtyard, a medic raced toward him. David waved him off, telling him to come to his office instead. As he walked into the building, he took time to look at the construction and placement of the new ordnance. *Well, at least that is coming together,* he thought.

He told Sergeant Zee Shachar, at his desk in the outer chamber of David's office, to follow him. The medic trailed behind and once inside, examined David's wound, collapsing the gash with a handsome row of stitches. He set up a plasma drip to replenish the lost blood. David was annoyed by the encumbrance of the drip and the second the medic left, he ripped it out, tossing the bag to the floor. Straw-yellow fluid spattered the gray walls as the bag split open.

David saw the surprise on Zee's face. "Some difficulties with Ms. Shahud," David offered. "A strong difference of opinion I am afraid. Irreconcilable." He slapped a bandage onto the needle hole.

"I am sorry, Colonel. I know that Neena means very much to you."

"I think we have to say 'meant'." David pulled a clean shirt from a closet and put it on.

Zee blurted, "Did you kill her?"

"No, Zee. I tried, but I trained her too well. My shot missed even though a second before I had the barrel no more than twelve inches from her stomach."

"I assume your shoulder wound is from her."

"Yes, as I was firing, she lunged at me with one of her Tanto knives. I did a spectacular job with her. I am very proud of her." David offered a weak smile as he tucked the shirt into his trousers.

"Yet, you tried to kill her. And you would kill her now if you had the opportunity."

"All true, Zee. I love her as a niece still, but we are on opposite sides of this and I will not allow anything—or anybody—to stop it." He retrieved his Jaguar from the holster lying on a chair, placed it on his desk.

"Again, I am sorry, sir."

"Thank you, Zee. Is Captain Ovadia here? I heard she might have sought refuge."

"Yes, Colonel. She arrived just after you left for Jaffa. She is in the officer's quarters."

"Tell her to report to me. Thank you. That is all."

Two whiskeys later, Captain Ovadia knocked on David's open door. "Reporting as requested, Colonel," she said.

"Thank you, Captain. Please come in."

She entered the office and saluted. He returned the salute and motioned with his right hand to have a seat by his desk. "Captain, can you tell me about the events of today and General Amit?"

"Of course, Colonel. I had been alerted to inquiries made this past Monday, the 28th, regarding the existence of a counterterrorism project commissioned within Strategic Command. I also learned that General Amit had made similar inquiries yesterday and had set in motion a full systems test of the missile targeting and control systems. The results of those tests, which I could not prevent, undoubtedly demonstrated that Strategic Command cannot control the missiles. As a result, I concluded that General Amit needed to be silenced to prevent further exposure of our project." David reached for a walnut, placed it in the palm of his right hand and compressed it into a pile of organic matter.

Captain Ovadia waited for David's attention and then continued. "At eight thirty-seven this morning, I entered his office and killed his assistant with my silenced 9mm. I grabbed her body and placed it on the floor behind her desk, continued into the General's office, where I found him. I said I had important documents to show him so that I might get close. As I walked behind his desk, I shot him in the back of the head."

"Thank you, Captain, for that full report. Now, a question—in what way do you think your actions have retarded the discovery of our project?"

"Well, sir, General Amit will not be available to provide testimony to any security agency."

"Do you think that his testimony is necessary given your understanding of the documented results of the systems tests that he ordered to be performed?"

"Not necessary, sir, but . . ."

"Thank you, Captain." David picked through the remains of the walnut, found a few pieces of nutmeat and ate them. "I have another question—what do you believe is the status of Strategic Command at this point?"

"The base is sealed and on full alert, sir." She rubbed the scar on her temple.

"Do you think that the fact that the entire base is sealed and on full alert will be noticed by higher authorities and will cause greater focus on the matter?"

"No doubt, sir."

"And do you think that the involvement and focus of higher authorities is a positive development for our project, covered by the Masada Protocol, which you and I signed under oath?"

"No, sir."

"So, Captain Ovadia, you murdered two people whose testimony you say is not necessary to substantiate the documented results of the systems tests and whose murders will bring increased scrutiny by higher authorities. Is that a fair assessment?"

"Yes, sir."

"One more thing, Captain. On whose orders were you acting?"

"No orders, sir," Captain Ovadia stated. With a firm tone, she continued, "I interpreted the situation and initiated the actions I thought necessary."

"Which you have just agreed were either ineffective in achieving their purpose or possibly detrimental to our project here. Is that correct?" David turned and brushed the walnut remains into his trash basket.

"Yes, sir."

"Are your actions covered by the Masada Protocol?"

"No, sir. The Protocol states that all orders regarding the killing of Israeli citizens are to be issued directly by you, sir."

"Captain, would you also brief me on the attempted killings of Abital Zahavi and the American Steve Barber?"

"Sir, I knew that Ms. Zahavi was the one who had ordered General Amit to perform the systems tests. Furthermore, I overheard Ms. Zahavi and Mr. Barber at the security desk telling the guard that they were there to see General Amit. I concluded that they were a threat to our project as well and made the decision to kill them."

"But you did not kill them, did you, Captain?"

"No, sir."

"And what do you imagine to be the consequences of an attempt on the lives of a noted and respected member of the Israeli government and an American working for the Undersecretary of Defense for Special Operations?"

"I imagine that both governments are agitated, sir."

"I concur with you. The reasons you offer for your actions have proved to be fatuous, as you have agreed. Further, our government and that of the American are in a much higher state of alert. You have disobeyed the Masada Protocol and severely jeopardized this project, Captain."

"I understand, sir. I am sorry, sir."

"Captain, what are your duties here at Pädäh?"

"I have none assigned, sir."

"Do you have combat experience, Captain?"

"No, sir. Although I took the compulsory IDF weapons training, I have spent my entire career in computer science and data processing environments."

"Too, bad," David said, lifting his Jaguar 941, shooting her in the middle of the forehead. As her head jerked up and her body flew backwards off the chair, he said, "I might have made an exception for a warrior."

On hearing the shot, Zee raced into the office, stared at Captain Ovadia's punctured head, the swelling pool of blood around it. "Zee, have someone bury the traitorous Captain and close the facility. Call in all agents and troops. We are under general quarters as of now."

"Yes, Colonel. And what should I tell the men and women about Captain Ovadia?"

"Tell them that the Captain paid the price of ignoring the Masada Protocol and threatening the future of Israel. That is all, Sergeant."

Zee knew that when the Colonel addressed him by rank, the conversation was over. He left to get help with the Captain's body and to relay David's orders to the watch commander. Pädäh had become a fortress, now christened with death.

Thursday, May 1, 2014; New York, NY, USA and London, England

Brian initiated a conference call from Bill Elsberry's office in Tel Aviv to check on the National Iranian Oil Company deal. Joe Burstein was on in New York and the senior debt trader spoke from London. The call would last hours as every piece of this historic transaction was reviewed.

As Brian expected, teams of lawyers were meeting wherever space could be found: conference rooms, private offices, break rooms, and hotel rooms. The teams were huddled over documents that would transfer nearly $100 billion of refinery assets to legal entities jointly owned by the National Iranian Oil Company and about twenty integrated oil companies and independent refiners. Simultaneous with the creation of the legal entities, nearly $100 billion was transferred to the sellers of the refinery assets, who, in turn, purchased about $25 billion in Iraq/Iran infrastructure bonds, which were delivered to bank custodians.

While he was on the call, Brian made sure that entire groups of employees working at the refineries were being terminated by the selling companies and hired by the newly created legal entities, which, going forward would own and run the refineries. Payroll data, 401(k) plans, pension and other benefits information were transferred to three outsourcing firms—one each in the United States, Europe, and India—that would provide payroll and benefits administration to the new entities. New general ledger systems and charts of account were needed for each new entity as well. There were large project teams on three continents overseeing these and a myriad of other operational details that must occur for the continuous operation of the refineries under new legal entities spanning more than seventeen national borders and thirty-five taxation and labor law jurisdictions. This work would continue for the next four or five weeks. Brian was pleased. *The details can kill a deal, or worse, its profitability.*

While this was happening, duly authorized agents of the new legal entities were signing tolling agreements that would govern how the entities would process crude oil, charge customers, including the selling oil companies, and distribute profits. Chandler Hines Kendrick was a financial machine, focusing on every detail so that each part of the complete transaction would stand up, if necessary, in court.

A successful challenge to any element of the deal might cause the delicate and intricate structure of the transaction to crumble. Brian did not want the deal to fall apart because someone failed to have the proper notary public affirmation used on some document. He wanted to ensure that, if the Iranian members of the newly formed Swiss consulting firm, to whom he would soon send nearly $500 million, were in for a penny, they were in for the whole fucking pound.

Brian was nervous but it didn't show. He was used to the intricacies of these transactions. He wasn't pacing, partly because of his bum knee and partly because he had a headache. *They have no idea what's going on here in Israel,* he thought running his hand repeatedly through his hair. Brian was glad that Joe was his working partner on this deal. The kid kept his cool.

At five-thirty in the afternoon Tel Aviv time, the deal was closed, piles of documents executed, and monies transferred. By eight o'clock that evening, the London and New York deal teams, the members of which had been working over one hundred hours each week for the last month, were on their way to spectacularly expensive closing dinners.

Afterward, Brian left the US Embassy, returned to his Tel Aviv hotel, and celebrated with one of his usual Bombay Sapphire martinis straight up, with which he toasted himself and the firm. It was done. Tomorrow, Khoemi and the rest of the boys would find that the entire $500 million, deposited today into their brand spanking new Swiss bank accounts, had been attached for the next twenty years by the Swiss insurance authorities. That will negate the political advantage the Iranians wanted to gain with the deal. But Brian had another reason to celebrate a successful closing of the deal. He was going to use the Iranians' greed against them one more time to try to save Israel from annihilation. *Only one drink tonight, old boy. You need to be sharp tomorrow.*

Chapter Seventeen
Friday, May 2, 2014; On the Coast North of Tel Aviv, Israel

The Prime Minister had decided to have the meeting at his summer residence on the coast north of Tel Aviv near Ga'Ash. Senior officials from Shin Bet, the, Strategic Command, IDF and its Directorate for Military Intelligence, along with key members of the intelligence and armed services committees in the Knesset had been summoned. The Prime Minister's entire cabinet would be there as well. Most had very limited information about the purpose of the meeting. Those from Shin Bet and Strategic Command were more informed because they were already involved. Bill watched as they arrived, some as early as seven fifteen in the morning.

Security was tight, and special units closely examined the credentials of everyone, even those of well-known public figures, stopping limousines as they wound up the drive running along the untamed coastline. The gathering had the thick air of meetings dealing with threats of death and destruction. They chatted and joked in subdued tones as the Prime Minister's wait staff poured coffee. The group took their cups and plates of fresh fruit and pastries, and assembled in the main dining room, which had been set up to accommodate the thirty or so people who were there. The summoned were calm and confident, having dealt with critical situations in the past. That was about to change.

At five minutes to eight, the Prime Minister entered the room and urged everyone to take a seat. The wait staff disappeared as though sucked away in a rip current. Aides distributed numbered documents stamped "Top Secret", which would be collected before the meeting ended. Entering with the Prime Minister were four people, one of whom was well known to the group: Abital Zahavi. She stood at the front of the room, swaying a little, her expression grim. She wore a well-fitting gray suit, the color no doubt matching her mood. Bill discreetly touched her elbow, hoping that she understood that his intention was to empathize. He, too, felt the gravity of this day.

Some in the room knew Bill, but only as the American military attaché from the US Embassy. No one there knew the enormous political power he wielded within the American government or the changes he hoped to make. He would *demand* a better alliance between America and Israel. *Assuming I survive the next few days.* He thought about the men and women at his embassy. Most had families and they cared deeply about a better world. *If we can save it, perhaps we can make it better.*

Bill was sure that no one in the room knew his other two colleagues. He imagined they would judge the man, Steve, to be an American with a military connection and the woman, Neena, to be an Israeli, or possibly an Arab, judging by her coloration and dress.

Soon, the room was quiet and the Prime Minister welcomed the assemblage and thanked them for making the journey to his residence. He introduced Bill, Abi, Steve and Neena, who had entered with him. Then, he went on, "Each of you has received a numbered document marked 'Top Secret', which is available to you only while you are here for reasons that will become obvious in a few minutes."

He waited for complete silence and in his deep voice, loud enough to reach the entire room, announced, "I have asked you all here because I have great reason to fear that Simon Luegner and David Alon, known to all of you, intend to launch all of our land-based ballistic missiles at sundown this Saturday, the beginning of Memorial Day, at 167 targets in the Middle East."

The Prime Minister had barely gotten the words out of his mouth, when the room erupted with cries and shouts. There were several who could only put their faces in the palms of their hands and remain quiet. Bill knew how they felt. It was what he had done when finally alone the night before—put his head in his hands in anguish.

Spreading his arms, palms down, the Prime Minister hushed the crowd, and then continued, "I appreciate that these allegations, which is all that they are now to you, are jolting. The individuals I introduced earlier will present the evidence, and you will have the opportunity to ask questions. I am convinced of the threat. This morning, I will seek your authority to engage a special unit of the United States armed forces under the command of Colonel Abi Zahavi for the purpose of assaulting Pädäh, David Alon's headquarters, and regaining control of our ballistic missile systems." He paused for only a second. "It is a sad day for Israel that we are forced to strike against our own."

The Prime Minister went on. "Abi will brief you on the events leading up to today. Bill Elsberry will brief you on the US combat unit and also the preparations underway with the US Navy to provide ballistic missile defense capabilities. Steve Barber and Neena Shahud are available to answer questions also. I must ask you, because time is of absolute essence, to pay close attention. Thank you. Abi, would you bring the group up to date, please?"

Abi stepped forward and presented the events of the past two weeks in chronological order. She provided a thorough briefing, including the nature and extent of the new fortifications and armaments made over the past two days to and within Pädäh, which had gone incommunicado as of five o'clock the prior afternoon.

At each relevant point in her presentation, Abi directed the group to examine evidence contained in the package. There were signed affidavits and documented missile system tests, the completeness and accuracy of which General Amit had verbally verified and Major Navon had attested in writing. There were enlarged photographs and annotated satellite images of Pädäh taken over the last three days. Several people asked for clarifications, which Abi, Bill, Steve, and Neena answered according to their experience and realm of expertise.

"Ms. Zahavi," the chair of the intelligence committee began, "You have made an excellent presentation, but you have provided little hard evidence that Simon Luegner, a man of courage and devotion to Israel, and David Alon, a legend, are connected to the virus in the missile systems. You have ably demonstrated that Strategic Command does not now command the targeting and control systems, but you have not proved who, if anyone, does. We, or at least I, need more than this circumstantial evidence before I can countenance a large scale military assault, by a foreign power I might add, such as the Prime Minister is proposing."

Abi turned to the Prime Minister, who motioned to a military aide to dim the lights and bring out video conferencing equipment. As the aide set up the equipment, the Prime Minister said, "I have sent members of my personal security team to Pädäh. They are there and they have full authority and the required security clearances to enter Pädäh. Let us watch as they attempt to do so."

The Prime Minister spoke through a live feed to his three security personnel. Two would attempt to enter Pädäh and the third would remain at a distance to observe and video the attempt. The two agents attempting to enter were equipped with audio and video pickups, which would allow the ensuing events to be televised in real time during the meeting.

The crowd heard the Prime Minister give the order to gain access. "They are to ask to speak with David Alon personally. I have placed five calls to Pädäh myself, not one of which has been answered." He turned toward one of the three monitors displaying the video and announced, "My men are starting toward the gate. Let's watch together."

The group was silent. The video shook on the monitors as the men approached the entry gate. While both men were outfitted with pickups, the monitor would display one agent's transmission and, if that failed, the second agent's transmission. The two reached the entry gate.

"Sergeant, I am Agent Peled," said the figure transmitting the video. "I am a member of the Prime Minister's personal security team. Here are my credentials and identity card. We are requesting entry and a meeting with David Alon."

"Sorry, sir, but my orders are to allow no one entry to the compound."

"Sergeant, I am on official government business and demand access. I insist on speaking with David Alon."

The guard stepped into his gatehouse to answer the telephone. He came out a few seconds later. "Colonel Alon will meet you here. Please wait. Also, please keep your hands visible." The guard pointed to the roof of the building inside the wall, and the two agents of the Prime Minister took an involuntary step back as they saw rifle barrels and scopes aimed at them. There was a collective gasp from the viewers. Steve took Neena's hand as they, too, watched the screen, mesmerized and worried.

Within minutes, David Alon, in military fatigues and armed with an Uzi, had reached the inside of the compound wall near the gate. He stepped through a small door, walked up to the gatehouse, facing the two agents. "How may I help you and the Prime Minister today?" Steve recognized David's expression. It was one of disdain.

"Colonel," Agent Peled said, "We have orders from the Prime Minister to enter Pädäh and examine the compound."

"I am sorry, but that is not possible."

"Sir, our orders come from the Prime Minister himself," the agent said as he held out a paper signed by the Prime Minister.

Steve surveyed the group at the Prime Minister's home to gauge their reaction to the video. All sat transfixed, and some cringed as David didn't bother to look at the paper. "The Prime Minister has no authority here," said David, his voice loud and clear. "I must ask you to leave immediately or we will conclude that you are a threat to this installation. The consequences of that conclusion would be deadly."

The group saw on the edge of the monitors that the non-transmitting agent, Agent Har-Even, attempted to draw his weapon. There were multiple loud 'pops' heard. The picture on the monitors jumped, jerked and turned skyward, coming to rest sideways, showing the body of Agent Har-Even, his head and torso ravaged by bullets. The third agent was screaming into his transmitter, "They've been shot! They've been shot!" The monitor showed the video pickup turning upward again. David's stern face was seen close up on the monitors. "*You* have done this," he declared, and the transmission ended.

A few moments of disbelief followed and then he meeting room erupted. "Silence!" the Prime Minister shouted. "We are *all* shocked by this, but *now* you have your proof! David Alon and his followers are acting outside our government. With the evidence presented this morning and what you have just seen with your own eyes, there can be no doubt. Does anyone *still* not believe that we are facing a nuclear holocaust?" The room was silent. Steve looked at Neena. She was still as a stone, her expression grim.

The Prime Minister's aide shut off the equipment. "Bill, please brief the group on General Jack Trevane and his command. Also, please review the assets of the US Navy that will be available to help us."

"Of course, Mr. Prime Minister." Bill described General Trevane's background and the capabilities of the Black Watch Command. He reported the number and type of ships positioned in the Mediterranean and Red Sea, assigned to assist with the destruction of any missiles launched. Bill was sweating although the room was quite cool. "The maximum number of missiles it's possible for us to intercept is likely to be less than thirty-five, based on the configuration of weaponry and location of our ships. Thirty-five total outgoing and incoming. So the ability of the US Navy to protect Israel from retaliation depends upon how many outgoing Israeli missiles have to be destroyed."

As Bill finished, someone shouted, "Why not let them launch the missiles?" The room was instantly still. Someone had asked *the* question. Bill sat down, exhausted. He turned to look at Steve and Neena, shook his head in frustration.

The Prime Minister answered, "I am not surprised at that question. I have asked myself the very same one. My answer is that I do not have information that leads me to conclude that we are better off creating a holocaust that will kill tens, perhaps hundreds, of millions of people. I am not so empty of hope that I can condone such a holocaust after we have spent decades condemning the last one."

"What will happen to our defensive capability—what will happen to the missiles?"

Steve stood up and checked his microphone. He motioned to the Prime Minister, who nodded that Steve should answer. "First, Alon and Luegner control your only land-based missiles. These represent the vast majority of your throw weight in terms of nuclear warheads, but not all. You still have considerable nuclear weaponry based on submarines and aircraft. As for the land-based missiles, tomorrow morning we'll be rounding up the missile silo crews—as Abi has briefed you. Without the crews, the missiles cannot be launched. Strategic Command can re-populate the silos with vetted crews or newly trained crews—it is a matter of how long that will take. Also, your missiles, which are equipped with MIRVs, multiple independently targetable reentry vehicles, are now locked on overlapping targets. Even in the event that we cannot change targeting for a few days, we *can* identify the targets for each missile. You can launch every remaining missile—those that are not launched by David Alon—on a one-by-one basis against selected targets until the virus is removed from the targeting and control systems. What you won't be able to do in the interim is to re-target your missiles to concentrate on any one country."

The Prime Minister rushed to add, "I have the assurance of the American President that the US will stand with us militarily. He is prepared to make both private and public statements to that effect."

"A little late for that," said someone. "That will be the day," said another. The taunts continued for a few moments more.

"Ladies and gentlemen," Steve strode forward, speaking in a loud and firm tone, his sudden movement and voice causing the room to fall silent, "while you believe that you have legitimate grievances regarding our foreign policy, I remind you that the United States, as we speak, is committing thirty ships and the twenty thousand men and women on board those ships to the defense of Israel. We are also committing combat troops—our *best* combat troops—to prevent the spectacle of Israelis fighting Israelis. *And* we have every reason to believe that our losses will be *extremely heavy* in assaulting Pädäh." Steve struggled to keep his anger out of his tone.

"My country has *always* honored its defense pacts and we will do so *now* in defense of Israel. So, as you heap contempt on the president of my country, I ask that you pray for those Americans who will soon die to save *your* country. I remind you also that this plot—this planned *holocaust*, by agents of *your* government—has been uncovered by actions initiated by the government of the United States without which you would *all be dead* tomorrow night." He took two steps back.

The room was deathly silent. The Prime Minister cleared his throat and said in a calm, somber voice, a voice so quiet that ears froze and strained to hear, "I ask your approval to allow foreign military personnel to engage any and all Israeli and any other forces present at Pädäh for the purpose of subduing those forces and taking control of the compound and all computer facilities there."

He took a deep breath and now projected his voice strongly. "General Jack Trevane has agreed that Abi Zahavi, a reserve Colonel in the IDF and combat experienced, will command the operation. I also ask approval of the use of deadly force, as necessary, by the teams being sent out early tomorrow morning to detain the sixty-eight missile silo crews. May I see the hands of those approving these actions?" Everyone raised his or her hand. The room remained quiet except for the sound of a few chairs moving and a choked sob coming from the back row.

The Prime Minister continued, his voice returning to normal volume, the voice of the leader that he was. "You and I are shocked by what we face. With the help of our friends, we *will* prevent the catastrophe that Simon Luegner and David Alon have planned. I am sure you understand why we must keep this situation to ourselves for now. Secrecy is *critical*. We need to regain control of our ballistic missile systems and we *will do so.*" The Prime Minister surveyed the eyes before him.

"We need to ensure that our neighbors do not use this event to launch military action against our country. We will be working with the American president and the Americans with us today to do that. For now, that is what we *must* concentrate on. We understand our obligation to report this calamity, and I will prepare a public statement. I will keep you informed. Please pray for our deliverance. Shalom."

The room emptied quietly, with people speaking in muffled tones. The packages marked "Top Secret" were collected and accounted for by number. Steve, Neena, Bill, and Abi waited to have a moment with the Prime Minister.

"Thank you all for your diligence," the Prime Minister said as he offered his hand to each.

"Mr. Prime Minister," Steve replied. "We need to get back to the US Embassy and prepare for the formal briefing of our president." He looked around at the faces in the small group and added, "Perhaps the good of this is that we have come to see more clearly why our countries have been friends and allies since the birth of Israel—we choose peace over war, love over hatred, and right over wrong—sometimes at great cost. Shalom."

"Shalom, my *friends,*" said the Prime Minister.

Steve couldn't help but think that he and Neena had chosen each other, too, for very much the same reasons. Yet even after Neena's lunch with David, there was a distance between them, as though their countries wanted them to choose love or loyalty. *Why can't it be both?*

Friday, May 2, 2014; Zurich, Switzerland

Brian looked forward to this day. He knew that, at precisely nine o'clock in the morning, Zurich time, an agent of CHK would deliver ten copies of a large, professionally bound actuarial report, certified as to its authenticity, to the Director of Financial Compliance, Swiss Federal Office of Private Insurance. That report contained new actuarial calculations supporting the equity capital calculation of a newly formed insurance company in Switzerland.

Brian also knew that the new actuarial report would receive expedited treatment. Vic Alfonse had seen to that. Later that day, the Swiss Federal Office of Private Insurance would issue instructions to the Swiss Federal Banking Commission to attach all the assets of the identified accounts in the specified banks enumerated in Exhibit A to the instructions. Again with Vic's help, Brian knew that the Swiss Federal Banking Commission would act instantly upon those instructions.

Following the attachment of the accounts, the banks in which the accounts were established would issue notices to each account holder in compliance with the instructions provided by the account holder. Eleven people in Iran would receive telephone calls from their bankers in Switzerland by the close of business Friday to the effect that the roughly $500 million deposited in their collective accounts had been attached.

The Swiss Federal Office of Private Insurance would have issued a statement announcing that a meeting with the Swiss Federal Office of Private Insurance for parties subject to the attachment orders would be held on Monday, May 12, at eleven o'clock. The statement would note also that the Swiss Federal Office of Private Insurance would accept no telephone calls or respond to other communications until after that meeting had taken place.

During the day, Brian placed phone calls from Tel Aviv to track the progress of these events in Zurich. At six o'clock in the evening, he placed his last call. It was done. Brian knew he would hear from the Iranians. He was prepared. *Fuck Rezvani.*

Friday, May 2, 2014; Washington, DC, USA

The President of the United States started the meeting precisely at seven o'clock in the morning. Abi, Bill, Neena, Steve, and Jack Trevane were participating by videoconference from Bill's secure conference room. In addition to the president and all but one member of his Cabinet (the Secretary of State had been sent the prior evening to Tehran), the council included the Joint Chiefs of Staff, the directors of the CIA and NSA, the chairmen of the Congressional Intelligence, Armed Services and Foreign Affairs/Relations committees, and Vic Alfonse. As the monitor panned across the men and women assembled with the president, Steve could see deep lines on Vic's face and guessed that he'd had little sleep.

The president began, "Vic Alfonse has been briefing me hourly and I have been keeping you aware of frightening developments in the Middle East. Earlier today, the Israeli Prime Minister held a special meeting for his top people. His government concluded that a rogue group of highly placed individuals in Israel's security agencies have gained exclusive and absolute control over the country's land-based nuclear ballistic missile capability and intend to launch the entire complement sometime after sundown Saturday—less than eighteen hours from now—at 167 targets in neighboring countries. I have convened this council to authorize the deployment of US Navy ships and American combat personnel to deal with this threat."

At this point, the President asked Bill Elsberry to introduce the people in his conference room in Tel Aviv and, as Abi had done with the Prime Minister, to brief the council on what had transpired over the course of the past several days. Bill ran the briefing. Steve covered the key events and presented the logic analysis that led to the conclusion that Israel's nuclear arsenal was now under the control of David Alon and Simon Luegner. Forty-three minutes later, following a number of questions being asked and answered, Bill concluded the briefing.

The president continued, "I think we can now be thankful of the build up of the Navy's anti-ballistic missile capability. Unfortunately, the capability is limited in comparison with the need, and the prospect of one or more Israeli missiles striking its target is real. Furthermore, several nations in the Middle East have consistently acted as an aggressor toward Israel. Consequently, we must also face the prospect that Middle East governments, particularly Iran, may consider retaliation, either with conventional forces or, in Iran's case, nuclear weapons. We *cannot* allow that to happen."

The president sat back in his chair, the American flag and seal directly behind him in the video. *No beating about the bush*, Steve thought. The president continued, "In addition to my request for deployment of American military assets, I am going to Israel until this matter has been resolved and stability has returned to the Middle East."

"Mr. President," the Chairman of the Senate Select Committee on Intelligence spoke in an authoritative tone, "your presence in Israel could be interpreted as our being complicit in the Israeli action. We could face complete repudiation by governments where diplomatic progress has been made."

"Our diplomatic progress has been a sham, and you, more than others, are aware of that," the president said, with a dismissive wave of his hand. "As to my presence being misinterpreted, I sent the Secretary of State to Tehran with a message that the United States, under mutual defense agreements dating back to 1952, will take any and all actions required to fulfill our commitments under those various agreements, including the use of military force."

The president jabbed his right index finger on the leather blotter in front of him. "My presence will be explained as America's commitment to peace in the Middle East. Our ambassadors to the other target countries will carry similar messages to those governments. I am not going to let Israel or any other country let loose a nuclear or conventional war leading to the destruction of the Middle East."

"Why should we get involved in this?" asked the Chairman of the House Foreign Relations Committee.

"I see how a Middle East laid waste might have great appeal superficially, but let me point out what I see as the risks. First, no one in this room, Tehran, the Kremlin, or anywhere else has a clue as to what would be the outcome—in military, economic, human suffering, and societal terms—of a catastrophe of that proportion. That means we don't even know what we don't know. It's impossible to assess risks when you don't even know what they are. That scares me."

Watching the president on the monitor, Steve to himself, *a president who admits to being scared. Now we're getting somewhere.* He found Neena's hand under the conference table. Neena looked at him, smiling in way that told him she agreed.

"Second," the president continued as the camera zoomed to a close-up shot, "whatever would happen, vacuums would be created by the destruction of countries, governments, and infrastructure. We all know that vacuums are filled almost immediately and, again, we will have little control over how those vacuums are filled. Europe, on its knees and shattered as it was at the end of World War II, does not come close to comparing to the chaos of the Middle East were Israel to blow it up."

The camera zoomed out and captured the faces of many of the people in the room deep underground in Washington. Steve saw strain on some faces, but others seemed unbothered. Some still beamed what Steve thought looked like phony electioneering smiles. *What are they thinking? That several hundred megatons of nuclear detonations is a* regional *problem? Dumb shits!*

"Third, most parties to the current mess have a stake in a better outcome and they have a stake in stability. Our goal for the Middle East should be stability and peace—I don't think there is an outcome beyond that available to us in our lifetimes."

The president looked at the Chairman and then at the others assembled. "Let's acknowledge that Alon and Luegner are heroes, gentlemen, though misguided in our minds. They are not typical radical elements. They are not crackpots." He turned back and looked directly at the Chairman. "What is most striking to me is the sheer desperation and anxiety that these men must feel for their country. This is what has led them to take these steps. Think of it! They and their supporters are so distraught, so hopeless of a future for their country that they would *obliterate* it and the surrounding geography for *hundreds of miles.*"

Steve was nodding his head. *He gets it. He understands.* He looked at Neena and found her absorbed in watching the president. *Maybe she'll believe now that Israel has a true friend.*

"The point I make to you now," the president continued, "and will make to the governments of Israel's neighbors, is that David Alon is not alone. Others in Israel must be as despairing. So, if Israel's neighbors do not want to live in the shadow of terror that David Alon has planned, they had better do one of two things. One is to wipe Israel off the map, and I will not let them do that. The other is to find a way to a lasting, tangible peace."

Steve watched the monitor as the camera slowly panned the president's conference room, which had erupted in voices and shouts. He looked over to see Neena wipe away a tear. *Those are tears of hope*, he told himself.

"Gentlemen," the president said as he stood, the camera zooming out. He folded his leather bound notebook as he waited for quiet. "If there are no more questions, I will accept with thanks your approval of my requests."

The monitor went dark in Tel Aviv. "That was one impressive display of leadership," Steve said. Others nodded. Abi and Neena were swapping tissues. "Let's get back to work. Brian is expecting an irate phone call from some upset Iranians and I need to be there to help." *I'm gonna love that call.*

Friday, May 2, 2014; The American Embassy, Tel Aviv, Israel

Brian did not take part in the videoconference and instead used the time to update reports, spreading out papers and his laptop on Bill's desk. He nibbled on wheat toast with blackberry jam and sipped his second cup of coffee. Bill's assistant poked his head around the door. "Mr. Kendrick, I have your New York office on hold. Shall I forward the call here?"

"Yes, thank you, Mr. Palun."

Brian picked up the telephone as a red light blinked. "Brian," Joe Burstein's voice croaked, "Sa'ad-Oddin Rezvani called here in a rage thirty minutes ago."

"Well, we've been expecting Mr. Rezvani's call," said Brian calmly. "I'm sure we will hear from the others as well. Did he leave a number?" *Didn't take him long.*

"He left that and a bunch of threats."

"Joe, we anticipated this. I would be worried if he *didn't* call. I'll speak with him. Please have Mr. Crossley of AAD call me here. We will need to step up security."

When he hung up the telephone, the others had returned from the conference room. Brian shared his news with satisfied smile, "The Swiss authorities have attached the assets of our Iranian friends. I need to call Mr. Rezvani and deal with his disappointment.

"Brian," Steve said, "Mind if Neena and I listen?"

"Please do. Ready for your part?"

"Yes, and wild horses couldn't keep me away from this call to our Iranian friend."

Before Brian could move, the telephone rang again. It was Todd Crossley from ADD for Brian. "Sa'ad-Oddin Rezvani called the New York office today all fired up," Brian began, "presumably due to the attachment of his account in Switzerland by the Insurance regulators."

"We've been expecting this call and have prepared for it," answered Todd.

"We need to implement the full risk management plan as soon as possible."

"We are on site now. All locations."

"Great. Please keep our employees and their families safe."

"Will do, Brian. We'll communicate as instructed."

"Deliver the package to Mr. Khoemi's office yet?" Brian drummed his fingers on Bill's desk.

"Yes. We have some very good people in Iran who are not happy with the ayatollahs. They were pleased to help, especially with the assignment we gave them." Brian disconnected.

Steve and Neena followed Brian into the small conference room. Brian was an adrenaline junkie and rivers of it were flowing in his veins. "Show time!"

Brian punched in Rezvani's number and pushed the speakerphone button, winking at Steve because he could sense the blood of anticipation pumping through Steve's veins, too. The connection was immediate.

"This is Brian Kendrick and I am returning Sa'ad-Oddin Rezvani's call. Is he available?"

"He has been expecting your call. I am Mohammed Khoemi and I will stay on the line."

"Very well, Mr. Khoemi. Although we haven't met, I'm familiar, of course, with your name and participation in the NIOC transaction. How may I help you and Mr. Rezvani?"

"Mr. Kendrick," said the guttural voice of Khoemi, "several of us who worked very hard to award you and your firm with large fees in connection with the purchase of refinery assets. Now we find that our accounts in Switzerland have been attached. We believe you may be able to enlighten us."

"Gentlemen, there has been a grievous error. The original actuarial study in support of your establishing an insurance company in Switzerland was inaccurate." Brian lifted his right hand in a "thumbs up" to Steve and Neena. He was smiling from ear to ear.

"Error, Mr. Kendrick?" Khoemi's voice had acquired an edge.

"Yes, Mr. Khoemi. The error was caused by a very technical and complex analysis, which is used by the Swiss authorities to determine how much equity an insurance company must have. The analysis uses historical data on default rates on bonds and other parameters in determining the estimates of probability of default and the consequences, in terms of dollar value, of the default for bondholders."

Brian knew that, while he was telling the truth in as simple a fashion as he knew how, they would not follow what he was talking about. He didn't give a shit. "The expected value of default is derived using a Monte Carlo simulation and that amount represents the minimum capital requirement under Swiss law for any insurance company doing business in Switzerland."

"Come to the *point*, Mr. Kendrick," Rezvani had finally chimed in.

"The point is that the original actuarial study had determined the required capital to be approximately twenty-five million dollars. Unfortunately, we recently found out that the data that we provided to the actuarial firm was somehow corrupted, so we re-sent the *correct* data to the actuarial firm in Zurich. When the actuarial company re-ran the analysis using the correct data, they determined that the minimum required capital is nearly five hundred million dollars."

"*What*!?" Khoemi blurted in his guttural voice, clearly filled with rage.

"Under Swiss law," Brian continued, ignoring Khoemi, "the actuarial firm was required to provide the Swiss Federal Office of Private Insurance with the revised analysis. Because the new actuarial study showed a capital shortfall of four hundred, seventy-five million dollars, the Swiss Federal Office of Private Insurance has taken the precaution of attaching all accounts of affiliated entities. Because your Swiss consulting firm and the individual accounts that you set up received fees associated with the issuance of the infrastructure bonds, those accounts are considered 'affiliated' and have been attached." Brian was beaming. *I wish Joe could hear this call. This was his idea.*

"So, Mr. Kendrick," Khoemi said, in short, crisp syllables as though his teeth were clenched, "How do we get our money out of Switzerland?"

"The easiest way to lift the attachments is to transfer money in an amount equal to the capital shortfall into your insurance company." *Fat chance.*

"We don't have that kind of money, Mr. Kendrick."

"I am sorry, gentlemen. In that case, your accounts will likely be attached until the actuarial calculation shows that the current capital amount will be sufficient to back the guarantee."

"When will that be?" Rezvani interjected.

"About twenty years under . . ."

"You miserable piece of shit!" Khoemi roared over Brian's explanation. "You have done this on purpose!"

"Mr. Khoemi, it is now immaterial how your accounts and all that money became attached. I am afraid I have more bad news." *Wait until he hears this.*

"More bad news, Mr. Kendrick? I will have you and your partners killed. I will kill their children and sell their wives into slavery. I will burn their homes. Who do you think you are fucking with?"

"Before I answer that question," Brian continued calmly, "I need to tell you the remainder of the bad news."

"Yes, yes. Go on!" Rezvani cut in. Brian pictured Rezvani pissing his pants.

"Gentlemen, unless the United States military, working with the Israeli government, can prevent it, in less than eighteen hours every land-based Israeli nuclear missile will be launched at Qom, Tehran, and over one hundred other targets in the Middle East."

"What! What are you saying?" Khoemi coughed out.

"I'm saying that the entire Middle East will be wiped out shortly after sundown this Saturday, Israeli time, unless we can stop rogue Israeli security personnel from launching the entire complement of Israeli land-based missiles. Make no mistake, gentlemen. I am speaking the truth. As evidence, your military can confirm a large buildup of US Navy ships in the Mediterranean and Red Sea."

There was dead air on the line. Steve handed Brian a note, *"Would not have missed this for the world!"*

"Now," Brian continued, "I'd like to answer your question about who—the correct English is 'whom'—I think I am fucking with. A colleague, here with me now, will enlighten you." Brian nodded to Steve.

Steve ran through thumbnail dossiers, prepared by Todd Crossley and his staff at AAD, on each individual holding a Swiss bank account receiving consulting fees from the National Iranian Oil Company transactions. The dossiers contained names, biographies, positions held in the Iranian government, and property held outside of Iran. Steve also enumerated names and addresses of mistresses and homosexual partners, residences in Iran, Swiss bank account numbers, and dollars received from the NIOC transaction. Steve took extra care to share knowledge of Khoemi's many peccadilloes involving young dancers on his frequent trips to London and Rezvani's cute, young, boy friends in Bangkok.

Just before Steve had finished, he expressed regret that he was unable to show the considerable number of photographs he possessed because of the technological limitations of the telephone connection. There was again silence.

Brian broke the quiet saying, "Mr. Khoemi, I need your help in preventing this nuclear holocaust in the Middle East."

"Why should I help you, you fucking shit?" Khoemi breathed over the phone.

"Because you will be turned to ash within thirty-six hours if you don't. Also, if you don't help, I'll make sure all the information that my colleague just read to you—and much, much more—finds its way to the full Guardian Council—oh, did I forget to mention that I have audio taped conversations for distribution as well?"

"I *swear* I will kill you." Khoemi said in a hushed, harsh tone. Rezvani could be heard ranting in the background.

"You may *try*," Brian corrected. He waited a moment and continued, "The help I need from you and Mr. Rezvani is to assist my government. You will convince your military and civilian authorities not to retaliate in any manner against Israel. The US Secretary of State is in Tehran to tell your president that the United States will use its anti-missile defenses to protect *all* countries in the Middle East and that America will protect Israel from any and all attempts at retaliation. Do you understand what I am saying?"

"I understand. How am I supposed to do this?"

"Mr. Khoemi, I have no idea. You are a wise and learned man. You will find a way. If you fail, you will lose every last cent of your money in Switzerland, and the information that I shared with you will find its way to the Guardian Council. Be assured of that. I will also inform your consulting firm partners that you two gentlemen are the sole owners of the insurance company that has caused their assets to be attached. You cut them out of that deal. They will not like that." Brian finished, waiting for their move. *Man, this feels good. A day to remember.*

"I can't do this. I don't have such power." Khoemi had the resigned tone of defeat.

"I have one more reason for you to help, Mr. Khoemi," Brian interjected.

Brian felt the moment become heavy. Hoisting the Iranians on their own petards had been fun, but now came the close of the sale. *He has to do this.*

"What is *that*?" Khoemi said, exasperation obvious in his tone.

"We are aware of an Iranian conspiracy to murder Sunnis in the merged Iraqi/ Iranian armed forces. The conspiracy is called 'Operation Kristallnacht'." Brian waited for, and got, the muffled gasp he had expected. "We'll be forwarding evidence of this conspiracy to friends in Iraq within the next day or two. Among the evidence is a communiqué originating in Qom with the initials 'AK' prominent in the message. We cannot condone such a mass murder, so Operation Kristallnacht will not happen. However, should you choose not to cooperate with us, we will associate both of your names, through the communiqué, closely with that conspiracy. I don't think that association would be in your best interests."

Brian waited. An old law of sales came to his mind at this juncture—"he who speaks first, loses". Brian raised his hand to Steve and Neena to remain absolutely quiet. At last, nearly forty seconds later, the speakerphone came alive.

"I will do my best, Mr. Kendrick," Khoemi said in a low growl.

"Very good, Mr. Khoemi," Brian affirmed.

There was static and Brian assumed that Khoemi and Rezvani had pushed the "mute" button on their telephone. Khoemi's voice came back on line, "How will you know that I, er, we helped you?"

"Easily—and we don't care whether you did—in the event that Iran retaliates, then we'll assume that you didn't help. If Iran foregoes retaliation, we will assume that you did."

"But that is not fair!" Khoemi raged.

Brian nodded to Steve who said, "We are after a desired outcome, not fairness, Mr. Khoemi. One more thing, Mr. Khoemi."

"Yes, what is it? I want to stop speaking with Kendrick and you, whoever you are!"

"You threatened my colleague, his partners, their families and possessions. You may think that you can operate outside the law and that we will not. You are mistaken. If a member of Mr. Kendrick's firm or any of their families is harmed in any way, I have been given the assignment to kill *each* of the people whose dossiers I read to you, including the two of you. My clients have the money and I have the expertise to do that. Do you understand, Mr. Khoemi?"

"Yes."

"Mr. Rezvani?" Steve asked for emphasis.

"Yes."

"As a memento of this conversation and my promise to you on behalf of my clients, you will find the youngest member of Mr. Khoemi's office guard asleep in his bed. His life is not threatened, but, unfortunately, he has lost his left pinkie finger. You will find his finger in a jar in your office, Mr. Khoemi, in the lower left drawer of your desk. You need to pay him appropriate compensation for his loss in your service. We *can* get to you. Goodbye."

Steve hung up the telephone and found Brian and Neena doing high fives.

"Shit, Brian, you are one of *us*," Steve pronounced gleefully. "That was a masterful script! I especially enjoyed the part you gave me."

"I, too, am very impressed," Neena added, smiling. "I knew you had brains. Now, I also know you have balls."

Brian smiled and bowed low. Then he said soberly, "I feel badly about that young man's finger—he has done nothing to me—but I hope lives will be saved by the message it sends."

He was quiet for a moment, and then offered, "Shall we rejoin the others?"

Friday Evening, May 2, 2014; Tel Aviv, Israel

By six thirty in the evening, stomachs were growling, nerves were on edge and more than one in the group had already taken aspirin. Neena had painstakingly mapped and diagrammed the fortress Pädäh—all five and one-half acres and each of the five floors. Jack Trevane and Abi had completed the battle plans and reviewed them with the best military minds in the Pentagon and IDF. Jack had given final ordnance instructions and had ordered his unit, still in Turkey, to join him at Israel's Strategic Command headquarters at the air force base. He'd left to greet them. Steve had completed his planning with Sergeant Harel and would meet him in the early morning hours. Brian had briefed Bill, Jack, and Abi after the call with Khoemi and Rezvani; he did the same, by telephone, with Vic Alfonse. In short, everything was as ready as it was going to be, and now time was on their hands.

Abi decided to go home to assemble her battle gear and get a few hours of sleep; she would join Jack at Strategic Command at seven in the morning tomorrow. She had borne much and worked hard. It showed.

Brian called his partners and Todd Crossley, and went back to his hotel. He had wanted to take part in the assault, but accepted Jack's refusal when he pointed out that Brian had not been in combat in several years. After the assault on Pädäh, Brian would return to New York—he had decided to engage AAD in some contingency planning.

Bill was bushed and admitted it. He had excused himself around six o'clock to have a small dinner in the private embassy quarters he was using during this crisis and retire.

Steve was starving and exhausted, but food took precedence. As he and Neena left the embassy grounds, Steve suddenly, even cheerfully announced, "Let's go to Gilly's in the port. If they're open, I know I can get us a table on the deck. I've had enough of four walls. Waddaya say?"

Neena smiled, "Gilly's! One of my favorites. Surly waiters and all. Let's go."

The port was about a mile from the US Embassy, but they decided to walk for the exercise. Both had not worked out in several days and the physical energy they were used to drawing upon each day had been pent up too long. As they strolled, Steve called the restaurant to make sure they were open—the restaurant closes after five in the afternoon if there are no customers. They were in luck—a Friday evening and people were looking to do something, and so, Gilly's was full. Before he hung up, he made a reservation for seven o'clock.

The evening was balmy, high tide lapping at the pilings on the boardwalk. Steve loved how Neena's hair was mussed and she hadn't bothered to fuss about changing from the jeans and yellow cotton shirt she'd worn all day. *She could wear rags and be beautiful.* They continued north toward the port. As they reached the large public garden off Herbert Samuel by Jabotinsky Street, Neena asked, "Do we have time to walk through?"

"Sure. Anything you want. " *I mean that,* he thought. *Anything.* Right now, though, he'd give anything to ease the undertone of strain still there, unspoken but sensed in his bones.

They took the winding garden paths overlooking the sea. "This is Independence Garden," said Neena. "It was dedicated in 1953. I wonder if we had more hope in 1953 than we do today."

"Why do you wonder?" Steve gazed at Neena, her long locks whirling as an on-shore breeze rustled through the palms and fig trees.

Neena dipped her head, saying, "I just can't help thinking that we have lost hope—not totally, but a little each generation, with each war that does not lead to peace, each rocket launched into a kibbutz, each dead Israeli—or Palestinian. I wish I had greater hope for my country, but right now I feel like I am just hanging on."

"Neena, sometimes that is all we can do." He held her close. "You know, when you speak of Israel, I hear a great love for your country. It comes through in all you do."

"If love is hope, then I *know* Israel will survive." She put her head against his shoulder.

"Tomorrow will tell whether there is hope for the Middle East. Besides," Steve said with a grin, "First, we have to *survive* tomorrow before we worry about the future. Now let's get to the restaurant. I've worked up an appetite."

"If we get through tomorrow," Neena smiled coyly, "Nothing will keep me away from you." She reached up and kissed him longingly. Steve could not remember being so happy.

Chapter Eighteen
Very Early Saturday, May 3, 2014; Tel Aviv, Israel

Steve slipped out of bed quietly. It was four o'clock in the morning and he had one hour to reach the clandestine briefing site with Sergeant Harel, Major Navon, and the two-person teams who would detain the ballistic missile silo crewmembers. As he was dressing, Neena propped herself on an elbow and called his name.

"Morning!" Steve said brightly, turning on the bedside lamp.

Neena covered her eyes but her lips curled in a smile. "Good morning. I will see you later, but I wanted to tell you how much I love you."

"Likewise," he said, leaning over to kiss the sleep from her eyes. "I'll meet you at Pädäh assault headquarters around ten hundred hours."

A courier from Jack Trevane's unit had dropped off combat gear for Neena and Steve. It was assembled by the front door of the hotel room. Steve looked forward to working with Jack. He pulled on the camouflage trousers and short-sleeved shirt, picked up his vest, helmet and other gear as he left. He insisted on keeping his side arm—the Walther PPK—and would carry his two favorite knives, a KABAR Marine combat knife and a Gerber TAC 2. He would be assigned other weapons at the assault assembly site.

As he left the hotel door, an Israel Police car was waiting. "Compliments of Sergeant Harel."

"Thank you." Steve stowed his gear in the rear of the car and got in the passenger side.

It was a little after four thirty and traffic was light. They raced out of central Tel Aviv and were quickly in the countryside. Soon the car turned into a farm and pulled behind a barn, flanked by a couple of chicken coops. There were scores of vehicles and over one hundred men and women all around. Steve got out and started to grab his gear. "Mr. Barber, you may leave that here. I am assigned to you until I get you to Pädäh assault headquarters."

"Thank you, again." Steve easily spotted Major Navon and Sergeant Harel and walked up to them. "Good morning, Major, Jehu. Is the full complement here?"

"Yes, Steve," replied Navon.

Steve followed them into a tent and strode up to a set of white boards that were propped up on collapsible tables. "Is this how you are going to track your teams?" Names and locations were handwritten written in black dry erase marker.

"Yes. Not fancy, but it will work," Major Navon responded. "Let me brief you."

Steve listened to the plan, then asked, "I see you've listed for detention both the Saturday and Sunday crewmembers. Why are we still going after the Sunday crews? We have confirmation that the launches are scheduled for Saturday."

"I can answer that, Mr. Barber," said Sergeant Harel. "We determined that the crews have back-up assignments in case of illness or other absence. Many of those back-up assignments for Saturday crews are crews scheduled for Sunday, so we were concerned that David Alon has recruited many, if not all, of those crews, too. As a result, we decided to minimize the risk of a rogue crew getting control of a silo by continuing with the original plan to detain both sets of crews. The decision to detain both sets of crews was made easier by having a sufficient number of teams to round them up."

"Well thought out, gentlemen," said Steve. "My compliments. If it's okay with you, I would like to stay here until about zero, nine hundred." The day was beginning and the sky lightened from black to pale blue. One lone star and a sliver of moon remained. *If I were to make one wish*, thought Steve looking up, *it would be that Neena and I make it back to the states.*

Steve felt the familiar sensation of the calm before the storm. He recognized the undertow of adrenaline readying itself in the pit of his stomach, building and churning, waiting until it was time to explode and fill him with the strength he was going to need during this one-bitch-of-a-day. Meanwhile, he appreciated this group of men. Talk was light, perhaps a little forced at times, but the time passed quickly.

Around six forty-five the first reports of the Shin Bet and police teams in position began to come in, broadcast over a PA system in the tent. By zero, six fifty-five, all teams were ready. Steve waited anxiously as seven o'clock came and went without a report, meaning that all teams had begun their respective detention orders. The next thirty minutes would be critical.

The PA system crackled with static as detention reports came in. Within the large headquarters tent, a police sergeant kept track of all silo crewmember names listed on the white boards, marking down the results. A large green "X" indicated that the crewmember was in custody. If the detention created an incident—one large crewmember had lunged at a two-man Shin Bet team and was tasered twice—a description of the incident was noted. A large red "O" meant that the crewmember had eluded detention.

The back up plan for crewmembers not detained was to have them arrested as they attempted to enter onto the missile silo grounds. Strategic Command was responsible for executing these orders, but no one had the time to vet the guards, so it was assumed some crews, if not detained at their residences, would be able to reach their silos. Everyone knew that they wouldn't be able to plug all the holes. This was a big hole, but, given the time to prepare, Steve was impressed. *Gotta go with what you got.*

By seven thirty, there were 129 large green Xs and seven large red Os, representing three crews and one lone crewmember. Because both members of a crew had to be physically present in the silo to insert their distinctive keys to activate the missile launch system, the lone crewmember was not as much of a concern as were the three crews. By cross-referencing the crewmembers against silo assignments, it was quickly determined that twenty-seven missiles at the three sites were vulnerable.

Immediate orders went out to Strategic Command to detain the four men and two women. That information was also sent to overall operational headquarters at the US Embassy, where it would be forwarded to the US Navy. Knowing the launch location of the missiles allowed the Navy's anti-missile systems to be pre-targeted. That was important; they needed every second because some of the missiles' targets were less than five minutes distant.

With the operation ended, Steve said, "I need to get to Pädäh. Do you have the tac frequency for the assault headquarters?"

"Yes," replied Major Navon.

"Please keep me informed of your operation. Thanks for your hospitality. Shalom." Steve saluted.

"Mr. Barber," Sergeant Harel started to speak and then hesitated. "I assume you will be part of the assault later today. May God keep you in his care, and the lovely Ms. Shahud as well. Shalom."

"Thank you, Sergeant. It has been a distinct honor to work with you." *It truly has been. I'd welcome Sergeant Harel on my team any day if he ever wanted to change jobs.* They shook hands quickly but warmly.

Steve hurried to his car, his driver sitting on the back bumper, drinking a cup of coffee, which he tossed in a garbage can as he saw Steve approaching. "Ready, sir?"

"Yes. Not sure for what, but I *am* ready." *The US has some great friends. I hope we keep them.*

Early Saturday Morning, May 3, 2014; Pädäh, Jerusalem, Israel

"Colonel?" Sergeant Zee Shachar said uncertainly.

"Yes, Zee. What is it?" David snapped.

"Defense Minister Luegner is at the gate."

"Explain to him that if he enters, he will not be able to leave."

"Done, sir. He says he still wishes entry."

"Fine, Zee. Let him in. If his bodyguards are with him, request Simon assign them to the operations commander for deployment."

"Yes, sir."

It took longer than normal for the Defense Minister's car to enter the compound. Several abatises needed to be lowered or moved and the car had to negotiate a host of new obstacles. Thick walls of four-foot tall reinforced concrete snaked across the former parking area. Pinzgauer trucks were snuggled in six-foot stacks of sand bags. Troops were moving .50-calibre machine guns and other ordnance. Ammo boxes were stacked in every corner. Dust spewed in all directions, masking everything in a slight coating of dirt. The rose garden had been replaced by a series of surface-to-air firing stations, also surrounded by concrete and sand bags. As soon as Simon's vehicle was in the compound, David went out to greet his co-conspirator.

All of this was being observed by two of Jack Trevane's sniper teams and relayed real-time by satellite link to the US Embassy and the USS *Ronald*

Reagan offshore in the Mediterranean, where the US Navy maintained its combat operations center.

"Good morning, Simon," said David. "I had not expected you to join us here, but you are a welcome sight. Things are going to get hot here very soon."

"Perhaps sooner than you expect."

"What do you mean?"

"I just missed being arrested," said Simon. "A deep source, who is not part of the Masada Protocol, but someone who owes me a favor, told me that the Prime Minister and key members of his government were briefed yesterday on our plans."

"I suspected that. The Prime Minister sent members of his personal security detail here. We killed two of them."

"There's more," added Simon. "The Prime Minister has authorized American forces to assault Pädäh, and Shin Bet and Israel Police teams are rounding up the missile silo crews."

"Damn Neena!" David shouted, as he punched the hood of Luegner's car. It left a dent but David felt no pain. *She is so good. Why couldn't she see?* "Let's go to my office," said David, turning on his heel and talking as he walked. "I can communicate with our silo crews, so I will find out how many have been detained."

Simon hurried to keep up, turning his head left and right, staring at the abundance of construction and armaments. "David, what are you expecting?"

"All hell to break loose. You were warned at the gate, Simon. There is no leaving now."

They reached David's office where he sent out a simultaneous text message to the thirty-four men and women who were assigned to the missile silos. The message asked for confirmation from the crewmembers, each a party to the Masada Protocol, that they were in place in their silos. Five minutes later he had his answer—three silo crews were in place.

"Damn it!" David pulled up a file on his computer and studied it. "We have only twenty-seven missiles left." He sent another text message and shut off his cell phone. "I have given orders to the three crews to go into lock-down. We can't fire the missiles early—one of the tradeoffs in the design of the virus—so we have to defend what silos we have until zero hour, sundown this evening, less ten hours. That's nine twenty-three this morning." David looked at his watch. "We have to hold for another thirty-seven minutes. After that, we cannot control the missiles through our computers here—nor can anyone else."

"David, are twenty-seven missiles enough? We have done so much. I would hate to fail now!" Simon was pacing and wringing his hands.

"Twenty-seven is enough—not what I wanted. I wanted to blow the Middle East to kingdom come, but our missiles will not take out all of Iran's capability, so we can count on their fifteen or so missiles to be fired in retaliation. That will add quite a bit to the party. That response may even convince the Prime Minister to launch the remainder of our nuclear arsenal." David shut down his computer and jammed a bunch of papers through a shredder by his desk.

"Will the Americans attack the silos we still control?"

"I doubt it. They are likely to assume—correctly—that I have given orders to arm the missiles without opening the silos if the silo defenses are compromised. Also, the silos are hardened. Destroying one would require tremendous explosive power—on the level of a nuclear bomb—to destroy. The Prime Minister will want to avoid that because of the local devastation and radiation. No, I assume the Americans have ballistic missile defense capability in the area and he will rely on that. I don't think they could get enough ships here in time. Did you say the Prime Minister was briefed yesterday?"

"Yes," said Simon, nodding.

David recognized an expression of disdain on Simon's face. "The Americans can't have that much capability close enough to matter. We can still achieve our purpose."

"Let's hope so. A lot of us are going to die today to see that happen."

"*All* of us are going to die today, Simon, including *you*," David said poking him in the chest. He stood crisply and walked out of his office. He needed to review the readiness of the compound. It had better be ready *now*. "Neena, Neena, Neena," David muttered to himself dejectedly and shook his head.

Mid-Morning Saturday, May 3, 2014; Pädäh, Jerusalem, Israel

Abi Zahavi, under a flag of truce and in full battle gear but unarmed, marched to within ten meters of the gate alongside the main entrance to the compound. She was extremely conscious of her vulnerability but wanted to offer David Alon no excuse for opening fire. Instead, she prayed. It was unlike her, but somehow comforting. She had also prayed earlier on the helicopter that carried her and Jack Trevane from the air base.

The morning was crisp. The shadows at 0847 hours stretching from the low hills to the east created a deeper chill that Abi felt at the base of her spine. The trees and shrubs that had once slapped the compound walls with their branches had been cut down, strewn on the ground outside the walls. This was done both to clear lines of fire and to make breaching the walls more difficult. Abi stepped with care. Concrete bunkers and barricades had transformed Pädäh into a complex of fortifications and anti-personnel barriers. Barrels of weapons forested the walls and rooftops. Those Abi could see wore resolute faces that mirrored the drab of their camouflage, the trousers and long-sleeved shirts clean and neat as though they had just taken up their positions. She saw no fear anywhere.

She waited as the iron gate opened and a five-member security party emerged, David Alon the first man through. There was no exchange of pleasantries. Abi raised her hand in a deliberate motion, holding out a handwritten note from the prime minister. The note demanded that David Alon and those under his command surrender and abandon the compound. David pushed his Uzi to the side and took the note.

"Abi, we have no fight with our mother country and we have none with the men and women assembled to assault us," David said after reading the note. "But we will die here rather than let Masada fall a second time to the enemies of Israel. You took that same oath. Go in peace or face death at our hands. The choice is yours, not ours." Without waiting for a response, he executed an about-face. The slamming of the gate rang in Abi's ears.

Shin Bet teams had cleared most of the residences and small farms around Pädäh by ten o'clock. Jack Trevane was pushing to get the area vacated ASAP, so that he could execute his plan of attack on time. It was possible his career depended on it. He knew many lives did.

The fire zone was a two-kilometer radius. Parts of the area around Pädäh were densely settled, houses of stone and faded stucco with peaked tile rooflines that rose and fell along the hillside in haphazard rows. Once desert, the area had become dotted with small vegetable farms as Israel built its self-sufficiency in the 1950's. In the last half of the century, small developments with a few homes, inhabited by Israelis working in Jerusalem, had taken the place of several farms. For now, the people were told that a large group of terrorists was trapped in Pädäh and the prime minister would have more to say later.

Use of the word "terrorists" by armed people with Shin Bet identification cards was more than enough to get cooperation from the residents. Some of them came back in ill-fitting uniforms from mandatory military service days. Out of closets, armoires and weathered trunks came the weapons that Israelis legally owned. Jack and his men praised the patriots for their valor but insisted that this was a military operation for which they had not been briefed or trained. They understood and obeyed the orders, withdrawing to a shelter eight kilometers away.

The area was a dust storm of activity, trucks, troops, and weapons taking positions like large pieces of a lethal puzzle. Jack surveyed the continuous set of synchronized motions from the bumper of a truck, his binoculars scanning the perimeter. The entire Black Watch Command had arrived in Israel from Turkey at 0700 hours and Jack and Abi had met them at the airbase to brief them on the assault. Abi had taken that opportunity to inform Jack that, although she was technically in command of the operation unfolding on Israeli soil, she looked to him to provide battlefield leadership and would delegate her authority to him. Jack understood and saluted. The two warriors thus agreed on how to accommodate Israel's sovereignty needs and to get command into the hands of the ablest.

The men and women of the Black Watch were fully rested and briefed. Some of the Command came from the air base to the assault point by truck with the supplies and heavy ordnance. Others were transported by helicopter. On their first flight to the Pädäh assault assembly point, the pilots detected that they'd been lit up by radar, so they changed the route to bring the troops in behind the hills to the west. Despite the more circuitous flight path, the Command would be in assault position by 1030 hours.

Steve and Neena were to lead a small detachment with the objective of penetrating and securing the computer room. With that done, Strategic Command systems people, standing by, would be brought in by helicopter. Their job would be to hack the software and cancel the launch codes. At this point, everyone knew that the launch date and time were locked in. Gideon Amit had determined this in the systems analyses he'd ordered before he was murdered.

No one could fire the missiles early. The US Navy was on full alert, but the operational assumption was that the missiles could not be launched until sundown at 1923 hours, at which time Israel's Memorial Day would begin.

In developing the battle plan, the assumption was that David was likely to destroy the computers long before Steve and Neena reached the computer room. Jack was sure that David couldn't move the launch up and he couldn't control the missiles once launched. So the question remained about what use would he have for them, other than to cancel the launch. More likely, David would see the computers as a risk to his plan because they might fall into the hands of Strategic Command. Nonetheless, the outside chance of being able to abort the launches so that not one single missile hit anywhere was seen as worth the effort. *And certain loss of life,* Jack thought. *That, too, will happen no matter what.*

If the launches could not be aborted, success rested solely on the US Navy taking out every one of the twenty-seven missiles. *That was the way it always was, taking calculated risks for calculated benefits.* So the Black Watch Command would assault the compound. The detachment, led by Steve and Neena, would go through the office building and three sublevels to get to the computer room below and see if anything was left. Jack trusted Steve's ability to get the job done. Only afterward would they know whether the cost was worth it.

By the clock, the operation was going well, but Jack felt pressed for time. He jogged over to join Steve. Steve had arrived at Pädäh shortly after Abi confronted David and reported in to Jack, his commander for this operation. He had then gone to the operations command tent. "Jack, I've reviewed the personnel assigned to our team," Steve began. "They look like a kick-ass group."

Jack had assigned a couple of his best men—actually one woman and one man—to the detachment. Master Sergeant Ed Greene was a close quarters/urban combat expert and Staff Sergeant Allison Parker, who went by Minnie for reasons unknown to anyone in the Command, was an EOD, meaning Explosive Ordnance Disposal, specialist. Both were exceptional. You didn't serve with Black Jack unless you were.

"I can't bear the thought of a Marine casualty, so I gave you my best," Jack grinned at Steve. Black Jack Trevane looked like his reputation, standing easily in fifty pounds of full battle gear, his helmet lying on a makeshift desk. He was decorated like a gothic Christmas tree, with grenades, sheathed knives, and ammo clip pouches hanging from everywhere. A shoulder holster held a standard Army issue M9 Beretta. He had strapped a holster around his right thigh for a second Beretta. Jack was ready for battle. He was always ready for battle.

Steve, Neena, and the two sergeants were again studying the drawings of Pädäh. Steve ran a hand through his hair. Drank a sip of his fourth coffee and ignored the bitterness. Field coffee. Smelled good and tasted bad. He felt his adrenaline pumping as he stabbed one drawing with a finger, following the blue lines of the ventilation system in the basement and floors below the computer room. The drawing was to scale and it was obvious to Steve that the small, high-velocity air handling equipment had ductwork too small to accommodate even Minnie. There were biological and chemical filters on the ventilation systems and internal backup systems in case air was shut off or sensors detected toxins in the air. The system was not a means of entry. The utility ducts were not either.

As the four poured over the drawings, Steve saw no secondary entrances or egresses to the four levels underneath the old house, converted to David's office building inside Pädäh. The floors, each separated from the other by a heavy airtight door, were designed to be tombs if need be. There was a small equipment elevator on the eastern side. That might provide access to lower floors. Steve sighed. *This is not going to be easy*, he thought. Immediately, he dismissed his moment of anxiety. *Nothing is ever easy.*

Minnie predicted the elevator was likely to be booby-trapped and that the shaft could collapse, filling with debris upon detonation. Nonetheless, she would check out the elevator once they gained entry to the ground floor. Steve did not like the idea of having only one entry point to places underground. He could tell by the faces of Neena, Greene and Minnie that they didn't like it either.

The assault planning team had considered demolishing the old house to encase the lower floors. They could then bring in Seabees to dig out the lower floors, eventually reaching the computer center. This had the possible advantage of fewer US casualties. But the likelihood of reaching the computers in time to prevent missile launch was extremely low.

Despite all the critical and creative thinking, the task would fall to hard, floor-by-floor combat. Steve knew what it would take, and he also knew that it was unlikely that all four would survive. *Please don't let it be Neena.*

Steve went through the plan once more, counting the steps, and each soldier describing the task he or she was to accomplish. They covered all the contingencies, mainly back-up assignments in the event of one or more were incapacitated. If they could not penetrate the computer floor by 1800 hours—Strategic Command computer experts estimated at least an hour to hack into the missile-controlling computers—they would plant enough C-4 to obliterate the room with the faint hope that, upon the destruction of the computers, the missiles would not launch. It was all they could do. Steve knew the entire operation was a long shot. He guessed the others knew the same.

"Well, what do you think?" Steve asked his team.

"I think we need to remember what Eisenhower said on D-Day," Neena answered. "He said, 'In preparing for battle I have always found that plans are useless, but planning is indispensable.'"

The four laughed. "Amen," Steve said. "Adapt and overcome."

After they completed the operations review, Steve left the command tent and called Bill Elsberry over a secure telecom speakerphone in the Black Watch communications truck. "Has the president arrived?" Steve asked.

"Yes. He's with the prime minister at his official residence in Jerusalem," Bill said. "Frankly, I'm in awe of the president's courage. You'd better take these guys out. I would not like to explain losing the President of the United States to an Iranian missile while he was in Israel."

"We'll do our best. We won't know if Brian Kendrick squeezed enough shit out of that Khoemi guy until missiles are fired. Getting the Iranians to keep everyone in the barracks and silos is what needs to happen. Is the Navy in position?" Steve tightened his pack and pressed his left leg to judge its readiness for strain. *Ready as it's gonna be*, he concluded.

"All set. The *Reagan* has a squadron of F-18s equipped to assault the missiles as they leave their silos. The USS *Shiloh* is in the Red Sea. They have pre-coded the three silo sites into their Aegis ballistic missile defense weapons systems. If a flash is reported, they'll be ready to track and, if necessary, fire. They'll double up on some missiles, but we don't have enough capability to do that on all twenty-seven if they get past the F-18s."

"How did you decide which missiles get double-teamed?" Steve asked.

"We picked the seventeen missiles aimed at Iran," Bill answered. "It's the only country with nuclear weapons and it has the largest army. If we can keep them at home, the others are not likely to retaliate even if a missile gets through. Let's pray none do."

"Amen. Gotta go. Wish us luck." Steve said.

"You got it."

Steve clicked off the phone and checked his gear once more. He left the communications truck and set out at the double to rejoin Neena and his detachment.

David had wanted to mine a vast area around Pädäh, but did not have the time. He never planned to fortify the compound and defend it. Neena and Steve had forced that necessity on him as they systematically discovered the object and means of his Masada Protocol. Over the past few days, David concentrated on the enemy's assault on his compound. *Now, Neena, too, is an enemy*. David now walked the entire compound, examined every position, every weapon. He probed every wall from the mind of an attacker and gave orders to change defensive barriers, move weapons. He also bantered with the men and women of his small, but passionate, command.

Pädäh was located in a small, elevated valley between low hills to the west and east. The south afforded a level assault area, an obvious approach. Outside the northern boundary of the compound, the ground tapered first slowly and then more rapidly downward, leaving Pädäh at an elevation of three hundred, fifty feet on that side. An assault from the north would be hard and costly. David sensed the enemy would come from the south and, probably, from the east and west. David was ready. But he knew he had made an error in judgment. *One that would prove costly.*

David had mistakenly assumed that any assaulting force would use armor, believing that the hills on either side of the compound would make assembling there too difficult. He was furious with himself. *I should have considered all eventualities.* He had realized even as he spoke to his people just four days prior that he was going to have to cede land quickly in the battle. American firepower would overwhelm the defenders above ground, but he still had some tricks up his sleeve. The compound might be breached and occupied, but getting to the computer room would take time and lives. *I'll still have the time I need.*

David knew in his bones the assault would begin soon. He covered the entire compound one last time to let his men and women see him—resolute, proud, and fearless. He hoped his demeanor would become theirs. He was not disappointed. Uniforms were clean. Weapons were at the ready and ample ammunition was securely stored. The Israeli flag rippled in a stiff breeze high atop the main building, snapping defiance at the enemies outside the gate. Everyone wore an armband bearing the flag and the motto "Masada will never fall again" in Hebrew. Some had painted blue and white stripes on their cheeks. Today David would not order them to remove it. As he returned to his station, David recalled his favorite line from Macbeth, *"Lay on, Macduff, and damned be him that first cries, 'Hold, enough!'"*

Jack rarely used armor—his assignments required rapid response and incredible mobility—so he'd learned to live, and kill, without it. Absent tanks and other armor, Jack was able to disperse his Command on three sides. Jack placed four sniper teams on the hills with orders to concentrate on Israelis manning the .50-calibre machine guns and surface-to-air ordnance. To substitute for armor, Jack used every sort of air power available. Today would be no different.

The time was 1039 hours and a group of three cruise missiles was in sight, coming in low from the north. Jack heard the rumbling roar of their jet engines and that was the signal to the sniper teams to begin eliminating targets. The helicopter pilots had earlier identified the location of the radar, relaying that information to the sniper teams.

A target location was all the snipers needed. They were equipped with XM-25s with High Explosive Air-Burst munitions, the weapon known as an Individual Air-Burst Weapon. It received a lot of hype when introduced for extensive testing. The US Army eventually chose not to make it standard issue, but Jack stashed a bunch of them. He knew he'd need them someday. The range was about half a mile, and the snipers, easily within distance, began firing the heavy shells, blasting their target with deadly affect. The radar units were out of action within the first five minutes. No one in Pädäh would be able to track what was going on in the sky.

Steve had just rejoined his detachment when the cruise missiles struck the compound. The old house at Pädäh was intentionally spared so Steve detachment would not have to dig their way in. The rest of the compound suffered tremendous damage. The missiles had bitten off large chunks of wall, cedar and metal panels included, and spit the pieces, ravaging nearby positions. Reinforced concrete abatises and protective barriers were uprooted and smashed. Steve felt the rush of success but it was too early to celebrate. *Way too early.*

David's men and women sprang from bunkers, tending the wounded and dead, replacing weapons and defensive barriers, rebuilding positions. A front-end loader emerged and hauled concrete pieces back to the perimeter wall, clearing firing lanes. The dusty smell of pulverized stone and concrete mixed with the smoke from the explosives, filling Pädäh like strange vapor from a witch's cauldron.

From the detachment's position just outside the operations tent, Steve heard Jack talking to his snipers over his tactical radio. "We have to neutralize those Starstreak missiles. Those are mean-ass weapons, and I won't have them used on my Apaches. Three Little Birds with M260 Hydra rocket launchers are on their way to vaporize those Pinzgauers. Take out anyone you see up on those 6x6s until the Little Birds get there. Understood?"

"Yes, sir," came the crisp reply over the radio.

About ten kilometers out, five Apache helicopters had assembled in attack formation and were closing on Pädäh from the north. Pädäh defenders on the remaining three Pinzgauer 6x6s jumped up to fire their Starstreak missiles. As they did so, Black Watch sniper fire rained on them, and the AH-6 light attack helicopters, called Little Birds, whipped in from the south and unleashed their rockets, turning the Pinzgauers into scattered bonfires. Steve watched the destruction unfold and, as the rockets struck, he clenched his teeth. *Damn that sonovabitch*, he muttered to himself, cursing David.

The battle plan called for the assault to begin from the east as soon as the Apaches had made their first run. They'd circle afterward to provide close ground support. Steve had studied Jack's dossier and knew that he used every advantage, including the fact that at 1047 hours the sun would crest the eastern hills, meaning that Jack's lead assault team would be coming at the enemy out of the sun.

Jack was at the head of the first ground assault wave, about a hundred soldiers. A second assault wave, led by Abi, would begin twenty seconds later, and the third, twenty seconds after that. Steve and Neena, along with their detachment, were embedded in the second wave, headed for the computer room.

They both had a short H&K 9mm MP5K sub-machine gun and a M4A1 Close Quarter Battle carbine with sound suppressors to save their hearing while firing indoors. They carried an assortment of explosive devices, including fragmentation, concussion, and stun grenades. Each of the ten members of the detachment carried two pounds of C-4 explosive in case they had to blow the lower levels. Steve carried his Walther PPK and his favorite combat knives. Neena, of course, was armed with her nine-inch Tanto knives. She also carried a Glock 17C 9mm.

Steve and Neena huddled at the southern assault point with their detachment, which, in addition to Greene and Minnie, consisted of specialists Cennamo, Hampton, Krzynski, and Rodriguez along with corporals Clark and Epstein. Steve's detachment was assigned the right flank of the second assault team until they met up with Jack's first assault team on their right. At that point, they would peel off, take the main building, and work their way down to the computer room.

The third team, coming from the west would join the second team and hold while Jack, reinforced by a contingent from the second team, led a counter-clockwise sweep maneuver, pushing any remaining defenders toward the pivot point—the third assault team—who would meet the defendants with massive firepower. Jack's snipers would concentrate on defenders forced into the open.

Jack's team was already rushing Pädäh on the east side. The cruise missiles and Apaches had leveled much and the compound had taken massive casualties. There were still ample defenders, but they expected to die. No one was surrendering inside Pädäh.

As Jack's team neared the compound perimeter, a rush of Mini-Spike anti-personnel missiles hit them with devastating effect. Fifteen, maybe twenty, of Jack's men were torn in pieces. The Apaches responded instantly, unleashing a storm of Hydra 70mm flechette rockets. Then, the Apache gunners trained their helmet-controlled targeting systems and fired a punishing stream of M230 30mm rounds.

Some valiant defenders stepped out to fire their Stinger missiles, but Jack's sniper teams dropped them almost instantly. Nonetheless, Stingers hit two Apaches causing one to burst in midair and the second to withdraw in spiraling clouds of black smoke.

As the Mini-Spikes smashed into Jack's unit, Steve's assault team began its run toward the compound from the south. Steve heard shouts and hurrahs as the first team breached the crumbled compound walls. Heavy automatic weapons fire filled the air and the loud tumph, tumph, tumph of the old, but lethal, .50-caliber machine guns told everyone that Death reveled in this day.

Steve's team rushed the compound wall, scrambling over the rubble. Firefights erupted everywhere. Jack's men were trained to work in firefight teams of three and the first wave was already methodically moving through the eastern part of the compound.

Steve ran on autopilot, relying on his training and instinct, as the team approached David's old house. His boots kicking up dust and shells exploding at his heels, Steve reached for a fragmentation grenade and yanked the pin. Neena instinctively turned to cover him as Steve and Greene flanked the entry. Steve tossed the grenade inside. A whoosh of stone, wood and glass hurled through the doorway. Steve peered inside, sweat stinging his eyes. *Nobody home.*

A clump of grass erupted behind them. Two men with Uzis fired from a hole at the detachment. Minnie returned fire, causing them to duck as Neena reacted. Turning her attention from Steve, she moved in a sweeping arc, like a ballerina performing a chaîné turn, to face the gunmen, and as she spun, she repeated the step twice until she was nearly atop the hole. As she gracefully ceased spinning, she fired a burst into the hole. The Uzis were silenced.

"What was that?" Steve shouted.

"I thought they would be more inclined to fire at me if I ran straight at them, so I threw in some ballet," Neena responded with a smile.

"Next time just shoot them. Okay?" *Ain't she something?*

Rodriguez was already giving first aid to Hampton. Krzynski was dead. Greene, Clark and Cennamo had entered the old, cut-stone building, the temperature cool inside. They began methodically clearing rooms, like tense homeowners looking for the rat they thought they saw run across the kitchen floor. "Wouldn't it be nice if this place were empty," Greene said.

By this time, the rest of the detachment, now down to eight, had picked up the C-4 from Hampton and Krzynski. Steve ordered Rodriguez, Clark, and Epstein to stand guard. The other five moved through the building as the battle roared outside. Minnie scoured doorways and floors for booby traps, the job made easier by the cleanliness of the house, so trim and neat that it could have been mistaken for that of an anal-retentive German hausfrau.

It looked as though nothing had changed since the house was built in the 50's. Three of the rooms on the first floor were decorated with overstuffed chairs, draped with antique lace antimacassars to prevent oily heads from staining the fabric. Side tables held candlestick lamps with fussy shades and a brass floor lamp stood in a corner of a room that had probably once been the parlor. The walls were covered with paintings of the Israeli countryside, and the polished wooden floors were bare, with only an occasional throw rug to soak up the wear of boot traffic. It was as though David had copied his grandmother's house. At odds with the character of the rest of the house, two gray metal desks and chairs each flanked a doorway. *David might've made someone a great wife,* Steve mused.

Steve had slipped through a side door in a butler's pantry and entered the kitchen, Neena at his elbow. The kitchen had an ancient white porcelain refrigerator and electric stove. *This place is like going back in time*, thought Steve. Contemporary kitchen design was represented solely by a Cuisinart coffeemaker perched on the counter next to the rust-stained porcelain sink. A lavatory, outfitted with clean white cotton towels and Neutrogena hand soap in a small painted soap dish, completed the first floor.

Steve looked at Neena, knowing what she was thinking. The house was empty, at least this floor. *Not usual. Not good.*

As Steve and Neena followed, alert and ready, Minnie examined the ground level floor. Suddenly, she went rigid and shouted, "Trap!" and pointed to a small portion of the floor near a desk in the northwest doorway. The word was a blast of liquid nitrogen, freezing the remaining eight of them in place

Minnie examined the floor. She reached for her combat knife and pried out a chunk of wood, pointing a small flashlight into the hole. "Bingo," she said. Turning to the others, she ordered, "Look for areas that are cleaner than other parts of the floor. Most novice installers think they dirtied the floor and wipe it so the bomb is not detected. They end up making detection easier."

Each scanned an area of the floor. Shouts of "here!" rang out as three more bombs were found on the ground level. Steve knew from the first one that the tripping mechanism was a simple pressure switch—step on it and it would detonate—and he was glad Minnie was on his team. This type was easy to diffuse and Minnie was a whirlwind, neutralizing all four in minutes. The tension ebbed.

Steve looked at his watch. Noon. His three guards relayed that the battle had moved away, Jack's assault team, reinforced by the second, had pushed the defenders toward the third team. *Jack is a master,* Steve thought.

"Three more floors to go until we get to the computers. Let's move," Steve urged. Neena led them to the access door to the next floor, one level down.

"Hold on a minute while I check the small equipment elevator," Minnie said. She had already moved to the elevator. Steve seeing that the battle had moved away, no longer worried about Pädäh defenders outside. He ordered the three guards to join the rest of the detachment. *Who knows what we're going to run into in here.* "Abi and Jack have things well in hand," Steve announced. "Now it's up to us. Minnie, what have you found?"

"As we suspected, the entire elevator is set with explosives. I think we should detonate it now rather than run the risk of being a couple floors below when it blows."

"Good idea. How long do you need?"

"Five minutes. I want to guarantee all the charges go off, so I will run a rig to the bottom and blow it in several places."

"Okay. Get to it. Let's set up to go into the basement." Steve picked up one of three bags of specialized equipment that they would use in checking each floor before entering.

The bag Steve had chosen was labeled "HERMAN", which stood for Holistic Environmental Reconnaissance and Munitions/Armaments Neutralizer. HERMAN was only forty pounds, but he could navigate independently and was equipped with A/V transmitters and a host of detection devices—including chemical and infrared. Steve and HERMAN's controller, Specialist Cennamo, lifted HERMAN out of the bag and set him up.

Steve watched Cennamo examine each of the arms. Thanks to billions spent on developing similar devices for use by American astronauts, each arm was outfitted with tools at the extremities. Cennamo maneuvered each of the tools in turn, grasping his arm, pulling and turning the equipment bag, and cutting a piece of metal. Steve knew that the arms and tools were designed to be disposable. On command, HERMAN would transform himself into an explosive-resistant configuration, trigger an explosion, lose the arm, and self-recover to continue exploring the defined search area. Even in the event that HERMAN lost all six arms, he could still provide reconnaissance and detection functions.

As Cennamo finished checking HERMAN, Steve chuckled. He was thinking of the Black Knight in Monty Python's classic "The Holy Grail". King Arthur, with successive slashes of his sword, reduced the Black Knight to a mere torso spouting defiantly "I'm invincible." *You're invincible, too, HERMAN.*

By the time Steve satisfied himself that HERMAN was fully operational, Minnie reappeared. "Fire in the hole!" she yelled. Hands flew up over ears as a single loud kaboom rang out, followed by a series of smaller explosions, and the old house shivered like a wet dog, the framed prints banging on the walls in applause. The house had been greatly reinforced to serve as David's headquarters, though, and easily withstood the blasts.

Neena had already placed several explosive devices around the frame of the door leading to the basement and waited for the team to be in position before detonating the charges. Blowing doors took a little more time, but cleared any booby traps on the other side. They wouldn't blow the doors to the other sublevels; those walls were concrete. They'd use other means. Detonations within concrete structures were deafening. The detachment was ready and Minnie gave a thumbs-up signal to Neena. Another set of kabooms filled the air. The door and its frame lay in tatters, wood and shattered cut stones flung around the once-homey room. *It's a shame what we have to do to this fine old place*, thought Steve.

"All clear," Minnie yelled, starting downstairs. She had a set of electronic devices she used to check the stairway—unfortunately HERMAN could not yet climb or descend stairs. "Minnie," Steve barked, "Per our plan, Greene takes the lead. This is his specialty."

Minnie muttered something, but halted in the stairway. Jack's people were aggressive, but they also knew how to take orders. Greene moved cautiously. At the bottom, he immediately tossed two grenades, one to each side of the room. When the grenades blew, Greene moved quickly into the basement to his left and Minnie went to the right. Rodriguez and Epstein followed and cautiously probed a little further into the basement under cover of Greene and Minnie. After ten steps they stopped.

Each person had lights on their helmets and four of them carried large floodlights. Although Jack had cut the power to the compound, somehow the basement had power and lights. "They need to have backup power for the computer room," Steve shouted. "Keep your helmet lights on and those floodlights off, but close at hand."

HERMAN was carried down the stairs and placed on the floor. Cennamo activated and released HERMAN to conduct a pre-programmed search grid. If necessary, Cennamo could command him wirelessly. In this case, the basement was exactly as Neena had diagrammed it and, although the full program would take thirty minutes, HERMAN was making quick work of it.

As HERMAN was leaving a small conference room and entering an office, he stopped and emitted a high-pitched whine. A small set of lights flashed red and HERMAN transmitted something to his controller.

"Gas masks everyone!" Cennamo shouted. "Cyanide. I'll release HERMAN from the program to follow the cyanide to the location of greatest concentration." Upon Cennamo's command, the whine and flashing lights stopped and HERMAN turned sharply to the right and stopped by a desk. He moved back and forth a couple of times, stopped and transmitted again.

"HERMAN has located the point of greatest concentration. That desk," Cennamo said pointing.

"Minnie, have a look," Steve ordered. *This is going to be one helluva day,* he thought. They were now using tactical communications devices that worked even through the gas masks, which they had quickly donned.

"Yes, sir." Minnie moved toward the desk, searching for whatever device would set off the gas. "This explains why we didn't have a welcome party."

"I suspect that David will continue to be more creative as we get closer to the computer room," Neena said. "He's vain about his work."

"Cennamo," Minnie suddenly called out to Cennamo. "Is HERMAN's heater on?"

"No, Sergeant."

"Engage it now!"

Cennamo manipulated a switch that would activate a coil in HERMAN, which would generate heat to 98.6° F., mimicking human body heat. Minnie pulled off her gas mask, standing absolutely still, listening. Suddenly, she looked at the ceiling about ten feet away. She raised her M4A1 and fired several rounds at a small disk.

"Those detectors tend to make a little squeak as the device picks up the heat level and expands. It's always a giveaway. I'll cap the gas now."

As Minnie removed the gas canisters from under the desk and placed them in sealed metal containers, Cennamo brought HERMAN back to his last programmed point and set him out to complete the search. Ten minutes later, HERMAN gave his all-clear signal.

The detachment began a physical search of the basement and its contents. Clark used a small device to take soundings of the floor, walls, and ceiling, looking for hidden pockets and spaces. None were detected and the detachment re-grouped. "Corporal Clark," Steve said loudly.

"Yes, sir."

"Check upstairs and if you can, please report our progress to General Trevane."

Clark responded, "Yes, sir" and bounded up the stairs.

"Neena, have you found anything?" Steve inquired.

"No. There are office supplies and some linen tablecloths and napkins in a closet, but no documents anywhere—either in the desk drawers or the file cabinets. There are no computers or hard drives. That doesn't surprise me, though."

"It doesn't surprise me either. Just hoping. Okay, let's prepare for the next floor."

Neena and Sergeant Greene examined the stairway to the next floor. There were metal doors at the top, framed in metal and built to be airtight. Before Neena could stop him, Greene grasped the door handle. She yelled, but before he understood her, he'd flung the door open.

An ear-bursting *whoosh* shook the house as a Mini-Strike launcher fired its missile. The missile had been modified to hold flechettes, and it exploded halfway up the stairway, sending out an even louder boom. Six-inch, razor sharp, arrow-shaped pieces of steel ripped *en masse* through Greene. The stairway, built of reinforced concrete, withstood the blasts and acted as a hard funnel, so the mass of flechettes concentrated on the basement level doorway at the top. Greene died instantly, his body riddled with pieces of steel from helmet to boot.

The six in the basement were stunned by the brutality of Greene's death. Ten seconds went by before anyone could react.

"Anybody else hit?" Steve shouted, trying to hear himself above the pounding in his ears. A round of "no's" followed. Steve opened the closet, pulled out one of the white linen tablecloths, and placed it gently over Greene's body. As he did so, the flechettes slowly pierced the linen like tiny silver trees. Steve stood still and watched the linen for a few seconds as it settled onto the body and reddened. "Sonovabitch!" he yelled. "Listen up. Follow the goddamn plan! Greene would still be alive if he'd followed the *goddamn plan*!"

Everyone knew what Steve was saying. The plan had a set of procedures for each stairway and floor. Opening a stairway door without an "all clear" from Minnie was not in the plan and had cost Greene his life. *Amateur hour,* Steve bitched to himself, but this warrior had died under his command and Steve blamed himself for any failure of his team.

"Okay, Minnie. Have a look at the stairway," Steve said, the anger still showing.

She stood at the top of the stairs and brought out two pieces of electronic equipment. After scanning the stairway, she put on infrared goggles. Next, she sounded the walls with the device that had been used in the basement. Then she said, "Preparing charges," and fired a large-bore weapon several times. The shells, tethered by a wire to the weapon, stuck to the walls, ceiling and floor as she fired.

"Stand back." Everyone took cover. "Fire in the hole," she yelled, pushing the button on an electronic triggering device. The shells were small explosive devices intended to trigger other devices. The only explosions were from the shells, indicating no other explosives present in the stairway. "All clear," she yelled. Steve decided not to remind the others why Greene could not hear her.

Specialist Rodriguez led the detachment to the bottom of the stairs in place of Greene, lobbed two grenades to the right and left, and stopped to reconnoiter. The blast from the rocket launcher and the backlash from the missile explosion had blown out the metal doorway and cleared an area about thirty feet in radius in the floor below the basement. "Epstein, you take my place to the right," Rodriguez yelled.

"Solid copy," Epstein barked as he swept down the stairs and took a position on the floor about ten feet away.

"I will take Corporal Clark's place on your left," Neena said, and she moved so quickly that Steve couldn't stop her. She took her position on the left, signaling back to Rodriguez.

"Cennamo, bring HERMAN down," Rodriguez bellowed.

Cennamo carried HERMAN down the stairs, setting him three feet into the room. Within five minutes, HERMAN was doing his programmed search of sublevel two—the basement was labeled sublevel one—and he sped through the entire room without incident.

Steve heard Clark's boots and walked up the stairs to meet him. Clark's eyes widened and Steve placed a hand on his shoulder. "He was a brave warrior," said Steve. "We'll mourn Greene later. Right now we have to get to those computers. Do you understand, Corporal?"

"Yes, sir."

"Did you report to General Trevane?"

"Yes, sir," the corporal responded quickly, averting his eyes from his dead comrade.

"What's the situation up there?"

"The entire compound is secure. Two prisoners. One of them is Defense Minister Luegner."

"What about David Alon?"

"No report, sir. Not all of the bodies have been identified, sir. He is not one of the prisoners, though, sir."

"Thank you, Corporal. Take a position and wait for Cennamo's all-clear signal."

Steve waited for Clark to move away from the body and thought to himself, *David Alon will not surrender. I won't let that happen.*

"All clear," Cennamo shouted.

Again with the all-clear signal, the rest of the detachment descended the stairs and began a physical search of the floor and its contents. Clark, as he was assigned, operated the small device that took soundings of the floor, walls, and ceiling to locate hidden pockets and spaces. As with the basement, Clark detected no abnormalities in the structure.

The floor, like all the subterranean floors, was seventy feet square and had been a storage facility and arsenal. It was mostly empty. In addition to wall-mounted gun racks and empty ammo boxes, some canned food and paper supplies were all that remained.

"Okay, Minnie. Let's get to the next floor," Steve said.

Minnie drilled two small holes, one for a small halogen torch and the other for a small camera. Both the torch and camera were on hand-manipulated cables so that Minnie could move them and examine both the stairwell and the back of the door at the top of the next stairway. She completed her visual inspection, withdrew the camera, and pushed an infrared mini camera through the drilled hole, watching the monitor as she moved the camera back and forth. Finally, she gave the command to open the door and completed her procedures without incident. Steve ordered Rodriguez to descend.

At the bottom, Rodriguez conducted his visual sweep and tossed two grenades. Clark and Epstein took positions to the left and right. Cennamo got HERMAN running. After HERMAN's thirty-minute search, Cennamo gave the all-clear. Clark performed the sublevel sweep. Meanwhile, the others inspected an array of metal filing cabinets and built-in shelves.

"Seems as if this was a document storage area, but it, too, is clean," Neena observed.

"Mr. Barber," Clark called out over his tac communications.

"Yes, Corporal."

"The metal cabinets are interfering with the device. Can I get some help moving them away from the walls?"

"Wait!" Minnie shouted. "I may have found something." She motioned to one of the built-in shelves. The shelf was slightly angled away from the wall. The others moved toward her, weapons raised.

As they did they so, a block of metal cabinets opposite Minnie eased open, noiseless. Three men with Uzis slipped out of a space behind the cabinets, sixty feet from the detachment, letting loose a burst of fire.

Cennamo dropped on the floor behind HERMAN and fired back. Clark and Rodriguez were hit before they could move. Minnie ducked behind shelves and fired, killing one of the men. Epstein dove to his left and fired a burst. The man on the left fired back, running a continuous line of fire down the concrete floor, over and through Epstein.

As the man fired at Epstein, Steve ran to the left. Cennamo and Neena let loose bursts at the gunman, hitting him several times. Steve continued running to his left trying to get the remaining gunman to turn toward him so that Neena and the others could have clear shots. As he ran, he caught a glimpse of the gunman. *Damn, it's not David.*

Another burst from the Uzi, but Steve had ducked behind a wide column. Just then, Cennamo fired, shattering the Uzi. Steve saw his chance, hed his H&K and M4A1, and rushed the man with knives drawn. *I'd like him alive for a while.*

As Steve came within striking distance, the man feinted with his knife and then, ripped the air with a truncheon in his other hand. Steve knew he was expected to back away from the knife into the stick. It was a move he'd used many times. But he was no amateur at hand-to-hand combat. Steve stepped slightly to his right and crossed his knife blades to block the baton blow, letting the force push him down into a crouch. From that position, he willed his legs to rise with enough strength, a searing pain sending signals to his brain. Steve spun, putting his weight on his right foot, and slashed the KABAR toward the man's back.

The enemy countered the maneuver. He stopped pushing, planted his left foot and turned sharply to his right, blocking the KABAR with his knife. They both pulled back and stood facing each other. Now the others could see both of their faces.

Neena screamed, "Steve. It's Zee, David's sergeant!"

"None of us will make it out of here alive, Barber," Zee spit. "But I insist that you die first."

"We'll see about that. You modern day Zealots haven't killed me yet, and you've had a lot of chances." Steve's heart pounded. He could feel his body coil and relax preparing for whatever was next.

"I've now taken the assignment personally, so I know it'll be done."

"Why hasn't your master stayed to kill me?" Steve asked, trying to bait the sergeant to tell him where David was.

"I can tell you. Why not? You won't get out of here anyway. He's gone to kill your president and Israel's prime minister." *The fool. He's picked on the wrong guy. I won't lose* this *fight.*

"Why?" Steve asked. *Alon is a fucking maniac!*

"He's going to make it look like an Iranian hit. You can't stop us. Time to die, Barber."

Talking was over. Zee jabbed the truncheon at Steve's eyes, causing him to blink, and then arched inward, holding his knife high and thrusting toward Steve's throat with his blade. In a great sweeping move, Steve brought both of his knives down on Zee's blade, jumping back into a crouch. He sprang at Zee, attacking with a series of windmill knife blows, Zee blocking them. Zee moved forward, jabbed at Steve's eyes. Steve stood still for a second, waiting for Zee to follow with the knife thrust to his throat. It came.

and as it did, Steve crouched under the blade and shot both his body and left hand forward with his TAC-2, shoving the blade into Zee's chest. He let go of the knife to save time and dropped back to fend off Zee's knife as he brought it down. Steve had mortally wounded Zee, but there was still great force to his final attempted blow. Steve stood fully erect and stepped up to meet him, jamming the KABAR straight into Zee's throat. He watched Zee clutch weakly at his neck for a few moments and collapse.

Neena flew to Steve, kissing him, holding him. The others shouted and hooted, and Steve managed a little smile. But the sense of victory was fleeting as they realized that Epstein was dead and both Rodriguez and Clark were critically wounded.

"Cennamo, Neena, take care of Rodriguez and Clark," Steve ordered. "Minnie, let's get to that computer room!"

Just then, something started to whine near Zee's body. Minnie rifled his pockets until she found the offending device. "It's an electronic delayed fuse detonator!"

"A what?" Cennamo asked.

"It's similar to a dead-man switch, but programmed to activate if not reset periodically. When the owner stops resetting the detonator, it will delay for the programmed amount of time and then transmit a signal to a receiver that will detonate the explosives. There must be a charge somewhere and it's going to go off very soon."

"Can we stop it?"

"Too late. The signal's been sent. We would have to find the charge and have the time to disarm it. That never works, by the way." Just then, a great blast shook the entire building.

Mid-Afternoon Saturday, May 3, 2014; on a Hill Overlooking Pädäh, Jerusalem, Israel

A man's large hands gripped military binoculars, gently pressing them against his eyes as he lay on his stomach peering through a break in the shrubbery on a hill overlooking his objective. His clothing was American issue camouflage battle dress. His face was painted in stripes of brown and black. Around his shoulder was an Uzi, not standard issue for any of the American armed forces. He carried a Jericho 941, also non-standard weaponry for Americans, in a shoulder holster, and a seven-inch knife, stained to the hilt with blood, in a sheath strapped to his right thigh.

The binoculars were focused on the office building inside Pädäh. David Alon watched as the building shivered for a few moments, the few hundred enemy around the compound taking cover. He continued watching until activity resumed. When he had first trained the binoculars on the compound, a battle had been raging. Now only shouts of orders could be heard. He made a note of the time. 1416 hours. David muttered, "Goodbye Neena, daughter of Israel. Shalom." *Damn! Damn! Damn!* he repeated to himself.

Beside David lay two American soldiers. Alive, they were a sniper team. Now they had joined their warrior sisters and brothers in death. David had killed them for their tactical communications equipment and the sniper rifle. *It pays to know what your enemy is saying, especially when it is about you*, David thought.

David took time to cover the dead soldiers, which would protect them from carrion feeders long enough for the Americans to discover their bodies. After that, he scanned the surrounding terrain, placed the binoculars in their protective carrier and strapped that to his body, picked up his weapons, and set off down the hill away from the compound. He would have a one- or two-hour head start, and until the Americans found the bodies, he would be able to monitor their communications. *That will be long enough.*

Mid-Afternoon Saturday, May 3, 2014; Pädäh, Jerusalem, Israel

The explosion reverberated throughout the office building and the foundation shuddered like it had chomped on something very bitter. Dust and concrete chunks fell through the stairway. Cennamo ran to the stairway and started to pull pieces of concrete as they careened down the stairway. He continued as even more concrete rained down.

"Cennamo! Stop," Steve ordered. Cennamo turned away from the stairway.

"That's what he meant," Steve continued.

"What do you mean?" Neena asked, an expression of terror on her face because even as she asked, Steve knew she realized what had happened.

"Zee said he knew that none of us would get out of here alive. David *planned* to seal off the sublevels. With us down here."

"That makes sense because the charge wasn't big enough to collapse the floors," Minnie added.

"These people are not the surrendering type," Steve continued. "David knew it would take too long for Strategic Command to dig through to us even if the computers are still working." *I'm really beginning to dislike that asshole.*

Everyone was silent for a minute as the reality of being entombed by the dead Sergeant Zadok "Zee" Shachar sunk in.

"Well since we're here, let's see what's in the computer room," Steve announced as he walked to the metal door to the last stairway. Minnie followed and swiftly completed her procedures. *Not that it matters,* thought Steve. *If we're trapped, what difference will one more detonation make?* He shook his head. This was not like him. He glanced at Neena as she and Cennamo put Clark and Rodriguez on IV drips. For once, he couldn't read her thoughts. *Will we die here?* Steve took a deep breath. "Get a grip," he whispered. This time it didn't annoy him that he talked to himself.

The stairway was clear. With Rodriguez wounded, Steve led the others down the stairs. At the bottom, he followed his instinct instead of the procedures, sensing that David Alon saw no further need to set traps. He would want them to have time to feel powerless, suffocating in the concrete ruins of his compound, while he killed the American president and Israeli prime minister. He kicked open the door open, knocking it off one hinge, and the four walked in. Smashed computers and monitors, papers, chairs, tables—everything was broken and strewn all over the floor.

"Shit!" Steve spat. "I *knew* it. David didn't need—or want—the fucking computers! All this fighting. All this death. For *nothing!*"

They looked for another trap, but Steve's his intuition was correct.

"I need to kill that bastard. Let's find a way out of here," Steve houted so that the focus was on a solution instead of the problem. "What bout the equipment elevator?"

"I blew it the hell up," Minnie retorted.

"I know that," Steve said. "But we don't know the extent of the damage, do we?"

The four ran to the equipment elevator. Steve yanked the door open and pieces of steel and cable fell out. He cleared enough debris to duck his head in, peering up. "Damn! It's totally blocked."

"Maybe it is only blocked here." Neena said. "There are ten feet of shaft between this level and the one above. That can hold a lot of debris." They backtracked up the stairs to the floor above. Rodriguez and Clark rested fitfully, in a slight opiate-induced stupor, under the IV drips Cennamo and Neena had set up.

Minnie reached the equipment elevator door first and held the handle for a moment, mouthing what Steve assumed was a little prayer. She pulled on the handle. Nothing fell out and the shaft was clear. She looked up. There was a faint glow. "Thank you, God," she said.

The others poked their heads inside and looked up. The hope was infectious and smiles returned.

"Minnie," Steve began, "What kind of risks are up there?"

"The explosives are certainly gone. We'll find sharp steel fragments. If the power is on, we might get zapped, but the power only goes to the motor, which is up top. But, this place is built like a brick shithouse, so I don't think we risk structural weakness. The booby traps were intended to be anti-personnel and not big enough to damage reinforced concrete. My charges were only big enough to set the others off. I think the risks are mainly that we could fall a couple of stories."

"Who wants to climb out?" Steve asked. He would stay with Rodriguez and Clark. It was his command. He should be the last out. *And Neena should be first.* A battle he would surely lose.

"I'll go," Minnie offered. "I am a spelunker. That's how I got my nickname—now you know. I can get through anywhere."

"I'll go, too," Cennamo said. "I'm not a hero—I'm starting to see the walls closing in on me here."

Steve and Neena looked at each other. "Okay," Steve said. "Let's look through the equipment and see what you can use to climb out of here."

They rummaged through everything, finding gloves and some tools that Cennamo carried to repair HERMAN. *They might come in handy to bend metal and grab hot wires. Not looking forward to this.* Steve pulled the straps from everyone's packs and hitched them together for use as a short rope that would bind Minnie and Cennamo together, reducing the risk of one falling, banking on Minnie's experience as a spelunker. Not much, but they hadn't anticipated having to climb out through an elevator shaft. The good news was that the shaft was four feet by four feet, so they could work their way up by stepping against the steel framing, at least where the framing remained.

"When you hit the surface," Steve began, "The first thing you do is alert American and Israeli security to David Alon's planned attempt on the president and prime minister. Don't come back for us until that's done. That's an order. Understood?"

Minnie hoisted herself up, Cennamo in tow. Neena and Steve watched them rise to the next sublevel. There would be the basement after that, then ground level.

If there are no big problems, they should be out in about fifteen minutes, Steve thought as he walked over to Rodriguez and Clark, checked their dressings and IVs. *Running out of time and saline. Sorry, but the president and prime minister have priority.* He gently picked up Epstein and positioned him near his wounded comrades, retrieving a blanket from the computer room and placing it over Epstein's body.

Neena sidled over to Steve as he stood looking down at his men. She pulled him back, wound her arm around his waist, resting her head against his shoulder. "You were great today," she said.

"Thanks," Steve said, "It was a bitch of a day and we haven't stopped the missiles. I'm glad you were here. It was very," he paused to think of the correct word, and continued, "Comforting. That's the word. It was very comforting to know you were with me. I knew someone had my back."

"David must be stopped."

"Yes, I'm going to find him and kill him with my bare hands."

"I am going with you," Neena said looking into Steve's eyes. He knew that she was not negotiating. *Wait 'til I get my hands on that sonovabitch,* Steve thought. *It's personal now.*

Steve stroked Neena's hair, kissed it, and then said, "Will you marry me?" *What did I just say?* His heart pounded. Was it pounding from the fear that she would refuse or the fear that she'd say yes? Steve didn't know. All he knew was that suddenly nothing had ever seemed more right.

"What!" Neena blurted out, stepping back a foot or so.

"I said, 'Will you marry me?'" Steve said amazing himself, his hands searching for hers.

Neena looked at him for a minute and said, "This is a fine time to be asking me a question like that."

"That's not an answer." *This feels so good.*

A few seconds passed, then she jumped on him saying, "Yes! Yes! Yes!"

"One 'yes' will do," he said grinning ear to ear.

"You will have to ask me again after we get out of here. I want a proper proposal of marriage."

"Okay, I agree as long as the answer will be the same."

"It will be."

They kissed. It was more than passionate. The kiss was a connecting, an exchange of energy, "... a trip to the moon on gossamer wings", as Cole Porter once wrote. The dusty concrete room, filled with death and pain, became a small doorway to heaven.

"Hey, is this where the underground party is?" a voice echoed from the elevator doorway. Steve and Neena fell back to earth.

"Sure is!" Steve shouted back.

The voice was that of Sergeant Major Tom Kirby. Behind him he had a medic and two corporals with gear to bring up Neena and Steve, and basket stretchers for the wounded men and one dead soldier. There was clanging in the elevator shaft as men shored up the shaft and removed broken and bent framing.

"We'll wait while you get Rodriguez, Clark, and Epstein up," Steve said to Sergeant Major Kirby.

"Yes, sir. Understood, sir."

Neena and Steve held hands as they watched their comrades disappear into the elevator shaft.

"Sergeant Major," Steve said.

"Yes, sir," he answered, his voice echoing off the metal walls.

"We left a comrade in the first sublevel—the basement. Did the blast include the basement?"

"No sir, the blast only took out the second sublevel—the one just above this one. We have already recovered Sergeant Greene's body, sir."

"Thank you, Sergeant Major." The metal basket stretcher disappeared for the ascent.

Neena was next. She tried to protest while slipping her boot through the sling but Steve yanked the cord and it started to rise. Steve stared at Zee's body.

"We'll ship the dead defenders up after you, sir," Kirby offered.

"Thank you, Sergeant Major. They were wrong, but they were warriors fighting for what they thought was right. They deserve a soldier's burial."

On the surface, Jack waited to greet them. As Steve's eyes adjusted to the sunlight, now low in the sky, he looked at his watch. It was 1525 hours. He smelled the smoke that rose in small pockets across the compound like a hundred Boy Scout campfires burning wet wood. Helmets with red crosses dashed to and fro with stretchers and IVs.

The pristine compound, Pädäh, a delight of Israel since 1951, was rubble. The walls lay shattered, wasted, as though they never stood. Mud bricks, stone fragments, and broken concrete were strewn in all directions, rebar sticking out like bent licorice sticks. Standing walls bore the pockmarks of large and small arms fire. Sticky patches dotted the ground where the dead and wounded had bled. Vomit, feces, and urine—the bodily output of agony and death—mingled with the blood in the ground and the lingering smell of gunpowder. Steve's senses recorded yet another bitter battle scene.

"Impressive mission, Steve," Jack said, walking directly up to Steve and looking him straight in the eye.

"Sorry we don't have computers to hack, General," Steve responded.

"So am I. So am I." Jack paused for a moment and continued. "We achieved our objective, Steve. We took the compound and secured the computer room. That's all we *could* do. Now it's up to the US Navy."

"That's right," Steve agreed. "In about four hours David's twenty-even missiles will be launched. Then we'll all know whether those expensive anti-missile systems work." Steve lowered his backpack to the ground and laid his weapons carefully across it. "How are casualties, Jack?" Steve said, using his first name as Jack had requested he do. It seemed as if that were days ago.

"Twenty-one dead—mostly from those damn Mini-Spikes—and eighteen seriously wounded, three critically. We have some walkers, too, but I don't count them." *If you can fight, you're not a casualty. How like Jack,* Steve noted with respect.

"And the defenders?" Neena asked as she lifted the burden of gear from her right shoulder, probing it gingerly.

"Fifty-five dead," Jack said. "Seventeen wounded—most are critical because they kept fighting if they could—and two prisoners who were not wounded. One of them is Simon Luegner. The other is his bodyguard."

Steve took one of his knives, recovered from Zee's body, and sliced the pant leg over his left thigh. The dressing, ripped from the adhesive tape, had bunched above the stitches. He yanked it off. *That feels better, not good, but better.*

"The fifty-five dead do not include David Alon," Neena said, knowing it was fact.

"The security forces have been alerted," Jack said, shaking his head. "I'm guessing that you want Alon's hide." The three of them walked toward the field medical tent, gear and weapons in tow. "Affirmative, Jack," Steve said, gritting his teeth. "I'm going to hang that sonovabitch's body in a public square."

"Good hunting, son," Jack said as he put his arm around Steve's shoulder.

Steve felt a shot of warmth hit him like a wave. Black Jack Trevane had just called him "son". Steve knew he'd just received a great compliment from a great warrior. "Thank you, sir."

They arrived at the medical tent where a medic looked Neena and Steve over. Aside from bumps, scrapes and scratches, they were both fine. *That's the second time I escaped with barely a scratch,* thought Steve, remembering the night he took out the London bombers. *Perhaps it's a trend. And now, I'm getting married. Got to stay healthy.* The medics tended to some pulled stitches and put new dressings on the wounds suffered in Beirut. Steve didn't flinch.

"Jack," Steve said as the medic taped the dressing, "Bill Elsberry and Abi are going to be on board the *Reagan* when the ballistic missiles are launched. Do you want to join them?" The medic returned to the other side of the tent to treat others with minor wounds. The critically wounded had already been airlifted to a nearby hospital.

"No, Steve. I can't do anything there, and I want to spend some time with my troops. They've had a tough day and I want to thank them for what they did. I also have twenty-one letters to write. I've found that I need to do that right after a battle so that I can still feel the heat of it and remember what my dead warriors went through."

"I understand, General." Steve stood at attention and saluted. Jack returned it with a snap. "Great serving with you, Jack."

"Likewise, Marine."

Steve and Neena headed for the communications truck to get transportation to Jerusalem. They held hands as they walked in silence. If the Navy couldn't stop the missiles, the Middle East would be destroyed. Steve saw the futile look on Neena's face. He squeezed her hand but there wasn't much else he could do.

"Mr. Barber. Ms. Shahud," Kirby, the NCO who pulled them out of their concrete crypt, called out as he ran up to them.

"Yes, Sergeant Major," Neena responded for the two of them.

"Mr. Elsberry is waiting for you."

"Thank you, Sergeant Major," Steve said. "Would you let Command know that we confiscated these weapons?" He raised his short H&K 9mm MP5K sub-machine gun and M4A1 carbine. "We'll bring them back tomorrow. We don't want Jack on our asses for a couple of assault rifles."

"Affirmative, sir," Kirby responded with a smile. "I'm sure General Trevane approves of the intended use of his weapons." The Sergeant Major turned and hurried back to his duties.

They looked for Bill. As they neared the shattered guardhouse, they saw him waving. Steve and Neena broke into a slow, tired jog and the three hugged and laughed, a release of tension for everyone.

"The president sends his personal thanks, and I have also heard from Vic. They are both proud of the Black Watch and you two."

"Thanks, Bill," Steve said, "But we didn't stop David—or the missiles." After pausing for a moment thinking about the gravity of what he'd said, Steve continued, "I want to put a few people in for commendations. My team showed a lot of guts and 'can do' today. Can you help me with that?"

"Absolutely."

"Thank you, Bill. This can wait until Monday, but I wanted to line up your help." Steve looked around at what had been Pädäh, but was now stumps, dust, and rubble. *How easily we can turn something beautiful into absolute shit.*

"Steve, I've arranged for you to board the *Reagan*. It's up to the Navy now. Why don't I drive you back to your hotel for a hot shower and clean clothes?" Bill turned toward the embassy town car, but Steve and Neena remained in place. "Bill," Steve said, "There's been a change in plans."

"Anything to do with David Alon?" Bill asked, turning back toward them.

"Yes," Neena answered. "We are the most qualified at finding and killing him."

"What can I do?" Shadows reached out like a great shroud creeping over the battlefield and its dead.

"We need ammo and a change of clothes," Steve said. "A shower would be great, too. It's almost sixteen hundred hours. Less than three and a half hours to missile launch."

"The State Department owns a house not too far from here on the way to Jerusalem," said Bill. "It's used for visiting dignitaries, but, given the nature of today's festivities, the Ambassador had barred its use until June 1st, so it's empty except for a small Marine detachment. You can secure clothes and ammo from them. I'll bet there's even a shower." Bill allowed a smile. "I'll call ahead and get what you need ready."

Bill chauffeured the embassy town car, the American flag fluttering on the hood. Steve and Neena were silent in the back seat, eyes closed, hands clasped. As they passed through Shin Bet roadblocks and crowds of curious onlookers, Steve noted the near total destruction. *We sure took it to them, poor bastards.*

As they neared their destination, Steve gave Bill a complete, but short, briefing of the day. Then they switched topics: how to find David. As Neena turned sideways to face him, drawing up her left leg, looking so tired and beautiful and trusting, Steve thought, *You're going to pay for all these lives, David.*

Late Afternoon, Saturday, May 3, 2014; US Department of State House, Jerusalem, Israel

Neena and Steve showered and changed clothes. They wore battle dress again because it was practical for the task ahead, and they re-armed. Bill had hurried off for the USS *Ronald Reagan* where he'd have better access to communications and could observe the assault on the Israeli nuclear missiles.

The Marines stationed at the State Department House were curious, but they knew better than to ask questions about top-secret operations. In addition to putting together a quick meal, the Marines offered to clean Neena and Steve's weapons, which Neena and Steve gratefully accepted. The Marines knew warriors on the hunt when they saw them.

Bill had arranged for a car for them. "We'll sort out the forms and approvals at the State Department, later," he'd said. Steve had the impression Bill enjoyed breaking the rules sometimes. *I really like Bill*, Steve mused.

In an emerald-green VW Polo, they raced toward the prime minister's residence, called Beit Aghion, in the Rehavia section of Jerusalem. The President of the United States had already arrived. There was no time to lose. "There's only one thing left to do," Steve said with a slight grin.

"What's that?" Neena responded.

"Figure out how the hell we're going to find David."

Neena chuckled. "I thought that you'd have a plan by now."

"I do, but I want to hear yours first."

"My plan is to send you down the street by the prime minister's house and when David shoots you, I'll locate his position by the flash and kill him."

"I like my plan better."

"What is that?"

"I don't know yet, but I know I like it better."

They were both laughing now. After the moment of welcome humor passed, Neena observed, "David will try to get as close as possible to ensure the kills and leave evidence of Iranian involvement. If he wants to implicate the Iranians in the assassination of your president and my prime minister, he needs to escape. That is a disadvantage to him."

"Can we get tactical control of security at the residence? At least on the outside?" Steve asked. "If you're right, he will go there because he knows he's on borrowed time. He'll only have tonight to kill them."

"Yes, Abi can clear us."

Just then, their tac radio burped a message. "Call home by landline. Confirm with two clicks."

Steve clicked the transmit button twice and looked at Neena. She understood and, after only a few minutes, found a payphone in a gasoline station that she'd used in the past. It was an old-fashioned booth, at the rear of the station and under the shade of an ancient Acacia tree. Steve dialed a special number that connected him to Bill Elsberry wherever he was at any given time. Steve held the receiver away from his ear so that Neena could hear.

"Password," came the voice at the other end of the line.

"Masada," Steve said.

"Steve," Bill began. "I'll be quick. Jack Trevane called in. Two of his snipers were killed by hand on the eastern hill overlooking Pädäh. Their sniper rifle and tac radio were taken. It looks like David Alon's work. We presume he thinks the two of you are buried under a couple of floors of reinforced concrete in his office building. That's an advantage you probably want to keep. That's why I had you call by landline."

"Thanks, Bill. Good thinking," Steve said. Neena nodded in agreement. "That means we need a new tac radio," Steve continued.

"On the way. We've been tracking you by satellite. Cute little car—please don't wreck it. You should see a couple of Marines pull up at your location in less than a minute. They'll have a tac radio that's been set to a series of IDF frequencies. We're going to keep up chatter on our frequencies just so that David thinks he's still plugged in. Jack Trevane is handling that. He has a Black Watch Command team running a simulation exercise on the premise that they're tracking David to kill him. David should be expecting a team of angry American motherfuckers to be on his ass. That should distract him."

"It would distract *me*," Steve agreed.

"If we are presumed dead in the explosion, how is it that anyone knows David is on the loose?" Neena asked.

"We've been spreading the word that Simon Luegner has been captured and spilled his guts." Bill responded.

"Got it," Neena said.

A car raced into the station forty kph above the speed limit, lurching to a halt on the gravel ten meters from the phone booth, spitting stones and dust. Neena and Steve tensed reflexively. A Marine sergeant, the one who had cooked for them, jumped out sporting a wide grin and ran up to them with a radio set. "Per Mr. Elsberry's orders, Mr. Barber," he barked as he handed the equipment to Steve.

"Thanks, sergeant. This will come in very handy."

The sergeant got back into the car, which sped away as fast as it had arrived. Steve got back on the phone with Neena listening in again. "Okay, Bill. Thanks for the heads up. We're on our way right now to the prime minister's residence to intercept David. Can you clear us?"

"Abi is right here. Hang on." Bill returned seconds later. "Okay, Secret Service is alerted and the prime minister and the president are evacuating. You've got immediate clearance through Abi so no worries about friendly fire."

"One more thing. This is my kill," said Steve.

"Roger that. Good hunting."

Steve hung up the phone and they continued toward Rehavia. Neena drove because she was familiar with the streets, which suited Steve fine. He could gaze at her profile. *So David thinks we're dead, does he?* Steve thought. *That'll cost him. Big time.*

One Hour Before Sundown, Saturday, May 3, 2014; USS *Ronald Reagan*, Off the Coast of Israel

The US Navy Seahawk helicopter lifted off the roof of the US Embassy building a little after six fifteen in the evening. Abi and Bill were on board. They would observe air control operations aboard the USS *Ronald*

Reagan. As they clambered out of the Seahawk onto the deck of the *Reagan*, a CPO, chief petty officer, met them and escorted them to air control operations.

Bill thought the air control operations room was like a James Cameron movie set. LED spewed bits of green, amber, orange, and red light in blinking patterns. Navy NCOs, non-commissioned officers, ringed the room, studying instruments and engaging in a murmur of information chatter that filled the room with the low hum of a mighty beehive. The acoustics were astounding. Twenty people were talking, but if you paid attention, you could understand what each was saying, even though the talk was just above a whisper.

Bill glanced around the room. He had seen operations centers before, but this was like a starship. "Abi, the *Reagan* is the newest and best we have. It's good every once in a while to see where the taxpayers' money goes. I have to say I'm in awe."

"It's very impressive, Bill."

On one side of the room was a set of white boards filled with alphanumeric characters in columns drawn in a variety of dry erase marker colors. In the center there was a large circular digital map. A radius of green light swung repeatedly around the map and as it hit various symbols digitally marked on the map, a small red light would emit a visual "ping". Also on the map were hand drawn markings and lines. On either side of the map, panels showed a constant stream of data and charts, differentiated in colors, identifying the type of information displayed.

This is where they met Davy Jones.

"Welcome aboard the USS *Ronald Reagan*," said a man who looked like a forty-year old Cary Grant. "I'm Captain David L. Jones. You can call me Davy. I tried being called David, but that didn't work," he said with a laugh.

"Thank you, Davy," Bill said, shaking his hand. "Bill Elsberry, military attaché at the embassy here. This is Abital Zahavi," he said, gesturing toward Abi, "Special Assistant to the Prime Minister—I think she would like you to call her Abi, is that correct?" he asked.

"Yes, Bill. Abi is preferred. Thank you." Abi extended her hand to Davy.

"I've heard of you during briefings over the past couple days," Davy said. "Very pleased to meet you. I understand you've had quite a day so far."

"Yes, we have. Sorry we didn't make your job easier by hacking the computers," Abi said.

The CPO came up to Davy, handing him a piece of paper with colored printing on it. Davy looked at it briefly and returned it to the CPO. "No need to be sorry, Abi. I understand that you met all the objectives of a very difficult mission," Davy said. "I'm very honored to have you both on board."

"Thank you, Captain."

"Will Ms. Shahud and Mr. Barber be joining us?" Davy asked.

"No, Davy," Bill answered. "They send their regrets at not being able to accept your hospitality, but they're attending to an urgent security matter." Bill knew that Davy would understand he'd been politely told not to ask further questions.

Davy nodded, and said. "I'll give you a short briefing on what we are doing here."

"That would be very helpful," Bill said, looking around the room filled with electronics. *Captain Kirk, eat your heart out.*

Davy looked at his watch. "I have about ten minutes. We're launching aircraft at eighteen fifty hours. To begin, you probably know that our Aegis class of ships provides an important element with the operationally certified Aegis Ballistic Missile Defense—BMD for short—Weapon System and the SM-3 Block IA missile. We use this weapon on target missiles in the post-boost phase and prior to reentry."

"If I may ask a stupid question, why doesn't intercepting a ballistic missile result in a nuclear explosion?" Abi asked.

"Abi, that's *not* a stupid question. A lot of people have asked that, and a lot of people assume that it does. The answer is that until re-entry, all ballistic missiles—at least the ones within the control of responsible governments—are not armed. That's because no one wants one of these exploding until it's damn close to its target."

They shifted a few steps as a series of Navy personnel wove through the operations room. Davy continued talking, moving back to the middle of a narrow passageway once the personnel passed. "There's a lot of science behind this, but essentially there are three control phases. The first is 'safing' or keeping the missile from being fired in error or without proper authority. Safing is generally accomplished by using a Personal Action Link or PAL, which is a lock or switch that controls whether the missile can be fired."

"Our silo crews control those, correct?" Abi offered.

"Yes, that's typical." Davy looked over at one of the displays for five seconds and continued.

"Arming the missile is typically accomplished through the use of a combination of Environment Sensing Devices, which prevent the missile from arming unless and until a unique set of physical actions have occurred. These devices can measure atmospheric pressure, heat sensors, trajectory, flight path, and much more. Unless the missile sensors send the appropriate data to the on-board computer, the missile will not arm, which means it will not permit the critical parts of the warhead to come together in a way that would enable the warhead to explode. Arming usually occurs in the re-entry phase when the pressure and heat around the missile increases and the missile knows it's headed down." Davy emphasized his point by making a diving motion with his right hand.

"The last phase, fuzing, is telling the armed warhead when to explode, such as using a radar to detect a specific distance to the ground or a contact fuse, in which case the missile would explode upon hitting something big enough." Davy looked at his watch and glanced at the same display again. Bill noticed tension creeping over the faces of the men and women at their stations.

"So, what I am hearing is that, prior to arming the warhead, it might be possible to explode it and release radioactive materials, but there would be no fission—no nuclear explosion. Is that right?" Abi asked.

"That's correct. We have one weapon system to use at boost phase, when the missile is accelerating upward. That system on the *Reagan* is our specially equipped F-18s—I'll talk more about that in a moment. We have another system to use at re-entry, when the missile is headed downward toward its target and at any point in between those two phases. Of course, we'd like to be able to intercept the missile before it's armed, but as a last resort, we would intercept a missile in the reentry phase and either hope that the fuzing is not triggered or accept the explosion high in the atmosphere where ground level damage would be drastically reduced."

The hum in the operations room was increasing in intensity. Data was streaming faster on the panels as indicated by the much-accelerated flashing of LEDs.

Davy watched the room for a moment and then said, "The Aegis BMD System is designed to intercept missiles post-boost phase and before re-entry. The SM-3 Block 1A missile is a 'hit-to-kill' missile and has been proven to be very, very effective."

"Are you going to use the Aegis BMD system?" Bill asked.

"Possibly. That question gets me to our fighter aircraft. We have the benefit of working with the owner of the ballistic missiles. That owner wants the missiles intercepted as early as possible. We have permission to be in Israel's airspace and we know where the silos and missiles are. As a result, we're going to rely primarily on our fighter aircraft. We'll back those up with the Aegis BMD system."

"I didn't know you could use aircraft against these missiles," Abi remarked.

She moved a step back to a stainless steel handrail that paralleled the passageway, leaned against it and shifted her weight to her left leg. Bill could see that she was tired. *Long day for her and it's not over by a long shot.*

"The idea has been around for a while. Defense Secretary Gates, as early as 2009, was very interested in using fighter aircraft to intercept ballistic missiles, and that's what got our program going. We've equipped a squadron of F-18 Super Hornets with advanced medium-range air-to-air missiles. This configuration is for use against missiles in their boost, or launch, phase. Other ships have the F-22 Joint Strike Fighter to do this work, but we have not switched out."

"Can you tell us your operational plan for attacking the missiles?" Bill inquired. *Let's get to how we're going to stop this.*

Sounds were now coming from other parts of the ship. Bill heard the whirring of an elevator and the "ding" as it reached a floor. Scraping and clangs and thuds resounded above and Bill looked at the ceiling, sensing the movement of heavy objects.

"Perfect timing. Just getting to that. The squadron is composed of twelve aircraft and we have three silos, with twenty-seven missiles to kill. We've assigned four aircraft to each silo. After they leave the *Reagan*, the aircraft will rendezvous in Israeli airspace within seven kilometers, or klicks, of the assigned silo. We have satellites in position looking for launch flashes and will feed that data to the aircraft, which will also use infrared sensors and visual sightings. We anticipate being able to have aircraft within two klicks of every missile as it leaves its silo. The F-18s can engage multiple targets simultaneously, so we see the missiles being downed well within the launch phase. If a missile survives our aircraft, we will respond with the SM-3 Block1A missiles from ships in the Red Sea. Sorry," Davy said looking at his watch, "I need to get to my post now. Any quick questions?"

"No, Davy," Bill said. "Good hunting." A droplet of sweat trickled down the back of Bill's neck and into his collar. He loosened his tie. *Hope this works.*

"Thanks. Feel free to observe from here, but please don't enter the operations center, where those displays, map and panels are—it gets tight and hot." Davy walked over and picked up a headset and began talking.

Soon, Bill and Abi heard the whoosh of aircraft catapulting off the deck. Davy looked over and flashed an "OK" sign—Bill knew Davy meant the twelve birds were up.

It was just seven in the evening. The aircraft would be circling above their respective silos by seven twenty-three, sundown, the beginning of Memorial Day. They'd wait in the sky to put an end to David Alon's frightful vision.

"Captain, satellites reporting multiple launch flashes," said a chief petty officer sitting in front of a large monitor with green dots. "Captain, we have visuals from Echo, Bravo and Foxtrot. Now, we have visuals from Delta . . . Alpha . . . . . Charlie."

Why do I feel like this is going to be harder than it looks? Bill asked himself.

1925 Hours, Saturday, May 3, 2014; The Rehavia Neighborhood, Jerusalem, Israel

David Alon, dressed as a security officer, strode at a measured, purposeful pace down the sidewalk. He held his Uzi at the ready and continually searched the surrounding shrubs and buildings for suspicious movements. The evening was clear and balmy, the sun now below the horizon. The residents of Rehavia, among the elite of Jerusalem and Israel, tended their properties with vanity, if not love, David thought. The wonderful, slightly sweet aroma of flowers filled the air. As he smelled the subtle fragrances, his thoughts turned to a recently deceased loved one. *Neena. Oh, how I miss you.* The roar of multiple jet engines caused him to stop and look skyward. He pulled his attention back to the task at hand—killing the prime minister and the American president.

David was one block away from the prime minister's residence. He had already passed through one checkpoint as Sergeant Zadok Shachar. *Zee doesn't need his name or ID anymore,* David told himself. *And they won't be looking for him.*

David knew he would have to penetrate the residence to kill the Prime Minister of Israel and the President of the United States. He needed both dead, and a sniper shot might work for one, but not both. He realized over the past few minutes, as the assault of delicate fragrances of the gardens continued to remind him of Neena, that he was angry, very angry. Angry at being thwarted in the launch of Israel's missiles. Angry at no longer being the center of Neena's attention. Angry at killing her. Angrier still at the enemies of Israel who had caused all this death, especially the death of his beloved Neena.

He saw more security personnel now. Zee's credentials would not work at the residence. The security detail would access computers and make phone calls. He had to enter the residence surreptitiously and work his way to wherever the prime minister and president were. He assumed that they would be in the PM's office, following the events on the ground and, now, in the air.

David was now on the block of the residence, several houses away. As fate would have it, years ago he served in a security detail there and knew the building. The security systems would have been upgraded, but he knew the methods and equipment that would have been used. Undetected entry was assured. He just had to get within ten meters of the building itself.

As he closed in on the property line of the residence, he sensed motion. Then, two security personnel merged on him. One came out of shrubbery on his left, the other from the opposite side of the street. As they ordered David to stop, he edged his right hand under his Uzi to wrap his large palm around his knife. *Sons of Israel, prepare to die.*

1928 Hours, Saturday, May 3, 2014, The Prime Minister's Residence in the Rehavia Neighborhood, Jerusalem, Israel

Steve and Neena had arrived at the prime minister's residence seconds before sundown. To avoid the possibility of being seen by David Alon, Abi had arranged for them to meet an IDF van several blocks away. Once driven there, they were secreted into the rear of the elegant mansion.

They waited in an upstairs office. Through the window there was a clear view to the street and date palms swayed in the breeze as if waving a warning. The long boulevard was lined with them. Security personnel patrolled in twos.

As they analyzed how David would plan his kill, they concluded that he would attempt entry by the door leading to the pantry. This door was on the side of the building and had only a single intrusion detector in the doorjamb and was semi-shielded from the security lights. David, naturally assuming no one knew of his plan, would not overly complicate things. *Ah, but David,* thought Steve, I *am about to complicate your life.*

For the sake of caution, however, Steve and Neena would separate, taking positions in diagonally opposed places so that together they had nearly a 360-degree view of the residence and its property. Steve would take his position a short distance from the side door toward the back. Neena would be out front by the corner of the property.

To avoid making any noise, even the low whisper into a headset transmitter, Steve and Neena would communicate with each other using the infrared targeting illuminators on their assault rifles. For this purpose they had devised a few codes. A slow movement of the illuminator over the face meant that the sender had seen an intruder. Rapid movement of the illuminator on the right or left arm or shoulder would mean that the intruder was to the right or left, respectively. They devised other codes, but there was very little time.

They carried small transponders in their combat vests that the security detail inside the residence would monitor. Any major movement by either

Steve or Neena would be detected, alerting the security detail to a possible encounter with David Alon. Once in direct contact with David, Steve and Neena would break radio silence and confirm to the security.

Although security personnel now remained with the prime minister and president, the grounds outside were devoid of any authorized personnel except Neena and Steve. This eliminated the risk of a friendly fire incident. *Plus we don't want to spook the prey,* thought Steve. If David disappeared, finding him again would be a very difficult task, especially once he knew he was a hunted man. As they stood by the back door adjusting their headset communications devices, they heard a series of jet aircraft at high speed, but under Mach 1, filling the skies.

"Those are the F-18s," Steve said. "Let's go."

"See you later," Neena said as she leaned into Steve and kissed him.

"You betcha," Steve smiled.

The two had streaked their faces with camouflage paint, in part to help them blend better with the flora on the property and the approaching night, but also to prevent David from recognizing them. Within seconds they were in position. Neena settled into a group of palm trees on the right, flanked with low shrubs and a low sandstone wall fronting the residence.

Steve headed to the left perimeter wall close to the entrance into the pantry. He hunkered down in a small space between two large firethorn, a bush with thorns two inches long. He knew that he'd get jabbed repeatedly, but that was part of the idea. *Who in their right mind would hide in firethorn?*

The only area that they couldn't see was the middle section of the rear wall. The security detail inside was aware of that blind spot, and they would assist by providing continuous electronic surveillance in that area of the wall and grounds.

Steve and Neena exchanged a flash of illuminator codes to confirm position. *Game time, David,* Steve thought. *These are your last ups.*

1928 Hours, Saturday, May 3, 2014; USS Ronald Reagan, Off the Coast of Israel

Bill Elsberry marveled at Captain Davy L. Jones in his element. His squadron of F-18 Super Hornets, armed with medium-range air-to-air missiles, was airborne and each fighter was at its target destination. They were ready as the silo doors opened and the twenty-seven missiles fired simultaneously, an action intended to complete David Alon's scheme to destroy the enemies of Israel.

"Confirm satellite launch flashes at programmed coordinates," Davy ordered.

"All confirmed, sir."

Bill and Abi huddled, straining to hear every word. The twelve aircraft had sixty seconds to get within range, acquire targets and launch weapons. Beyond sixty seconds, the missiles would gain acceleration and altitude—too high for the fighters' weapons. Distances to targets were short. The missiles would arm minutes after launch phase, ready for detonation at target.

Operations personnel cried out information constantly; pilots responding in a cacophonous stream of reports—missiles exiting silos, engaging systems, target acquired, AMRAAM missiles fired, target destroyed. It made Bill's head spin—all twenty-seven missiles launched at exactly one minute after sundown. The twelve F-18s attacking, following, attacking, all at the same time. It sounded like chaos, but the operations people were focused on saving the Middle East and at least outwardly, they remained calm.

"Captain, Echo 2 reports AMRAAMs stuck in launcher. Backup systems failed to release and launch. We have one live target on course for Qom, Iran. Soon to leave launch phase, sir."

"Can Echo-1 take the target?" asked Davy.

"Negative, sir. Echo-1 has climbed above the attack zone and targets will be out of range by the time he can get his bird back, sir."

"What other fighter teams are assigned to that silo?"

"That would be Foxtrot, Golf, and Hotel, sir."

"Can one of them get to it?" Davy's expression was solemn but his fists were clenched.

"Negative, sir. All returning to carrier."

"Shit! Patch me to the *Shiloh*."

Bill's mind was jolted as he heard that last word. *The USS Shiloh. A ship named after a place where almost 24,000 men died in June of 1862. I hope that's not a bad omen.*

"*Shiloh* on box, sir."

"Frank, this is Davy." The conversation echoed from the speakers in the operations room. "Are you tracking our operation?"

"Affirmative, Davy. Saw the missile in late launch phase. We started sequence. SM-3 away in five seconds."

"Bring down that missile and I'll buy next time in port."

"Always happy to drink on your tab, Davy."

The *Reagan* air operations center was a buzz of activity as the F-18s returned to the carrier. Luckily Echo-2 could land with the AMRAAM still in the launcher. Meanwhile, a computer tracked Echo-2's last target. It was out of launch phase and—the distance to Iran so close—would soon be in re-entry. By then, the missile would be accelerating to its final destination where it would detonate over Qom with more than six times the force of the bomb dropped on Hiroshima. Bill's head felt as if it would explode. He ran a hand over his face and closed his eyes for a second. He wasn't a praying man. *But if ever there were a time,* he admitted to himself.

The SM-3 fired from the *Shiloh* showed up as a small line extending across the map in the center of the *Reagan's* air operations. The room held its collective breath; intently watching the lines of the SM-3 and the Israeli ballistic missile converge. In an instant, the tracking lines disappeared.

"Frank, can you confirm the kill?" Davy called out.

1935 Hours, Saturday, May 3, 2014; The Prime Minister's Residence in the Rehavia Neighborhood, Jerusalem, Israel

David dragged the second body into the ivy crawling up the trunks of two large hibiscus syriacus, commonly called Rose of Sharon, shrubs flourishing next door to the prime minister's residence. In the dark shadows of the shrubbery, the camouflaged uniforms would delay the discovery of their bodies. Soon, it would not matter.

David no longer felt remorse over killing an Israeli. That emotion had fled when he watched Neena buried under tons of concrete at Pädäh. He put everything else out of his mind, including what he would do after he had completed his assignment that evening. David gave himself thirty minutes to kill the Prime Minister of Israel and the President of the United States and, he hoped, start the war that would cripple, if not obliterate, Israel's enemies.

He took a moment to survey the grounds from the shadows. In the front, a low sandstone wall led to an arched wrought iron gate with a walkway to the front door. The walkway was made of granite pavers in a pattern of concentric arches leading to the veranda and elegant main entrance, constructed of cedar and etched glass. The lawn was manicured and garden beds offered an array of flora native to Israel. The scene was an Israeli travel bureau postcard.

Concrete walls nearly ten feet high, topped by spikes, protected the rear and both sides of the property. On the inside, the walls were almost entirely obscured by enormous pyracantha, commonly known as firethorn. Embedded under the razor-sharp thorns were motion and heat sensors that fed data to the security room in the basement of the residence.

David decided that boldness, a trait that he prized, was the key to his success this night. He strolled toward the wrought iron gate, scanning for cars, vans, and armed personnel. To his amazement, he seemed to be alone at this moment, only forty meters from his targets. *They will regret their complacency*, he mused.

David turned into the front walkway, keeping his pace deliberate and bearing military so that anyone observing him would assume he was on authorized patrol. As he neared the front porch, he noted a much smaller walkway to his left, constructed also of pavers, leading to the side entrance off the pantry. He remembered that entrance from years ago. It was where security personnel used to sneak a smoke. It had always been the weakest security point. The pantry door offered easy access in the shadows. When he had reached the smaller walkway, he took it. *Neena, I wish I could have said goodbye to you.*

1936 Hours, Saturday, May 3, 2014; USS *Ronald Reagan*, Off the Coast of Israel

Everyone in the Ops Center on the *Reagan* was silent. Moments that felt like hours hung stagnant in the air. In the midst of the air-conditioned room, beads of sweat formed on every brow. Did the *Shiloh* down the lone Israeli missile that the F-18s had missed? Was all hell going to break loose? Bill glanced at Abi and her face reflected the anxiety he felt in the pit of his stomach.

At last there was a squawk from the box.

"USS *Shiloh* reporting. Drinks are on you, Davy," Frank said.

Bill heard a hint of laughter in Frank's voice. Bill exhaled without realizing he'd been holding his breath and took back what he'd thought about the name *Shiloh. Superstitious idiot!* Relief flooded through his entire body and he turned to Abi and gave her a hug. She stepped back, surprised, but laughed, and Bill heard the relief in her voice as well.

The room erupted with hoorays and yells, but Captain Davy Jones needed order in the room and got it.

"Frank, where did debris fall? Israel?"

"Sec, Davy." Several moments passed. "Intercept occurred thirty klicks from border. Computer analysis shows most debris is within Israel. Certainly the warhead."

"Thanks, Frank. See you at the operational de-brief."

Abi walked over to Davy and spoke for a moment. Then she picked up a telephone and made a call to a Shin Bet officer. They had teams on station near the silos and their job would be to find the warheads of the destroyed missiles and keep them safe until Strategic Command could send teams to retrieve the debris. Shin-Bet would also arrest the silo crews.

On several TV monitors, Bill and Abi saw local and international news reports were breaking on the stations. The commentators were full of conjecture—possible war games, even a pre-emptive strike by Israel. Bill knew that the president and prime minister, supported by a host of State Department personnel, had updated Middle Eastern governments all day, but the media was clueless.

Bill stood thinking. His elation turned to concern. Although the missiles had been stopped, would Iran retaliate? Had Brian Kendrick squeezed Khoemi's balls hard enough? *And fucking Alon is still on the loose.*

1938 Hours, Saturday, May 3, 2014; The Prime Minister's Residence in the Rehavia Neighborhood, Jerusalem, Israel

Neena watched the man dressed in an IDF officer's uniform. He walked from the other side of the property along the sidewalk toward the arched gate in the front of the residence. As best as she could in the dim light, she examined his uniform. All seemed in order. The standard issue Uzi was slung over his shoulder and held firmly in both hands. Still, better safe than sorry. She flashed a signal to Steve with her infrared illuminator and got his signal back. *No security personnel are supposed to be here*, she said to herself. *Why would an officer be on patrol alone?*

The uniformed IDF security man turned into the gate. There was one street lamp near enough to cast the man briefly in faint light. As though a ghost walked there. Something about the man raised the hair on the back of her neck. The strong build. The bearing. Those large hands. *It's David!* She signaled Steve. David was turning off the main walkway onto the smaller walkway leading around the side of the building. *Steve, darling, be careful*, she pleaded in her head as she slipped out of position to close in on the prey. *David, why didn't you die at Pädäh?*

1940 Hours, Saturday, May 3, 2014; USS *Ronald Reagan*, Off the Coast of Israel

The operations center was calmer now, everyone relieved that all the aircraft had returned safely and the *Shiloh* took out the one missile that the fighters had not. Operations personnel documented the operation and the bees' hum was light and, almost, giddy.

"Davy?" Bill called out. "Can you tell whether Iran has launched any missiles?"

"You bet. No reports. The screens are quiet."

"Can we wait here for a while? We would like to watch. See what Iran does."

"Sure. Happy to have the company. We have orders to engage and destroy any inbound missile. The USS *Shiloh* has primary accountability for BMD of Israel, but I can keep us patched in if you like."

"That would be great. Thanks, Captain." *This ain't over by a long shot.*

Ten minutes passed quietly, but then, "Launch flash reported forty-eight kilometers northwest of Tehran, sir," barked the CPO in front of the large monitor with green dots. The mood in the room shifted to fear.

"What's the source?" Davy asked.

"Satellite, sir."

"Get the *Shiloh* on the box, Chief!"

"I have the *Shiloh*, sir."

"Frank, what have you got on that satellite report?"

"Not sure, Davy. We can't get radar confirmation. We can't see it on either our Sea Based X-Band Radar or on Air Force Upgraded Early Warning Radar. We're trying to get more from the surveillance satellite. Problem is we have to switch over because the first is moving out of range."

Davy was touching the display map in the middle of the operations center. "What is your point of no return on this?"

"If we don't have this thing targeted in thirty seconds, we aren't going to hit it."

"What is your estimated time of impact?"

"Two minutes, seventeen seconds."

"Have you detected any countermeasures against your radar systems?"

"Negative. We just can't see it."

"Shit!"

Bill and Abi were watching and listening to the exchange. "All this killing of our people and Israel will still be bombed!" Abi cried out.

"We're not done yet, Abi," Bill responded. "Something weird about not seeing the missile." *Our shit is very, very good. We should see it, if it's there.*

"Can you send up fighter aircraft, Davy?" Abi asked.

"We have fleet defense assets in the air, but they aren't equipped with the necessary weapons systems. I can't get my anti-missile F-18s off the deck fast enough to intercept, Abi. I'm sorry," Davy responded and then called tensely over the box to the *Shiloh*, "Frank, what's new?"

"Still can't see it. And now we can't reach it in time."

The CPO broke in, "Sirs, have report from fleet that there's been an explosion of unknown origin northwest of Tehran. That could be what our satellite saw, sirs."

"We should be able to see the missile from here, Frank. Chief, what do we have?"

"Nothing, sir."

Bill looked over at Abi and saw how tired and dismayed she looked. *So much for relief.*

The command centers on board the *Reagan* and *Shiloh* were absolutely still for the next minute, forty-three seconds. Not a word. Not a breath. All were waiting to hear the deadly blast.

It never came.

"Sirs, fleet confirming explosion northwest of Tehran was located at an oil refinery!"

The shouts of joy echoed everywhere. Bill and Abi reflexively embraced again for a few moments. They joined everyone else in cheering and backslapping. *Just another refinery disaster,* thought Bill. *Never thought I'd see the day when that was good news.*

"We probably owe Brian a drink, too," said Bill. "Davy, do you have a secure line I can use?"

"Absolutely, Bill!"

A CPO took Bill to a small private office just off the operations center. Abi followed and Bill was glad to have her there. She'd been a rock through this. Following a call to the president and prime minister, Bill called Brian. It was earlier in London, and Brian picked the phone up quickly. When he heard Brian's voice, Bill hit the speaker button. "Well, Brian, it appears that you and your firm have had a major role in avoiding a holocaust here."

"That's great, Bill, but you and the others did the heavy lifting. How are they?"

"In general, they're all well, but we're not finished here."

"How's that?"

"David Alon escaped the compound, and we believe he'll attempt a hit on the president and prime minister. Steve and Neena are tracking him now." *And I pray they find that sonovabitch quickly.*

"You have a lot to do, Bill. I'll let you go. Goodbye."

"Before you go, Brian, could you be in Jerusalem by early morning tomorrow?"

"Sure. I'd like to see the team again."

"I'll have your fighter standing by at zero, four hundred London time."

"No need for that, Bill. I can fly commercial tonight."

"I insist, Brian, as does the President. He wants to thank the four of you personally."

"Okay, Bill. I know when someone is pulling rank. See you tomorrow."

"Goodbye."

As Bill and Abi returned to the operations center they met Davy in the passageway. Abi said, "I have to get to the prime minister."

"I can help you," Davy offered. He spoke to the CPO.

"I'll go with you, Abi," Bill said. "I should be with the president. Are you armed?" Abi nodded.

In minutes, the CPO returned and escorted them to the flight deck and the awaiting Sikorsky. Bill hadn't thought much about David Alon while he focused on the missiles being taken out. Now his anxiety level was back at high. As the Sikorsky rocked and lifted off, Bill remembered that it was now Memorial Day in Israel. *Well,* he thought, *I hope I live long enough so that all this becomes just a dim memory. Why haven't I heard from Steve?*

1942 Hours, Saturday, May 3, 2014; The Prime Minister's Residence in the Rehavia Neighborhood, Jerusalem, Israel

David approached the door to the pantry. He slid his Uzi down and grabbed his knife. He would pry out a pane of glass and reach in to throw the deadbolt. He would then open the door a quarter inch so that he could use his knifepoint to push a button connected to the alarm system. Then he would go in, close the door, all without setting off an alarm. From there, he would slaughter anyone in the residence, by hand, if possible, or with the Iranian PC-9 ZOAF semi-automatic pistol. He would leave the pistol behind for the authorities to find as evidence of the Iranian crime.

As David pried the pane of glass, Steve emerged from the firethorn seven meters away, stepping directly into David's view. David turned to meet the threat, reaching for his Uzi. Steve aimed the infrared target illuminator directly over David's heart and shouted, "You just can't seem to kill me, David. Want another chance?" Steve drew his KABAR with his left hand as he held the assault rifle. The surprise on David's stern face was replaced by red-faced fury.

"You are wrong, Steve." David spit and grinned as he looked down to see the small red dot on his chest. "While I gave the orders, it wasn't me that tried to kill you or it would have been done."

"So *you* say," Steve retorted.

David waited a moment. "Why don't you shoot? I am sure that would comply with the rules of engagement in my circumstances."

"You have betrayed your country and caused the death of a lot of people, Israelis as well as Americans. Your *countrymen*—because you wanted to play King David. We are on the brink of nuclear *war* here because of you. So, if you think I'm going to let you off with just shooting you, you're a fucking idiot. Offense intended."

Steve saw Neena approach and stop, her weapon leveled at David. He knew that Neena was with him on this. Killing David was personal. Steve could tell from David's changing expression that he had seen Neena. David seemed instantly calmer.

"Neena, how glad I am that you are not buried at Pädäh," David announced with a hint of joy in his voice as he looked over his left shoulder toward her. Steve sensed that he meant it.

"Strange, because I wish *you* were," Neena snapped as she stepped behind him and aimed her weapon at his back.

David's expression turned instantly to one of sadness. *This guy is Jekyll and Hyde,* thought Steve.

David turned abruptly to face Steve again, anger returning to his face. "And if you think *you* can kill *me*, then *you* are a fucking idiot. Offense intended." He slowly pulled off his Uzi, dropped it onto the walkway, kicking it back toward Neena. He did the same with his Jaguar 941 and the Iranian semi-automatic pistol. Then, he gripped his knife so tightly that the veins popped on the top of his right hand.

"Excellent choice, David," Steve said as he shed his weapons, keeping the KABAR in his left hand. "Now you'll die as a warrior rather than the traitor that you are."

Steve and Neena's movements were recorded by the transponders, which sent alarms off within the security office of the residence. By this time, the entire yard was flooded with light and security personnel. They stood well back, weapons at the ready.

Steve backed step by step to the rear of the yard, David following, his arms at his side, and knife against his thigh. By instinct, they moved to a large area of crushed granite, the nucleus of a series of paths that wove through the gardens. It was as if they were in a bullring, but there were no shouts of *olé*. The struggle for life was real and respected in silence by those watching it. *This is my kill. Mine.*

They faced each other in the center of the crushed granite path. Eyes penetrated eyes, each warrior looking for an opening.

David outweighed Steve by twenty pounds and was shorter by three inches. Steve knew that he had to avoid David's hands. Steve had seen David crush walnuts in his office and had sized him up when they first met, a well-honed habit. Steve knew he had to reach out, using his greater arm span, to land a blow. Or, somehow, attack David from behind.

As Steve calculated, David lunged his knife forward, bringing his left arm around toward Steve's right side. Steve instinctively brought his KABAR up to fend off David's blade and sprang to his left, away from David's ponderous arm. David lunged again. Steve evaded again.

Neena watched, a cat ready to spring at any time. She had removed her weapons. She circled with the two fighters, keeping her body aimed at the space between them, but back about five meters. The rest of the security detail had formed a ring, fifteen meters or so in diameter. The only sounds were the grunts of the two locked in deadly combat, circling, breathing, waiting.

It was Steve's turn to attack. He jabbed repeatedly at David's eyes, his hand flashing like a cobra and just as deadly. David's agile moves thwarted every blow, but Steve didn't expect the blows to land. He was setting David up for a different stroke.

Eight, nine jabs came and Steve slouched as though tired, waiting for David to lunge again. This time, Steve didn't leap to his left. Instead he crouched, grabbing David's left arm, spinning him, looking to sink the KABAR into his neck or left side.

Steve hadn't anticipated the momentum of David's arm and it knocked him off balance. David thrust his powerful body at Steve, chest to chest, David's knife an inch from Steve's throat. Steve's KABAR held David's knife at bay. David grabbed Steve's throat and Steve struggled for breath, felt himself fading.

David's blade pierced Steve's throat, a second of searing pain and then Steve pushed back as hard as he could. With a surge of ebbing strength, Steve's right hand wrested the Gerber from its sheath, plunging it deep into the nape of David's neck. Blood spurted, splattering their faces. David choked on the blade and the blood. The iron grip on Steve's throat slipped as David staggered backward, his arms and hands flailing at the object thrust into his skull. David's knife clattered to the ground and he tried to speak but blood garbled his words as it flooded his lungs. Steve yanked his knife from the wreck of David's head. It was done. David's hands, those enormous hands, would never crush another walnut. Breathing hard, Steve watched the life leave the man who would've unleashed horror on the Middle East, his last exhale blowing bubbles in his own blood. *You lose, fucking idiot*, Steve thought as he gasped for air. *Offense intended.*

He looked up to see Neena staring at him. She was weeping as she began to wipe his face.

"Where have you been?" Steve squeaked while massaging his throat, trying to make light of the fact that David had nearly killed him. She didn't laugh.

He reached for her and held her as they stood on the bloody ground. "I'm sorry," he whispered. "I didn't want you to be the one who killed him."

Neena turned, and with the tears streaming down her face, kissed Steve. "I am *crying* because I nearly lost *you*." She pointed to David's body

"He is not the David Alon who loved Israel, who loved me. He is only a man who loved death. So it claimed him. You were the weapon."

They sank to the crushed granite, huddled there as security took David's body away and the personnel dispersed silently. Questions, forms, and procedures could wait.

After the others were gone and they had several minutes alone, Steve asked, "Will you marry me?"

"This is a fine time and place to be asking *that* question again," Neena teased looking up from Steve's shoulder, leaning her wet cheek against his chest.

"Well, you insisted that I ask again, so I am. You didn't set any conditions about where or when. You just said it should be a proper proposal." Steve bent down on one knee, his good leg. Took her hand and squeezed it, sheepishly holding out in his other hand a grenade pin that he'd shaped into a ring. He'd never wanted anything this much in his life. "So, what do you have to say *this* time?"

"The same as before! *Yes. Yes. Yes.*" She was smiling brightly now, the tracks of her tears glistening in the harsh floodlights. They could hear the whoosh of a helicopter landing on the roof of the residence. *Hope that's Bill with good news,* Steve said to himself. *And I have some news for him, too.*

Steve drew his hand softly over Neena's cheek and wiped the few remaining tears from her chin. He caressed her hair. Then he pulled her close again and just held her. *I'm so lucky in so many ways*, he thought.

Chapter Nineteen
Early Morning, Sunday, May 4, 2014; The Prime Minister's Residence in the Rehavia Neighborhood, Jerusalem, Israel

The streets of Rehavia were jammed with cars, radio and television crews with broadcast transmission trucks. Police were shouting at drivers attempting to double-park, waving them on as if they were lingering in the arrival area of an international airport. Security forces virtually lined the streets for blocks, weapons loaded and ready to fire. The country and its people were on edge. Not knowing whether to run or dance, they simply embraced each other while waiting to know the fate of their country.

The office of the prime minister had announced that an important news conference would be held at nine fifteen in the morning. The actions of the previous day had created understandable excitement and, in some quarters, alarm. The announcement stated that prime minister, speaking from Beit Aghion, his official residence, would explain those events. Further, the President of the United States was visiting the prime minister and would also speak at the news conference. Every major network and cable channel had someone there, including Al Jazeera.

Steve, Neena, Abi, Bill, Brian and Jack had arrived around eight o'clock for breakfast. They were shown to an elegant, but modest dining room, in which they were greeted first by Prime Minister Erez and, then, the President of the United States. Grand arrangements of flowers flanked the large doorways, while the early morning sun poured through French doors covered by sheer linen curtains on brass rods. Shadows of security personnel and automatic weapons dappled the floors near all the exits.

The table, hewn from a large cedar tree and gleaming with twenty layers of hand-rubbed finish, was bare except for thick placemats decorated with bucolic prints of the Israeli countryside. Starched linen napkins poked out of towering crystal glasses set on charger plates in the middle of the placemats. Sterling silverware, polished like the dew drops of the morning, flanked the charger plates. In the center of the table, a sprawling arrangement of fresh cut flowers rose no higher than eight inches so that the diners could see each other. A steward in a stiff white jacket and three liveried attendants stood at attention in the corners of the room.

After being instructed to sit, the group bowed heads as the prime minister said a short prayer and afterward, the steward and attendants leapt into action. Plates of hummus, tomatoes, cucumbers, onions, fried eggs, fresh bread, toast, olives, butter, smoked salmon, and cheeses were served. One attendant made sure that every glass brimmed with orange juice and every cup was full of coffee. Steve could not remember being so well fed.

The prime minister and president wanted a full briefing on the assault and ballistic missile defense of the Middle East. They also solemnly sought the details of David Alon's life and death. As the military attaché to Israel, Bill conducted the briefing. The prime minister and president asked questions of each of the people around the table and Steve thought they expressed true interest in the answers. Steve knew that the leaders of the two countries already knew most of the details from other sources. He assumed they took this opportunity to listen to those with intimate knowledge of the chaos that, for now, Israel and its neighbors had avoided. Steve was impressed by both men and admired the courage of his president. *He put it all on the line and he didn't have to.*

At nine o'clock, the prime minister and president excused themselves to prepare for the news conference and fifteen minutes later, entered the pressroom. Everyone arose, respectful applause resounding in the great hall. The six of them, a team now, comrades who had fought and won, stood offstage with a full view of the prime minister and president. The president beckoned. Bill, Abi, and Jack crossed the stage and took their seats. To protect their identities, Steve, Neena, and Brian stood behind a hand-painted wooden panel that had been placed between them and the reporter pool.

General Jack Trevane wore dress blues decorated with a square-foot of medals and ribbons. Bill adopted diplomatic attire, elegant in semi-formal morning wear, with a black single-breasted stroller, starched white shirt, a four-in-hand tie, dove-grey waistcoat, and black-striped grey wool trousers. He didn't have a top hat or gloves, which Steve thought would have been going way overboard. Steve and Brian each wore navy-blue single-breasted suits. Steve chose a bright red, white, and blue patterned Hermes tie. Abi was sophisticated in a deep purple Patra beaded silk chiffon cocktail dress and jacket. Neena chose an aqua Ralph Lauren mock wrap Jersey dress with a small gold necklace. Steve couldn't take his eyes off Neena.

The press conference was staged so that the prime minister and president would be together, but at separate podiums inches apart. It was a large room, a grand hall on the first floor, but still not big enough for the invited guests and swarm of journalists, so media pool representatives were selected. Fifty people squeezed into the hall along with five television cameras.

At precisely nine fifteen, Prime Minister Erez, accompanied by the President, walked to his podium, which was adorned with the Official Seal of the State of Israel. He had no written notes with him.

"Ladies and gentlemen of the press, distinguished guests, citizens of Israel, friends of my beloved country, and lovers of peace everywhere, I am honored to be here this morning with the President of the United States of America to tell you, on this Memorial Day, of momentous events, great acts of heroism, the meaning of friendship, and hope for peace in the Middle East.

"First, I must tell you of a great and tragic attempt by Defense Secretary Simon Luegner and Senior Mossad Agent David Alon. They devised a plan to unleash a nuclear holocaust of historic proportions across the Middle East." Reporters started to shout questions, but the prime minister held up his hands until quiet returned. "While I do not have time to tell you all the details, I can tell you that the plot involved members of Mossad and the Israeli Defense Force Strategic Command. I can also tell you that the plot has been completely foiled and all known conspirators are either dead or in custody.

There was a collective gasp from the audience, reporters scribbling furiously on notepads, cameras zooming in for close-ups of the prime minister and the president. From behind the screen Steve watched a monitor and once again admired the composure, the squared shoulders, the leadership style of his president. *Here is a man I would work for any day,* he thought. *No questions asked.*

"Over the past few hours, the networks have reported combat within Israel, attacks by aircraft and missile firings. Let me summarize these events for you and put them into context so that you will understand how they are related and also put an end to rumors." A few shouts of "yes" and "tell us" rang out from the gathering.

Steve had lived what the prime minister now told the audience. As he listened, he reflected on how fragile freedom was and the desperate acts that are committed in freedom's name. He turned to Neena and reminded himself of her journey with him over the past several days. *I want that journey to continue. Freedom is my purpose. And it drives Neena, too. Her family was killed because they weren't free; butchered by fanatics who believe their way is the only way. And David Alon took in that vulnerable girl but betrayed her in the end; dismissing everything she'd fought for, trained for. Ally turned enemy.* Steve shook his head. Neena, too, fought for freedom. "Neena," he whispered, leaning so close a wisp of her hair brushed his cheek. "I will never betray you." She squeezed his hand, a look of understanding in her eyes.

The prime minister finished the story of the conspiracy and how the Middle East had narrowly escaped the ravages of multiple thermonuclear detonations. Steve reminded himself of why he loved his job.

The President of the United States was introduced, the room erupting with applause and shouts. The prime minister and president first shook hands and then exchanged embraces. Then the president stood close to his podium, lifting his hands to ask for silence. Finally, the din diminished.

"Thank you, Mr. Prime Minister. I add my welcome to all of you and am thankful to be here—or anywhere—at all." Laughter spontaneously rang out. The president continued, "It is obvious to me and to my fellow leaders in the Middle East with whom I have been speaking over the last two days that the events we have just witnessed and, thankfully, survived arose from an overwhelming sense of despair and hopelessness for a future of peace." Several shouts of "yes" and "shalom" erupted and died out.

"Simon Luegner, David Alon and those that followed them were accomplished people and respected in many ways. They also had impressive records of service. They were not acting out of greed or personal gain. They were acting out of desperation and an ever-increasing sense of vulnerability and dismay. We may never know what led them to do what they did. But we *can* learn from our own experiences of the past days." The President walked out from behind his podium and stood in front of it. The prime minister joined him.

"People cannot live in constant fear of other peoples for long without seeking some solution—however brutal and inane—to the despair that fills their hearts and minds—despair for themselves and their loved ones, for their neighbors and friends, for generations yet to be born. Simon and David taught us this lesson well. I have learned it." Steve and Neena looked at each other and then turned back to the President. Steve imagined the intense faces of the people gathered in the room. *You could hear a pin drop*, he thought.

"I will be joining the prime minister on visits to neighboring countries. Our message is a joint one: *now* is the time for peace." The audience broke out in more shouts of "yes" and "now". The President raised his hands and began speaking again.

"The United States stands ready to help in several ways. First, I will ask the Congress to approve a Mutual Defense and Non-aggression Pact with Israel and every other country in the Middle East who will join us in this journey toward peace. One of the elements of that Pact will be the agreement by the United States to shield all signers of the Pact from any and all foes.

"Further, we need to recognize that, in the partitioning of Palestine and the subsequent acts of violence on *all* sides, a cycle of hatred was born—a cycle that has lasted almost seventy years. We need to *break* that cycle *now*. Therefore, an additional element of the Pact will be the recognition by all its signers of the right of each participating country to exist within their *current* borders." The audience went wild, shouting and clapping. The prime minister raised his hands to help silence the increasingly fervent group.

"Subsequent to signing the Pact," the President went on, "A separate Palestinian state will be negotiated and, once created, that state will become a member of the Pact. We will give ourselves one year in which to accomplish this. If we have failed to establish a separate Palestinian state by the end of the year, the Mutual Defense and Non-aggression Pact will terminate automatically, and America will withdraw militarily from the region except where we have previously established treaties and pacts."

Steve thought, *That's not very subtle. Good! It's about time people got hit with a two-by-four.*

"On Israel's part, there needs to be greater tolerance, and even an embracing, of non-Jewish citizens and residents, both Christians and Muslims. This must be accompanied by an equal-handed protection of their rights within Israel. The prime minister has assured me that he and the Knesset will be taking firm action on this very soon. This is a critical component for our partnership on this journey of peace." The audience was more subdued now. A couple of people could be heard shifting their chairs on the hardwood floor. *Everyone has to put something in the pot,* Steve mused.

"Lastly, we need to address the fact that millions of Palestinians and others live desperately in refugee camps and have done so for decades. Integration of these people into existing states and cultures needs to proceed and they need to have the opportunities we all seek for economic and social gain. To help with this effort, the United States will commit one hundred billion dollars—ten billion dollars annually for the next ten years—for the purpose of integrating Palestinian refugees within those countries that are signers of the Mutual Defense and Non-aggression Pact. I will seek additional assistance for these refugees from OPEC members of the Middle East who clearly share in the responsibility for the future of these people." Some reporters began to slip out of the room. Other reporters, who had waited outside, rushed to take their places.

"There is much to be done and the journey to peace will not be without sacrifices by all. I am reminded, however, that should we fail in this journey, we are likely to breed another Simon or David, if not in Israel, then in another land.

"Let me close with a reading from the Christian bible. I chose it because it speaks of a time of glory and peace, a time that, with hard work, is within our grasp. It also paints a vision of glory for Jerusalem—a city of immense importance to Christian, Jew, and Muslim alike. A reading, then, from the Book of Revelation, Chapter 21, verses 1 to four:

'Then I saw a new heaven and a new earth, for the first heaven and the first earth had passed away, and there was no longer any sea. I saw the Holy City, the new Jerusalem, coming down out of heaven from God, prepared as a bride beautifully dressed for her husband. And I heard a loud voice from the throne saying, "Now the dwelling of God is with men, and he will live with them. They will be his people, and God himself will be with them and be their God. He will wipe every tear from their eyes. There will be no more death or mourning or crying or pain, for the old order of things has passed away."'

The President paused for a moment and then concluded with, "Thank you for allowing me to speak with you this morning."

The people in the room at first remained quiet and then they started clapping and cheering. Many stood, as did the six upon the stage. It took the prime minister some time to quiet the room. After he did, there was a short question and answer period. When that ended, the prime minister and President retreated to the dining room with Brian, Jack, Abi, Steve, Neena, and Bill.

"My thanks to each of you, again," the prime minister beamed as he shook their hands, going down the line. The President of the United States followed a step behind and his handshake was just as Steve expected, strong and confident.

"I am so very proud of you and thankful for your steadfast efforts. Without you, I cannot even imagine what this world would be today. Brian, Steve, and Neena," the president said. "I hope you will return with me to Washington. I would like you to help in Congress and others to understand the importance of establishing a lasting peace in the Middle East."

"Mr. President," Brian said, "If I may, I'd like to excuse myself for a few days from Washington so that my firm can conclude the last details of the Iranian transactions. To keep our leverage in the deal, these details need attention."

"Of course, Brian. I understand fully and, like Vic Alfonse, I am very grateful to you and your firm for the service you've performed for your country. Please allow me give you a lift to Washington so that we will have the opportunity to get acquainted. I would very much like to know more about those Iranian transactions."

"I'd be honored, Mr. President."

"Then it's settled. Bill, can you arrange everything for our friends to get on board Air Force One?"

"Yes, Mr. President. I'm looking forward to the quiet that will return when these two," Bill said gesturing toward Steve and Neena, "are safely out of Israel." Steve had been silent, but as Bill finished his sentence, he mused, *I don't think quiet is going to return to any of us.*

Chapter Twenty
Wednesday, May 7, 2014; Qom, Iran

Ayatollah Mohammed Khoemi sat at the desk in his barren office, gesticulating with a fountain pen at Danesh Mahdavi. "This infidel has cost us greatly."

"At least we have our money, even if we cannot yet use it."

"Do you think we will live twenty more years!" Khoemi spit. "I want that money while I am young enough to enjoy it." He threw the only object near enough, a tattered copy of the Quran. He looked at the book now standing on its binding against the wall, pages wilting where the holy tome lay. *I should have done that many years ago.*

"We have sued Chandler Hines Kendrick," Mahdavi stated, interrupting Khoemi's abuse of the Quran.

"Yes, and after five years in a New York court, we will receive fifty million dollars, the maximum damages under our contract. Our shares will be insignificant compared to the harm they have done to us with the Guardian Council and our fellow Swiss account holders. You did not have to face them and tell them what has happened to their money! You were not there when I had to beg them to hold back on retaliating against that cesspool, Israel!" Khoemi slammed his fist on the desk. "You and I are lucky to be alive, and so is Brian Kendrick. For Mr. Kendrick, however, all that is about to change."

"What are your instructions, holy one?"

Chapter Twenty-One
Saturday, May 17, 2014; New York, NY, USA

After arriving in Washington aboard Air Force One, Brian was met by his AAD security team. All CHK partners and their families had been assigned these teams after Brian had body slammed Ayatollah Khoemi and Sa'ad-Oddin Rezvani over the telephone two weeks earlier. He and the AAD men caught the shuttle to New York where an armored Suburban took Brian to the office to work with Joe Burstein. There was still a lot of paperwork to wrap up on the multiple transactions involved with the NIOC deal.

It was past eleven and Brian was dog-tired when they finally finished, locking all original documents in the office safe. Joe waved wearily as he left, accompanied by his own AAD team, and Brian thought once again how lucky he was to have dedicated partners willing to back up each other and take risks when the stakes were high. A light was on in the conference room and before clicking it off, Brian stood in front of the copy of the Declaration of Independence. He saluted, feeling a little foolish that one of the AAD men might see him, but mostly feeling pride for the country he loved.

He was trying to decide whether to go home or have a drink at the Bear and Bull with his newfound shadows when one of the secure lines rang. Brian answered, pushing the speaker button out of habit. *Who else besides Joe knows I'm working this time of night?*

"Hello, Mr. Kendrick. Codeword 'Ulysses'. Repeat 'Ulysses'.""

Brian's whole body tensed. "Yes, I understand. Go ahead."

"Mr. Kendrick, you should know that about two hours ago, one of your partners had an unusual and fatal accident at his home in Chappaqua, New York."

Oh my God! "What! What happened? Where are the AAD guys? Why do you call it 'unusual'?"

"Mr. Kendrick, I can give you no further information at this time, except that the local police consider it an accident. However, the plumber thinks that you and Mr. Barber should look into this matter with great urgency. The plumber also said that he stands ready to make good on his promise to you. Goodbye."

Brian stood, staring at the telephone as if the device were responsible for this tragedy. He pushed the speakerphone button slowly to stop its whine. He pushed it again. He heard a dial tone. *So, it has begun,* he thought as he dialed. *Maybe I should have stuffed the guard's dick in Khoemi's desk drawer instead of his finger. Well, I'll make sure that Khoemi regrets the day he was born.* "Hello, Steve," he said as his call was answered. "The plumber tells me I have a serious problem and I need your help. How soon can you be in New York?"

Saturday, May 17, 2014; Washington, DC, USA

Steve and Neena remained in Washington to enjoy the beautiful spring weather and to make plans for their quiet wedding, which would be held the next April in Israel. They walked the Vietnam Memorial, had lunch in Georgetown, lingered in the Smithsonian, and Steve saw Washington through Neena's eyes; a little in awe of the sheer size and energy of the city and very much impressed. America, too, had its history. Although they had planned to stay in DC for two full weeks, Steve received a telephone call that whisked him off to New York to work with Todd Crossley of AAD, the risk management firm retained by Chandler Hines Kendrick.

After Steve left for New York, Neena departed for Israel. Separation would be painful but they would get used to it somehow. They each had work to do. Neena was to consult for Abi, named Defense Minister last week, replacing Simon Luegner. Abi would rebuild Mossad and Strategic Command and Neena had high hopes for Abi's success. She'd heard, too, that Abi and Bill had been seen together in several posh restaurants in and around Tel Aviv. It was none of Neena's business but inwardly she approved. She'd grown very fond of them both.

Abi offered Neena a senior position in Mossad, but she declined. She had no intention of living her life tied down to an office. She also had a few Hezbollah yet to kill before her family, or at least she, would be at rest. Her santo knives were in the belly of the plane, special clearance tags wrapped around the case. She was glad to be flying back to Israel, the country of her heart and soul. But she would return to Washington D.C. and her other love would be waiting. Steve had said he might need her help with an unexpected development. Something brewing. Something big.

Acknowledgements:

Many friends contributed their individual gifts to this novel. To each of them I give my thanks for investing so much in a work by an unknown author.

Several military advisors offered inspiration and critical technical advice. Among them, three stand out. John Buxton, Lt. Col. (Ret) USAF, has over thirty years of experience providing management and consulting services to domestic and international clients in multiple industries and government agencies. Bill Chadwick is a retired Special Forces soldier with worldwide experience in leading men in armed combat and advising foreign militaries. Mike Crossley, a Force Recon Marine combat veteran, has been a Security Advisor for the Department of Defense for the last fifteen years. These men are among the vital few to whom we owe our liberty.

The quality of the manuscript was greatly enhanced by a small group of "beta readers" who accepted the task of helping to make this a better book. Some read the .pdf file on their computer. Others printed the document and carried the three-inch manuscript around with them. All made a difference with their unique viewpoints and comments.

Mel Abert of AbertEntity offered his great creative talent in art directing the cover. Not an easy task on a budget of zero. Connie, his partner and wife, was an early, and especially encouraging, beta reader.

I have saved the best for last, Diana Greenwood. She is my editor, friend, coach, and inspiration. She is also an accomplished author of children's books. This book would not have seen the light of your reading lamp without her.

About the Author:

Lee Broad has held positions in international banking, strategic and organizational consulting, and on Wall Street. He has an eclectic background in global business assessment, international joint venture development, and mergers/acquisitions. In addition to performing specific project-oriented engagements, he has served in interim executive capacities in the consulting, childcare, and electronics industries. Lee holds a Bachelor of Science degree in Management from Rensselaer Polytechnic Institute and an MBA with a concentration in Finance from Columbia University.

Drawing on his extensive domestic and international business experience, community involvement, and observation of foreign affairs, Lee has chosen the Middle East, long the scene of war and now a hotbed of fanatical terrorism, as the setting for his first novel, *The Masada Protocol*.